'I simply devoured this. Beautifully written,
with twists you won't see coming'
Lesley Lokko

'A deliciously atmospheric mystery connecting
two characters who stole my heart'
Ruth Ware

'I loved it. Unique, magic and exquisitely written.
Winterthorne breathes and I loved that imprint
of time on time. A beautiful novel'
Amanda Geard

'Evocative and intriguing ... Twisty, vivid and
characterful, this dual-time novel will have you hooked'
Woman & Home

'Magical – a hauntingly beautiful story of love, loss
and the triumph of hope. I read it in a single sitting
and found it absolutely enchanting'
Susanna Kearsley

'Deliciously engrossing: romantic, immersive and
beautifully written. A wonderful storyteller'
Jane Johnson

'What a stunning book. Exquisitely written. Zoë Marriott
is an exciting new voice in this genre. An absolute triumph'
Elena Collins

'A sweeping dual-time story based on an intriguing premise. This book kept me spellbound throughout. Emotional and atmospheric. Highly recommended for fans of mysterious reads that keep you on the edge of your seat!'
Christina Courtenay

'A beautiful book . . .
I loved this one so much. Such an intricate, interlaced and stunning novel that I am completely blown away. The sheer love and emotion in this really got to me. Bravo!'
Nicola Cornick

'A beautiful, beautiful book. I am completely blown away by it! So beautifully written – an absolute masterpiece! Transporting. Loved it so much'
Renita D'Silva

'What a wonderful book. Just gorgeous. Marriott conjures two eras and two heroines with pitch-perfect precision and empathy. Clever and compelling. I read it in one breathless gulp'
Joanna Nadin

'I loved it. An evocative, entrancing novel that plays with concepts of time in a fascinating and gripping way, while also leading the reader through a very human story of love. A fabulous read'
Joanna Courtney

Zoë Marriott wrote her YA debut *The Swan Kingdom* when she was twenty-one, and has written eight more critically acclaimed, award-winning YA novels published in the UK by Walker Books and in the USA by Candlewick. *The Moonlit Maze* is her adult debut.

Also by Zoë Marriott

YA FICTION

The Swan Kingdom
Daughter of the Flames
Shadows on the Moon
Frostfire
The Name of the Blade Series
Barefoot on the Wind
The Hand, the Eye and the Heart

ADULT FICTION

The Moonlit Maze

The Moonlit Maze

ZOË MARRIOTT

REVIEW

Copyright © 2025 Zoë Marriott

The right of Zoë Marriot to be identified as the Author of the Work has been asserted by her in accordance with the Copyright, Designs and Patents Act 1988.

First published in 2025 by Headline Review
An imprint of Headline Publishing Group Limited

This paperback edition published in 2026

1

Apart from any use permitted under UK copyright law, this publication may only be reproduced, stored, or transmitted, in any form, or by any means, with prior permission in writing of the publishers or, in the case of reprographic production, in accordance with the terms of licences issued by the Copyright Licensing Agency.

All characters in this publication – apart from the obvious historical figures – are fictitious and any resemblance to real persons, living or dead, is purely coincidental.

Every effort has been made to fulfil requirements with regard to reproducing copyright material. The author and publisher will be glad to rectify any omissions at the earliest opportunity.

Cataloguing in Publication Data is available from the British Library

Paperback ISBN 9781 0354 1785 8

Typeset in Sabon by CC Book Production

Printed and bound in Great Britain by Clays Ltd, Elcograf S.p.A.

Headline's policy is to use papers that are natural, renewable and recyclable products and made from wood grown in well-managed forests and other controlled sources. The logging and manufacturing processes are expected to conform to the environmental regulations of the country of origin.

HEADLINE PUBLISHING GROUP LIMITED
An Hachette UK Company
Carmelite House
50 Victoria Embankment
London EC4Y 0DZ

The authorized representative in the EEA is Hachette Ireland,
8 Castlecourt Centre, Dublin 15, D15 XTP3, Ireland
(email: info@hbgi.ie)

www.headline.co.uk
www.hachette.co.uk

*Dedicated to my agent, Kate Shaw,
with the utmost gratitude.
May this novel be the first of many!*

Prologue

Xanthe, 19 July 1924

Xanthe stepped through the moon gate, passing through the shadow of stone and drooping wisteria blossoms into blueish moonlight. Overhead, stars drifted among wisps of summer cloud like handfuls of lustrous pearls tossed carelessly on a midnight cloth. A warm wind shivered the leaves. The pale green silk of Xanthe's evening dress fluttered around her calves, and short strands of red hair blew free of the beaded silk scarf wrapping her head. She looked around expectantly.

'Tom?'

There was no reply. No movement at the entrance to the maze.

She glanced back. Framed in the curve of the moon gate, the castle shone. Light streamed from the tall windows, painting gold squares onto the lawn. She could hear the faint trilling of the string quartet playing their hearts out in the ballroom. The party was in full swing. The chance of any of the guests wandering away from the steady supply of gossip and champagne and out into the gardens – or of her parents abandoning their guests – was tiny. Still, she couldn't stay here too long.

She would be missed eventually, and she didn't want to cause another scene.

But she wouldn't go back without seeing him, either.

She moved away from the lower lawn, towards the topiary maze. The gravel crunched faintly underfoot, treacherous and shifting. Her heels, specially dyed the perfect shade of *eau de nil* to match her dress, had not been designed for midnight strolls. Beyond the maze, the sea was booming as the tide came in on Winterthorne's cliffs, far below the castle. Salt made the air tangy.

'Tom?' A little bit louder now. This wasn't like him. He was always there – always waiting for her. And he especially wouldn't be late tonight. Not after. After.

A tiny smile creased her lips.

This is happiness.

It didn't matter what her mother and father said any more. She knew now where her future lay. There would be no more arguments, no more shame, shouting or pleading. Tomorrow she would tell them, and he would be by her side when she did it.

With one hand trailing over the carefully trimmed curve of the yew hedge, she followed the path deeper into the maze. Overhead the familiar shapes of the cockerel, the peacock, the owl, the swan, formed from the living hedge and carefully tended by Mr Marten – Tom's father – loomed against the starlit sky. She had played here every day when she was a little girl and had a kindly governess, before the narrow little boarding school and the Swiss finishing school.

The gravel sounded ahead of her. A masculine shape moved out of the dead-end hidden in the hedge ahead. Laughter rose to her lips as she went towards him, stretching out her hands.

'Playing hide and seek? You should know that I'll always find you.'

'Oh, really?' said a deep, familiar voice. 'Now that you mention it, I didn't know that.'

Xanthe stumbled to a halt, her heart knocking hard against her ribs. She took a hasty step back, but her heel turned under her – wretched shoes! – and before she could turn to run a large long-fingered hand had snatched her wrist.

Her mind skittered with thoughts. *How did he find out? Did he tell my parents? Stupid, I should have brought Rowan with me!* And then, piercing through everything else: *Where is Tom?*

'What are you doing lurking out here?' Her tone was brittle; she didn't dare appear frightened. 'I thought you were welded to the wall. Or did the footmen stop bringing you drinks?'

'I came looking for you, my dearest, darling fiancée,' he answered, voice low, deliberately menacing. 'And now that I've found you . . .'

'What, Jonathan? What exactly are you—' She broke off with a gasp as he wrenched her arm, dragging her closer. He stank of whisky, and she could hear his fast, excited breathing.

The brutal grip on her wrist tightened, twisted, slowly, calculatedly, until her bones protested with hot, elastic twinges of pain. He could break her hand like this. He wanted to. She could feel his gaze on her face, knew the sight of her pain there would excite him. Fear would arouse him even more. She had to keep her expression blank.

'I haven't decided yet,' he whispered. 'But whatever it is . . . whatever it is . . . Oh, Xanthe, I promise you will not enjoy it.'

Part One

One

Jude, present day

My flatmate catches me as I'm getting ready to leave for my six-to-eleven shift at La Dolce Pizza.

I've still got to tie my bootlaces and put on my coat, but the lip-pursing and foot-fidgeting tell me that Penny's rehearsed a speech. So even though the words, 'I've got something to tell you...' make my gut twinge uneasily, I finish folding my clean apron into my backpack, sit on the arm of the sofa bed where I was asleep an hour ago and try to look interested.

'It's good news. Totally good! Last night Duncan asked me to marry him! Isn't that amazing? And we're totally in love, so in love, right? Anyone can see that, right? I said yes!'

'*I was in love for two weeks, once.*' That's what I want to say, but obviously I don't; it would only make me sound ridiculous. Or, worse, jealous.

It wasn't ridiculous at the time. It felt real. Like the realest thing, the only real thing in the world since the last time I saw Ma alive. And then it wasn't, of course. I was just ... desperate for it to be. Like someone longing so hard for a sip of cool, sweet lemonade that they accidentally gulp down citrus bleach.

It's too late to warn Penny now, though. I ought to have said something, done something, the night she and Duncan met. I ought to have tried harder in all the months since. And now this. She's staring at me and her eyebrows are starting to come together. There's a bit of defiance, a bit of anxiety there, but also hope, because that's the type of person she is. Or, rather, that's the type of life she's had. The kind that teaches you to believe things will be all right in the end.

Shit, I've definitely been quiet for too long at this point.

'That's great. Congratulations.' I try to smile. I know I don't sound convincing. But Penny's never been that hard to fool – as the fact she's engaged to Duncan now proves.

'OMG, you had me worried there, Jude! So you're OK with this? You'll be OK, right? Duncan said you would be, but you know me – always totally freaking out over nothing.'

My gut is still twinging. I hate the fact that Duncan has already managed to gaslight her into repeating his 'whenever Penny has an inconvenient emotion she is just freaking out over nothing' mantra.

'What did you think I wouldn't be OK with? It's not like you'll be getting married and moving out tomorrow, right?'

Penny's immaculate, Insta-worthy brows are meeting above her nose again. 'God, sorry, I mucked it up. Duncan said I would.'

'What? *Are* you moving out tomorrow?' I try to make this sound like a joke, but the weird little laugh I pin on at the end is pure panic. Even Penny can pick up on that.

'No! No, of course not!' The words are in direct opposition

to the way she's pursing her lips. Sure enough, she follows up with, 'We do, like, want to move in together, though, obviously – and, like, I already own this place so it seems a waste for him to keep paying rent? I mean, there's no rush! You know, just, maybe start looking? For somewhere else.'

My life, unlike Penny's, has trained me to expect a kick in the teeth. It still always hurts, though.

☽○☾

It's my fault, is the thing.

Panic is acid in my stomach, cramping and queasy, as I try to figure out how I'm supposed to find a place that's a) rentable for anywhere near the meagre sum per month that I can afford, b) in a location that will allow me to commute to both my jobs and still get six hours' sleep – or even five – and c) will be available within Duncan's required timeframe of, in Penny's words, 'No pressure, but as soon as possible, because his lease is up in May.' It's already the end of March.

I don't know if I can do it.

The bus stops with a lurch that makes me slide forward on the seat. My arms are wrapped round my backpack, and I brace my feet in a practised motion and slide back into place as the doors open, allowing in a chill blast of wind and drizzle, and a woman who looks just as downtrodden as I feel. She's muffled up like a caterpillar in a huge dripping puffer coat, mumbling her destination to the driver as if she'd rather go anywhere else. Our eyes meet as she passes; we both look away quickly.

I'm probably going to be late. I should have got the Tube. The bus is slow, but it's also cheaper.

The window opposite me ripples and streaks with reflections as we pass streetlights and shadowy bus shelters. My reflection is not looking happy. The extra-curly baby-hair bits at my hairline are standing out in a halo all around my oddly elongated face. I look as if I've stuck my finger in an electricity socket. As if I forgot to buy . . .

'Coconut oil,' I mutter.

That's why I had that couple of quid extra in my pocket. I'd spent it on a sandwich. It wasn't even a good sandwich, but I still thought it was my lucky day. Idiot. Now I'll be a frizzy mess until payday. Wonderful. Fantastic. I squash my face into the top of my backpack in exasperation for a second, but only a second. That's a vulnerable posture. Too vulnerable for a public place like the bus.

I'm just so tired. I'm tired all the time.

I was right there the night Penny and Duncan met. It was Penny's birthday. We had a party in the flat that turned into a scrum. Dozens of people we didn't even know turned up. Including him. Penny says that their eyes connected across a crowded room: love at first sight. From my perspective, it was more like watching a moray eel lick its lips as it set its sights on a nice juicy mackerel that has flippered too far from the shoal. If eels eat mackerel. What do I know about fish? I do know something about boys, though – I learned a lot of hard lessons from my ex, the lemon bleach – and I knew Duncan wasn't going to be good for Penny. He was too slick, too loud, too ready to take possession of every conversation and talk over anyone who didn't bow to his obvious brilliance. His favourite book is *Atlas Shrugged*.

Penny's smart, but she's not . . . street smart. She never

was, even when we were kids living in that same rundown but friendly block of flats. Her mum getting promoted and her family moving to live in a nice big house in a safer area made her even more of a Pollyanna type. She trusts people too much. She trusts life too much.

But I didn't do anything that night. And later on ... I pointed out how deeply unpleasant Duncan could be a few times. I even thought I'd made her think twice occasionally. But it never lasted, and the last time she snapped back at me with: 'Duncan said you'd say that about him! He says you're jealous!' I just ... gave up.

Maybe I could have made a difference if I'd kept trying. Maybe I could have put her off, made enough of a fuss to force her to really *look* at him. But I was tired then too. I'm always so tired. I didn't want to have heartfelt discussions about feelings. I didn't want to care enough for that. So I told myself it was none of my business. Not my problem.

The thing is that Penny and I were friends, once. Best friends, even, when we were little. All that changed after she moved. Even though we still went to the same school and the same college, we moved in different groups. She was in the shiny group that had designer bags, got dropped off by their lawyer, doctor, banker parents in shiny cars, and were taking shiny A levels in law, or finance. I was in the arty-grunge group, the ones who always looked a bit grubby, wore jeans that were ripped and faded because they were actually old, not 'distressed', and never turned up for the extra-curricular activities, because we had to work part-time.

It was just a coincidence that a friend of a mutual friend knew about my situation – that I was turning eighteen and about to be kicked out of foster care with nothing but a 'bridging allowance' to keep me off the street. And Penny had inherited her granny's flat in Haringey. The place needed a lot of work, and Penny wanted to do it up herself while she finished her degree at King's College. She needed a roommate to bring in some cash.

She probably felt sorry for me. The 'tragic news' had to have been all over the college after I dropped out. She definitely didn't ask as much rent as she could have. But I didn't complain about the mouldy grout and damp stains in the bathroom, or the toxic smell that came out of the old metal sink in the kitchen, or the pink flocked velvet wallpaper peeling off. She was supposed to have cleared the second bedroom out for me, and I'm still sleeping on the sofa bed in the tiny living room nearly three years after I moved in. She always makes sure that the fridge is full, but I do most of the cooking for both of us, and the washing-up, since there's no room for a dishwasher. I nearly choked myself not laughing the first time I saw her try to handwash something. She kept making these little noises of horror and disgust every time a bit of soggy food touched her hand.

It's been a long time since I felt like the two of us lived in the same world.

But none of that really matters. I know what Ma would think. I can feel her looking at me in disappointment and confusion, saying: 'You didn't even try to help her? You're better than that, kid. Don't let the world turn you cruel.'

How is it that I still have to have arguments with her in my head nearly four years after I scattered her ashes?

It's my stop. I whack the bell, skidding a little on the damp lino as the brakes of the bus screech, and I fly out of the doors so fast that they graze my shoulders as I push between them. I run all the way down the road, dodging the puddles on the unevenly patched pavement and a scattering of students larking about on the corner, dart into the side-alley, sidle past the skips and arrive at the kitchen door cold-damp-panting. I don't have time to catch my breath before I'm walking into a cloud of roasting garlic. The kitchen is sweltering, with lights bright enough to cause retina damage, full of people spinning around each other in a complex, borderline hostile dance of flying pizza dough, red sauce and cheese.

'You're late,' Callum snaps as he rushes past me towards the sinks with an empty tray. 'You're on section four, table eight wants a high chair putting out and the boss has some post for you in his office.'

'Post? Here? What is it?' Why would anyone send stuff to my work? It's not like I get anything but junk mail anyway.

'Don't know, don't care! High chair – table four!' he yells, heading back towards the restaurant doors with a tray of wine glasses.

'I thought it was table eight . . . Hell.' He's already gone. It must be table eight. Table four is in section one. I shed my coat, hang it up in the tiny space by the door, drop my backpack and rip my black apron out. I've got my pad and pencil – and a wide, vapid smile, vital for tips, especially on a bad-hair day – ready by the time I step through the double doors into the restaurant. I still feel sick with panic, and a lurking sense of betrayal that might be about Penny or me or both of us. What I want is to sit down in a quiet corner and cry. I don't want to talk to anyone, and I don't want to smile. Unfortunately, what I want has nothing to do with it.

☽◯☾

Five and a bit hours later, I'm hauling my backpack straps up over aching shoulders when the boss, Gary, bellows at me from the doorway of the back office: 'Where'd you think you're off to, Jude?'

I'm knackered, my hair smells of garlic and there's a puttanesca stain on the bottom of my white uniform shirt, which I'll have to spend hours scrubbing in the kitchen sink tomorrow – instead of catching up on sleep – if it's going to be fit to wear for my next shift on Monday. And I might be homeless come May. Various responses to Gary immediately form on my lips, just begging to spill out.

Luckily – my gig working at the supermarket is a zero-hours contact, so I need to hang on to this job more than ever if I *don't* want to be homeless come May – Gary doesn't give me the chance for smart comebacks. He raises one beefy arm, his tattoos on full display now that we've closed and he's rolled up his sleeves, and waves something white.

Post. Gary's office. Right.

'This isn't a P. O. box, you know,' he continues as I trudge down the corridor, past the old wine boxes no one's hauled out to the skip yet. 'Why are we getting your personal letters here, eh?'

'I don't know. Sorry. Thanks.' I still have enough hand–eye coordination to nip the envelope off him without having to endure the little game of keep-away that I think he was looking forward to. I start to jam the letter into my pocket, eager to escape. But something makes me stop.

The envelope isn't white – it's cream. That kind of thick, nubbly cream that means the paper is handmade using cloth fibres, and probably acid-free. The kind of paper I used to use for watercolour and pen-and-ink work at college. The kind of paper Ma used to save up to buy me for Christmas and birthdays. Good paper. Expensive paper.

The address is handwritten in precise, flowing cursive script, in indigo ink. It's for 'Juliet', which is a name I haven't answered to in four years. There's – there's a kind of crest? In the corner. A red line drawing, with what I recognise as a heraldic motif, a wreath of oak leaves, with a swan and a padlock at the bottom. And Gothic printing in tiny letters circling it, but my eyes are tired – I'm tired – and my tinted dyslexia glasses are at the bottom of my bag. I can't make sense of it.

'Swan, Lockwood and Swan,' Gary reads off easily, craning over my shoulder. 'Sounds fancy. You on trial for something?'

Shit. A solicitor's letter.

The credit-card companies – actually the debt-management companies that the credit-card companies sold Ma's debts to – claimed their money back out of Ma's 'estate'. They sold every stick of furniture we had in the rented flat, the framed prints she loved, the rugs I rolled around on as a kid, her big potted plants that she raised from seedlings, her electronic devices, her books, even her jewellery. By the time they were done, everything I had of my old life fitted into the two battered, stained suitcases that they didn't want, and my college backpack. I only found out later that I didn't need to let the bailiffs in, but how was I supposed to know that at seventeen? And

I couldn't have taken any of it with me into the bedsit where the council 'fostered' me after our landlord had me evicted.

But other than the credit cards all Ma had was student loans and those *were* written off. So who's coming after me? Why?

'Nah. I've come into some money,' I say carelessly, arranging my face into the biggest smile I can manage. 'See you!'

It's a tiny, petty pleasure to see Gary's expression wiped clean with shock, but it doesn't last. I'm experiencing the re-run of *Panic*, followed by its sequel, *Panic Part Two: Panic Attack*, and I'm out of the door before he can stick his nose in any deeper.

It's nearly midnight. The streetlight on the corner is flickering, splashing light intermittently on wet tarmac, puddles, the metal grates covering shop and restaurant windows. The students have been replaced by a random drunken bloke humming to himself as he zigzags unsteadily past me, and the slow crawl of taxis heading to trendier bits of the city.

I need light. I need my glasses.

I head towards the Tube station at a jog, new sweat breaking over my face, calves cramping with weariness. My boot edge catches on something in the echoing tiled stairway as I'm heading down into the Underground. I nearly go headfirst. The letter floats out of my hand, turning in a gust of hot air from below like a feather. I feel a huge swell of temptation just to let it go, to hope it disappears, stamp it into the slurry of brown muddy footprints if it doesn't.

But I don't. I grab it and manage to get myself down the stairs in one piece, wave my Oyster card at the reader without even taking it out of my pocket and finally collapse on one of the grey metal benches against the cold, curving wall.

Normally I'd be fine to read this. I was fine reading the Specials Board, card machine and receipts all night long. But the combination of exhaustion and a freak-out turns all writing, even the glowing arrivals board overhead, into sideways squiggles. I fumble to get my glasses out, putting a smudged thumbprint on one lens in the process, and finally, finally, tear the envelope open. My eyes skitter down the page:

Dear Ms Stewart,
We are writing to inform you of the sad death of your great-aunt Anne Erskine in September of last year. Ms Erskine was involved in a road-traffic accident and sadly passed away from surgical complications in hospital two days later. Please accept the sincere condolences of our entire firm.

What? I don't have any aunts. Ma didn't have any family, no one. Her mother gave her up when she was a baby. She grew up in foster care.

Executors ... estate ... transfer of legacy ... contact us at your first convenience. Then a list of documents they need, proof of my ID.

It has to be a scam of some kind. Although now I see they are asking me to make an appointment at premises in Lincoln's Inn Fields, in Holborn. That's far too fancy to be fake, surely? They must have me mixed up with someone else. Some other Jude – Juliet Stewart.

I look up at the display. Service due in five minutes. A few other people have arrived and are clogging up the ends of the platform. I fold the letter and put it in the envelope, then slide it carefully into the side pocket of my backpack as I stand up, all the time mentally combing through everything that I know about my family history.

My grandmother's name was listed as Hanna Rugelman. The documents that Ma eventually got her hands on say that Hanna was a foreign student, but not from where. There were no details on my grandfather, so I guess he could have been an Erskine. But how would the family ever have tracked me down, when 'Erskine' is nowhere in those files?

Ma was fostered with a view to adoption when she was a year old, but the couple stopped the proceedings and brought her back six months later stating 'marital breakdown and/or domestic issues' on the papers. That's one of the few things I ever saw Ma bitter about. She didn't remember the couple at all, but she never forgot the fact that she was supposed to have parents, to be part of their family – and they just sent her back when life got tough.

'Like rehoming a puppy that pees on the carpet once too often,' she used to say, her voice flat with contempt.

It can't be anything to do with them – there was never a finalised adoption. No legal tie.

Ma bounced around different places after that. When she was six, the state put her into a permanent foster placement with an older couple, Gemma and Dan Stewart. They'd fostered dozens of kids over a period of thirty years – Ma was the last. Dan died of a heart attack when she was leaving college. That's when Ma changed her name to theirs. Stewart. Gemma lived on until I was three, and I have some soft-focus-Monet-print-type memories that I like to think might be of her.

Ma never thought of them as her parents, though. They

were good people, but they weren't 'Mum' and 'Dad'. They had a biological son, years older than Ma, and he inherited everything they had. Ma used to say that they'd given her something far more valuable than money or property: self-belief.

It's because of them that she ended up going to Oxford to study history of art and eventually became the creative programme lead at the tiny non-profit where she worked until she died. Because of them that she was able to be the amazing, unforgettable person she was. Because of them, in a funny way, that I exist. She met my father at Oxford.

My father.

Everything's gone quiet. The Tube is coming. The ground trembles underfoot. Hot air eddies around me, blowing tiny frisps of hair into my eyes as the train streaks into place alongside the platform. But it's so quiet I can't hear a thing except my own pulse. *My father.*

I haven't thought about him in years.

Stephen Whittaker. He walked out on us before I was born. Died in some stupid army training accident on the Brecon Beacons when I was five, before I ever had the chance to learn why, find out what he was thinking or if he was worth forgiving. I remember – God, I remember – my mother's plate shattering on the floor, peas rolling across the kitchen tiles. She had caught sight of the newspaper headline. She left the shards of crockery and the ruined food lying there as she reached for the pages. She was crying, crying over the grainy black-and-white picture of the soldier who'd died.

I have the clipping. She cut it out and put it in the back of the oldest photo album with the pictures of her and Gemma and me when I was a baby, and I haven't opened that book in years; it's stuffed at the bottom of the suitcase with the posh leather-covered sketchbook that she gave me right before she died. But there was something in that article about the freak accident and the promising young officer, *something*, some turn of phrase, that's making my eyes blur and the hairs all over my skin jump like static. The something was . . .

'Survived by his aunt'.

I stumble onto the Tube, barely aware of what I'm doing. I need to get it together. I need to think, but all the way home it's like being in a dream, being high, being in a trance. I don't come out of it when I get off the Tube, out of the station. It's started drizzling again outside, but that doesn't make me snap to, either.

My father. Survived by his aunt. Condolences on the death of your great-aunt. Then I unlock the door of the flat and walk in, and the first thing I hear as I stand there in the dark entrance hall is Penny's voice cracking as it rings off the newly replastered walls: 'Duncan! Duncan! Don't stop!'

Jesus *Christ*. That wakes me up all right. I shut the door as quietly as possible behind me because I know from embarrassing experience that if Duncan realises I'm there he'll go even harder. Penny would want to stop, would probably be so embarrassed that she won't look me in the face for days. And I won't be able to be in a room with either of them without feeling my scalp prickle hot with mortification.

I shed my boots and coat and creep into the living room, not daring to put on any lights. There's enough streetlight coming in that I don't trip over anything, even the laptop bag that Duncan's discarded in the middle of the floor. Enough to show me that they've treated themselves to a takeaway and a couple of bottles of wine tonight, and left the washing-up – pretty much every plate, fork and spoon we own – piled haphazardly in the sink.

I sit down on the arm of the sofa bed, which I can't unfold to sleep on now as the noise will obviously give my presence away. Penny's bedframe, which is a solid thing covered in plush grey velvet, is thudding against the wall a-rhythmically. Worse, I can hear Duncan too. Like a pig hunting for truffles. I'd give nearly anything for working earbuds.

I take the envelope out of my bag. I don't unfold the letter. No need. The words are still throbbing, neon-bright, in my mind. It's real. This is real life.

Tomorrow is Friday. My manager at the supermarket has me booked in for eight-to-three. I need those hours. I need the money. I need to scrape together a deposit to move out and rent somewhere else. And as soon as my shift ends, I need to head out to every letting agent in reach via bus route and try to find the impossible, an affordable place to rent for a single 'unskilled' worker with two part-time jobs and no references. I need to do what I've been doing since Ma dropped dead in the street of a brain aneurism with no warning at the age of thirty-eight, leaving me without a person in the world who really cared if I lived or died: survive.

Penny and Duncan have spilled red wine on the new carpet – and on the edge of my tatty old suitcase, which is sticking out slightly from under the sofa bed. That's the suitcase with the photo albums in it. I'm sure I left it tucked well under.

My phone, my mum's old Samsung with the cracked screen, is in my hand. It takes two seconds to type the text:

Can't make it in for shift tomorrow, food poisoning, srry, Jx

I've sent it before I even realise that I've made my mind up. No, that's not true: I think I've known what I was going to do since I first realised what was in that letter, and what it might mean. I have to find out.

I'm going to Lincoln's Inn Fields tomorrow.

Two

The secretary at Swan, Lockwood and Swan didn't seem flustered about fitting me in at such short notice when I called. I had excuses ready about my work and how this was the only day I was free, but one mention of my name and she was happily booking me in at 9.30.

After a couple of deep breaths, which do little to make me feel better, I march up the steps to the posh office in Lincoln's Inn Fields. The door's open, and there's a narrow lobby with geometric tiles underfoot and another door, this one painted white and set with large, stained-glass panels. I stop to stare at them. They're beautiful. Turn of the century, Burne-Jones influenced. Stunning flower imagery on the top and side panels, a brunette in blue draperies pouring water from a ewer in the central one. Probably one of the virtues. Mercy, or Charity, or Hope. Exactly the sort of art that always made Ma roll her eyes: 'Victorian, sentimental as hell.'

But I love it. I've always loved art like this. I used to want to *make* art like this, before Ma died.

The front door clicks shut behind me and the sudden silence

makes my ears hum. There's a buzzer here, and when I gently test the handle of the inside door, it's locked.

I quickly unbutton my coat, pull my glasses off and swipe the rain from the lenses. Resist the urge to pat my hair because I know interfering with the curls will just make them worse. Shove the glasses back on, press the buzzer.

A cheery voice – the same one that I spoke to on the phone – echoes in the little space.

'Swan, Lockwood and Swan, how can we help you this morning?'

I clear my throat, but my voice still comes out strange and gravelly. 'Jude – Juliet Stewart, to see Mr Swan at—'

The door clunks as the lock disengages. I step inside, taking one last lingering look at the gorgeous glass, and am hit with a wave of warmth that makes my glasses instantly steam up at the inner corners. Directly in front of me is a reception area. The reception areas I'm used to, at the dentist, or the office at the council, have pitted plastic screens and cheap IKEA chairs. Here, even the photocopier looks as if it's been polished. A middle-aged Asian woman in a smart suit stands up from behind an antique desk to greet me.

'Good morning, Ms Stewart.' Her eyes flicker over me. I lift my chin and force my back straighter than it's ever been: it punishes me with a twinge. 'Nasty weather, isn't it? Do take a seat here. Mr Swan will be with you as soon as he can. Would you like a drink while you wait?'

I could murder an extra-strong PG Tips but don't want to ask. I just shake my head, and perch on the edge of the seat of an armchair furthest from the desk. As the woman starts tapping away at her keyboard, I practise some more deep breathing. In through the nose, out through the mouth. In through the nose, out through the mouth. Penny swears by this, but it's still doing nothing for me. I squirm around in the chair, awkwardly pulling my coat off.

'Would you like me to hang that up for you?' the receptionist asks.

Lady, can you not see I am trying to have a quiet panic attack here?

'No. Thank you.' I fold the bulky fabric over my knees and tug at my shirt in an effort to straighten it. An obnoxious chip in the black polish on my thumb catches my eye. I curl my fingers to hide it.

The clock on the wall above the desk says 09:26. I have been in here literally two minutes and I'm barely hanging on. What was I even thinking? I don't belong in a place like this. I should be at work. Donna's going to fire me. Oh God.

There's the sound of a door opening, and a discreet murmur of voices. I look up to see an older man, very tall, with cheekbones like golf balls under deep red-brown skin, and tightly curled pure white hair. The receptionist looks in my direction and this polar bear turns towards me, already holding out his hand. I stand, cramming my coat hastily under my arm.

His palm is dry and warm against my cold, clammy one. 'Ms Stewart? Delighted to meet you. I am Gerald Swan. I had the privilege of handling your great-aunt's legal affairs for many years. She was a remarkable woman, quite remarkable. Let's go into my office and be comfortable, shall we? Oh, if you could just give your documents to Stephanie . . .'

I fish around in my bag and pull out my passport and birth certificate, then hesitate as I place them on the green leather blotter on the desk. But the receptionist whisks the documents away from under my fingertips, and Mr Swan herds me deftly into his office.

It's the same size as the flat that I shared with Ma. Cool, wintry light floods the room through two massive sash windows. On my left is a desk large enough for four people to work at. On the right is a red leather sofa and a chesterfield, arranged around a fireplace that's nearly as tall as me.

'I always think a fire is essential in weather like this, don't you?' he says.

I've never seen an open fire before. It's loud, popping and snapping away furiously, almost as if it might break free and start on the rug or the coffee table next. I nod, drape my coat over the arm of the sofa as neatly as possible, and sit again, feeling like a puppet whose stiff limbs are under someone else's control. My hands have knotted up in my lap; I can't hide the scuff-marks on my boots, or the way that I slide backwards on the slippery leather. The fire is putting out a huge amount of heat, and that and the alarming noises are making my head swim. I'm back in that trance state from the night before and nothing here is real, not even me.

He sits down opposite me and leans forward. 'You must have a lot of questions.'

I do. I ought to have written some flashcards or something, because at this moment the only one that comes to mind is *Can I go yet?*

'Right. Let me just – I just need to make sure I understand – this whole situation. Your client was Anne Erskine, and she was my great-aunt. But my mother didn't have any aunts. So Anne Erskine must be—'

'Your father's aunt, yes. Although she was more like a mother to him, in all honesty. She raised him from the age of ten.' He smiles at me with disconcerting warmth. 'Anne Erskine's will was made shortly after Stephen enlisted in the army. She left everything to him. There's a codicil stating that if Stephen pre-deceased her, then her estate would go to his children. You are Stephen's only child.'

'He and my mother weren't married, though.' I shift in place. Leather squeaks.

'The Family Law Reform Act of 1987 abolished any distinction between the children of married or unmarried parents. Anne knew that.'

There's a look of expectation in his face, a kind of emphasis on those last words. It takes a minute for me to absorb the implication. Does he mean – 'She knew about us? About me?'

'She knew that Stephen had a child. I'm afraid he refused to tell her much more than that. It was a cause of some friction between them. Stephen was adamant that you and your mother were better off without him. Better left alone.' He hesitates, then one hand makes a kind of elegant circling gesture, a movement that conveys resignation, acceptance. 'He was a troubled young man. Anne didn't want to take the step of trying to contact you against his wishes, although after he died she made a couple of attempts to trace your mother – unfortunately, without success. She wanted to provide for you as a member of the family.'

I look away from him, staring blindly at the fireplace. 'That was nice of her.'

'She considered it the bare minimum she could do. If it had been her decision, she would have done much more.'

I'm still looking into the fire.

'Would you like a glass of water?'

I swallow hard. 'I'm fine. Thank you.'

'Shall I give you some details about the inheritance?'

The inheritance.

She's left me everything that would have been my father's. I feel a sudden current of excitement that runs down my vertebrae like electricity. I haven't felt anything like it in years. It's nearly too much.

He's holding a plastic folder filled with creamy pages. He flips through it, but when I finally look at his face he's not reading – he's watching me. 'Ms Erskine had only a small sum in savings, but she paid into a private pension fund for many years. Because she died before drawing the pension, her beneficiary is entitled to take the pension fund as a lump sum, without the deduction of Inheritance Tax. Probate has already cleared.'

I delicately remove my glasses, and fold them quite calmly into my shirt pocket. Then I've got my hands over my face, clamped tight. I'm sure I look like an utter weirdo. I just can't, I can't let him see whatever my expression is doing. Breathing into my fingers, I mumble: 'How much is in the fund?'

'A little over one hundred thousand pounds.'

A noise like thunder cracks open my chest; a sob that hurts as it escapes from me. Tears pool warmly against the palms of my hands. I can't even try to pull myself together. All I can do is sit there and cry.

'I'll fetch you that glass of water. Just a moment.'

The door closes. I don't look up. I'm trying to hold in more noises, keep a howl trapped inside. I don't know if it's a howl of relief or sadness, joy or fury, or all of them.

You heard that, right? Ma? I'm going to be OK now. I'm going to be OK without you. God, you have to ... Please, I need you to know this. I need you to know ...

I wish grief was like it is on TV, or in books or films. It's always extraordinary somehow. Magical. Transformative. But in real life grief is just misery. Misery and aloneness that go on and on and never get any better. You'd toss your sanity in the nearest bin to feel that the person you've lost is with you, even for a single second.

Now, out of nowhere, after forgetting what optimism even feels like, I can stop. Stop worrying, stop slogging. *Start again.* But I can't share this with Ma. This isn't our relief, our good news. It will only ever be mine. It's the best thing that's ever happened to me and it feels so empty.

Mr Swan is clearly used to dealing with emotional breakdowns. The minutes tick by and I realise there's no way it's taking him so long to find a glass of water. But his timing is brilliant. By the time he opens the door, I've just about calmed down, and finished hastily scrubbing my face with a tissue from my pocket. There's nothing I can do about my red nose and eyes. Self-conscious, I take the tumbler from him with a smile and a nod – avoiding his gaze again – as he seats himself and flips briskly through his folder.

'Here we are. Would you like to hear about the rest of Anne's legacy?'

The rest of it? What else is there? 'Please. I mean, yes, go on.'

'Your great-aunt had a house. It's located in a seaside town named Winterthorne, on the east coast, in Yorkshire. It was a gardener's cottage on the former Kearsley estate. The property is quite small, two bedrooms. We've had a caretaker, a local woman who previously acted as Ms Erskine's cleaning lady, checking on the place and airing it out as needed. The house has been valued at approximately three hundred thousand pounds. Although property in this area is increasingly desirable, if you wish to sell.'

He's been talking slowly, with conspicuously long pauses between sentences – just in case. But I don't have the volume of emotions left to break down again. I'm stunned, but I'm calm.

'Did my father ever live there?' Where did those words come from? That's not what I meant to ask.

'As a child, yes. I believe he stayed there often when he was on leave too.'

I don't know how I feel about the answer. Home. That's what he's saying. That cottage was my great-aunt's home, and my father's. Should that mean something to me, even though I never knew either of them? I can't tell.

I'll be honest, the potential £300,000 means quite a lot.

'Is that – is that everything?'

'Substantially, yes. The cottage is set in a plot of land, which comes to just under half an acre. There was an old outbuilding at the bottom of the garden, which Ms Erskine had converted into a studio for work. It has electricity and water.'

'Studio?' This one word stops me dead. Mr Swan regards me evenly, letting me gather my thoughts as the peppery scent of pencil shavings, the gritty dustiness of charcoal between my fingers, the musical chime of a paintbrush gently hitting the sides of a water jar soak up gently into my memory. There are a million uses for a studio. Photography, pottery, ballet. But.

'Did she paint?'

He nods. 'She was an illustrator and artist. A talented one. She won many awards over her career.'

An artist. Anne – this woman I never knew, this woman who was my family – was an artist. Like I wanted to be. I haven't picked up a pencil or a paintbrush in years. I don't know if I ever will again.

I massage my forehead. 'What do I need to do? Do I need to make decisions now, or—'

'Not immediately, no. We can begin the process of transferring the estate into your name straight away, however. Perhaps an advance on the liquid assets would be helpful? To give you some time to think.'

At last, an easy question.

☽○☾

I manage to find my way back out into the city. My legs have gone funny, sort of coltish, that too-long-and-too-knobbly feeling that you sometimes get after a really bad bout of flu. I think the solicitor could tell because he offered to get me a car to take me home, an offer which for some reason filled me with a desperate urge to laugh and laugh and laugh. It sounded so ridiculously grand.

It's still raining; it's still cold and windy. Everyone around me has their head ducked down, faces grimly screwed up. Their lives are grinding away like clockwork, one second after the next, one foot in front of the other. My clock's stopped. Just like that. I float around aimlessly for a bit, and then I end up on the Tube, headed to the British Museum.

I haven't been back there since she died. After losing the flat, dropping out of college, getting jettisoned from foster care, I didn't have time for anything, really, but work and sleep. One of Ma's sayings: 'Always take the time to refill your soul with beauty.'

Wading through the crowds, standing in line to have my bag checked, there's a low buzz of anticipation in my gut. As soon as I get inside the museum itself, the buzz expands, filling me with a warm glow of familiarity. I'd forgotten how much I always loved it here – this is why we came back, again and again, until it became routine on good days and bad, birthdays, just-because days. I love the huge, echo-y entrance area with the ridiculously expensive giftshop on one side and the sweeping staircase out of a fairy tale on the other. The voices all around me talking in half a dozen languages. The Great Court of Portland stone, with the lacy white ceiling arching up overhead to reveal the dark sky, and the contrast of cracked, ancient artefacts on white pedestals below. This place was part of me, part of our lives. I've missed it and I hadn't even noticed.

I'm braced for memories to hurt, the way they usually do. But for the first time since I was called out of my fine-art class to the college principal's office and found two grave-faced police officers waiting there to shatter my life, I feel . . . OK.

I wander slowly through the familiar spaces. I look at Japanese netsuke, Richard the Lionheart's gigantic sword, the fluted edges of ancient stone axes, the Sutton Hoo helmet – real and reconstructed versions – plaster casts of lost stone monuments. None of it is new to me, but it all feels new. I'm still just drifting, until I wind up back at the Egyptian exhibit. This is an old favourite. When I was a kid, Ma had the hardest time stopping me from climbing on this Sphinx's back. I thought it was a horsie.

I sit down on one of the benches opposite a life-size statue of Bastet. I've been refusing to look back for so long, frightened that I wouldn't be able to go on. Memories of Ma seem almost like dreams. Thinking about her is not the same as the yawning emptiness of missing her, and that constant, almost frenzied longing for safety and care that I, that any child, who loses their parent before they're ready, feels. Those are the wounds that losing her left.

I let the memories in, feeling for the impressions her life made on the world. On me. Feeling for what remains, the edges of who she was.

She always told me, 'Don't act stupid,' or, 'Don't pretend to be thick.' Never, 'Don't be stupid.' Because Ma took it for granted that I was brilliant. It was hard to live up to, sometimes. If I asked her, 'Ma, what do you want me to put in this salad?' she'd give me a long look, then say dryly, 'I don't know, Juliet – why don't you try adding some initiative?'

I put tinned sardines and Hula Hoops in one, once. She ate it. All of it.

She didn't understand tact, either. She knew how to be kind. One of the kindest people I've ever met. But if I asked her how I looked in something, or what she thought of my make-up, she'd say exactly what she thought in that moment, then be confused, torn between remorse and impatience, when I dissolved into tears.

'Why'd you ask me, then? Don't you want a true answer? You don't want me to lie to you, do you?'

I'd screech back, 'I want you to be a normal mum and think I look beautiful in everything, no matter what!'

I kept on asking her how I looked in everything new, just the same.

She wouldn't let me touch my eyebrows. She'd plucked ninety per cent of her eyebrows off when she was a teen, and they never grew back. She hid the tweezers out of every manicure set we had.

'You'll thank me when you're older,' she said. 'You'll see I'm right!'

And she was, obviously. Which was intensely annoying back then.

She had the world's most amazing hair, a deep brown-bronze colour that got darker in the winter, brighter in the summer. Sometimes she'd do an intricate, twisted braid, or pull the top half up and leave the rest down. Sometimes she'd sweep the whole lot up into a truly impressive bun right at the crown of her head. I envied her that bun so much. I used to call it 'the Bagel'.

'Oooh, it must be a big day – the Bagel is out. Watch out, funding bodies! Bow down, admins! Cower before the Bagel!'

I wouldn't have swapped her for any other parent. Not one who could buy me a mansion and five puppies and a pony. Not one who had sisters and uncles and cousins and grandparents to offer. Not even one who could stick around for more than thirty-eight years.

I know who she wanted me to be. What she wanted me to do. Stay in college and get the predicted grades, no matter what. Go to university. Pursue my art. But those dreams withered away once she was gone. It was just too hard, being alone. I'm not the girl that she knew any more. And I can't guess what course she'd advise me to take now.

Here's another fact about Ma: she always tried to make me forgive my father for leaving. Not for his sake, but for mine. I never really did, but I did forget about him, forget to be angry at him.

Anne Erskine didn't deserve my anger, and she doesn't deserve to be forgotten. Anne Erskine wanted to help me.

And she was an artist.

I'm on my feet again, eyes tracing the lines of the giant winged lions near the Balawat Gates. Humans only wish they were half lion. Really, we're more like snails. We carry a kind of home on our backs, like they do – an accretion of experiences and memories. Our parents' experiences and memories. Scars from when we fell, patterns of damage that we ourselves don't even really understand. Like a snail, we don't ever question the fact that we move through life under the weight of this shell. Even when every hollow curl echoes with grief, even when the weight of those flaws and dreams inherited from our parents is too much to bear, we can't get away. The shell is part of us. We have to keep carrying it all until we die.

Anne left her shell, the hollows and echoes of her life, for me to find.

It's quiet here between the gates. A little boy of about five or six teeter-totters past me, giggling. A woman follows, probably his mum, half laughing, half scolding in a language I don't know. She catches him and sweeps him up in her arms. I meet the mother's eyes for a second, and she smiles back at me. Then she carries him away.

I've never lived in a house before. I don't need one that's

somewhere off in Yorkshire, miles from anywhere, in some town that no one's ever heard of. I'm obviously going to have to sell it.

But I could go there first. If I want to. Go to this place, what was it called – Wintercombe? *Winterthorne*, that was it. There's nothing to say that I can't stay there for a few days. I can tidy the place up, go through everything that's in the house and get it ready to sell.

That electric feeling sweeps along my spine again, stronger this time, breath-stealing, exhilarating, on the edge of painful. Hope. I stare at the exquisitely carved wings of the three-thousand-year-old lion. I'm going. I'm going. I'm going to Winterthorne.

Three

'This is the stop, love,' the driver says, leaning one burly arm casually on the wheel. 'The Winterthorne stop. Winterthorne town's over by the sea there all right, but since the company cut back all the routes five years ago this is as far as the bus goes.'

I stare out of the window behind him. The road is sunk deep into the hilly land, with a drystone wall backed by a dark snarl of woodland, and a dense hedgerow that runs as far as the eye can see in either direction. The only sign of civilisation is the tiny wooden bus shelter that the bus driver parked next to. There's no sign of the sea.

The other passengers are staring out at the dull, drizzly afternoon so hard that I'm surprised the windows haven't melted. But, seeing the look of panic on my face, the driver sighs. 'I can take you on the roundtrip if you like, through Welton and back to the station. I oughtn't to, strictly speaking, but I don't feel right dumping a young girl out in the middle of nowhere.'

This is what it's been like all the way. I've been dragging around all my worldly possessions on various trains since this morning and it's now nearly two o'clock. I've left London, left the south, left everything I've ever known behind. That was supposed to be the difficult part. I'm here in deepest darkest Yorkshire – and this should be the home straight. Except that fate, the universe, or maybe just the rural public transport system seems to be determined to keep me away. The people at the last train station wouldn't even admit that there was a bus service to Winterthorne. It was pure luck that I saw the name of the town on the sign for this bus – only it turns out that wasn't the *good* kind of luck.

I could have given up at least four times already. I'm tempted to again now.

Instead, I tighten my grip on the handle of my case, and shake my head. 'No. Thanks. I need to find the town. That's what I came here to do.'

I keep telling myself this as the bus roars away. This is the Winterthorne stop. Winterthorne has to be somewhere here, somewhere between here and Welton, the next stop. If I follow the road, I'll find it.

The road is pitted and potholed. I don't even dare walk down the centre – a driver would never see me, not with all these switchback turns. I pull my case along the edge of the verge doggedly, muttering every time the little wheels bounce over a stone or a rut of dried mud and the handle tries to twist out of my hand.

The track climbs. And climbs. Drizzle spatters my glasses and hot cheeks. My tightly braided hair, which was holding up surprisingly well until now, is unravelling in long spirals around my temples. How can any road be this steep and just not slide right off the side of the hill?

Right on cue, I see a square wooden pole stuck in the hedge, lopsided, half hidden in a tangle of thorns and ivy. Two faded, peeling signs at the top point in opposite directions, like outstretched arms – one forward, the way I've been heading, and one back the way I've just come. The sign facing forward says . . .

'Kerningham?' The Kerningham bus was travelling in the opposite direction, I'm sure of it. I can't have gone in a complete circle without realising it.

The other sign, the one pointing back the way I've just come, is so faded that it's impossible to make out what was once painted there. If I squint, I can just about imagine there's the faint shape of 'W'. For Welton? Or Winterthorne?

Maybe it's W for *What the hell were you thinking, Jude?*

Common sense tells me to follow the sign. Turn back. Even if I'm fooling myself about the W, I know for a fact that I don't want to be heading in the direction of Kerningham. It's going to start getting dark out here in a couple of hours. I should go back to the bus stop, wait for the next service and, if they can't tell me where Winterthorne is, give up for the day and find a Travelodge or something for the night. In Welton. Or anywhere.

I ignore common sense. I'm not sure if it's pure stubbornness, or instinct, or some submerged memory of the maps that I pored over on my phone's screen for hours over the past weeks, but I want to keep going. I mean, maybe someone pulled the sign out of the ground somewhere else and just tossed it into the hedge. *Onwards and upwards*, like Ma always used to say.

Another few minutes' walking and the drystone wall disappears, replaced by more hedgerows. The wild bushes are a tangled green mass around me, scattered with tiny star-like flowers, blocking my view ahead and behind, and on either side. It's like being in some bizarre fairy maze. Sometimes ancient-looking trees, twisted and gnarled and mossy, arch over the road, dipping almost close enough for me to reach up and touch their newly unfurled leaves. Sometimes the trees bend in the other direction and the sky opens up above. The drizzle has stopped. It's growing brighter.

Then the suitcase wheels hit a ridge of mud. The whole thing twists sideways as if it's suddenly come alive; the handle wrenches painfully out of my hand. The instant I let go, it topples over, hitting my left ankle, which instantly buckles and gives way. I go down, hard, in the wet roadside grass.

I let out a screech of frustration.

A handful of tiny birds burst out of the hedge, fluttering close enough for me to feel the heartbeat thrum of their wings on my face. They spiral around me, then stream up into the sky. The echo of sweet song fades into quiet.

I sit there for another minute, feeling ridiculous. Take a deep breath in. Let a deep breath out.

Then I heave myself to my feet. I adjust the straps of my backpack over my shoulders for the thousandth time, and lean down to grab the handle of the case and haul it upright. A quick, cautious wriggle of my left foot causes nothing more than a faint, dull ache. No permanent damage, then.

Onwards. Upwards.

Except that as the road curves gently to the left it begins to slope downhill. The clouds are shredding fast, revealing a gem-bright sky. My mood begins to lift. I feel a tingle of emotion moving through me: not quite anticipation, not quite fear.

I can hear something. I think I can hear the sea.

The sun finally breaks fully through the clouds, cascading gold that makes my eyes water. My vision swims; I blink rapidly. Warm, salt-scented wind tosses the wet strands of hair around my face, carrying the sounds of distant birds – gulls – and the unmistakeable rush and boom of the ocean.

And then . . . I'm there. The town spreads out below me like a colourful patchwork quilt, a jumble of rooftops – grey slate and red tiles and yellow-grey thatch – spilling down the hillside to the sea where little terraced houses, brightly painted, hug the curve of a bay. The captive water glitters, blue-gold, boats of all sizes bobbing in place. Beyond the bay, a group of tall rocks thrust out of the open sea in a wavering line, like fingers, the remnants of some cliff face that fell into the water long ago.

On the right are pale cliffs and the white wedge shape of a beach. On the left, a heavily forested hill. There on the peak of the hill, among rippling branches and leaves, there's a ruin. It's huge, with towering spires – more like spikes – of ragged stonework, and gaping holes where windows must have been.

Winterthorne.

The shattering double beep of a car horn stabs my ears. Panicked, I skitter sideways with my suitcase, nearly falling again in my desperation to get myself to the safety of the verge before someone hits me.

A battered old truck, duck-egg blue, streaked with rust around the doors and wheel rims, judders to a stop beside me. A young man leans out of the rolled-down window. 'Hi! Are you Jude? Jude Stewart?'

He's in his mid-twenties, I think, fair but tanned, with a scattering of freckles across the nose and cheeks, and an impressive mass of wavy, chestnut-coloured hair that's tipped with copper at the ends, as if he spends a lot of time outside in the sun. His eyes are a clear, vivid green. He doesn't exactly look like a serial killer, but then what serial killer does? I don't even try to keep the suspicion off my face.

'Who are you?'

A dimple pops in his cheek as he grins. 'Nick Fairley. My mum's Liz Fairley.'

This means nothing to me. I shake my head.

'Ms Erskine's cleaning lady? She's been taking care of your house for you while the solicitors tracked you down. They told us what train you'd be on, so after I finished at the farm I waited at the bus stop for a bit. When you didn't turn up on time, I drove around looking for you. I've got your keys and some paperwork that you'll want.'

I'm trying to absorb this flood of information when he pushes the driver's-side door open and climbs out, rounding the front of the truck in two strides of long, jean-clad legs. He's slimly built, but his shoulders are broad, and the arms exposed by his faded old T-shirt are sinewy with muscle. He towers over me. I feel a sizzle of alarm and take a step back, snatching my phone out of my coat pocket. Mr Swan did give me a phone number for the cleaning lady, but the name 'Fairley' doesn't ring a bell and, anyway, of course I have no signal, no way to call for confirmation. Or the police.

But he doesn't come any closer once I've backed off. He just offers me his hand. After a minute's hesitation I take it, ingrained politeness winning over ingrained caution. He's got big hands to match his height; his fingers are blunt and strong, and his palm is rough, with leathery stripes of calluses on it. His grip on my fingers is gentle, though. After a quick shake, he lets me go, then steps round me and reaches for my suitcase.

'OK if I put this in the back?'

I bite my lip. 'Can I see the paperwork and keys first, please?'

I'm expecting signs of temper by now, but his face only telegraphs good-natured patience, and the dimple is still present. He lifts his hand up away from the case in a Don't Shoot gesture, then points to the truck. 'On the front passenger seat. Big white envelope, small white envelope.'

I sidle sideways, keeping my eyes on him until the last second, then peek inside the truck. Sure enough, there are two envelopes there. When I pull the door open and grab them, I can feel keys inside the smaller one and a quick look inside the larger shows legal-looking stuff with my name and the logo of the solicitors. I let out a slow, nearly soundless sigh, and relax.

'Sorry,' I say, my voice coming out a little gravelly. 'But. You know. I've had . . . a long day.'

'I'll bet. You came all the way from London today, right?' he says cheerfully, grabbing the suitcase as if it weighs less than a bag of sugar and shoving it onto a pile of fraying sacks in the back of the truck. 'No worries, we'll get you where you need to be.'

Five minutes later, we're turning off the pitted country track onto a broad, open road. Big white houses, set back from the road, flash by among the trees, and gradually get smaller and closer together until we're rattling down a residential street with tall, thin terraces painted various bright colours: blue, pale pink, light green, vivid yellow. An elderly woman walking a large Dalmatian raises her hand in a cheery wave as we pass her. Nick waves back.

'Have any trouble finding the place?' Nick asks over the sound of the pop song on the radio.

'A bit, now that you mention it.' I lean against the window wearily.

'It happens. My mum always says people can't find Winterthorne unless it wants to be found.'

I lift my head. 'What does that mean?'

'Oh, I don't know – people always get lost, the buses don't come, whatever. Transport around here is a nightmare. It's been like it since they closed our railway line down in the 1950s, apparently. One cannot simply walk into Winterthorne.'

I smile reluctantly. *'Lord of the Rings* reference?'

He laughs, eyes crinkling. 'Got it in one. I think you'll fit right in. Hang on, this corner's a bit sharp.'

We swerve hard enough to make my seat belt tighten, and then the sea is directly in front of us, looming up between a row of higgledy-piggledy little shops with whitewashed walls. Nick neatly manoeuvres the truck into a space between a couple of other cars at the kerb and engages the handbrake with a protesting shriek of gears.

'This isn't the place, is it?' I ask, looking at the row of shops. Mr Swan said 'house', not 'flat', and he definitely hadn't mentioned a bakery, shoe shop, new age shop, pet shop or a chemist's. My eyes keep straying back to the vast, glittering expanse of the ocean. I have to resist the urge to roll my window down and stick my head out like a dog.

'No, we just have one quick stop to make. I'll be back in five seconds,' he tells me, already slipping out of the door, leaving the engine running. 'Two seconds, even!'

He heads to the bakery, a building with a pink sign that

reads *Belle Croûte*. The glass frontage is filled with a mouth-watering display of French bread, pastries, tarts, a dozen different colours of macarons all jostling together.

I'm just settling in to wait and drool when the door opens again and Nick exits, accompanied by a small lady who looks to be in her sixties, with milk-pale skin and a halo of short, fine silver and blonde hair. She's wearing a pink apron and carrying a large pink box. She barely comes up to his elbow, but his expression is resigned, as if he's tried to stop her coming.

'This is her? This is Jude?' she demands through the window as she arrives at the truck. Her voice is low and rough, her accent a mixture of what I think is French and Brummie.

'That's me,' I say, smiling a little self-consciously.

'Jude, this is Belle,' Nick says, pulling open the door of the truck and then reaching back to try to take the box from Belle. 'The owner of the best bakery in town.'

She fends him off. 'Well, look at you! Aren't you lovely? We're so happy to see you here at last, Jude. Everyone's looking forward to meeting you. This is a little something from everyone in town to you.'

She flips open the lid of the box to reveal a huge golden pie, decorated with pastry flowers and birds. Packed in beside it is a round loaf of dark, crusty bread, assorted macarons, a row of Cornish pasties and a few other things I don't really have time to note before Belle pops the lid closed again and shoves the box over the gearstick at me.

'What, really?' I grab at the box, nearly drop it. 'I – thank you, that's so kind of you. I don't know what to say.'

'Just enough to see you through a few meals. We can't let you starve! Come and visit me when you've settled in.' She suddenly stops, her large, dark eyes sharpening. She reaches out with one capable-looking hand. Despite being so tiny, her fingers are long, and easily encircle my wrist. 'Jude. Don't be afraid.'

'What are you—' Uneasy, I twist my wrist. She lets go instantly.

'And I think we're done,' Nick says, guiding Belle backwards away from the truck. 'She didn't ask for her fortune telling. Thanks for putting this together. Mum said she'll see you tomorrow, OK?'

I shake off my discomfort enough to call out, 'Thank you again!'

Belle gives me a nod, then trots away to her shop. There's a beat of silence. I roll my eyes warily towards Nick.

He shrugs as he buckles his seat belt. 'She's eccentric. Believes in karma and tarot cards and stuff. No harm in it. Everyone just ignores her if she's being weird.'

'What did she mean about everyone looking forward to meeting me?'

'It's a small town. And . . . sometimes her predictions are correct,' Nick says with unblemished composure, turning the wheel and checking his mirror as if this is a perfectly normal conversation.

I put the box down on my knees with a thump. 'Predictions?'

As he pulls out of the parking space, a couple crossing the road ahead wave at the truck.

'Afternoon, Nick!' the man shouts. 'Oh! Welcome to town, Jude!'

'Good afternoon, Mr and Mrs Walensky!' Nick calls, waving back at them. He tells me, 'You'll get used to it.'

I don't say that I'm not going to be here long enough to get used to anything. It feels as if that would be ungracious, although I'm not sure I can articulate why. But ... *Don't be afraid?* I don't like the sound of that.

Nick turns the truck round and we head away from the sea towards the towering, ruin-crowned green of the hill. I look back over my shoulder, keeping the water in sight until my neck twinges and I have to face front again. The streets are steep, narrow and winding, and in many places the buildings seem jammed in together haphazardly, grand Georgian architecture alongside sagging thatched roofs, Victorian villas next door to arty modern constructions of glass and steel. Some of the streets are cobbled. There are trees everywhere – including a massive oak right in the middle of two lanes of traffic. I blink as I realise that the road just splits in half on both sides to go round it.

Twice, cars beep at us. A couple more people wave in greeting. I can't bring myself to wave back to people I've never met, so I curl my fingers carefully round the box of bread and pastries and smile. It's awkward, uncomfortable. But also ... nice? I'm welcome here. Like Nick said, it's a small town. Small towns are supposed to be different. Friendly.

'People thought a lot of Ms Erskine,' Nick says as we reach the edge of town and the hedgerows envelop us again. 'It's nice to know someone's coming to sort out her things and take care of her house. And your aunt must have thought a lot of you, to leave you everything.'

'She was my great-aunt. I didn't really know her.'

Nick gives me a look that's sympathetic but not overly horrified. 'Sorry. Families, eh?'

I nod, out of words.

The truck takes a right turn onto a track so narrow that the green of the hedgerow seems to swallow us. Thin whippy branches patter on the windshield and wing mirrors, and he mutters under his breath: 'Mum didn't tell me it was this bad – I'll have to get the strimmer out.'

Before I can say anything, the way ahead opens up, and I see it.

What did Mr Swan say? An old gardener's cottage? I don't know what I was expecting. It wasn't this. I can imagine Little Red Riding Hood trotting up the path, her basket laden with good things to eat, opening the wrought-iron gate in the neatly trimmed box hedge, and calling out for her grandma.

The building is tucked away amongst sun-dappled trees in a garden filled with drifts of spring flowers in pink, white, yellow and lilac. The walls of the cottage are sandy-yellow stone, the sharply peaked roof slate speckled with lichen. The windows are tall and arched. The front door is painted scarlet. I have a sudden dizzy memory of how, as a little girl, whenever I drew a house I always went straight for the Christmas Red crayon, to colour the front door.

'Here we are.' Nick parks the truck with more painful grinding from the brakes, then sweeps one hand out like a magician introducing his beautiful assistant and grins expectantly. 'Home sweet home! What do you think?'

Still dazed, I answer without thinking: 'It's gorgeous.'

Nick's grin turns into a different kind of smile, small and pleased. 'We did our best to keep it up.'

He nudges me from the truck, hefting my case down again as if it's nothing and even lifting the pastry box from my hands. I approach the wrought-iron gate. It swings back with a well-oiled, musical note, and I step onto a white gravel path and walk slowly towards the red door. Behind me, Nick is following, closing the gate with his knee since both his hands are full. He's almost on my heels, crunching over the gravel with my suitcase, but I feel oddly distant from him. In a slightly different reality.

I pass into the shadow of the white-painted, slate-roofed little porch, and stare at the door. My hands are automatically fumbling with the envelopes, trying to find the keys, but without any urgency. I almost expect the door will just, I don't know, sense I'm there and open for me –

The brass knocker rattles. The handle turns. The door opens.

Four

A curvy woman, several centimetres taller than me, stands in the doorway. She's freckled, with fine laughter lines that give her a friendly look, and steady eyes of a clear, pale green. She's got a sort of quality about her, not so much youthful as – ageless. Could be thirty or fifty. But the wavy chestnut hair caught up in an untidy ponytail, and those freckles, give her identity away.

'Liz?' I guess. Before I can backtrack and try 'Mrs Fairley' instead, she gives me a smile. The same dimpled grin that convinced me, almost against my will, to trust Nick long enough to climb into his truck.

'Jude.' Before I even know what's happening, she's out on the step, her arms drawing me in. I'm not really a huggy person, but it doesn't seem to matter. Her hair smells of unfamiliar shampoo and furniture polish, not coconut oil or Marc Jacobs perfume, and my mother never had this soft, pillowy quality. In fact, Ma wasn't much of a hugger, either. My eyes sting and I close them, just for a second.

Nick clears his throat loudly. 'Hello? Mum, can you let the poor girl go long enough for me to put this stuff down? Come on now.'

'Sorry, sorry!' She releases me, laughing, not sorry at all. I move back off the step, shuffling sideways on the gravel to let Nick get past me. I sniff, pulling my glasses off to check the lenses for dust. When I put them back on, I find that they're giving me identical bemused looks.

'What?'

'You're allowed to come inside, sweetheart,' Liz – Mrs Fairley says. She pushes the door, which had started to drift shut behind her, wide open. 'It's your house now.'

'Oh God, right, sorry!' I bumble in, banging the doorframe with my backpack because I'm trying so hard not to hit either of them. I pretend to look around, but I'm not taking anything in; it's dim in there, and my eyes are still watery for some stupid reason. Mrs Fairley follows me. Nick heaves the case over the threshold, hands the pastry box to his mother, and claps his hands together. 'I'll just go and strim those hedges, while I'm here. Leave you two to get sorted out and everything. Back in a bit. Bye!'

He pulls the door shut behind him as he makes his escape. The back of the door is white, and there's a brass cage on the inside to catch the post from the letterbox. I absently shrug my bag off, left shoulder cracking with the motion. I'm aware of Liz bustling away somewhere as I slowly turn in place, details sinking into my awareness the way that paint seeps across the paper after you've laid down a wash of water.

It's so quiet in here. An unquiet-quiet made up of small, restful sounds. There are birds twittering away madly outside, and a low, constant *shush-shush-shush*, like water, the wind in the trees. I can't hear cars, sirens, voices. A clock ticks decidedly nearby. It's a tall clock, a grandfather clock, next to the door. It's dark wood, but the pale face shines out: there's a painted blue sky at the top and a smiling sun. Next to it there's one of those old-fashioned coatrack-telephone-stand combos. There's no phone or coats on it, but there is an African violet in a chipped blue-and-white pot.

Underfoot are diamond-shaped red tiles, and behind me is a set of narrow white stairs running up the righthand wall. The walls are painted yellow, a deep shade somewhere between mustard and gold. You don't really see their colour at first because they're full, just full of art. Too much. Ma would have called this busy, over-crowded, chaotic. Small frames and big, all styles and colours, jostling for space in every gap. Here's a print I recognise, a Rackham plate of a sad-faced Alice at the tea party with the March Hare and the Hatter. And another, now that I look: a reproduction of one of Ruskin's moody blue oils, cloud-thick skies and the dark silhouette of something that might be a church. Between them there's a series of smaller pieces that I've never seen before. These look original. Acrylics, probably, each one about the size of my spread hand, but individually framed.

They're jewel-like, almost photographically detailed: an angular yellow flower and its rippling reflection on a dark-green river; a brown rabbit peering through tall grasses with wild, watchful eyes; a swirling rockpool, the sun striking its surface, shells and a starfish visible at the bottom; a green hill with a spiky sandy-coloured ruin at the peak, and a storm of clouds and sea behind. Wait, that's here – that's the hill here in Winterthorne! My gaze darts down to the bottom of the picture. There's a signature, small and tidy: *A. Erskine*.

I let out my breath, touching the frame with careful fingers.

'You like them, then?' Liz asks.

I'd almost forgotten she was there. She doesn't look offended, though – she's smiling, leaning against the banister.

'I love them.' My voice comes out a little wobbly.

She nods, satisfied. 'Good. She'd have been glad. Come on – let me show you around the place a bit, so you know what's what.'

It's a brisk, business-like tour. I'm grateful for it. For one thing, obviously I do need to know where the fuse box and first-aid kit and emergency matches, candles and torch are (all in the cupboard under the stairs). For another, it helps settle me down a bit. I feel uncomfortably vulnerable, as if my skin's got thinner.

It turns out that there are only two rooms downstairs, but they have a pretty impressive amount of square-footage, by London standards. The 'parlour' has a working fireplace (not that I intend to risk burning the whole place down by trying to light it), a big, saggy sofa and easy chair, a thick rug covering most of the dark wood floorboards. Everything looks a little faded, threadbare and comfortable. The walls in here are taken up by bookcases, crammed nearly to bursting. The big window overlooking the front garden has a deep window seat. There's a book still sitting on the cushion; I can see the bookmark sticking out of the pages. I don't touch it.

Running along the back of the house is a long, narrow kitchen, which has a door out to the garden. 'I'll leave you to investigate that on your own,' Liz says, after opening the door to give me a quick look. It looks lush and wild out there – less a garden, more a jungle. 'It's walled. Backs onto the woods.'

The kitchen is flooded with late-afternoon sun, flashing

and glittering among the leaves outside, pouring in through two massive arched windows. The windowsills are filled with potted plants. There's a scrubbed pine table under one window, with Belle's pastry box sitting in the middle. I eye it with intense interest; it's been a long time since the soggy cheese sandwich on the train.

Liz probably notices that look, because upstairs we whip quickly through the rooms. A tiny bathroom where an iron clawfoot tub takes up every bit of space not occupied by the toilet and sink, then the big bedroom, which has the nicest William Morris wallpaper – Willow Boughs – a triptych of Japanese woodblock prints where most people would have hung a mirror, and a brass bedstead made up with a flowery quilt. There's a lingering smell of roses, that dry potpourri scent that comes from little sachets filled with papery petals. It makes me think of my not-grandma, Gemma. I can't remember what she smelled like. If it was roses, or cigarette smoke, or something else.

'We cleared out the wardrobes and the drawers,' Liz says, opening the door of a closet large enough to stable a horse. 'I put everything in bags, here, you see. I thought Anne would have wanted them donated, but the solicitors said to wait. Do you want to go through—'

'No,' I say quickly. I'm thinking about the bailiffs rifling through my mother's things, stuffing it all in bags. 'No. Can we still donate them or—'

'Of course, love. I'll get Nick to put them in the back of the truck before we go. The local hospice shop will be glad to have them.'

The second bedroom is smaller. As soon as Liz opens the

door, I can tell that it's disused – that it's been disused a long time. It smells musty. Under that there's a hint of sweaty socks and the strong, powdery deodorant that sporty guys wear.

'Anne never touched it. It didn't seem right to go in after she was gone,' Liz murmurs.

I barely glance at the neatly made bed, the old posters on the walls, the bits and pieces scattered around under a layer of undisturbed dust, before shaking my head wordlessly. Liz pulls the door shut again, and we both turn for the stairs.

'All right!' Liz brightens up as we return to the kitchen, taking a seat at the table and folding her arms. 'Nick's probably drawn that job out nearly as long as he can, and he'll be in soon. But, before we go, I think you ought to make us a nice pot of tea.'

'I should?' I say doubtfully. 'I mean, yes, but I don't know—'

'Where anything is? Well, that's the point. I can't leave you without making sure that you at least know how to make yourself a cuppa, now can I? That'd be inhumane. Go on. The matches for the burner are on that windowsill next to the plants . . .'

Step by step, she talks me through lighting the gas burner, locating the mugs, spoons, teabags and sugar. The tea packet's unopened and the sugar pot is full. I realise she must have stocked the basics for me. The teapot, a heavy brown earthenware thing, sits ceremonially on the counter on its own iron trivet. I've only ever used an electric kettle before – the scream that comes out of the copper one when it boils makes me jump so badly that I nearly burn myself. It helps, though. Liz's right; it helps. Doing this thing for both of us, such a simple, basic thing, in this strange new place. By the time that Nick comes in, announced by the rattle and slam of the front door and a smell of clean, slightly sweaty male skin and fresh green sap, Liz and I are laughing – giggling, in Liz's case – over mugs of tea and the macarons from Belle Croûte.

'Lovely,' he says, pulling up the bench without waiting for an invite, and helping himself to some tea. 'Can I have one of the green ones? What's so funny, anyway?'

Liz looks at me and makes a small, desperate noise deep in her throat. I snort into my mug, nearly spilling it. This is the noise I apparently made when the kettle screamed, and she's been doing an impression of it repeatedly ever since. I don't know why it's so hilarious. It just is.

'You had to be there,' I manage, pushing the bakery box in his direction. At that moment, I'm so grateful for their presence, their sheer matter-of-fact normality, I'd give either of them all the green macarons they wanted. I point at Liz. 'And you can stop that now, please. I don't want tea up my nose.'

'Me neither, Mum,' says Nick firmly.

'All right, I'm finished.' Liz sighs contentedly, putting her empty mug down. 'You drink your tea, love, and we'll just have time to collect the bags of clothes and get them down to the charity shop before Jasminder closes up. Give poor Jude a bit of peace and quiet.'

I'm not sure if being alone at last sounds like the best thing ever, or the absolute worst. I don't say anything, but maybe my face changes. Nick turns to his mother, hiding his expression from me. After a moment, Liz reaches out and takes the half-full mug of tea out of Nick's hand.

'Go up to the bedroom and get a start on the bags, would you?' There's a note in her voice, patient but a tiny bit stern as well. Nick's jaw clenches, but he gets up. So do I, rubbing uncertainly at my arms.

I help get the bags down the stairs and load them into the back of the truck, wave to Nick – who smiles back, though his jaw is tense, still annoyed at his mother – and turn to say goodbye to Liz.

'Thanks for this. For all of this. Stocking everything up, getting the place ready. It's – I really appreciate it.'

'They did pay me to do it, you know,' she says, dimple popping in her cheek. Then she takes my hand. 'I'd have done it anyway. Anne was my friend. More like family. My number's there on the fridge, and I'll send someone down in the next couple of days to check if you need anything.'

She climbs into the truck and Nick reverses it through a three-point turn that becomes more of a five-point turn, at one point going right back into the hedge and setting the whole thing shivering. I stand and watch from the other side of the gate.

'Welcome home, Jude!' Liz yells out of the window as Nick finally gets the truck pointed the right way.

Then they're gone. The light's going too, syrupy gold shading into cool bluish twilight in the shadows, although the sky's still bright overhead. I have the house keys in my pocket – Liz's set, which she handed back to me. I take a deep breath, trying to figure out what to do next now that I'm really here.

I go into the house. Lock the door behind me. Focus on the gentle sounds of my own movements as I pass through the tiled hallway, down the two steps into the kitchen, and to the back door. Liz left it unlocked.

In the garden, my boots make a sharp *chock-chock-chock* on the granite stepping stones as I hop from one to the next,

The Moonlit Maze

avoiding the dense, mossy grass that swells up over the edges of the intermittent path. On either side of me, trees and bushes rustle softly. White and yellow flowers – crocuses? – peek out around their feet. There's an iron archway with a dried-up-looking purple vine all woven through it, which I think, based on the thorns, might be a rose of some kind. Beyond that, nestled back against a weathered redbrick garden wall, is a small wooden cabin. It's painted blue, twilight blue. The two windows at the front are curtained like sleeping eyes, and I know the door is locked. I have the key here in my hand, on the ring Liz gave me.

My great-aunt's studio. Anne's studio. The place where she made art.

I stare at it for a long time, keys jingling in my twisting fingers. It oughtn't to be harder than confronting Stephen Whittaker's old bedroom, but it is. I want to go in. I don't dare go in. I want to go in.

Maybe . . . just not now. That's all right, isn't it? I have some time.

I look up through the trees at the hill above the house. I realise that I can just make out the top of the ruin from here – the stones are still sunlit, tinted red, though the wood below is darkening by the minute. I wonder what the place used to be, what it's called. There's a trill of song, sweet and rippling and low, unlike any drab little sparrow that ever chirped in a London park. What kind of bird sings at night? Maybe I'll find out.

It's like a long-held breath finally releasing. Like all the muscles in your neck going loose all at once. *I have time.*

I undress that night in the rose-scented bedroom, listening to the sound of the wind moving in the trees. I don't draw the curtains. There are no people out there, no lights. All I can see out of the window is the dark shadow of the hill, seeming closer at night, and above that, a sky pinpricked with glinting stars, and the fat curve of the moon. As I pull a sleepshirt over my head, I imagine I can feel its pale light striping my naked back, lukewarm.

Under the quilt, the bed is made up with old-fashioned sheets, a little stiff at first, but then warm and soft. They smell of some brand of fabric softener I've never used. They smell of wind and sunlight, and maybe even a little bit of the sea. My joints throb with tiredness, but I expect it might take me a while to fall asleep in an unfamiliar bed – on unfamiliar pillows with hollows worn in strange places, flat on one side and plump on the other – in a new place. I close my eyes. I listen to the sound of the wind in the trees. It's like water. Like waves on a beach. Like falling rain . . .

Five

Xanthe, spring 1924

The train emerged from the tunnel into soft rain tinted green with spring sunshine. Xanthe, rocking gently in place as the track curved northwards, blinked against the sudden brightness. Opened the battered leather cover of her journal. Fanned the softened edges of paper with her thumb. Stared down at the careless loops of ink inscribed on the pages. Closed the book again.

She was almost there.

A smooth, pale hill was coming towards the train. Hedgerows and yellow fields ran below it, and swollen clouds behind. Searching her memory, she found the name waiting: Brimfogel Hill. Where the men used to light bonfires to warn of raiders coming from Denmark, and Norway, and then Spain and France. She most likely counted as an invader from France these days. She wondered if anyone besides the family even knew she was coming back.

Perhaps better if they didn't.

The train seemed to be picking up speed. For a moment, she

felt dizzy, pressed back into her seat by gravity, as if the train was standing still and the earth itself was whirling beneath it, jolting the motionless wheels and flinging them forward, forward, off the edge of the land into the sea.

But there was no sight, yet, of the sea.

She always remembered this journey differently. Remembered it with her ocean dancing and glittering through the memories, making things seem brighter than they'd truly been. Leaning an elbow on the wood rim under the window, she combed the fingers of one hand through the freshly shorn strands of her hair, taking comfort in the repetitive motion. What was Mother going to say about Xanthe's 'shingled' locks when she saw them? Nothing good, most likely. The unruly masses of curling red hair had brought Xanthe nothing but teasing and inconvenience since she was a small child; as soon as the weight of them was lying on the floor of Felicie's drawing room, she had felt both lighter and freer. More herself, or at least some new version of herself into which she was slowly feeling her way. She hadn't regretted it. Not once. But she couldn't deny that it had been, ultimately, another act of rebellion. Perhaps the whole of the last three years had been, in one way or another.

Then had come the letter.

Xanthe had sensed a gradual softening in her mother's stilted, dutiful correspondence over the past few months, but she had been taken off-guard by the sudden outpouring of warmth she had received before her birthday.

> . . . *it feels like so long since we've seen you. It has been so long. Surely you must be missing us by now, as much*

as everyone here has missed you? Let's put all that silly fuss behind us now. Your father and I truly want nothing more than to see you return home this year, darling . . .

Helpless in the face of kindness as she never was when confronted with cruelty, she had replied saying yes, yes, she did miss them, yes, she did want to come home. She hadn't managed to arrange everything to return quite as quickly as her mother had hoped, and so Xanthe had celebrated her twenty-first birthday in Paris with her small number of friends and large number of friendly acquaintances under the stern gaze of Les Deux Magots rather than with her parents, but . . . well, here she was. Back on her native soil as requested, with her entire life in France, her rebellion itself, folded away neatly into a few suitcases and trunks. As if nothing about it had been real. As if she'd only ever been waiting to be offered forgiveness to come running, though she had told herself, again and again since she arrived in France, that Paris was her home now, and she didn't need her family's approval or their absolution.

But her mother's words, that implicit offer to forget the past, had caught Xanthe like a hook biting deep into the mouth of a hapless fish, and drawn her, gasping, from her hiding place in fresh waters. Drawn her back to the salt tides of home.

'It's just a visit for now. Nothing's final. I don't have to stay.' She opened her journal again and pressed her fingertips to the pages as if she could absorb the ink, absorb strength. 'I don't have to do anything I don't want to do. *I don't.*'

Her voice rattled off the luggage rack and the white plastered ceiling. She winced. Perhaps it would have been better if she had needed to share the compartment. But there was never anyone on the train to Winterthorne; that was part of what made it Winterthorne, she supposed.

Abruptly, the light changed. The panelled walls of the first-class carriage suddenly glowed, gold-edged and wavering. Insensible of the potential damage to her travelling suit, she scrambled up onto her knees on the prickly horsehair of the train seat. Her hands – one still clutching her journal – pressed to the glass pane.

It welled up slowly into the frame made by the window, bounded by trees on one side and rising cliffs on the other. An immensity of water, at once far away and impossibly close, restlessly tossing and gold-capped under the sun, dull and still as occluded glass where the clouds lay close to the horizon.

The sea. Her sea. Under her ribs, in the tricky, jostling maze of organs and bones, something stirred. Recognition, felt just as Wordsworth said, in her blood. Felt along the heart. She was almost there.

Home.

When the train pulled into the little station ten minutes later, she only just managed to slither down off her perch on the seat in time to avoid scandalising the porter. She brushed ineffectually at her skirt with one hand, trying to flatten the wrinkles, while the young man opened her door, swung down her valises and two corded trunks, and loaded them efficiently onto a trolley amid clouds of steam and smoke. She noticed absently that his left hand had been replaced with a metal hook, which he used nearly as deftly as his flesh hand. Such sights had become commonplace since the end of the war.

'There you go, your ladyship.'

Stepping down onto the platform, she jolted and almost

stumbled. It had been three years since she had used her title. She had been plain Xanthe Winter in France. The young man was looking at her expectantly, but the round, ruddy face beneath the neat peaked cap was entirely unknown to her.

'Thank you.' She fumbled in her purse, squinting as if perhaps the smoke were bothering her eyes. 'Er . . . I'm not entirely sure . . .?'

'It's Hardy, milady. You might perhaps remember my father, who had the job before me?'

'Oh, yes, of course!' she responded mindlessly. Xanthe despised lying – especially this kind, the polite fiction. But you couldn't get out of it. If you tried to admit the truth, people would take offence, turn the offence into a slight, and never forget it. Conversely, they would help you if you played along, they would cooperate in making the story work, even if they knew full well that you were making up every word. It was exhausting. She forced herself to enquire, brightly: 'I hope he's well?'

'Enjoying retirement, ma'am, him and my mother both. He's taken up bowls, you know.' He made a kind of rolling motion with his metal hand, then laughed. 'Funny hobby, but he does enjoy it.'

Her fingers – which had been raking at the bottom of her purse desperately – found a coin and pressed it discreetly into his good hand. The man tipped his hat, still beaming, and turned to haul her luggage across the platform. She let her head fall back in momentary relief, and then followed, tugging on the narrow silk brim of her cloche hat to make sure it was still in place. The tiny station was unchanged since her last departure: Victorian iron-work blistered with rust, the little stationmaster's hut needing a new coat of paint as it always did. The blackthorn hedgerows beyond were plump and pale with May blossoms, though it was still April. So different from the soaring grandeur and constant grinding cacophony of Paris. And there was the same car that always waited for her too: a Morris Oxford, top up. She was torn between the traitorous comfort that familiarity brings, and resentment of the way she could already feel her edges softening, trying to melt back into the spaces occupied by her past self. Her smaller self.

Then the windshield rippled as the driver pushed open the door, unfolding with some difficulty from the narrow space behind the wheel, and removing his hat.

'Mr Marten?'

He was just as he had always been. Tall, square-shaped, neatly attired in a knitted vest and a starched shirt and tie. Over the top, a voluminous tweed coat, the pockets always bulging. Mysteries resided within: seed packets, odd gloves, secateurs, nails and screws, bits of wire and brown paper bags filled with mint bullseyes that he would dispense to a small girl who had grazed her knee, been stung by a bee or, worst of all, been abandoned by her glamorous older cousins in the garden while they ran off, laughing, into the countryside on some grand adventure.

'Afternoon, Lady Xanthe. Welcome home.'

The deep creases around his eyes and the nearly invisible flash of a dimple under the full, nut-brown beard told her there were nothing but good wishes in the greeting. No hidden reproof. There never was, with him. It was all she could do to halt her headlong rush forward before she embraced him, just as she would have done when she was five, toddling through his gardens.

'It's – oh, it's *wonderful* to see you.' His fingers were as hard as granite in hers, and his calluses rasped against the soft leather of her gloves. 'How are you? You haven't aged a day. What are you doing here? Where's Higgins?'

The head gardener's cheeks had taken on a faint pink cast. He cleared his throat and gave her hands a little jiggle in his, then clapped his hat on his head and stepped away to open the rear door of the car. 'Very kind of your ladyship. Higgins is laid up with his lungs again.'

'Poor man,' said Xanthe feelingly. The chauffeur had been gassed at Ypres. 'I hope he's let them get the doctor for him this time? No, don't be silly. I'm not sitting back there – I want to be able to talk to you.'

Suiting word to action, she pulled open the front passenger door and hopped up into the car's dark interior. Mr Marten closed the back door with a sigh that Xanthe could hear through the open sides of the car. 'I should think the town will have something to say about you riding up front with me like one of the housemaids, lass,' he said, his voice conveying both humour and resignation as he closed the back door and came to take his place beside her.

He had called her that, sometimes, when no one else was around to hear – *lass*, affectionate and exasperated, just the same way that he spoke to his own daughter, Sally.

'Well, no matter what I do, they're longing to be scandalised,' she retorted as he slammed the door shut. The porter, who had been working to secure the luggage at the back, reappeared and gave them a thumbs-up. 'I don't see why I should let it bother me. Anyway, you haven't told me how you've been!' she shouted over the rattling roar as Mr Marten started the engine and ground through the gears, easing the car down off the verge onto the doubtful safety of the rutted cart track. 'How are your gardens? You must be busy at this time of year!'

'Busy at all times of year, if I'm doing my job right,' he said. 'Your parents' gardens are doing well; I should think we'll have a good display of the roses this year. How have you been keeping over there in France? Been going around lots of grand balls and meeting marquises?'

'Oh, I'm very glamorous. I have an attic room and I stay up all night reading by gaslight to clear a space in all the mountains of books so that I can get out when morning comes. Felicie, my friend, says that if the piles fall over and crush me to death one day, she'll just leave me there. A fitting tomb for me.'

'She sounds all right, that friend,' he said, smiling. 'And what do you do all day?'

'I visit bookshops, of course. And I wander from cafe to cafe, scribbling away like a madwoman. If I'm lucky, I can squeeze in a visit to a museum or a gallery, or sometimes I'm invited to a dreadful party, a literary salon they call them, and everyone laughs at my accent and makes fun of everything I've written.'

'You know, it's strange to say it, but somehow that's just what I imagined,' he said, thoughtful.

And that was all the comment he would make, Xanthe knew. She wouldn't have dared to offer this unvarnished account of her life to . . . well, anyone else. Her letters to her parents had employed a fine mixture of evasion and omission that allowed them to create a more palatable story in their minds: one where she spent her time attending respectable tea parties and concerts, and her allowance on hats and silk stockings, all chaperoned by the family of her genteel friend from school, Josephine.

Xanthe buffeted Mr Marten's shoulder gently. 'Enough about me! I know you must be dying to tell me what Sally is up to these days.'

He beamed, eyes crinkling deeply at the corners. 'Well, now that you ask. She's a typist at Braithewaite and Carlisle's, down in the village. Senior typist, in fact – they think the world of her there.'

'She's probably running the place for them, if I know her.'

'And she's found herself a nice young man, too, name of Fingal. They got engaged at Christmas. He's up at the university in Durham just now, training to be a teacher.'

'Engaged!' Xanthe hesitated, trying not to show her dismay. Sally was a year younger than her. 'Congratulations! You'll tell her I'm pleased for her, won't you?'

'I will, yes. She'll be glad to hear of you.'

A tiny bird – a wren or a robin – thrummed across the windshield, narrowly escaping collision. Xanthe fixed her gaze on her gloved hands where they rested in her lap. Her lips felt dry. *Just ask. Just say it.*

'What about Tom? Is he finished with university now?'

She knew that he was. He had been born over in the tiny gardener's cottage on the edge of the estate almost exactly two years before Xanthe; their birthdays were two days apart.

Xanthe had always tried to save some of her birthday cake for him, since she wasn't allowed to invite him to her parties. Hiding away in the hedge maze to share cake with Tom, giggling and shushing, unfolding napkins carefully tucked round slightly stale and crumbly icing and marzipan, had always felt more like a real birthday treat than anything her parents had offered.

She was so caught in the memory that Mr Marten's response, when he spoke, took her by surprise.

'Graduated with honours. He won a big competition too, with a story that he wrote for the student paper, about a factory and the conditions for women workers. The Ellis-Merchant Prize – have you heard of it?'

'No, but it sounds impressive,' she admitted, not trying to prevent the smile spreading across her face. Happiness, yes, but also relief that she could feel it, and feel it genuinely, untainted by sadness or envy. 'Good for him. I'm glad for him and proud of him. Not that I had anything to do with it, of course.'

'Except for drilling him all those years on his spelling,' he said dryly.

'What are friends for? He helped untangle my arithmetic many a time. Is he . . . ?'

There was a darting glance at her face, gone so quickly that she felt more than saw it. 'He lives up there now. Working at the newspaper. They offered him a job before he even graduated, and he was promoted last year. Doesn't make it back home to visit as often as I'd like, though I know he tries. He's a busy man these days.'

'I see.' And she did. It was kind of him not to make her ask. 'Well, I expect in five years' time I'll be boasting to everyone that I knew him when he was a boy.'

She looked down at her lap, at her gloved fingers resting protectively on the pocketbook that held a battered old journal, half full with ragged fragments and crossings out and unfinished scribbles. It was nine years since she had let anyone look inside it – since she was twelve, and Tom fourteen. Since she was sent away to boarding school. They had both grown up and moved on.

It was for the best.

The sunlight fell suddenly on her face, bouncing from the brass highlights on the car's dashboard. She raised her hand to shade her face and, as she did, the road turned, and the hedgerows fell away to reveal the town.

Six

Winterthorne spread out below the road in a vivid patchwork of walls and rooftops in pink, slate-grey, copper and yellow, spilling down the steep folds of the hillside to the bay, where fishermen's cottages hugged the half-moon curve of the dun-coloured beach. The bay water, captured by the encircling arm of the sea wall, was turquoise, clear as glass. The Thorns – the four tall, jagged remnants of a cliff that had collapsed into the ocean in the time of William the Conqueror – thrust out of the open water beyond the headland, bridging the gap between clouds and the shadows of clouds on the green-gold glitter of the ocean. Gulls, kittiwakes and guillemots wheeled around the tall rocks, keeping a wary eye on their nests. The craggy chalk cliffs were the colour of freshly churned cream at this time of year, in this light.

And towering above it all – the cliffs, the town, the bay, the sea – was the ivy-sheathed golden stone, copper Tudor brick and various Gothic Revival additions of Kearsley Castle. A ridiculous pile of antiquated kitchens, under-used bedrooms, half-abandoned cellars, perpetually leaking roofs – and Mr Marten's glorious, famous gardens – all constructed from the ruins of a Cistercian monastery which had been violently 'reformed' by Henry the Eighth's men, and then handed over to one of his minor noblemen as a reward for loyalty.

It was too beautiful to safely dwell on in her memories while she was gone. Whenever she returned and saw it again, she felt dazed, almost hurt, wondering how she had ever managed to make herself leave. And then leave again. Yes, she had enjoyed Paris. She had enjoyed her time in Lausanne, too, and had been intoxicated by the beauty and history of Rome in her visit there. But, just as a salmon will dash itself to pieces on the rocks in its quest to return to the place where it was born, so Winterthorne and its sea owned a deep-down part of her.

It was home. It always would be, no matter how far she ran, or for how long.

'You'll mind how you go, won't you?' Mr Marten said abruptly as he turned them onto the long, poplar-lined driveway that led to the castle's front entrance. It was a concession to what they both knew: the orbits of the daughter of the Winter family and the estate's head gardener were unlikely to touch often, if at all, now that she was grown.

'I will,' Xanthe said, drawing her shoulders back in her seat. 'And you'll . . . you'll pass on my love.'

'Of course.'

The car travelled around the fountain at the centre of the carriage circle, and then juddered to a halt in front of the house. As Xanthe's ears struggled to acclimatise to the sudden quiet, the iron-studded door at the top of the broad steps opened, and Bowdler, the family butler, appeared, white-gloved and sober-faced.

A moment later, Xanthe's parents were coming down the steps towards her.

Xanthe's first reaction was relief. Her cousin Jonathan wasn't with them. Then, hard on the heels of that, shock. They looked old. Both of them, but especially her father.

There had never been much hair on Papa's head, not in Xanthe's lifetime, but now the remainder of it had gone. He was thinner, seemed to take up less space somehow, though he still towered above Xanthe's mother. His shoulders had a peculiar kind of hunch to them, and it took her a minute to realise what caused it.

He was using the cane, the walking cane that she had given him for a Christmas gift when she was twelve. Oh, the tight-lipped scolding her mother had given her over that cane! Over Xanthe's insensitivity and unkindness in reminding her father of the faint limp from his old riding injury, and the wounded pride that Lord Kearsley was far too stoic to betray but which, her mother assured her, he felt deeply. Xanthe had expected that the cane had been 'lost' in the attics, or given away.

'Darling! Stand still – let me look at you.' Her mother clasped her shoulders firmly, pressed a brief, dry kiss to her cheek, and then stepped back to examine her from head to toe. 'I like this shade of blue on you, but, goodness, what's happened to your hair? Take off your hat, dear – is this what they call shingling? It looks so different!'

'Quite fashionable, I believe,' her father said, slightly out of breath. His grey eyes met Xanthe's for a moment, unreadable, then he smiled. 'Not unflattering.'

'Do you know, I think you're right, dear?' Lady Kearsley

said, as if surprised. 'You look quite marvellous, Xanthe. So grown up! Paris has agreed with you.'

'Thank you,' she responded, half a second late. 'I believe it has. How are you both?'

'Rubbing along tolerably enough – no need to worry,' Lord Kearsley said. He reached round the side of his wife to give Xanthe's shoulder a gentle pat. 'Let's get inside now, ladies. Cook's had tea waiting for us in the drawing room for half an hour or more.'

'I had her make a chocolate cake, Xanthe, dear – they were always such a favourite of yours when you were small.' Xanthe's mother took her arm and pressed it. 'Remember? You couldn't say "chocolate" so you used to ask for a "cocky cake".'

'Did I? How embarrassing!'

'No, you were only three,' her father said. 'Rather sweet, actually.'

They stepped inside, into the dark hall, slightly crowded together still. Xanthe, her vision still blurred from the bright sunshine outside, turned automatically to the right, reaching her free hand towards the blurred black-and-white clad figure whom she assumed was Bowdler, ready to take her hat.

Her hand grazed something solid. There was a panicked scuffle of feet, echoing coldly on the tile, and then a deafening metallic clang. Xanthe jumped as something icy cold splattered her lower legs. 'What on earth?'

As she blinked again, she saw a small person clad in a maid's uniform, desperately trying to mop up a tide of clear fluid in which slices of lemon floated. A silver tray, jug and three silver punch cups lay scattered across the red, black and cream floor tiles.

'Oh! The lemonade!' Xanthe's mother said mournfully, using her hold on Xanthe's arm to pull her back out of the spreading puddle.

Bowdler rebuked the maid with a barked, 'Ellen!'

The girl flinched. Her cap was sliding off, revealing a tangle of honey-coloured hair beneath, and she was plainly mortified – she hadn't even dared to look up, let alone tried to excuse herself – but the side of her cheek that Xanthe could see was flushed a painful, blotchy red. Something about the gawky quality of her movements made Xanthe sure she wasn't much more than sixteen.

'Don't be cross with her, Bowdler,' Xanthe said quickly. 'It was my fault – really. I knocked the tray out of her hand. Ellen, I apologise.'

The girl lifted her face for the first time. She was remarkably pretty, with wide blue eyes – but Xanthe's attention was caught by the healing cut high up on her right cheek, the size of Xanthe's thumb. The thin little wrists poking out from the white cuffs of the girl's uniform were mottled purple.

Xanthe's body went as cold as if the lemonade had been poured down her spine instead of at her feet. For a split second she was back in Paris, back in the muggy thunderstorm air on the little balcony of Laurence's apartment, Suzette's sneering face blazing against the dusk. Her blood-streaked teeth. The voice, thick with tears and contempt: '*Who do you think, imbecile?*'

Xanthe opened her mouth; somehow nothing came out.

Bowdler had no such issue. 'That's as may be, my lady, but the girl is still blocking the way. Ellen, remove yourself at once!'

With an almost animal gasp of panic, the girl abandoned the fallen tray and scuttled backwards on her hands and knees.

'Ah, good. Come along – I had them light the fire in the drawing room. Your shoes will soon dry . . .' said Xanthe's father, and Lady Kearsley tugged Xanthe into motion. They all edged round the puddle.

Xanthe swallowed hard, took a deep breath and hissed quietly: 'Mother! That maid is covered in bruises!' She tossed a look back over her shoulder at where Ellen was still on her knees by the entryway, head bowed, being quietly dressed down by Bowdler.

'We're not beating her, my dear.' Lady Kearsley smiled indulgently. 'The girl's ferociously clumsy, but what can one do? It's so hard to keep staff these days – you have no idea! She's the third housemaid in the past six months . . .'

Lulled by the deluge of words, Xanthe allowed herself to be guided into the drawing room, where tall windows looked out over the intense sunlit green of the upper lawn, and the fire crackled, and a magnificent chocolate cake waited on a silver stand, ready for cutting. She put her worries about the unfortunate young maid to one side.

☽○☾

Dressing for dinner that night, Xanthe hummed under her breath. She could still sense the shades of herself at five, and ten, and twelve, and sixteen, moping around the ladylike pink room, singing her made-up songs and telling herself made-up stories. She'd read everything from Grimm and Carroll and Nesbitt to Rossetti and Yeats while sitting on this window seat.

She'd cried herself to sleep in this bed. But all of it was gone now, long gone, like the flimsy cobweb shreds of nightmares that rotted away to mist in the morning light. The old fears and insecurities – what did they matter any more? She was all right. It was all right. She had not found herself reduced to an awkward, stuttering child the moment she passed the threshold. Her parents were not implacable ogres. Her cousin Jonathan wasn't even here.

For the first time since leaving Paris, she felt as if her lungs had opened up enough to take a full breath. She had come back entirely willingly, but some part of her had been expecting . . . what?

She tucked a strand of hair up into place behind a diamante clip and stared at her reflection in her dressing mirror, searching her face as if answers might be hiding there behind her eyes. In the ivy outside the window, a bird was trilling sweetly, long round notes that reminded Xanthe of sea breakers coming in over the sand. A nightingale.

Song birds in the dark. Immediately her mind came alive with words and images, the way that dust motes turn to gold in a shaft of sunlight, spiralling and colliding. Still in her narrow silk slip, she got up and pattered across to the window seat where she had left her bag. After several minutes of frantic scribbling in her journal and quite a lot of inkblots, there was a short knock at the door. She capped her pen and thrust it and the journal back into her bag, dropping everything onto the window seat – but before she could even decide if she wanted to call out 'Enter', the door opened to reveal Lady Kearsley and her personal maid.

'Oh, good – you're not dressed yet. I've brought Pinchbeck

to help you, since you don't have a lady's maid just now. You weren't going to wear your hair like that, were you?'

Xanthe raised an eyebrow, determined not to be flustered. 'I was, yes. Why so formal, Mother? Do we have guests coming?'

Lady Kearsley smiled ruefully. 'You won't tell him that I gave it away, will you? Darling, your father so wanted to celebrate your return . . .'

'A party?' She couldn't help taking an involuntary step back. 'Oh, *Mother*—'

'Now, don't fuss! Only a tiny gathering, quite informal, just a few friends. We only just missed your birthday this year. Your father couldn't resist. He wanted to surprise you. You'll play along, darling, won't you – for him?'

Xanthe felt her shoulders slumping even as she let out a long sigh. Her mother took it for the capitulation that it was and bustled forward to open the wardrobe doors and inspect Xanthe's newly hung garments.

'I like this blue. But perhaps the green? What a pretty shade, I don't think I've seen a dress this colour for years. We used to call it *eau de nil*. Pinchbeck?'

The lady's maid, who had already herded Xanthe into place on the seat before the mirror, glanced back, and said decisively, 'The blue.'

'It's not that I don't appreciate the thought,' Xanthe said, trying not to flinch as Pinchbeck pulled out and discarded the hair clips. With a derisive cluck of the tongue, the lady's maid began to subject her hair to a vigorous brushing. Her eyes watered as the boar bristles scraped her scalp. 'But why tonight? I've only just arrived. I'm exhausted and I look done in.'

Lady Kearsley came to stand behind her, bringing the unmistakeable mother-smells of clean skin, Pond's face cream, the rose and bergamot of her L'Heure Bleue perfume.

'My child, you're twenty-one. You don't even know the meaning of the word "exhaustion". That's for when you have children of your own. Now, remember to look surprised! Don't ruin your papa's fun.'

With a brief press of her gloved hand to Xanthe's cheek, she flitted away.

Seven

Descending the curving staircase into the great hall thirty minutes later, Xanthe was a little daunted to see that the drawing room, library and dining room were dark and quiet. It seemed they really did intend to 'surprise' her. Even Bowdler and the footmen had gone into hiding. She wandered past her father's study, the little-used music room and Pink Saloon and, following a whisper of instinct, found herself at the entrance to her mother's orangery, which sat at the back of the house, overlooking the cliffs and hedge maze.

The great, glass-walled space was filled with echoes and shadows, offering a stunning view of the moon beginning to rise over a thin sliver of distant ocean. There wasn't anyone there – just her mother's ferns and miniature trees, sitting in their ornate pots. For a moment, as Xanthe hesitated in the open doorway, she wondered if she had made some kind of mistake: misheard her mother, or forgotten some vital directions as to where she should present herself. The crippling feeling, only too familiar, of being in the wrong place, at the wrong time, of having got things backwards and being the only one who hadn't known it, made her swallow down nausea. She turned to leave.

Noise erupted like a thunderclap. Lights suddenly appeared everywhere. She almost staggered, and only as the sound faded away realised that it had been a great cry of 'Surprise!' coming from a dozen or more voices.

'Good Lord!' She put gloved hands up to her cheeks, and the room filled with laughter. The shadows had been people after all, and now her father was there – handsome in his dinner jacket, and sans cane – his face lit by a rare, mischievous grin.

'Aha! I do think we pulled that off rather well – don't you, everyone? Happy birthday, my dear! Happy belated birthday.'

'And many happy returns!' shouted someone else – the daughter of Sir Anthony someone, Jeanette or Judith, clad in a scarlet party dress and raising a glass of champagne in Xanthe's direction.

Xanthe stood her ground, even though everyone was looking at her, looking at her, looking at her. She let herself close her eyes for just a second, gathering her breath in, and then forced a smile, taking her hands down from her face and knotting them into a tangle of white satin at her waist.

'What a lovely surprise. Thank you so much. I'm so glad to see you all.'

She had done it. Said the right thing. The wall of staring faces broke down into chattering, smiling groups, and Lady Kearsley appeared at her elbow with one of the footmen, who – thank God! – handed her some champagne. She took it and tried not to gulp it too obviously.

'Happy birthday, Xanthe,' Lord Kearsley repeated, quieter and more sincere now. Her mother gave her a delighted, conspiratorial smile, silently praising her for such a convincing performance. Her skin was still tingling with the urge to flee, but now she was able to look around with cautious interest. More than half of the people in the room were about her age, people she knew to varying degrees. There was an elegant buffet table, draped in white, with more champagne, and a punch bowl, and pretty little displays of finger foods. Colourful Chinese paper lanterns had been strung from the iron-work of the glass roof, and someone had even rolled in a gramophone, although it wasn't presently playing anything.

Most wonderful of all, there was absolutely no sign of her cousin Jonathan lurking anywhere.

Her father touched his hand to the back of her shoulder fleetingly. 'You see, we've tried to think of what you would want. Did we do well? Do you like it?'

She nodded, and impulsively leaned in to give her parents a quick peck each on the cheek. 'You're utter lambs. Thank you again.'

Some of the party-goers were drifting towards them, and Xanthe let herself be ushered off into their presence, re-acquainting herself, if somewhat stiffly, with the not-quite-friends of her childhood.

'Your hair is terribly chic,' Judith – it had been Judith, Judith Farringdon – said, giving her own roll of smooth, dark hair a pat. 'I admire your bravery, I've been looking at the fashion plates for ages, but I simply don't dare. Weren't you terrified?'

'Oh – well, I don't – I-I –' Xanthe stuttered. Took a breath. Began again. 'It was a last resort, really. This is the first time I've ever been able to get it to do what it's told.'

'I want to talk about your dress,' the Honourable Harriet Kimbell-Menzies cut in. 'This open shawl neck, with the lace. And the silhouette! Is this the latest fashion in Paris?'

'I'm not as good at keeping up with fashions as I could be,' Xanthe hedged. The blunt truth was that she hadn't done any clothes shopping since her first month or two in the city, when she had still been staying with Josephine. She liked pretty dresses as much as anyone, but there were always so many other exciting things happening there – art showings, plays, readings – and never enough hours in the day to write, and, besides, she had to pay for food, and books, and her room, which stretched her allowance to its limits.

'Well, thank goodness for that. You've made me feel quite dowdy enough as it is!' Harriet said with a laugh. 'I'm so envious. If I caught a glimpse of a real Paris fashion house, I should probably die on the spot.'

'Have to strike that off the list of honeymoon destinations then.' A blocky young man appeared beside Harriet with a full plate in one hand and champagne in the other. *Tony, something . . . Tony Galbraith, that's it.* 'Can't have the bride keeling over. I'd never live it down.'

Harriet rolled her eyes, rapidly unbuttoning the bottom of her evening gloves and folding them up to expose her fingers so that she could help herself to the contents of Tony's plate.

Judith and the bespectacled young man next to her, who Xanthe couldn't quite place, laughed.

'Good for you, Tony!' Judith's young man said. 'When did you finally pop the question?'

'At Christmas,' Tony said, exasperated. 'Ralph, don't you ever look away from your books long enough to read the papers?'

'Ralph's up at Oxford,' Judith told Xanthe with a hint of proprietary pride. 'Final year. He's only down for the weekend.'

'Exams approaching like a speeding train,' Ralph said gloomily. 'So, no, I don't precisely scour the wedding announcements. I've a stack of books higher than my head and I'm lucky if I see sunlight most days.'

'What are you reading at Oxford?' Xanthe put in, hoping to steer the topic away from weddings.

'Oh, Classics. *Litterarum radices amarae, fructus dulces sunt!*'

Tony snorted, unimpressed, while Judith and Harriet pulled discreet faces: humorous, resigned and knowing. All boys were taught Latin as a matter of course. Equally as a matter of course, girls were not.

Xanthe, speaking before she could think better of it, translated: '"Bitter are the roots of study, but sweet the fruit."'

'I say, do they teach girls Latin these days?' Ralph asked.

'No, but that doesn't mean we're incapable of learning it.' Even as Xanthe made the tart response, she realised that the other girls were looking at her with barely concealed annoyance. She suddenly remembered an older girl at school telling her that the best policy for dealing with Latin bores was to pretend you hadn't heard them – and never, ever ask for a translation. It only encouraged them.

The conversation moved on, and soon someone got the gramophone crackling to life. 'I'll Build a Stairway to Paradise' gave way to 'The Sheik of Araby' (Xanthe assumed her parents had asked the younger guests to bring their own records along, because if her father had the faintest idea what film the latter had been inspired by, he would have refused to have it in the house) and then 'Rose of the Rio Grande'. Ralph persuaded Judith to dance, and then Harriet did Tony, and before long there were a handful of younger couples doing a sedate shuffle around the tiled floor. Xanthe even joined in, though it was tame compared to the dancing in Paris. She supposed that even if the tango or the Charleston had made it as far as Winterthorne, no one would have dared shock their elderly parents by performing them here. The elderly parents in question had mostly withdrawn to the other side of the orangery by the potted ferns, where rattan furniture had been thoughtfully arranged to allow them to sit and chat. Xanthe thought wryly of the young man she had met all those years ago when she was sixteen, at her parents' Summer Ball – what had been his name? Reginald? She'd never had the chance to dance with him. He wasn't here, which was hardly surprising. She doubted he'd accept an invitation back to Kearsley Castle after what had happened the last time . . .

Placing down her punch cup, Xanthe paused in buttoning her hand back into its evening glove to touch the leaf of one of her mother's prized 'miniature' oaks. It was dry and delicate as paper between her fingertips, and the colour of aged bronze.

Long before Xanthe was born, her mother had visited some grand exhibition in London and had been enchanted to see tiny trees, trained to grow in pots. But rather than purchase one of these exquisite plants and bring it home she had decided to attempt to grow her own. She had taken over the castle's Victorian orangery to house them, collected acorns from the Winterthorne woods and planted them in old teacups, repotting them into ornamental Chinese ginger jars when they got bigger. It had taken years of experimentation to develop her own methods to keep them small: pruning them, depriving them of sunlight and water or even trimming their roots. These were the survivors.

None was quite as tall as Xanthe's waist, and some of them only reached her knees. Their trunks and branches bent into curling, graceful shapes, and their leaves were shades of brown, copper and gold, as if it were autumn all year around. They were extraordinarily beautiful, the envy of amateur lady gardeners the length of Britain. Xanthe had never seen the orangery without the trees. They had always been there, a feature of her childhood. As she looked at the miniature oaks again now, she had a sudden realisation. The brown leaves, and their dainty size, the very things that made her mother and others love them so much, were all because they were dying.

Xanthe let go of the leaf with a jerk, as if it had burned her. She returned to buttoning her glove, trying to ignore a strange feeling growing inside her, a kind of hollowness greatly out of proportion to her idle musings.

Perhaps she should have some more champagne. Only she didn't want champagne. She didn't really want a birthday party, did she? It was weeks too late. God, what was that awful smell, that hot, eggy stench? She put one hand over her mouth, thinking for a moment that she might be sick.

Someone came to her side. She turned quickly, dropping her hand, already fumbling for excuses for her strange behaviour – and then stopped dead. 'Jonathan.'

He looked exactly the same. Tall, slightly built, with long, graceful limbs, and handsome, always so handsome. The faintly aquiline real-life version of Rudolph Valentino that all the girls – and mistresses – at her school had sighed and giggled over. He smiled down at her with every appearance of warmth, the expression tinged with that hint of wryness Xanthe knew communicated to everyone he met that he honestly couldn't help this ridiculous face of his and not to hold it against him. The glow of excitement in his eyes and the way he shifted slightly from foot to foot, movements liquid and restless, told Xanthe that he'd already had at least three glasses of whisky. Enough to make him jovial and easy, but not enough to start picking fights. Yet. One hand – the hand that used to shake sometimes, no matter what the doctors tried – was tucked casually into the pocket of his trousers. The other was extended towards her, and that was not casual at all.

'Xanthe. I hadn't thought it was possible, but you've done it.' There was a pause. Xanthe kept silent, refusing to try to fill it. With a tiny shrugging movement and a widening in his smile, he finished: 'Got even more beautiful. You are ravishing.'

She tried to tell herself that the weight in her stomach was resignation, not despair. She should have expected this. What foolish dream had she been living in where Lord and Lady Kearsley would ever have any kind of party without the heir to the title and estates? Every single thing in this house, every stick of furniture, every family treasure, every brick, box, beam, tile, every mote of dust and each hole in the roof, all of it, would one day be his.

She knew without needing to look away that all eyes were fixed on them. The gossip from the last time they had been seen in public together must be worn very thin by now, but what was a party without a scandal? How would this story play out? A romance? A tragedy?

She had no choice. She held out her own gloved hand. He grasped it firmly and with a look of satisfaction, then tightened his grip, and tried to bring her hand up to his mouth to kiss it. She resisted.

'Let go, please.'

'Why? I'm not hurting you,' he said, eyebrow quirking up infuriatingly. 'Don't be a spoilsport now, darling. Just play along.'

Then her parents appeared, beaming and vivacious, suddenly more alive, the way they always – only – seemed to be in Jonathan's presence.

'Oh, Jonathan! You promised me faithfully that you wouldn't be late!' Lady Kearsley was laughing as she scolded, and Jonathan finally let go of Xanthe to turn and kiss his aunt's cheek.

'Don't nag at him, Caroline. He's a grown man.' Xanthe's father clapped Jonathan heartily on the back and then shook his hand.

'I beg forgiveness,' Jonathan said. 'But this time it really wasn't my fault. The blasted car wouldn't start! I've had a devilish time getting here at all.'

He was lying. He wasn't even trying hard. But it didn't matter to them, Xanthe knew; they wanted to believe whatever Jonathan said and so, to them, whatever Jonathan said was true.

'Well, you're here now, and that's all that matters,' Caroline said, unwittingly echoing her daughter's thoughts. She looked around as if she had somehow lost track of Xanthe, and then reached out to take the hand which her daughter had only just managed to reclaim from Jonathan, drawing her into their intimate little family group. 'We're all here together, at last. I'm so happy.'

Lord Kearsley looked from Xanthe to Jonathan with slightly narrowed eyes. 'I think it's time, don't you?'

'Time?' Xanthe croaked faintly. But Jonathan was already taking hold of her other wrist, once again ignoring her reflexive attempts to try to free herself.

'I've been ready any time the past five years,' Jonathan said.

'Time for what?' Xanthe said, louder. Her eyes were fixed on her mother, who wouldn't meet her gaze.

'Everyone! Your attention, please!' her father said, turning to face the guests – the vast majority of whom had been attempting to eavesdrop already, drifting not-so-subtly closer from the moment that Jonathan arrived.

It was already too late to escape the trap. It had been too late as soon as he'd walked into the room. And she couldn't even try to get away, not with her mother lacing their fingers together on one side and Jonathan's grip like a manacle on the other, and the party-goers surrounding them on all sides like a wall – not without making the most horrific scene, humiliating herself and her parents.

'I'm absolutely delighted to announce the engagement of Jonathan Winter, our nephew, to our daughter, Lady Xanthe. I think we can all agree that they make a handsome couple, and they deserve all the happiness in the world. Do join us in a toast to their good health.'

'Their good health!' everyone responded, raising glasses newly filled with champagne. The footmen had been busy there, Xanthe thought distantly. Probably even they had known what was going to happen before she did.

'You could try to smile, you know,' Jonathan said, taunting. He'd pulled his left hand out of his pocket at last, to accept a champagne glass of his own. 'I might get hurt feelings.'

She snapped: '*Good.*'

Lady Kearsley turned shocked eyes on her. 'Xanthe, really.'

A swell of white-hot rage rolled through her body, and suddenly it didn't matter that other people were all around them, still looking. She flexed her arms, making ready to struggle in earnest – now, when it was too late. Why hadn't she had the sense to fight two minutes ago? Why had she let them do this to her *again*?

'Let go of me – or I shall say something a lot ruder than that!'

'You are both rather clinging to her,' her father said. 'I do think we can trust her not to run away again. She's not sixteen any more.'

Unbearable. '*Let go!*'

The sound of her raised voice made heads turn. Both of them released her instantly. It was instinct, to get away from fuss before it could taint them.

'Darling, listen,' Lady Kearsley began.

'Don't.' Xanthe tried to burn them with her gaze, but her father just looked stoic, and Jonathan smirked, a child who knew the blame for his mess would never be brought home to him. Lady Kearsley was the only one who seemed the slightest bit ashamed.

With no further regard for what anyone might say about her conduct, Xanthe stalked from the room.

Eight

Xanthe had never really known Jonathan. That was the problem.

Her father had been the eldest of three brothers, but perhaps because he had inherited the responsibility of the earldom before his twentieth birthday, he was the last of the three to wed. By the time he had met Xanthe's mother he was nearly forty, and his younger brothers had already started on their families. Childless for almost a decade after their marriage, Lord and Lady Kearsley naturally adored all their nephews, the tribe of laughing, handsome boys who spent their summers running wild on the Kearsley estate, considered Kearsley Castle their own home, and Lord and Lady Kearsley – their Uncle Alfred and Aunt Caroline – their second parents.

But Jonathan . . . well, he was special. Everyone knew it. He was the oldest of the cousins, the most handsome. His father had died when he was eight, and the family consensus was that his mother was a bit of a duffer, more concerned with an ever-lengthening list of exotic imaginary ailments than with giving Jonathan and the twin boys who had come after him the attention they needed.

Lord Kearsley took Jonathan firmly under his wing and kept him there. After Xanthe was born, when the doctors said there wouldn't be any more babies for Caroline, Jonathan truly became the son that Lord Kearsley would never have.

Xanthe had grown up surrounded by this half-feral gaggle of cousins. She had seen them so often they might as well have been her brothers. But she was eleven years younger than Jonathan, and six years younger than the next youngest cousin, Jeremy. And she was, it was universally agreed, *such a funny little thing.* Awkward, odd, liable to babble on and on or lapse into strange half-absent silences. More important than any of that, she was a girl. Everyone knew about the entail, and that the estate was still coming to Jonathan, and so 'the blinker', as her cousin Andrew off-handedly dubbed her – in honour of the habit she had developed between the ages of seven and nine, of scrunching up her face in an exaggerated blink when people tried to look her in the eye – changed nothing.

The boys weren't generally unkind to her. They simply had no interest in her. She was fit only to be scraped off so that they could go on with their country summer adventures, exactly as if she hadn't existed. Throughout her whole childhood, Xanthe probably never exchanged more than a hundred words with her cousin Jonathan.

Then the war came. Xanthe had just been sent away to boarding school. In her conscientious monthly letters, her mother informed her as, one by one, the laughing, handsome cousins signed up to fight. Equally conscientiously, she informed Xanthe when, one by one, the laughing, handsome cousins began to die.

Xanthe had sat in her dormitory reading these letters with

detached horror. David and Andrew, Jonathan's two younger brothers, were the first, dying on the same appalling day in Marne. Jonathan had enlisted after that, immoveable despite the whole family begging him to stay safe at home. The next to die was Jeremy. Then Daniel. Then George. She remembered her disbelief when she had realised that the little blistered blots that marred each letter, here and there, were the marks of dried tears. She had never seen her mother cry in the flesh. Caroline's motto, oft repeated, was *No matter what emotions a lady may experience in private, she should never give way in public.*

She remembered trying to force herself to cry too, because she was sure that she ought to if her mother had – it must be the right thing to do. Xanthe knew she had the capacity for tears. She had blubbered so much when she was little that her cousins had added the sobriquet of 'the watering pot' to her list of nicknames. But at some point she had lost the knack of tears. Even when she broke her wrist her eyes had stayed dry.

They stayed dry now, too.

She made a futile effort to try to conjure up some special memory of each one of these dead boys. One thing, anything, that differentiated this dead cousin from the dead cousin before. But in her mind they were a kind of moving blur, beautiful and distant. Like a field of tall golden grass that she had never quite been able to reach, now falling down in a graceful wave before the edge of a scythe.

Her classmates lost fathers, brothers, cousins, sweethearts. The schoolmistresses did too. A few of them left to volunteer as nurses or ambulance drivers. As she watched these other people try to conceal devastation behind glassy smiles, their swollen eyes and hollow cheeks, a part of her was shamefully grateful that the Winter cousins had never paid her any attention. That she had never been given the opportunity to love them. She mourned them for her parents' sake, not her own.

But Jonathan, Caroline's letters told her, had a charmed life. Jonathan was beloved of his men. Jonathan was brave. Jonathan charged the guns and won a mention in dispatches, and didn't take a scratch.

Then, as if even such a golden thread could not stretch infinitely, Jonathan's luck ran out. His unit took a direct hit from a shell. Jonathan was the only survivor, but badly hurt. He contracted a virulent infection in the military hospital. No one expected him to survive it. He did, only to fall prey to another.

He was sent home. Not to his enfeebled mother, who wept if she was asked what she would prefer to eat for breakfast, no. Jonathan came home to Kearsley Castle, where Lord and Lady Kearsley greeted him with all the joy and love and care they had. He was the only one left.

Xanthe, by contrast, had not been allowed to return to Winterthorne for Christmas that year. Her mother wrote that they all felt it was best she not have to see her cousin in his present state. She would not be able to help, and it would only distress her. The truth, Xanthe was aware, was that in extremity they had reverted to what felt most familiar, most safe. Most vital. Caroline, Alfred, and the son they never had. A tight-knit little unit ranged against the world that had violently tried to pull them apart. Outsiders were neither needed, nor desired. She battled her resentment over being excluded by reminding herself that it was hardly a banishment, any more than being sent to boarding school in the first place had been. It was just one Christmas out of dozens she had spent, and would spend, at Kearsley.

She would be home again soon.

It was jolly enough to camp out in the near-deserted school with a couple of the other girls from her form. With only one schoolmistress and the school nurse on duty throughout the holiday the supervision was necessarily lax. One of the other Christmas exiles, Ophelia, had a vast Fortnum & Mason's hamper, ordered for her by her parents from their post abroad. Another, the daughter of a French diplomat, managed to get her hands on some real contraband: two bottles of brandy. Christmas Eve was very merry indeed (though Christmas morning somewhat less so). Xanthe could hardly complain about giggling with her friends in the dormitory after 'lights out' by the flicker of illicit candles, sharing bites of cheese and cake and swigs of brandy, and swapping their most terrifying ghost stories and gossip about the romantic exploits of the upper form. Much more comfortable than to be at Kearsley Castle where, her mother had confided, they all had to be terribly quiet and calm all the time, because even the slightest unexpected noise caused Jonathan to be thrown back in his memories to the battle where he had been injured, and suffer a kind of violent fit. Apparently, no less than two maids had been so frightened they had left without working their notice. Xanthe's mother finished by grimly stating that she hoped both the girls would regret their cowardice: she had instructed the housekeeper, Finch, to withhold their references.

By the following year, Caroline's letters had brightened considerably in tone. Jonathan's mood and health had improved as the weather did, and everyone was relieved that the worst of his recovery was behind them. In fact, he was so much better that he felt up to travelling, and when term finished for the summer holidays Xanthe discovered that he had gone to visit friends in London.

The following Christmas, however, he seemed to have suffered something of a relapse. Xanthe had been granted permission to come home that year, but initially she didn't see him at all. No one did. He hardly ever left his room. There were strict instructions that no one knock, or make noise as they walked the corridor outside. When he did leave, it was normally at night. Xanthe had no idea why until he returned in the early hours one morning, draped over the shoulders of two strapping young local men.

He had a bloody nose and a cut lip, and was capable only of muttering slurred swearwords and vomiting noisily in the front hall. Bowdler and one of the footmen hustled him away out of sight while Lord Kearsley, still in his pyjamas and dressing gown, awkwardly pressed some money on the young Winterthorne men, for their trouble.

Lord Kearsley had gravely explained to Xanthe that sometimes the pain from his wounds made Jonathan drink too much. He couldn't help it. Such injuries were very difficult for a young man to bear – and the doctors were either unsympathetic brutes or ineffectual idiots.

The next morning, when Jonathan appeared at breakfast, Xanthe observed that he did seem to have trouble using his injured left hand. But his right hand also shook convulsively, and looking at the sick grey shade of his face and the way he winced from the light, Xanthe couldn't help comparing his 'pain' to the effects that she and her friends had suffered the day after their rampant brandy consumption at school.

When Jonathan failed in his efforts to neatly remove the top of his boiled egg, he responded by smashing his plate against the wall and storming from the room. The servants silently and efficiently cleared up the mess while Xanthe's parents avoided her gaze and discussed the unusually snowy weather.

Any vague idea Xanthe might have entertained that she and Jonathan would become closer now they were the last two remaining cousins was clearly doomed. She had remained just as invisible to him as she always had been. Grateful, for the first time, to pack up her trunks and return to school in the New Year, she had hoped that by the summer Jonathan would have recovered enough to no longer call Kearsley Castle his permanent home.

That hope, it turned out, had been in vain. The following summer – the summer she turned sixteen – was when everything changed.

Part Two

Nine

Jude, present day

I can't move. I can't wake up.

I lie there, feeling my chest move in slow, even breaths. Feeling the weight of my hands, heavy as stone, one resting on my stomach, the other curled on the pillow next to my face. Through barely cracked eyelids, I watch as the light brightens and shifts across the ceiling. Time passes.

I can't move. I can't wake up. I can't remember . . . what's real. Only what I just saw. What I felt.

Was it a dream? The tinny sound of the gramophone, the steady thump in one temple from too much champagne – and from the effort of performing for all those strangers. Performing most of all for my family, my harshest judges. I can still feel cousin Jonathan's implacable grip round my – round her wrist. The claustrophobia of everyone staring. How could they do that to her? How could I let them do that to me?

But that *wasn't* me, a voice at the back of my mind cries out, insistent. It wasn't me. It was a dream.

I still can't move. *I can't wake up.*

And then, suddenly, I can. My eyelids roll closed in a slow blink, and when they open again, I'm free. Choking on a panicked gasp, I roll over onto my stomach and squash my face into an unfamiliar pillow that smells of rose potpourri. Tears spill out of my eyes, relief and shock. I clench and unclench my hands, just to feel them respond. There's no mark on my wrist, there's no bruise. It didn't happen. It wasn't real.

I'm Juliet Gemma Stewart. I'm in my great-aunt's old house in Winterthorne. I'm safe. I'm safe. There's nothing to panic about.

I've always had powerful dreams. I used to have night terrors as a kid, freak Ma out by sitting bolt upright in my little bed and absolutely screaming the place down. Sometimes I sleepwalked, which was awful – but the sleep paralysis, like what happened just now, was the worst thing of all. I could never even remember what I dreamed about back then; I only knew that it would leave me frozen under the covers, my limbs weighted down, petrified with fear that *something bad was coming*. The specialist said it was stress, growing pains, I'd age out of it. I thought I had.

All the change and upheaval lately, being in a completely new place, new smells, exhaustion ... it all must have done something to my brain.

Slowly, slowly, I begin to calm. It wasn't even a nightmare I had. Vivid, yes, unnervingly vivid – the smells and colours were impossibly real, down to the ticklish sensation of champagne bubbles on my tongue. I can still remember the names of those dream parents, the dream friends and servants, and the name they called that dream girl: Xanthe. But nothing about it was really terrifying. I might even have tried to write it down, out of interest, when I woke up. If I'd been able to wake up.

The clock in the hall is ticking away faintly, and under it is that same watery *shush-shush-shush* from the trees that lulled me to sleep last night. A bird is shrieking shrilly and not very musically right outside the window. I realise I'm smiling into my pillow. There's something about this house. A kind of spirit. This feeling of . . .

Sanctuary.

The word appears in my mind, unbidden, as if someone had leaned in close and whispered it in my ear. I repeat it aloud, liking the taste of it on my tongue. That's right, exactly right. *Sanctuary.* A place of safety. A place of rest.

It's been a long, cold stretch since I felt that way anywhere.

On the bedside table my phone suddenly vibrates. I heave myself up in the soft bed and grab it. Four bars of reception – that's unexpected.

It's a text from Penny, of all people. For a moment I wonder unkindly if she wants advice on how to unclog the sink or something – God knows Duncan wouldn't have the first idea – then I squirm when I see that she's just asking if I've arrived safely, and what the house is like.

I didn't think I'd ever hear from her again after I picked up the last of my things. And I thought she'd be relieved not to hear from me, the pity-case-hanger-on who outstayed her welcome. I'm not even sure why I told her about the inheritance, and where I was going. I was so shocked and exhilarated still; I suppose I just wanted to share it all with someone. Duncan wasn't there, and Penny was so happy and excited for me that for an hour or two it felt like old times. Only, of course, then she told him everything I'd said. After that whenever he was in the flat – which was constantly – he was needling me, trying to prise details and figures out of me. Penny just ... let him do it. Uncomfortable, sheepish, avoiding my eyes, but still not saying anything. I was so glad to get away from both of them, to hand my keys back and walk out for the last time.

The thought makes me grit my teeth. I have to force myself to text back.

Got here OK. House nice

It feels pretty curt. After a moment I follow up with:

Journey was a mare, but people here are kind. Thanks for checking in x

The text takes a moment to go; my four bars of reception have vanished as fast as they appeared. I plonk the phone down, relieved to be done with social interactions. I haven't even brushed my teeth yet.

It's nearly 9.30. There's nowhere to be today. Nothing to sort out. No unpleasant drudgery to force myself to do. There's only quiet, and space, and plenty of time.

I throw on some jeans and a sweatshirt and wander downstairs, feeling grateful to Liz again as I work my way through the process of making a pot of tea. The mugs we used yesterday are on the draining board, but I leave them there and open the cupboard to look at my great-aunt's mug collection. It's vast and colourful. I have this theory that people's mugs say more about them than they realise. As I pick through chunky square-ish mugs, delicate hand-painted bone-china mugs and souvenir mugs from every museum and art collection in the UK, I wonder which one of these was her favourite, or if she was one of those weird people who doesn't have favourites. After discarding at least fifteen mugs, I start to get decision paralysis. It shouldn't feel like such a weighted choice, but the mug I pick this morning will be my mug while I'm here. It just seems . . . significant.

Eventually, right at the back of the cupboard, I find a mug that's familiar – a mug from the British Museum giftshop, with images from an exhibition of finds from Sutton Hoo that my mother and I went to several times one year when I was a kid. We had this mug. We had lots of mugs, just like Anne. I have no idea what happened to any of them in all the upheaval after Ma died. I have no idea if Anne even went to this exhibition, if she might have been there at the same time as us. It's nice to think so. Nice to imagine our paths might have crossed at some point, even if we didn't realise it.

After putting all the other mugs away, I sit down at the table, and pour myself my first cup of tea in my mug. Then I treat myself to a mystery pastry from Belle's box, which turns out to be some kind of maple-syrup thing with pecans. By the time I've finished my second cup of tea, I've decided what I'm going to do today.

I go upstairs, flinging open the door of the second bedroom – the room that belonged to the man who fathered me – defiantly, like I'm expecting someone to stop me. But once I'm inside I don't really know what to do. This bedroom faces the front of the house. It's brighter in the morning than it was yesterday afternoon. That doesn't make it any more cheerful. It feels different from the rest of the house, where everything is so alive, like Anne just stepped out for ten minutes and could be back any time to tut over the mess I left in the kitchen. I find that oddly comforting, as if she approves of me being here. But this room feels dead. Forbidden, even.

I'm being stupid. I didn't know him. Just because Anne couldn't face this room that doesn't mean it should have any effect on me. This whole house will have to be packed up if it's going to sell anyway, so why not start here first. Right?

I go downstairs again and fetch black binbags from under the kitchen sink. Back in the room, I pull open a drawer – then feel myself hesitating again at the sight of neatly folded jumpers and jeans. I wait for Ma to chime in with something. She doesn't, of course. Because it's always just me, pretending to hear her voice. And I've got no idea what she would say right now.

I start taking the clothes out of the drawers and dropping them into the bag. I work fast, carelessly, trying to ignore the creeping sense of wrongdoing that makes the nape of my neck itch. The chest of drawers and wardrobe empty rapidly. Once the bags bulge with outdated, musty-smelling clothes and old shoes and underwear, I put them on the bed and start pulling posters off the wall, rolling them up and dropping them, one by one, into a new bag. Football club, football club, video game, sports car, rock band. It's all so generic. No treasured photos of family or goofy ones of friends, no leftover toys from childhood. Nothing. There's nothing here at all that tells me anything more about who he was.

There's no trace of us. Of Ma.

I wrench too hard at the top drawer of the bedside table. It flies out, and the contents scatter over the dark blue carpet.

The Moonlit Maze

A few coins, an old keyring, thumbtacks. One of those tiny pocket diaries people give you for Christmas. It's unused, the pages empty. That's from two years after I was born. There's some old condoms, too. They expired the actual year I was born.

'You idiot,' I say aloud. 'You didn't deserve her.'

Even the bookshelves are boring. A heap of old car magazines. Non-fiction about the Second World War, books written by ex-soldiers, a bit of Isaac Asimov, a bit of Frank Herbert, two of the three books from the Lord of the Rings trilogy. Another thing he never bothered to finish. I don't realise I'm holding out a little hope for the books, for *something* worth finding, until I stuff the last one into the bag with the posters and run out of energy. I sit down on the bed and put my face in my hands, then sneeze, my nose itching with all the dust ingrained in my fingers.

'Idiot,' I repeat. Why did I expect anything? Did I really think I'd stumble over a diary in which he confided the reasons why he abandoned his pregnant girlfriend and his baby? And then stopped his well-off aunt from helping them? Only lowlives did what he did, walked away like that. If there'd been anything special about him, he would have had the guts to stay.

I look around me at the wreckage of the room, my attention drawn to an old green glass jar on the windowsill. It's empty, and a bit dusty, but the glass is ripply and old. It's beautiful. That jar is the only thing in this room I wouldn't gladly chuck into a fire. A bar of sunlight is shining through the glass onto the carpet, and I realise it's still a beautiful sunny day out there.

When I woke up, I told myself that I was free, and I had time, and nothing unpleasant to do. And then I turned right round and came in here to torment myself.

I leave the mess where it is, and close the door behind me. I'll figure out what to do about all of it later. After washing my hands, re-plaiting my hair and changing out of my sweaty, dusty top into a fresh T-shirt and jumper, I check my phone and see it's still early, not lunchtime yet. I'll go for a walk and clear my head a bit. There's all that scenery and countryside out there. Maybe I'll even see if I can find the sea.

Scrunching down the garden path through the drifting flowers, I'm trying not to think about anything as I stuff my phone into one pocket and the house keys into the other. The garden gate opens easily under my hand and I step out—

I swear, there's no noise. No warning drone from an exhaust pipe, no roar of an engine. Nothing but peaceful quiet, wind in the leaves and birdsong. And a massive black motorbike with a black-helmeted rider, streaking down the narrow country track, almost on top of me.

It's instinct to throw myself backwards; there's nowhere else to go. My ears vibrate with a deafening metallic scream, a crash. I lose track of everything in the terrifying blur of movement. Then it's quiet again.

When I come back to myself, I'm huddled on the verge, my body so heavy with shock that I can hardly breathe. I'm in one piece, apart from a bashed knee and grass-grazed hands. I must have bounced off the hedge behind me and hit the ground pretty hard. The driver's on the other side of the road, dragging his motorbike out of the hedge. He's tall and solidly built – that's all I can tell about what's under the black leathers. He's not even looking at me. He *almost killed me* and he's not even looking to check if I'm OK?

The Moonlit Maze

He turns round. The dark leathers are scraped and scuffed down his side. There's a long silver gouge out of the paint on his helmet. He came off the bike. I can't see any blood, but – I start to try to get up – I start to reach for my phone to call an ambulance – then he snaps up the visor.

My muscles lock in place, like a rabbit facing a fox. I can't tell what colour his eyes are from here, but the pupils are so dilated that they look black. Black with fury.

'You should be dead.'

He sounds American. That's the only thing I can absorb before he gets back on his battered bike, guns it viciously to life and thunders away down the track.

Ten

It all happened so fast that I can't say for sure which of us was to blame. I stepped off the verge without looking, and my head was so far in the clouds that I didn't even hear anyone coming. On the other hand, only a total moron would come roaring round that corner that fast. And if he'd hit me he might have been OK – but I definitely would have been dead.

After a bit of thought, I realise that his parting words weren't exactly a threat, even if they sounded like one. But he didn't stop to see that I wasn't hurt, either. He probably wanted to get away before I called the police on him. So, in conclusion: wanker. Nothing I haven't dealt with on multiple occasions back home. I just wish I'd had time to give him the finger before he went.

The near-miss leaves me breathless and shaky, but in a weird way it also helps. Wakes me up, floods my bloodstream with adrenalin and totally clears my mind of all the confusing feelings that crept over me in Stephen Whittaker's room. Once I've checked to make sure that my hands and knee are only bruised, not bleeding, it doesn't even occur to me to go back inside. I want to walk, and some black-leather-motorbike-wanker isn't going to stop me.

I'd been vaguely planning to head downhill to the town and the sea, but that's the direction he went. Instead, I turn my face up towards the hill – though I can't see the intriguing ruins from here by the road – and start tramping in that direction.

These hedgerows haven't been tamed by Nick's strimmer. They close in, whipping at my arm and face and snagging on my jumper, trying to push me sideways off the verge. Overhanging trees shade the way, making it cool and damp. The grass is still wet with dew even though it's mid-morning, and my trainers slip. I should have put my boots on. But they're city boots anyway, not really meant for hiking.

The hedgerows grow taller. The trees above get thicker. There's no view in the dank green corridor, and barely any fresh air. The birds aren't even singing. Despite the uphill walk, I'm starting to feel goosepimples on the back of my neck, and wishing I'd thought to put on a scarf.

I decide this is nearly as boring and uncomfortable as the walk from the Winterthorne bus stop. I'm a city girl at heart; who am I trying to kid? Why did I think some sort of wholesome country ramble was going to be my idea of a good time?

I'm just about to turn back when the hedgerow to my left peters out and sunlight suddenly floods down on me. Shading my face with one hand, I can see a little footpath that leads off from the road. There's a fence and a stile. Beyond that is woodland, the crowns of the trees all lit up gold with sun, their lower branches dark and mysterious, wreathed in ivy. City girl or not, it takes precisely three seconds for me to hop over the stile and run straight into the woods, overtaken by an entirely childish need to explore.

Under the trees it's still cool, but streaked with light and colours, the leaves constantly dancing together, dashing sparks across the path. I can sense and occasionally hear birds fluttering above. There are clumps of purple-blue flowers, and here and there piles of jumbled rocks, some bigger than my torso, the surfaces crusted with yellow and orange lichen and tufts of velvety moss and little curling fern things.

The path is steep but it's dry and I don't have any difficulty walking quickly, though I keep stopping to look at things. A squirrel hangs upside down from a branch over my head, stares at me, then vanishes in a ripple of soft fur. I spot a ragged, tumbledown-looking nest in the branches above and am warned off by the sharp cackle of the magpie pair who must have built it. Bees and butterflies flit past erratically. It even *smells* good, clean and sharp and green.

It's the wood where Snow White slept in a glass casket, and a silent princess sewed nettle shirts for her brothers who were under a curse. It's every wild, enchanted forest imagined by a little girl who read Susan Cooper and Diana Wynne Jones and Alan Garner, but grew up in a flat miles away from the nearest park. A dream that I'd had over and over as a child, but forgotten, until now.

After a long, happy stretch of wandering, I break out of the wood onto a much wider path. There's gravel underfoot, although it's choked with wild grasses and weeds. Tall, dark trees with a striking, almost conical shape spear up on either side of me, spaced evenly apart. An avenue.

I pass a strange circular structure set in the gravel. It's almost entirely hidden by nettles and ivy, and saplings are growing out of it, but I can make out stone or maybe concrete underneath. I lean in to peer at it – and jolt with shock as I see a face staring back at me between the branches of one of the saplings. Then I understand what I'm looking at. Pressing a hand to my chest, I let out a wheezy laugh: it's a statue of some kind, blotched with white rings of lichen. The statue has a water jug braced on her shoulder, and a green pipe poking out of it shows where water would have flowed once. It's an abandoned fountain.

More young trees have rooted in the gravel between the avenue trees here. I step through them carefully, and get my first close-up view of the ruins.

'God,' I whisper.

There's a beauty to it, to the tall, jagged spires thrusting up from the ivy and trees that have tried to reclaim the site. The windows and doors are all long gone. Most of the walls still seem to be standing, although the floors between have fallen down; they're a kind of honey-coloured stone, with sections of intricate brickwork, redbrick patterns that remind me of a trip to Hampton Court when I was at school. I meander around, fascinated, barking my shins on bits of fallen masonry and tripping over roots. On one wall, way over my head, there's an old fireplace, the black surround and colourful tiles still intact, clinging to a section of surviving plaster. There's even a trace of wallpaper. It looks as if it was floral, pink or red.

Here and there I can see black scorch marks etched into the stone. Fire. This place was wrecked by a fire so hot that even after years of being left open to the elements, beaten by the wind and sun and rain, the walls still show the evidence. But now it just feels peaceful and still, as sacred as a cathedral.

I clamber over a tumbled section of wall into a meadow that sits in the footprint of a large room. There are the remnants of ornate metal struts above me, blistered and twisted, black with soot and red with rust. Some still hold shards of glass. Broken pieces of glazed pottery shift underfoot. Against the furthest wall a strange tree grows amid the wreckage, winding branches through the metalwork. It's an oak, but not like any oak I've ever seen before. It's tall, but the trunk is slender and twisting, bent into a kind of S shape. The leaves move together with a dry sound, and I see that the vivid green is streaked with copper, as if they were about to turn.

Beyond that final wall, framed by the strange oak and the tortured metal frame of what might once have been some kind of greenhouse, or – no, I think it was an orangery, like the one in my dream – there's a long stretch of flat open ground. And then the cliff, and there at last: the sea. The smell and sound of it, which I hadn't even noticed growing closer and closer as I explored. The light glitters over the surface, mesmerising.

'My sea . . .'

The sun's behind me now, warm on my back and in my hair. The water is ahead. My shadow stretches, long and thin, over the lawn, a bridge between the land and the ocean. I realise that I'm humming, an odd little tune I can't remember the name of. I'm swaying in place, gently, my feet moving without conscious thought. I turn in a slow circle, my arms lifting, body suffused with a sense of calm and familiarity, as if I were retracing steps I'd danced a thousand times before.

The light changes; clouds drift across the sun. My shadow disappears and the sea suddenly turns dull. I catch my breath. The tune slips out of my memory as I drop my arms and look around, a little dazed. I'm starving, and my knee hurts quite a lot now that I stop to think about it. I'm not sure if that's from before or if I've banged it again clambering over a tree root or something. I check the time on my phone. It's nearly three. I've missed lunch.

I circle the outside of the ruined building and find the path again easily, taking it a bit slower this time, especially on the steeper woodland section, since my knee seems to hurt more when I'm moving downhill. I'm tired and dreamy, thoughtful. It's been a strange sort of day, but good. I'm really looking forward to getting home – getting back to my great-aunt's house and raiding the pastry box again.

I'm thinking about toast and remembering happily that Liz left me both cheese and eggs in the fridge when I come through the front gate. I pause, wary: there's something on the doorstep.

It's those little blue flowers I saw in the woods. They're flat blossoms, each with five round petals and a bright yellow star at the centre. A bundle has been tied neatly with some papery twine and propped up against the door for me to find.

Someone's left me flowers. No one's ever given me flowers before.

Touched, I pick them up and smell them. They don't have any scent other than the earthy green smell of the woods, which is good enough for me. I go inside and look for a vase. My great-aunt seems like the kind of person who would have vases coming out of her ears. Falling out of every cupboard. But, no, I can't find one anywhere and the stems of the flowers are too long and spindly to fit in a mug or a glass tumbler without keeling over.

Then I remember the green glass jar on Stephen Whittaker's windowsill.

The Moonlit Maze

I quickly hobble up the stairs and into the sad little room. Knee aching, trying to get in and out without looking at the mess I've left, of course I manage to catch my foot on the edge of one of the abandoned binbags, and knock the jar right off the sill to the floor. I suck in a breath, sure it's about to shatter – but it bounces on the carpet and rolls under the bed.

With a sigh, I sit on the musty carpet and slide a shrinking hand into the darkness, hoping I'm not going to encounter spiders, cockroaches or a pile of Stephen Whittaker's old *Playboy* magazines.

My fear is only partly justified. My hand does knock into the edge of something, possibly a box. After pulling out the green glass, miraculously intact if even dustier than before, I hesitate for a second, wondering if I really want to know what else is there. But my curiosity is too strong to resist, and it's not like my opinion of him could sink any lower. I bend down and reach under the bed again, grabbing the box.

It's just an old shoebox, covered in dust bunnies and, yes, a few dead spiders. I shrug and flick the top off.

There's only one thing inside. It's a bulky, old-fashioned photo album, identical to the kind that are stuffed in the bottom of my suitcase. The ones Ma filled up with pictures of her foster family and friends at university, a photocopy of my birth certificate and inkprints of my new-born hands and feet, photos of me with Gemma as a baby, newspaper clippings, my childish artworks, Polaroids of us on holiday.

The jar hits the carpet again with a thunk. My hands feel like they're shaking, but I don't look away from the album to check. I open it.

There, on the first page, is a collage of photos. They're of her. My mother. Heartbreakingly young and gorgeous, with her hair frizzy and imperfect, and wearing way too much lip gloss. Smiling, smiling, smiling. Her and him, together. His arm slung round her shoulder, laughing, both of them clutching drinks in a pub, him lifting her off her feet in front of one of the Oxford buildings while she clearly shrieks at him. Him in profile, kissing her cheek while she pretends to swoon. Photobooth strips of them mucking about, sticking their tongues out at the camera. One shot of them asleep together on a picnic blanket, her head tucked under his chin, his hand resting protectively on her back.

The only picture of him I ever saw was the grainy black-and-white image in the newspaper story about his death. I knew he was fair, but didn't realise he had hair the colour of clear honey. I didn't know his eyes were brown. I didn't know he smiled at her like that, like she was his whole world.

On the inside cover of the photo album, opposite the photos, is a handwritten poem. Mum's handwriting.

> *I have been here before,*
> *But when or how I cannot tell:*
> *I know the grass beyond the door,*
> *The sweet keen smell,*
> *The sighing sound, the lights around the shore.*
>
> *You have been mine before,—*
> *How long ago I may not know:*
> *But just when at that swallow's soar*
> *Your neck turn'd so,*
> *Some veil did fall,—I knew it all of yore.*

Has this been thus before?
And shall not thus time's eddying flight
Still with our lives our love restore
In death's despite,
And day and night yield one delight once more?

Below that, in different handwriting, is written: *SUDDEN LIGHT, D. GABRIEL ROSSETTI.* This handwriting is blocky, slightly cramped, all caps. His handwriting. He probably wrote it in later so that he didn't forget.

She wrote this down for him because it meant so much to her, he meant so much to her. No wonder she couldn't stand to look at Rossetti's paintings, no wonder she was always telling me that stuff was sentimental rubbish. It hurt too much.

He hurt her. He left her. But he kept this. In his sad impersonal desert of a room, he kept this safe in a box hidden under his bed, all those years.

'You idiot,' I whisper. I wipe the tears off my face and rub my fingers dry on my jeans. Then I put my palm flat on the page, my skin pressed against the place where their writing rests on the paper, together.

Eleven

Xanthe

The year Xanthe turned sixteen, the world seemed new.

The war had finally ended, and at her school, everyone walked around for months as if it were Christmas Eve all the time, with a kind of lightness, a kind of suppressed joy. Even poor Miss Lennox, whose fiancé had died in the trenches at Passchendaele and who had been missing from the school for three months after what Xanthe's friend Ophelia had heard described, in whispers, as a 'nervous breakdown', could be seen smiling and humming under her breath occasionally since Armistice Day. The gossip was that she was walking out with someone new, one of the masters from the boys' school on the other side of town, though Xanthe had noticed that she still wore her old engagement ring. In such a transformed world, anything might be possible, even quite wonderful or strange things.

The first sign of the fundamental shift in Xanthe's own family showed up in the form of a shining green racing car, impossibly new and expensive-looking, sending the gravel of the boarding school's driveway flying as it slid to a halt at the front steps. The door opened and a man stepped out. The sunshine reflecting from the windshield of his car made his golden head seem almost to glow.

'Who is *that*?' Xanthe's friend Ophelia leaned so far out of the sash window of their dormitory – where they were supposedly packing the last of their possessions neatly into their trunks and tidying the room, ready to leave – that she was in danger of toppling straight down two storeys to land on the bonnet of the exciting car. 'He looks just like a film star!'

'Too young to be anyone's father,' Josephine announced, peering over Ophelia's head. Her faint French accent seemed suddenly thicker.

Xanthe, who was sitting beside Ophelia on the narrow sill of the window, more to keep a cautious hand knotted into the back of her friend's jumper than because she was much interested in the tide of families and guardians and servants coming to pick everyone up for the summer holidays, said a little blankly, 'Oh. That's my cousin Jonathan. I wonder what he's doing here?'

☽○☾

Since the dreary January day when Xanthe's parents had deposited her with her luggage on the driveway of Churchmere School, her escort home for the holidays each term had been the chauffeur. Xanthe's father had never visited, and her mother had accompanied the driver only once, in the year everyone had to leave early because of an epidemic of mumps. She hadn't even got out of the car.

The sight of either of her parents dodging around bustling mamas, heavily laden servants and over-excited schoolgirls to politely introduce themselves to the headmistress in the grand hall would have left Xanthe speechless with surprise. Jonathan's appearance made her wonder if she had managed to catch some kind of exotic fever. He couldn't possibly be here to see her; she doubted he could pick her out of a crowd at ten paces.

If it hadn't been for Ophelia's firm grip on her left hand and Josephine's eager presence just behind her right shoulder, she would have run away and hid in the dormitory until the hallucinogenic fancy of her lofty cousin charming all the house mistresses among the blowsy flower arrangements and tasteful selections of art, needlework and essays from this year's Exemplary Achievement Prizes had dissipated. But Ophelia and Josephine were agog to meet this glamorous and unexpected relative.

'I was not even sure you had a family,' Josephine said frankly. 'I thought you might be an orphan and just lying about it out of shame, like something in Dickens.'

'Yes, I had to look you up in Debrett's Peerage and everything, to prove it to her,' Ophelia put in. 'Come on – you can't leave us like this! You have to introduce us!'

Xanthe allowed herself to be towed and prodded across the echoing chaos of the room, in the full expectation that her cousin, who was probably just lost and asking for directions, would not notice that she was there for several humiliating minutes.

So she was not prepared. Not at all. For the spectacle of Jonathan catching her eye and – *smiling*. She'd seen Jonathan smile before, of course, only never at her. The effect was a bit like being caught in the full glare of a searchlight. Uncomfortable, mortifying, especially when all the staff turned to stare at her too.

'There you are, cuz,' Jonathan said lightly, stepping away from the crowd of teachers. 'How do you do? You must stop getting prettier every time I see you. Have a care for my poor old heart.'

Miss Langston tittered, then went bright red. Xanthe didn't blush; she never blushed. But she did feel heat, a scalding wave of embarrassment and surprise and, under it all, an awful tingle of electric excitement. Jonathan! Jonathan *here*, and noticing her in front of everyone and – she didn't know what to say. If she said anything, it would be something stupid, or she would stammer. While she was still trying to imagine an appropriate response, Ophelia stepped considerately into the breach.

'You really are Xanthe's cousin, then? Oh, I beg your pardon. I'm Ophelia Letwin, and this is Josephine Montmorency, we're Xanthe's dorm-mates. How do you do?'

Jonathan greeted the other girls with the patient indulgence you'd expect of a grown man dealing with schoolchildren – a patience she'd never witnessed from him before – and Xanthe's bewilderment grew until she just couldn't stand it any more.

'What on earth are you doing here, Jonathan?' she asked abruptly, interrupting Ophelia's ecstatic praise of the shining green car that had first caught her attention. 'You can't be here to see me.'

The headmistress, Miss Portner, who was still standing nearby, looked scandalised.

The Moonlit Maze

Jonathan only smiled at Xanthe again, easy and unruffled. 'I think you'll find I can.'

That strange electric feeling was making her limbs all wobbly. 'Jonathan—'

'I'm better now, Xanthe.' His voice was low, clearly meant for her ears alone. 'It's been a filthy few years, but the war's over and it's all behind us.'

He offered her his hand. Without even thinking about it – to refuse, with all these people looking on, would have been horribly rude – she took it. He shook it with a satisfied look, and then . . . didn't let go.

'You'll be finishing next year, won't you?' Jonathan went on, slightly louder. 'So this might be my last chance to visit. I thought I'd take you out for a spot of lunch, your friends here too if you like, and then we can have a nice leisurely drive back to the castle.'

'Yes, please!' Ophelia said.

Josephine looked at Miss Portner, who gave them a little smile, and nodded. 'Yes, you may go, since neither of your mothers is due until three o'clock. That is, providing you've both finished your packing and everything is shipshape in your room?'

Ophelia bit her lip.

'Of course,' Josephine said brightly, 'but perhaps we should tidy our hair, if Mr . . . er . . .'

'It's Winter,' Jonathan supplied. 'Plain old Winter. I don't mind waiting. You two pop along. Xanthe, since you look perfectly tidy to me, why don't you show me about a bit?'

'I – I don't . . .' Xanthe tugged at her hand, still firmly in Jonathan's grasp, and after a moment he released it.

But her friends were already skipping away, and Miss Portner was saying, 'The courtyard gardens are lovely at this time of year. Why don't you make the best of this nice weather? I'll send the girls out when they're ready,' and Xanthe didn't have any choice, though her legs still felt wobbly and she wasn't sure if she wanted to be alone with her cousin, or what was going on.

Miss Portner waved them beneficently out through the French windows at the back of the hall. Ordinarily, it was worth someone's life to use, or even open those doors. The gardens were separate from the stables and hockey fields, and reserved for girls in the top form, the mistresses and important guests. Xanthe had been looking forward to finally being allowed entry when she came back in September, but in her current state all she could take in about the privileged space was a barrage of sensations. Sunlight in her eyes. Sweat prickling on her upper lip. Gravel shifting treacherously underfoot. The warning drone of bees and the woody green smell of recently cut grass.

'Well, you're not roughing it here, are you?' Jonathan said admiringly, while Xanthe was still trying to battle the sensory confusion. 'Come on, let's have a bit of a toddle.'

He took her arm without asking, but Xanthe found she didn't mind – she knew her eyes were still working really, but when she got like this she couldn't pay much attention to them. It was almost like being blind. Jonathan was engaging in some undemanding small talk. Xanthe was sure he was being charming, but it was more of an impression of quick, laughing chatter. She couldn't contribute, and would have felt less awkward if he hadn't spoken at all.

'Are you giving me the silent treatment?' he asked, drawing them to a halt. There was a slight edge to his tone now – a bit of uncertainty. 'I remember you always having plenty to say when you were younger.'

Xanthe's muddled vision cleared in time for her to see him reach out idly with his free hand to one of the shrubs in the flower bed next to them. His fingers found a deep purple-pink bloom, cup-shaped, and caressed the dense whorls of petals.

'Rosa Reine Victoria, the Queen Victoria Rose,' she informed him without thinking, just desperate for something to say. 'A classic Bourbon from the late 1800s.'

He looked at her, then laughed, his hand coming up to press hers where it sat limply against his forearm. 'Are roses an interest of yours, then?'

Mr Marten had taught her. 'They used to be. I don't have anything to do with these ones, but I . . . don't forget much.'

'You always were a funny, studious little thing. I remember you trying to tell us all about – what was it? – butterflies once. Never heard a five-year-old say "pupae" before.'

'I know, you said so at the time.'

There was something edged in her tone now, and Jonathan looked suddenly discomfited, as if he hadn't imagined that it might not be a sweet childhood memory for her too. 'We were pretty beastly to you in those days, weren't we? I'm afraid little boys are liable to be toads – and I'm the only one who really had the chance to grow up.'

Xanthe's gaze jumped from the rose to Jonathan's face and she stared at him while he determinedly studied the shrub. How old was he now? She couldn't remember his birthday, but she knew he was eleven years older than her. He had been the oldest of all of them. And now ... of his brothers, all his childhood playmates, only he was left behind.

'I'm sorry,' she said, and the words shook with sudden feeling for him, feeling she hadn't even known she had. It was easier for her. She'd never really been one of them. She hadn't had anything to lose.

He gave her a sidelong look, shrugged a little jerkily, like a horse twitching a fly off its shoulder. But his hand came to clasp hers again, a little harder than was comfortable.

'They're all gone,' he said, unwittingly echoing her thoughts. His fingers released her to twiddle the rose back and forth on its whippy, flexible stem. 'It's just you and me now. Have you thought about that much? I have been lately. It's all down to us. We're going to have to look after Aunt Caroline and Uncle Alfred, and one day the whole dreadful old pile and everyone on the estates will be our responsibility too. Just yours and mine.'

Xanthe struggled with herself, but eventually couldn't hold the answer back, though she tried not to sound too grudging. 'Yours. You're the heir. According to the entail, I'm not even a spare.'

'Bugger the entail,' he said sharply, and then snorted at her face. 'Sorry, cuz, I forgot your delicate years. Come and sit here, will you? Your friends'll be out in a minute and I've got something to say.'

'You've already said more to me in the last half an hour than you did my whole life up until this point,' Xanthe muttered as they sat down, and he made that restive jerking movement again, a shadow of impatience crossing his face.

'That's what I'm getting at. You're going to be out of this

place next year, and home for good and – well, you rather grew up while I wasn't paying attention. So I thought, since it's just the two of us now, perhaps I'd better start paying attention. For your sake and mine, and the parents', too. We ought to try to get on.'

Xanthe frowned at his elegantly shod feet, crossed at the ankle, and then at her hand, which was resting on the flaking black cast-iron of the bench. What he said made a kind of sense. But there was something niggling. They had never exactly not 'got on' before. She'd never ... Did he imagine that she was going to burst into tears at the sight of him like a child still? She'd only ever done that before because they had teased her, or chased her away, or deliberately left her lost in the maze. Why imagine them as some kind of enemies? Why had he really come all the way out here?

She risked another look at his face, and forced herself to hold his eye this time, although the sandy sparkle of golden stubble on his chin was much more fascinating. He arched an eyebrow. Clearly some response was required. She pressed her lips together, and then said, a little tentatively, 'I always wished I'd had a sibling.'

He smiled and produced, as if by magic, the pink Queen Victoria bloom he had been fiddling with earlier. She hadn't seen him snap the stem, or noticed it in his hand. 'Friends will do, for the moment.'

'All right, then.' Reluctantly, she took the flower from him. 'Friends.'

He insisted on pinning the rose to the front of her dress.

Xanthe braced herself for an explosion, but Miss Portner, who ought to have been incandescent at the wanton theft from her prized garden, only smiled when she saw it.

The bloom bobbed gently at the edge of Xanthe's vision all through lunch at the posh hotel in town, during which Jonathan set himself to being as amusing as possible, charming Josephine and Ophelia thoroughly. And not only them, Xanthe had to admit to herself. Just as she'd never realised before the stunning effect of Jonathan's smile at close range, she had never known that he could be genuinely good company. He actually paid *attention*. When Ophelia hesitated over the menu and Josephine tried to be sophisticated and order something grown up, he overruled them both and ordered the nearest thing to a nursery tea: iced buns, cakes, finger sandwiches and – thrillingly – champagne. He made a point of saying that this place was famous for its chocolate cake, and Xanthe was astonished to realise this was because he had somehow remembered it was her favourite. He also ordered lemonade, and stuck to drinking that himself, a gesture that Xanthe felt in some instinctive way was meaningful. And while he kept Ophelia and Josephine pink and laughing, he made it clear that the main part of his interest was in Xanthe. When she dropped her napkin, he bent over and picked it up for her and put it back on her lap himself instead of summoning a waiter to do it.

Xanthe couldn't understand *why*. But that didn't mean she was immune, either.

By the end of lunch, the unwatered rose had shed a handful of its petals in the early summer heat. She gathered them up gently in the napkin, folded it and slipped it into her satchel, deliberately not asking herself why. She noticed Jonathan noticing. He didn't ask either, although he looked pleased. And Xanthe realised that made her feel happy, rather in the way that her father's rare smile or her mother's occasional praise made her feel happy. Family feeling, then, she told herself. Perfectly normal.

By the time they got back to the school it was nearly time for both Josephine and Ophelia's parents to arrive and Xanthe felt worn out. The effort to keep focused on what everyone was saying, maintain an appropriate expression and form mildly clever responses was draining enough at the best of times – with Jonathan there she felt as if she were half an inch from being revealed as a slug at every instant. But there was nothing for it. She had to get home somehow, and Higgins apparently wasn't going to show up, so now there was a two-hour drive back to Kearsley. Alone. With Jonathan.

She knew without even asking that any request to be left in peace to pretend to read a book wasn't likely to be taken in a generous spirit. If anyone even could pretend to read a book in an open-topped car. While Jonathan supervised one of the school's handymen, who was lashing Xanthe's trunk to the small space on the back of his vehicle, Josephine showed Xanthe how to bind her hair back with a silk scarf, then kissed her on the cheek.

'I am happy for you,' she whispered with an embarrassed giggle, before disappearing after Ophelia.

Xanthe watched her go with a sinking stomach that wasn't at all eased by Jonathan's matter-of-fact chivalry in opening the car door for her. 'If there's anything you want to say, best to do it now. We'd both scream ourselves raw if we try to talk once we're on the open road.'

'No, nothing. I don't mind not talking,' she said fervently. He raised his eyebrows, nettled. 'Oh, I didn't mean—'

But of course she had, and perhaps she was too tired now not to let it show a little. His expression took on a sardonic cast she remembered all too well from when she was younger. He was definitely nettled – insulted that she wasn't just aching to spend the drive home hanging on his every word. Yet, somehow, the familiar scowl made her feel better. What on earth was she worried about? Jonathan must know enough to accept that she was still awkward and occasionally untactful, just as Xanthe accepted that, while he might have been on his best behaviour today, he was still capable of being a 'little toad'.

'Girlish nerves?' he asked sweetly. 'Or have our good intentions come to nothing already?'

She huffed with laughter. 'I'm tired. I've never had champagne before. I'd curl up and have a sleep if I could, but I don't think this car is quite designed for that.' He could be insulted if he wanted. Hard cheese.

His frown deepened. 'I hope you don't get carsick. She's brand new.'

'Too late now. You'll have to take your chances,' she said cheerfully, and sat down into the squeaking leather seat, arranging her satchel on her lap while he closed the car door. The look, almost of disappointment, stayed on his face as he took his place beside her, drumming his fingers on the burr wood of the wheel before tugging on driving gloves. Then he glanced down at the drooping rose at her breast, and smiled.

'Look after that, won't you, sweetheart? I suspect Aunt Caroline will want to press it into a book.'

Then he started the engine up and took them squealing down the driveway.

Twelve

The first weeks of that summer holiday remained a glittering, sun-soaked blur in Xanthe's memories for the rest of her life. She was entirely unprepared for her sudden elevation to an entirely new place in her family, and that change made everything, even the most familiar things, seem suddenly unfamiliar.

But she also knew, looking back, that some of the dreamlike quality was because this period had been just that: a dream. A wonderful, foolish daydream. And she had been happy. Enjoying, for the first time in her life, the feeling of being wanted.

If only she had understood exactly what it was that she was wanted *for*.

She realised straight away that her parents were different that summer. Buoyant, smiling and pleased to see her. At first, she didn't really make much of it; Jonathan had come with her, after all, and then stayed for tea. Although the day she returned from school at term's end was never treated as a special day – Xanthe usually didn't even see her father until the evening, when they gathered for dinner, and he would acknowledge her presence with an exaggerated start, and everyone would have to laugh as if the joke wasn't ancient – it seemed only natural that they would both emerge to welcome Jonathan and his shining new car. But then, rather than sending her upstairs straight away to change and unpack, Caroline let Xanthe have tea in the Pink Saloon with her, Xanthe's father and Jonathan. Xanthe knew that this was intended along the lines of a treat and appreciated it as such, though she was still a little full from lunch, and too tired to really contribute much. After tea, Caroline walked her upstairs to her room, arm looped through Xanthe's elbow, and asked her about school and her friends in a puzzlingly attentive way. Going through Xanthe's trunk with the maid, she hummed gently under her breath.

'Did you and Jonathan have a nice visit at Churchmere?' she asked, shaking her head over a sadly patched gym slip. The question seemed casual, but Xanthe observed the darting, sidelong look. She plaited her fingers together on her knee, trying not to fidget on the edge of the bed.

'Everyone was surprised to see him there,' she said carefully. 'Ophelia thought he looked just like a film star, and Mrs Portner let us walk in the rose gardens, and then he took all three of us – Ophelia and Josephine and me – to lunch. It was very good of him.'

Caroline beamed, her eyes fixing on the drooping rose pinned to the front of Xanthe's dress. 'Wasn't that gallant of him. Unpin that, darling, and I'll have Pinchbeck put it in some water for you to keep.'

'I . . . thought we might press it between the pages of a book?' Xanthe said, prompted by a vague experimental spirit.

Her reward was a look of warm approval. 'That's a lovely

idea. How grown up you seem this year! Time truly does run away when one isn't paying attention.' She dabbed gently at her eyes.

But, in fact, Mother, like Jonathan, did seem to be paying attention to Xanthe now. Even her father was giving her ... looks. Not all the time, but just now and again, suddenly, as they were going in to dinner, or perhaps over breakfast. Bright, *intent* sort of looks. *Satisfied* looks, as if – she suddenly remembered Mr Marten, smiling gently in one of his glasshouses – a failing tomato plant had responded to the new compost and started to fruit as it should.

Was it just that she was growing up, no longer the scrubby little child who cried all the time and talked too much about odd things and could never seem to find the right place for herself? Was it the end of war – or perhaps Jonathan's recovery from the war, at long last?

Her peaceful, lonely routines, developed over years, of reading and writing in her bedroom, wandering in the gardens, trekking through the woods or clambering down to the private little cove below the maze with a packet of sandwiches and a good novel, were all thrown into disarray that year. There was no time to wander anywhere. No time even to think.

Only one day stood out in her memory as feeling truly real. The day she ran into Tom Marten again.

Xanthe and Lady Kearsley had been supposed to drive out to visit the Farringdons that morning, but Caroline had been listless and pale at the breakfast table and, after Xanthe's father had shut himself in his study, Caroline had confided that she had one of her sick headaches.

'I shall have to lie down,' she said, shielding her eyes with one hand. 'No, no, Finch is quite well able to look after me. You can occupy yourself for the day, can't you, dear? I hope you won't be too lonely ...'

Xanthe was sorry her mother was unwell, very sorry indeed, but the escape from the promised lunch with the stiffly proper Farringdons, and the prospect of a truly free day in which she might stare off into space without being considered peculiar, daydream without being scolded for inattention and write without being teased for her 'scribbling' was something close to bliss.

Respecting her mother's strictures on what a lady owed to her skin, Xanthe dutifully donned a sunhat, then swiftly took her journal and pencil case into the garden before anyone could decide to find something useful for her to do instead.

The weather was sultry and airless, and Xanthe found herself grateful for the shelter of the hat as she wandered into the stillness of the rose garden, looking for a shady spot to sit. She chose one of the benches beneath an arbour of creamy pink-tinged Madame Alfred Carrière roses, leaning gratefully on the cool wrought iron as she opened her journal to look at a short story she had been working on, a sort of fairytale-ish fable about a girl born with the teeth of an alligator.

There was no breeze at all. The salty taste of this morning's high tide hung in the muggy air, mixing into a heady haze with the intense perfume of the blooming flowers. She scribbled a little, crossed out a few lines, fanned herself with her hat and then admitted that the shade wasn't deep enough. The words were swimming before her eyes. She got up, clutching at the bench back as a wave of dizziness swept over her.

That was when Xanthe saw him.

She didn't even realise who it was at first. He was just one of the gardener's boys passing by, pushing a barrow: a tall, slim figure, dark-haired, sunlight reflecting from his white undershirt and gleaming on the freckle-brown breadth of his shoulders. He hadn't noticed her. She began to sit down again, hoping to avoid any interaction. But something made her hesitate.

The figure was limned in gold, seeming to shimmer in the heat. He stopped to dash sweat from his forehead with a muscular forearm. Something about the movement sent a strange pull through Xanthe's centre, a pull of attraction – and then she knew.

'Tom?'

He started, dropped the barrow and broke into a grin. 'Xan!'

They hurried towards each other in a surge of gladness, and met by the rose garden's central statue of Diana, both already talking.

'Have you finished at the grammar—'

'Are you back for the summer, then—'

They both broke off and he gestured for her to go on, but she shook her head.

'Yes, exams all done,' he answered, grinning. 'And heading to university this autumn. I'm working for Dad for a bit while I'm at a loose end.'

'Me too – at a loose end today, I mean. One more year at school for me, though. I'm so glad you're going on to university, Tom. What are you going to study? Tell me all about it!'

Tom abandoned his garden tools and Xanthe left her journal on the bench as they slowly walked the circuit of the garden together, talking and laughing easily. It was just as if they'd never been apart – even though he'd got so tall! She supposed it was normal for an eighteen-year-old, but she could hardly believe that she had to look up so far, squinting against the sun, to meet his eyes. Had they always been such a striking shade, those eyes? A deep hazel that shaded to amber? If it weren't for the familiar mess of his hair, she might not even have known him.

She swayed away from him on the path, then drifted back as he turned his head to watch her. Their bare arms brushed and goosepimples shivered across her skin. Tom's voice seemed to crack. She saw the lines of his tanned throat move as he swallowed and fell silent.

Xanthe remembered, suddenly, the last time she had seen him. They had been playing around on the tiny little private beach at the bottom of the castle cliff, along with Tom's sister, Sally. It had been late autumn, an Indian summer, and they were all drunk on the unexpected sunshine. She and Sally – eleven and twelve then – had ganged up on fourteen-year-old Tom, chasing him around on the sand, trying to trip him, jumping on his back until they all went down in a giggling heap. It was an achingly sweet memory: simple happiness.

Within days, her parents had announced that Xanthe's governess, Inchmallow, was to be dismissed, and Xanthe herself sent away to boarding school in the New Year. It wasn't a punishment, her father informed her briskly. It was only that there had been some *talk*, and . . . well, perhaps Kearsley was too isolated for a girl of her age. She must learn her proper place in life, and make friends with people of her own class.

Xanthe had taken the news in silent misery. What could she

say? Glowing in her mind, a red-hot coal of mingled glory and shame, was the knowledge of how, as Sally had rolled away from their tangle of limbs in the sand, Tom and Xanthe had lain together. Stayed together. Just for a moment. She had felt the weight of his body against hers, the warmth and shape of it, filling her own body with radiant light.

She knew it had to have been that. There wasn't anything else anyone could have talked to her parents about. But who could possibly have seen? Who would have told? Xanthe had never been able to bring herself to ask.

Tom cleared his throat and Xanthe snapped back to the present moment. He began a story about his father and sister, and she pushed away the remembrance of her parents' stern faces as they'd walked away from her within the chilly, rain-sodden walls of Churchmere. It was surprisingly easy. Tom was talking and she'd always loved Tom's stories, the warmth and wry humour that brought them alive. She smiled up at him, then laughed as he got to the end.

'So then Sally said, well, if he can do it, I don't see why I can't. And she got over the hedge in one jump! One! I've never seen Dad go so red in the face – he didn't know if he should be outraged or proud,' Tom finished, talking over the sound of Xanthe's laughter.

'Good for her!' she said firmly. 'I don't see why anyone should be allowed to call us the weaker sex if we can prove we're not.'

'Listen. I'm glad to have seen you, and grateful for the break – but I've got to get back to work. Dad'll kill me if he catches me slacking off,' Tom said. He stretched his arms out with a faint groan, fingers seeming almost to scrape at the cloudless sky. 'I'm supposed to finish weeding the rose beds this morning and then start on the borders.'

Xanthe's stomach sank. Not even an hour had passed. That wasn't nearly long enough. Tom might be out here every day for the rest of the summer, but once her mother was feeling better, would she ever have the chance to see him, let alone talk to him, again? 'Well, tell him it was my fault. He won't be cross with me, will he?'

'No, but that won't make him any less cross at me,' Tom said. 'Or get the borders done, either.'

'We've barely had a chance to talk at all! Tom, my father's in his study and Mother's upstairs – it's safe in the house. Come and hide in the orangery with me. I could even probably sneak us some lunch.'

'What? That's going from the frying pan into the fire,' Tom said, smiling but frowning too now, a little. 'If one of the inside servants caught us—'

'Oh, Tom, please! It's been so long since we've talked.'

'Xanthe,' he said, suddenly serious, putting out his hand to stop her walking so that she had to turn to face him properly. His fingers hovered in the air by her shoulder, then fell away without touching. 'I can't. I never could have, not even when we were kids. I've got a job to do, that my father trusts me to do. Maybe it seems petty to you, but not all of us can just flit about, doing whatever we want like—' He cut himself off.

'Like I do?' Xanthe repeated after a moment, softly.

'I didn't mean— Oh damn. I didn't mean it that way. Xan . . .'

She turned away from him to stare at the roses. Everyone loved roses, didn't they? They were so pretty. So utterly useless.

'I know you didn't. But you don't understand, either. When your father offered you this job, here, working for him – if you'd said no, what would he have done, Tom?'

'I don't know, hired a lad from down in the town to do it instead, probably?'

'Then he wouldn't have punished you for not doing what he thought you were supposed to do? Given you a stern talking to? Sent you away?'

'No, of course not!' He sounded bewildered. 'What do you mean?'

'I mean that you have a choice, Tom. He gives you a choice. I know I have a lot of things that a lot of people would like to have. Money and a big house and – oh, stupid fancy dresses. But they're not really mine, you see? Everything I have belongs to my parents really. I'm not *allowed* to have a job, like you. Or my own money, or my own things. I'm not allowed to have a choice in what I do.' She shrugged his hand off when it came to rest tentatively on her shoulder, turning back to face him in a sudden flash of temper. Xanthe had never spoken like this to anyone before, had barely articulated these feelings to herself. 'It's all theirs, right down to the clothes I stand up in! Any time I don't do or think or say what they think I'm supposed to – they can take anything they want away from me. They can take my friends away. My home away. They've done it before.'

He looked back at her, wordless, stricken. Then, as if he couldn't help himself, he reached out and gathered her awkwardly into his arms. His body radiated heat – his spread hands seemed big enough to almost cover her whole back – and the base of his throat smelled of green sap, clean skin, cheap washing powder. She threw her arms round him and hugged him back fiercely, uncaring of the belt buckle that dug into her tummy, or the dampness of his skin against the thin linen of her dress.

Then it was over. To Xanthe, letting go felt as if the sun had gone behind a cloud, and a sudden awful chill swept over her. She wanted to move forward, to touch and be held by him again. She forced herself to take another step back instead.

'I'm sorry, Xan,' he repeated, low and sincere. He looked lost, gangly and young – just a boy for all that he had grown so tall. Her eyes met his again for an instant. She felt a kind of tug deep inside her, that pull of attraction, of wanting. It hurt to ignore it. Oh, it hurt.

Xanthe did the only thing she could. She turned from him and walked away, and heard his footsteps receding as he did the same thing behind her. He would go back to the warm, sunlit garden, and she into the cool, shadowed emptiness of Kearsley Castle. Their proper places.

There was nothing else to say.

Thirteen

Xanthe tried not to think about Tom Marten too much, after that. It only made her feel restless and discontented, as if he had stirred up some wild part of her that the long, quiet years of exile at boarding school had put to sleep. A part she *needed* to sleep, so that she could fulfil her role, the role her family had finally given her now.

Not that thinking about him would have made a difference. There were no more days off. It transpired that Xanthe was now considered old enough to attend the Summer Ball that her parents always held at the beginning of June – the high point of the season for all the county gentry – and represent the family. But, at the same time, her previously perfectly acceptable wardrobe was found to be, in the words of Pinchbeck, 'a right royal disgrace'.

Mother took her up to London to see her own dressmaker. While they were there, Xanthe was also fitted for several sets of extremely uncomfortable undergarments, had her hair trimmed, was given a pile of different pots and lotions and creams and a stringent lesson from a large and perfumed lady on how she ought to use them to care for her face and hair and hands, and found herself in receipt of a bewildering number of hats and hair grips and silk stockings.

'I'm afraid you're not a little girl any more, darling,' her mother laughed when Xanthe begged to be allowed a tiny respite – a walk in the park across from their London townhouse, an afternoon of peaceful reading, anything. Her smile was bright, but her tone was final. 'You can't go running wild just because that's what you'd prefer to do. A woman's work is beauty, and beauty is pain. Don't gripe now. There might be a special treat coming for you soon.'

The special treat turned out to be Jonathan, who motored up to join them at the townhouse. He took them both to dinner in a succession of grand restaurants, and to see a play, and he escorted Xanthe by herself for a matinee performance of a musical. He wanted to take her to a party with some friends of his, but Caroline put her foot down with a firmness that Xanthe had never seen her display with Jonathan before.

Xanthe pretended to be disappointed, since she could tell that both Jonathan and her mother expected her to be. In reality, she was relieved. Jonathan had taken Caroline's refusal with gritted teeth and glittering eyes and stormed out of the flat.

He didn't return that night. Caroline watched the ticking of the clock with a deep crimp between her brows, then declared they would have a quiet, simple dinner at home, just the two of them, although they'd already dressed for Jonathan to take them out.

The next morning there was still no sign of Jonathan. Caroline feebly told Xanthe that he must have slept at his club and forgotten to send a note. She sent Xanthe out for a dress fitting by herself, with a list of detailed instructions to pass on to Madame Delamare. Madame Delamare did not seem overly interested in listening to Xanthe recite them, and Xanthe was still worrying over whether she would get the blame for the showy flounce that she was fairly sure her mother hadn't approved when she arrived home again to find Caroline flushed with happiness over a bunch of yellow peonies presented to her by Jonathan. He was bright-eyed, smiling, apparently back in the best of spirits – and offered no explanations for his absence.

None of them referred to the disagreement again.

Jonathan did eventually take Xanthe to two parties, but both of them were jolly, informal affairs for young people, well-chaperoned, and held at the homes of friends of Xanthe's parents. There wasn't even any dancing. Apart from the various mothers and fathers, Jonathan was the oldest person present by miles. Xanthe observed Jonathan swing wildly back and forth between bored out of his skull and not caring who knew it, and determined to wring admiration and adoration out of every person present.

Jonathan's idea of the two of them coming to be friends didn't have much of what Xanthe understood of friendship in it. There was no quiet chatting, confiding secrets or helping each other with problems. It mostly seemed to be him taking her places in public, ordering endless glasses of champagne – though he never drank himself – and aiming enigmatic remarks that might equally have been compliments or insults at her, just to see if she would take offence. Xanthe firmly reminded herself that he was still only her toad of a cousin, and responded by ignoring or laughing at him as often as she could. There was never any way to know how he would react, either, until he'd gone white with rage and refused to talk to her for the rest of the evening, or suddenly grinned and kissed her gloved hand.

Champagne gave her a headache. She usually ended up abandoning her glasses half drunk. But Jonathan was so confusing that Xanthe spent most of the time she was with him feeling as if she might be drunk anyway: tense and on edge, and occasionally hopping mad. She wished she knew how to be as rude to him as he was to her without upsetting her mother. Yet it was also... exciting. The attention. No matter how mixed it was, or how mixed her own feelings about it, she struggled not to let it make her giddy.

The pattern – Jonathan's intense interest mingled with bouts of sudden cold distance, the endless entertainments, the heady approval from her parents – continued throughout the summer after Caroline and Xanthe had returned home. It continued all the way up to the night of the Summer Ball itself. The night when everything fell apart.

Or rather, she thought later, trying to make sense of it, that was when everything fell together. The missing puzzle piece slotted into place, and the pattern finally made a horrible kind of sense.

Xanthe's hands trembled that night. She counted each step down the curve of the stairs, half afraid that she would trip over the hem of her long white dress in her new shoes, half excited and ready to be a grown-up at last. The ostrich plumes in her hair danced in the warm air rising from the packed hall below, setting her slightly off balance, and she struggled not to toss her head as she joined her parents and Jonathan at the bottom of the staircase. They made a tiny, cosy group amid the crush of guests.

The Moonlit Maze

Then the string quartet responded to some pre-arranged signal and fell silent. Everyone turned to look at them.

Jonathan grinned, and got down on one knee.

In the sudden, overwhelming quiet, the awareness of everyone – almost every person she'd ever met, hundreds of people – listening, witnessing, vibrated against her skin like a roaring fire. Her mother and father were on either side of her, waiting for her to answer, smiling, smiling, smiling. Her gaze had fallen back down to Jonathan's expectant, impatient face as he knelt at her feet, his fingers tightening to the point of pain on hers as she hesitated.

'Well?' he asked.

That was all he asked. No 'Will you?' or 'Would you?' And no 'Please.'

No. One little word. Say no. Only she couldn't. In front of all the eyes. She just couldn't.

Barely loud enough for even her to hear, she whispered, 'Yes.'

The room dissolved into a sea of champagne-gold bubbles: her parents congratulating them, her mother kissing her cheek, her father clapping her shoulders and Jonathan, shining with a kind of febrile, triumphant excitement – the excitement of a man who has won a prize, taken the trick, put his bet on the long-chance horse and seen it come flying home – turning away and picking up a full wine glass, to propose a toast to his lovely bride-to-be. Everyone cheered again. Jonathan drank the glass straight down in a single pull and reached for another.

It was a horrible mistake. She might be naïve, but not as naïve as that. Jonathan didn't want her. He hadn't even tried to kiss her. It was all so clear now. Jonathan was doing this, playing along with all this, because her parents had ... not *made* him – Xanthe didn't believe that they could or even would try to force him – somehow *convinced* him that it was right, or for the best. How, she didn't know. Couldn't know. But they had.

What was she going to do?

Xanthe spent the rest of the ball outside her own body. It was the most frightening sensation, feeling numb and absent, but she was grateful for it regardless. She hovered at her own shoulder, admiring herself distantly as she chatted to people – friendly, poised, at ease, more graceful and gracious than she had ever been. Her parents, in their turn, hovered around her, glowing with pride. Across the room, Jonathan rapidly switched from champagne to whisky.

Xanthe watched herself watch him. She watched her parents watch him too, and their looks of concern, but they did not attempt to intervene. Xanthe knew Jonathan a little now. She knew that while he felt it was entirely his right to ignore anyone he liked, no one else was allowed to do the same to him.

So when, at three o'clock in the morning, the party was beginning to wind down and Xanthe was tiredly observing herself laugh at the jokes of Reginald Manley, the son of a local dignitary, and he – greatly daring – took her hand and kissed it, and asked her to dance, Xanthe wasn't actually surprised to see Jonathan, who had glanced in their direction and clearly noticed the younger man's clumsy attempts at flirtation, start across the room in their direction. She wasn't surprised that he was stumbling, pushing people aside, his eyes like hollow black holes in his skull. She wasn't at all surprised that her father tried to step into his path with a low mutter of 'All right there, steady on—' Or that her mother hastily sought to draw her away. All this seemed completely inevitable.

She was surprised when Jonathan whipped his fist back and hit Reginald Manley squarely in the jaw.

The punch made a noise like a ripe melon hitting a hard floor. Reginald went straight over backwards, but somehow, whether in shock or because he thought she could keep him on his feet, he didn't let go of Xanthe's hand. He dragged her with him as he landed heavily on one of the buffet tables. The table legs skidded backwards – ear shredding – and the tablecloth came loose as Reginald slid down the edge. A tower of champagne glasses and silver salvers shattered and spun on the polished marble floor.

Xanthe found herself abruptly, unpleasantly, thrown back into her own body. She was down. Gasping for breath, almost sobbing, though her eyes were dry. Sprawled on a glinting bed of splintered glasses. A broken plume dangled in front of her eyes. Her white satin gloves were stained with spilled wine. They were red.

No. That wasn't wine. Her hands were bleeding. They burned. She couldn't move without cutting herself more. She let out a low noise of pain and confusion and heard her mother's voice rising above hers in an attempt to drown her out. 'Good heavens, how clumsy of you, Xanthe!'

'My hands ...'

Caroline talked louder, 'Reginald, are you all right? I'm so terribly sorry – I'm afraid my daughter isn't used to the champagne! Bowdler, have the footmen clear this mess away.' And then, in a hiss to her daughter, 'Keep a hold of yourself, for heaven's sake.'

Xanthe looked up to see her mother bending awkwardly over her, constrained by her corsets. Her face was expressionless, but her eyes were pleading. Her hands wrung together.

Of Jonathan, of her father, there was no sign.

'Mother—'

'Hush, dear. Don't make things any worse.'

For a moment, Xanthe didn't understand. Then, with a queasy drop in her stomach like falling all over again, she did. Alfred had taken her cousin away so that he wasn't ... wasn't *embarrassed* by the consequences of his actions, and Mother was going to smooth it all over, to sweep what had happened under the rug. No one would be upset. No one had drunk too much. No one had hit a guest and knocked his fiancée down. No, no.

Xanthe had just had a little accident, the silly girl.

'Will someone help me up, please?' she asked, her voice breaking.

One of the footmen crouched beside her and took her arm. Her mother turned quickly away, talking persuasively at their guests. The music was still playing, though no one was dancing any more.

'Here, milady – gently now,' the footman said, hushed. 'Let's get you away from this. Just you let me take your weight, that's right.'

The footman was new. She didn't know his name – William, maybe? – but she did know the name of the look on his face. Pity.

The Moonlit Maze

Later on, after the housekeeper had cleaned and bandaged Xanthe's hands and tucked her into bed, she sat and waited, flexing the bandaged fingers just to feel them sting. Just to remind herself of what had really happened. She had to remember. She couldn't let herself forget. Be made to forget.

She had been lucky, really. Mrs Finch had been a nurse, once, before she was a housekeeper, and she assured Xanthe that her gloves had protected her, and the cuts were hardly worse than papercuts. She would be right as rain in no time.

'A little less champagne next time,' she had chuckled, patting Xanthe comfortably on an unbandaged bit of her wrist. Her darting eyes told another story. The servants all knew, of course. They had been dealing with Jonathan for years. They would toe the line, just as Caroline and Alfred expected Xanthe to do.

At nearly four o'clock, the bedroom door opened and her mother – dressed for bed, with her hair in curling papers and her face gleaming with night cream – wafted inside.

'How are you feeling, darling?' she asked, conciliatory. 'I should think you're exhausted. I asked Finch to bring you some warm milk.'

Xanthe didn't answer. Caroline's gaze flickered to the cup of milk that sat, untouched, on the dressing table.

Caroline pressed her lips together, then came to sit on the edge of the bed. The sensation of her weight depressing the satin-covered mattress sent a wave of bittersweet nostalgia through Xanthe. It had been years since her mother had visited Xanthe this way, at night, but her tone was just the same: the soft tones of a mother telling stories to a child. Only Xanthe didn't believe them any more.

'Well,' Caroline spoke into the silence, 'Jonathan is sorry, of course, but no real harm was done. You're young, Xanthe, and no one expects you to understand how to manage these sorts of things yet. I know – your father and I both know, of course – that you were only intending to be polite to Reginald. You didn't mean to . . . well, to flirt with him or anything like that. Jonathan forgives you.'

She wanted to cry. To throw herself down on the bed and thrash and scream like a toddler. To make the kind of scene that would go down in family history.

Only it wouldn't. They wouldn't let it. They wouldn't let anyone upset Jonathan.

Xanthe stared down at her hands. Flexed them. Closed them into padded fists. Flexed them again. 'Does he?'

'You'll be back to school in a few weeks,' Caroline said brightly. 'Won't it be exciting to tell all your friends about the lovely time you've had this summer and everything you've done! You're an engaged woman now – I should think they'll all be quite envious! And – we were thinking, your father and I, that perhaps you might like to go a little further in your education?'

Xanthe blinked, surprised for the first time. 'My . . . education?'

'Nothing too challenging, of course! But there's an excellent finishing school, in Lausanne, which one of my friends was telling me about. It would teach you all kinds of useful things for your future life, and when you come back you'll be eighteen and all grown up, and – and really ready to get married. What do you think, dear?'

Xanthe looked up into her mother's eyes. Was she imagining

the faint, tight shapes of anxiety around the other woman's brow and lips? Maybe. Caroline's face radiated cheerful enthusiasm, and nothing more. If there was turmoil hidden behind her gaze, Xanthe couldn't see it in the low light. Was this intended as a peace offering? A way out?

Did it matter? It was two more years away from this place. Away from them and the lies that they would never, ever admit were anything but the truth.

She was surprised at how lightly her voice came out. 'I think I'd like to go, thank you. I'd like to go to Switzerland.'

Fourteen

Jude, present day

I stare sadly at the crumbs left in the bottom of the pastry box, then fold it up and stick it in the kitchen bin. That's it. All gone. I've also finished the eggs, cheese and other bits and pieces that Liz stocked my fridge with. This morning I'd been forced to dig an ancient granola bar out of the bottom of my backpack for breakfast, and drink instant coffee, black, to supply my poor frizzling neurons with caffeine. There's no getting around it. I'm going to have to go out today.

I've spent the last three days adjusting to the solitude and peace of the cottage. Soaking it up, really, like a dense, dry artist's sponge soaks up excess moisture and paint off a watercolour board. I've curled up on the sofa or in the big brass bed, leafing slowly through the pages in the album that Ma made for my father. Sometimes I find new things, nearly hidden: notes he added to remind himself of when or where they'd been when a photo was taken, or private, enigmatic phrases that don't seem to connect with anything, like 'Under the bridge with the stars'. I tried looking them up whenever my phone would throw me a bar. Most of them weren't quotes, just him thinking to himself. If I became restless, I went out for long walks through the woods and explored the clifftop ruins, taking pictures on my phone.

And I've been having dreams every night.

Intense, absorbing dreams, filled with people who seem so real, so alive to me in those stretched-out sleep moments. Like nothing I've ever experienced before. My subconscious is building a kind of mythology around this place, Winterthorne and the ruins. I didn't even know I had enough imagination to conjure up that kind of ongoing narrative, the chilly aristocratic world and those twisted family relationships – especially the creepy cousin – but I find I look forward to going to bed every night to see what happens next. I'm enjoying the dreams, just as I've been enjoying being here by myself.

I feel something building inside me. Something fragile that I know I need to protect, a tiny flame that might so easily blow out. I'm not sure exactly what it is yet, this feeling, but it's good, and I don't want it to be smothered by contact with the loud, messy outside world.

Unfortunately, I can't survive indefinitely on instant coffee, half a tub of butter and the stalky bit from the bottom of a head of lettuce.

'All right,' I mutter, opening the cupboard under the stairs and looking into the plastic storage tubs at the bottom. A couple of sturdy bags for life, or even some ordinary grocery bags would do. 'Where are you?'

Ma'd have been out the door by now. She'd have rolled her eyes and said it was worth paying for bags from the shop to get out of having to dig through someone else's rubbish. Then again, she was the one who ran up all those credit-card debts, wasn't she?

What would she have to say about this house if she could see it? About Anne Erskine? About my decision to come here, and what I've found here? Her voice in my head is tellingly silent. Again.

Maybe it doesn't matter.

That thought gives me a queasy, blasphemous feeling. But maybe it *doesn't*. I love it here. All the things that would have made Ma impatient and bored are the things I like most. Being surrounded by countryside. The silence-that-isn't-silence. The rich, clashing colours and patterns everywhere. The overcrowded art and overstuffed bookcases. The house is perfectly set up for a certain kind of life, a peaceful, contented life, and there's a space in it ready for me to fit right into, as if I'm ... the missing puzzle piece.

My fingers close over the handle of a jute bag. I wrestle it out of the cupboard and find another bag folded up inside it. Exactly what I need. This place is always giving me exactly what I need. And all of it belongs to me.

I sit back on my heels.

I'm still there in the hall, staring blankly into space, when a brisk rap on the door makes me levitate. One hand clutched over my pounding heart, I go to answer. The flood of morning sun as I open the door makes my eyes water. At first, the person on the doorstep is just a tall, dark shape.

I blink, and my dazzled vision resolves into a man. Early thirties, with gleaming blond hair smoothed back in orderly waves, and a malicious sort of smirk. But it can't be. It can't be – 'Jonathan?'

My heels hit the stairs before I even realise I've started backing away. I lose my balance and sit down on the bottom step with a thump.

'Hey, hey, what's the matter? Are you OK?'

That isn't the right voice. No, it is the right voice – for Nick, Nick Fairley, who's crouching down in front of me, the door swinging behind him, his tanned face open and his green eyes filled with concern. There's no one else there.

I let out a short laugh that cracks dryly in the middle. 'Oh God. Sorry. I – you just made me jump when you knocked and my heart was still going and I—' *thought that you were this person from my dreams*. 'I thought you were someone else. I'm all right.'

'Right,' he says politely, clearly not believing that last part. 'Do you feel like getting up? Let's get you a cup of tea.'

The Fairley School of Crisis Management. Step One: Administer Tea. I laugh again, more genuinely this time. 'I don't have any milk in the house.'

'Glass of water, then.' His large, work-roughened hands gently enclose mine, and he pulls me to my feet, shepherds me into the kitchen. I'm reminded that this house is familiar territory to him; he's spent more time here than I have.

'I really am all right,' I insist as he guides me to a chair at the table and grabs a tumbler from the draining board, filling it at the sink. 'It was just an adrenalin rush after basically no breakfast.'

'That's why Mum sent me to check on you,' he says, putting the glass down in front of me, then nudging it unsubtly closer. 'No one's seen you since the day you arrived. We thought you must have run out of food by now.'

'Guilty.' I lift the jute bags that I'm still holding in my left hand. 'I was getting ready to head out. You know that thing when you're about to go out the door and someone knocks on it?'

'And you nearly leap out of your skin, yeah,' he says, grinning. 'Drink that anyway. You gave *me* a shock. I'm not used to girls fainting at my feet.'

'In your dreams, Fairley,' I shoot back, sipping the water. I don't know if I've convinced Nick, but I don't feel shaky any more.

'Do you want a lift? I'm actually heading back into town anyway; my sister and her husband have got a stall at the farmer's market. It'll save you the walk, since you're not feeling good.'

'I'm feeling fine, and I like to— wait. Farmer's market?'

'Every other Thursday in the old town square. All the pies and pastries you can eat. Providing you get there before everything sells out.' He tuts, shakes his head a little, drops his voice to a low confiding tone: 'Looked pretty busy up there to me today.'

I laugh. 'All right, I will accept your lift. Thank you.'

Nick grins again as I finish my water with a gulp and get up to rinse out the glass. When I turn back, he's leaning over the kitchen table, one blunt finger carefully touching the petals of the little blue flowers in the green glass jar that I placed in the centre. They're starting to look wilted, but I can't bring myself to throw them away.

'Picking forget-me-nots?' he asks quizzically.

'Is that what they are? I just liked the colour.' I don't really want to get into how they were left at my door like an offering. That's just for me.

'Oh, so you have actually left the house at some point, then?'

He heads down the hall and I follow, rolling my eyes at his back. 'Yes, I've left the house. I've been out walking every day. I'm not a hermit.'

'Have you been up to Kearsley Castle, then?'

The sound of that name – the name from my dreams – nearly makes my knees buckle again. Nick is opening the front door, which is a good thing; by the time he looks back at me, I think I've got my face under control.

'The old ruins on the cliff? Yeah, a couple of times.'

Do I sound normal? Who knows. There's a rational explanation for this. Mr Swan must have mentioned the name of the old estate. Yes, that's it, that's all it is – I already knew the name, and it ended up in my dreams. Not a big deal.

'Be careful up there,' Nick says as I turn away from him to lock the door. 'Every year a bit more of it falls down. It's not really safe. You don't want to end up tripping over any skeletons, either.' He notices my expression as I turn back to him, and rushes to explain. 'The place was wrecked in a massive fire. Took days to put out. It all just collapsed in on itself. People went missing; they found some of their bodies after the rubble had cooled down, but not all. This was, I don't know, a hundred years ago? They didn't have search and rescue then.' He pauses, then shrugs, sheepish. 'If you go on local legends, one of my relatives is supposed to have started it.'

He ducks into the cab of the truck and I practically wrench the passenger's side door open and dive inside, my entire scalp tingling with curiosity.

The Moonlit Maze

We're in the truck, rocketing down the road into town, but instead of watching and taking note of the route so that I don't get lost when I have to walk back, as I was planning to do, my gaze is glued to Nick's face. 'This ancestor of yours—'

'We don't like to talk about it much, honestly. Tom Marten was the gardener's son, right? But he had some sort of obsession with a girl who lived up there, one of the toffs. She got engaged to another toff. Tom went batty. Set fire to the place. It was never proved or anything – and we're not directly descended from him. But when the castle folks left, a lot of the town's income went too, and people blamed my family – I suppose they didn't have anyone else they could blame.' He drums his fingers on the steering wheel, then shrugs again. 'I don't know why I brought it up. Just be careful up there.'

There's an awkward silence. Nick's clearly regretting having said anything, and I'm wondering how I can find out more about what happened to the castle and whatever family really did live there. Tom Marten, the gardener's son. It's a common enough name – a common enough character, the handsome working-class boy, like *Lady Chatterley's Lover* – but it's still a heck of a coincidence. Only it's hard to believe that the laughing, well-meaning Tom in my dreams would hurt anyone . . .

In the distance, there's the unpleasant mosquito drone of a motorbike – getting closer and louder for a moment, then thankfully waning into the distance. I shudder, letting out an involuntary sound of disgust.

Nick gives me a sidelong look. 'What was that?'

'Just – that motorbike . . .'

He pulls a face. 'Probably Aidan what's-his-name. Something

Polish, I think. Zooming around the countryside like he thinks it's his private playground. Dickhead.'

'He is! He nearly ran me over outside the cottage, and didn't even ask me if I was OK. Just snarled at me and zipped off.'

'Dickhead!' Nick repeats, more emphatic. 'You didn't get hurt?'

'I just ended up in the hedge, that's all.'

'He's a bloody hazard. I wish he'd bugger off back where he came from.' He sees my look and clarifies. 'America. His family are rich, I think. They've got a holiday home up in the woods, but they hardly ever came here. Rumour is he got in trouble of some kind, so they stuck him on a flight, and he's been hanging around like a bad smell for the past six months.'

'What kind of trouble?'

'God knows. Drugs? Anyway, if he gives you any problems again, let us know. I'd be happy to have a word with him.' He does sound grimly satisfied at the prospect. His fingers have tightened round the wheel and his jaw's ticking with tension.

Trying to lighten the mood a little, I ask, 'What would your mum have to say about that?'

'Nothing, because I wouldn't tell her.' His serious look melts instantly into a grin. 'Sending Mum in is like pressing the nuclear button. No survivors.'

We fall into a more comfortable silence until Nick parks the truck in a space between a big redbrick building with sash windows – a sign proclaims it the Coach House Hotel – and a pretty little church. I climb out into the narrow, cobbled street and sniff for the sea. Instead, I'm hit with a waft of melting chocolate, baking bread and some kind of smoky meat. My stomach rumbles.

The market square is behind the church, encircled with trees – beeches, I think – that have made the pavements buckle up around their roots. Lining the square are historical buildings with banks, shops and cafes shoehorned into the bottom floors; I spot the logo of a familiar supermarket express branch, and even a chain coffee place on the corner. So it's not really the land that time forgot, after all.

The market itself is absolutely heaving. Nick leads me past flowers and potted plants, pickles, preserves and jams to a double-width stall in the thick of things. One end is dedicated to bee products: a pyramid of different-coloured honeys, golden candles in wicker baskets, prettily wrapped soaps and lotions. A tall, curvy woman who looks a bit like Liz is waving goodbye to a customer as we approach. She's wearing a yellow T-shirt with a bee logo on the front. The other end of the stall is farm produce: eggs, bacon, ham and sausages, goat's cheese and butter. A shorter man with a shaved head and a hipster beard is there, currently weighing sausages. They're both in their mid-thirties, I'd say. Nick must be the baby of the Fairley family.

The woman's face lights up when she sees Nick. 'You're back! Come and take over the till for a minute, will you, love? We're nearly out of change and I need to fetch some more wax cloths from the van – they're really flying today.'

'In a minute, Meg. Jude, this is my big sister and her husband, Ben. They own the farm where I'm doing my work placement.'

'Hi, nice to meet you.' I lean carefully across the honey pyramid to shake the hand Meg holds out. 'Work placement?'

'He's doing a degree in agriculture and sustainability, didn't he tell you? Clever boy is our Nick. Lovely to meet you too, Jude – Mum's been telling us all about you. Ben! Say hello to Jude, up from Anne's old place!'

Ben gives me a friendly wink, his hands deftly wrapping cheese in greaseproof paper for the next person in the queue by the stall. Meg's already hustled Nick behind the counter. She disappears into the crowd and Nick gives me a helpless look as a trio of women immediately approach to ask if the soap is gluten free. I bite my lip, trying to hide my smile. It seems bossiness runs in the family. No wonder Ben's a man of few words.

'Come back once you've got your shopping sorted,' Nick calls as I wave goodbye. 'I can drive you home!'

I wave again to acknowledge I've heard, but without committing myself to return with him. People are kind here, but I know from experience that it's better in the long run not to rely on kindness. It's liable to run out exactly when you most need it.

After the last few days of quiet at Anne's house, the market really is an experience. I feel like I want to look at everything at once. Knowing that – for maybe the first time in my life – I have the money to get what I need without sums ticking away anxiously in the back of my mind makes it really hard not to get carried away. I keep reminding myself that I'll most probably have to drag everything back on foot, but I still end up buying focaccia bread with sea salt and olives baked into it, a chicken-and-leek pie, a rainbow of vegetables – some of which I'm not one hundred per cent sure how to cook – two different kinds of cheese, and a box of fancy cookies. Then I make myself stop, and go and visit the burger truck that's doing a roaring trade in one corner of the market. This is what they mean when they say that you shouldn't shop hungry.

I eat my burger sitting in the sunshine, on the steps of a bandstand at the top of the square, with my bags tucked under my legs. It might be my imagination – again – but it's probably the best burger I've ever eaten, especially with the added bacon. The truck lists the local suppliers on a board to one side. The bacon comes from Kurtzman farm, which I realise was the sign on Meg and Ben's stall.

I nip into the supermarket to get milk, tea and a few other staples. My bags are now definitely as heavy as I can carry. A bus would be handy, but since I don't think that's an option I'm trying to decide if I should head back to Nick's stall after all – buy some bacon, see if he's still there, and maybe offer to pay for his petrol to make up for having to be my taxi service. Then my attention's caught by a cluster of craft stalls.

The little flame that's been growing inside me flickers.

Hesitantly, I approach the cabin filled with art supplies. My bags are weighing my arms down, so I can't even fold them across my chest. I have to stand there looking, with my torso open and unprotected. My heart exposed.

They have all the basics. Little starter kits of pencils, pastels, watercolours. Brushes, plastic palates, portable easels. At the back, there are larger, more expensive boxes of oils and acrylics. A display of those little wooden anatomical figurines reminds me of being in college; we used to dare each other to sneak in and put them in obscene positions to see if our lecturers would notice.

There are gorgeous, expensive sketchbooks with soft leather covers, like the one that Ma gave me right before she died.

I've never used it. I've been carrying it around, pristine and untouched, in the bottom of one of my suitcases, ever since.

'Heya, duck, do you want any help?'

The stallholder has finished with another customer and turns eagerly to me. I stare at her, wordless. Her bright expression slowly transforms into uneasiness as she waits. She tilts her head. I keep staring. Finally, she clears her throat. 'Are you—'

She's going to ask if I'm OK.

I am OK.

I quickly put my bags down, and point into the stall. 'I'd like the basic A5 hardback sketchpad and the A4 spiralbound watercolour board pad, the Derwent graphite pencil tin, the Faber Castell watercolour pencil set, that six-piece nylon starter brush kit and a pencil sharpener, please. And a rubber eraser.'

The woman is already snatching products from the display, relieved and delighted. 'We like a customer who knows what they want! Are you an artist?'

I don't know the answer to that. I don't want to ask myself those kinds of questions yet. I shake my head. 'Not really. But my – my aunt was.'

Fifteen

Xanthe, spring 1924

Xanthe stormed away from the lie of her 'birthday party' with every intention of going straight to her room to begin packing. If she had her way, she would be gone from England again by the end of the week – and, more importantly, out of this house before another day had passed.

She didn't make it as far as the stairs. Her father caught up with her as she passed his study and wordlessly opened the door, his face creased by a look of grave concern and strained patience, which made it very clear that they would have this discussion, whether she liked it or not.

'Now. What's all this about?' he asked as he closed the study door behind her and walked, stately and unhurried, to sit behind his desk. 'Your mother is quite upset. And Jonathan too. I can hardly blame them.'

The thought of sitting down before him, as if she were some petitioner come to beg his pardon – a footman who had failed to polish the silver appropriately or a ... a maid who had dropped the lemonade jug – made her angrier still. She paced the room, once, twice, trying desperately to calm her ragged breaths. His eyes followed her.

The words emerged through gritted teeth. 'You ambushed me.'

Her father sighed. 'I don't think we need to be quite so dramatic, my dear. Come along. Sit down. There's no need to wander to and fro like a caged tiger.'

'If one of your friends told you that they had announced their daughter's engagement like this, without even telling her beforehand—'

He cut her off. 'Perhaps we were a little high-handed, but you've been engaged to Jonathan since you were sixteen. This was only an announcement! We thought you would like it. You did like it, didn't you? You said—'

'When I thought it was a birthday party!' she snapped. 'Anyway, that's not the point!'

'Well, I'm glad there is a point to this, at least, as I'm sure I can't see one. Please sit down.'

'I will not! I have made it perfectly clear that the engagement is over. It was never real to begin with. He didn't even— You know this. You know why I went to France after finishing school!'

'I confess that I don't. I've never understood it. We made excuses for you, that you were young, it was nerves. Perhaps you were distracted by the glamour of travelling. You never took the time to explain yourself.'

This was so breathtakingly unfair, the words tripped over each other as she responded. 'That isn't true! You – everyone saw what Jonathan did – my God, I've never been so humiliated! He didn't only hurt me, he could have killed that poor boy!'

'Overwrought nonsense. It was an accident.' The first signs

of impatience. 'And Jonathan was not to blame, as your mother told me you admitted at the time.'

Xanthe flinched as if from a slap. 'I didn't—'

'Your cousin proposed to you and you accepted him. You were happy to agree, and why wouldn't you be? Jonathan is a fine, fine young man, a man of honour – a war hero – a man whom any young woman would be lucky to call her husband!' His voice had grown louder and louder until his final words emerged as a near bellow. He paused, cleared his throat. 'Come now, my dear. This is hardly some medieval arrangement that has been forced on you.'

Aching – aching in just the way she had when she was little, when she had cried alone in her room, knowing no one would ever look for her when her cousins were here – she whispered, 'I didn't want to marry anyone. I – I just wanted to please you.'

'You gave your word, Xanthe. Do you realise how much hurt and worry your behaviour caused us? We've tried to understand, we've tried to welcome you back, and instead of gratitude we've had tantrums and hysterics.'

Desperately, she cried, 'Papa, I only want to be free!'

He swept the words aside with a sharp flick of his hand. 'None of us is free. We are a family. We have obligations of honour and duty to each other, and to the world. Do you think Jonathan wanted to fight in that awful war?'

'He volunteered! I didn't.'

Immediately, she wanted to call the words back. It was too late. His expression changed, and he turned his head sharply, staring at the wall behind her as if he couldn't bear to look at her any more. 'Do you truly intend to break your word? Break your mother's heart, and mine?'

'Am I not supposed to have a heart, then?' she asked bitterly. She felt as if she were curling up, crumpling away at the edges like the papery, dying leaves of her mother's oak trees. She didn't want to worry or hurt them. She just wanted to be allowed to *exist*. 'Or does mine not matter?'

It was as if she hadn't spoken. 'You should know, Xanthe, that if you drag this family's name through the mud by running away again, I shall refuse to support you any longer. Not a single penny, do you hear? You'll have nothing from us.'

She flexed her shaking hands, each finger separating in the air as she stared down at them. It was the only way she could keep them from curling into claws. Her voice came out high-pitched and cold. 'Have you ever bothered to make that threat to Jonathan, Papa? Even once? When he got into fights, ran up all those debts, crashed his car? Or are you content to keep stuffing his pockets with our family's money until he finally manages to drink himself to death?'

There was a long silence.

'That's quite enough. I should like to be alone now.'

She battled with herself for a moment, hands still spread. Shakily, she forced herself to walk to the door, open it and then close it softly behind her.

The energising heat of her fury was gone. In its place, the same old miserable ache, the same old wound inside that could never heal. Her eyes burned, hot and dry.

Her mother was hovering near the foot of the grand staircase, expression anxious, face pale in the low light. All Xanthe wanted was to go to her, to be enfolded in her arms. She couldn't. Her mother wasn't on her side in this. Her mother was never on her side.

The Moonlit Maze

'What did you say? You haven't upset him, have you?'

'He said he wanted to be alone.'

The tightening lips, the shake of the head. 'Oh, Xanthe . . .'

For the second time that night, Xanthe turned on her heel and walked away from both her parents.

☽○☾

Fair-weather clouds trailed inky fingers over the face of the moon. The ocean flashed silver-bright, sank back into languid darkness, then surged with light again. It was too cold for Xanthe to linger here, especially in her evening dress. Her hair was pulling free, strand by strand, from Pinchbeck's careful styling, curls tangling behind her ears in the sea wind. She shivered. But stayed.

Behind her, the familiar bulk of the hedge maze – its smooth green walls home to the topiary birds that Mr Marten had spent thirty years painstakingly bringing to life – protected her from being discovered. She had followed its twisting, shadowed turns almost blindly, until she found herself here at the secret exit. It was a slim gap in the hedge, hidden behind a topiary albatross, and only a handful of people knew about it. Below, the crumbling, twisting, nettle-and-thorn guarded path led down the cliff to the castle's private cove, where Xanthe had swum and built sandcastles and chased and played during those golden times with Sally and Tom Marten, out of sight of her parents' disapproval.

Mr Marten once told her that there had always been a maze here. The site was ancient. When the monks had lived on this clifftop in their monastery, long before the castle was built, this place had been a miz-maze, its traditional pattern perhaps thousands of years old, cut into the turf and chalk of the cliff. A place for prayer. The monks would walk it for hours at a time, turning, turning, round and round, following the stylised curves that symbolised life, death and rebirth in heaven, reaching in their ceaseless movement for God's love.

That ancient maze had been destroyed long ago, and Xanthe found no peace crunching along the gravel paths tonight. She didn't know what she would do for money, or where she could go – not back to Paris, not without her allowance. But she knew they would never let her rest while she was here. Not even for a single day. They would keep backing her into corners, pushing the bridle over her head. And all the time they would be telling her that it was for her own good, whipping her with their hurt and distress at her failure to cooperate, until eventually she would move obediently in the direction they wanted.

She let out a choked growl of anger, then a louder one. Finally, she screamed. Her throat burned. Her hands made wild tearing motions at the air. She ran out of breath and panted, staggering in place.

No one heard, no one cared, not even the birds. No one ever had. She felt sometimes as if she had been screaming her entire life.

When Jonathan erred, when he broke his promises over and over again, her parents rushed to excuse, explain, forgive. He didn't mean to. It didn't matter. No harm was done. It wasn't as bad as all that. He failed messily and publicly, and in return he was loved. He never even had to try.

Xanthe tried so hard, but she was always wrong somehow, always that strange blinking, babbling little thing, away with the fairies. As far back as she could remember, she had sensed her family's struggle, their desire to push her into some different form, a better form, one that wouldn't make them recoil. Someone they could love.

There was a tiny part of her that had believed if she just went away for long enough to grow up fully – long enough, perhaps, that Jonathan lost interest in her, and decided to marry someone else – she would be able to return one day and just be herself.

Xanthe was shivering in earnest now. She had to go back – there was no getting around it.

The moon broke through the clouds as she turned. The dark maze was lit up suddenly, nearly as bright as daylight. Xanthe gasped, startled. Someone was there.

It was a woman, she thought. Knew instinctively. The face was in shadow, but she was the wrong shape to be portly Finch, or skinny Pinchbeck, or that little maid – none of whom, in any case, would have been lurking out here. For a moment, Xanthe and the intruder stared at each other, motionless. Xanthe saw a cloud of hair, soft and waving, dark but silvered by the moonlight. The smell of petrichor reached Xanthe's nose – rain falling upon dry earth.

A thrill prickled down her spine. Something like fear. Something like excitement.

She said: 'Who are you?'

The wind rushed up. The moonlight dimmed. By the time she reached the albatross, the gap in the hedge was empty, and there was no trace that anyone had been there at all.

Chilled and heartsore and more than a little unnerved, Xanthe fled along the narrow gravel path towards the maze's exit, occasionally blundering into and bouncing from the spiky hedges. The process wasn't doing her dress or hair any good. With a trace of tired humour, she registered a prayer that all the guests had gone home. If not, they would get a first-hand demonstration of what was meant by the phrase 'dragged through a hedge backwards'.

When she stepped through the moon gate, brushing aside the trailing creepers that caught at her face, she was surprised to see light still streaming from most of the windows onto the lawn, and two cars still parked on the drive. Stragglers who'd had too much to drink?

She'd hoped to creep upstairs unnoticed. But Jonathan was there, pacing up and down the first flight of the grand staircase, muttering to himself. With a sigh, she backed away and made for the library. That was where the servants' staircase let out.

'Xanthe.'

She paused mid-step, halfway across the grand hall. She hated, *hated* being around him when he was drunk. But if she ignored him he might start shouting the house down, and she would get the blame.

'*Xanthe.*'

His voice cracked.

Damning herself for a fool, she came to the foot of the stairs and looked up at him. She saw at once that he wasn't drunk, or not much. He was too still for that, too serious, one hand clenched over the balustrade, the other not tucked into his pocket but hanging loose, fisted at his side. His gaze was unnerving, wide and blank.

'My God – what's the matter?'

Jonathan swallowed. 'It's Uncle Alfred.'

He didn't have to say anything else. Her hand met the newel post with a resounding slap – *that will probably bruise later*, a distant part of her noted – as she propelled herself up the steps at a run. Her shoulder brushed Jonathan's, hard enough to rock him, but he didn't say a word. She reached the top of the stairs, darted along the galleried landing and came to a halt at the open door of her father's dressing room.

Her mother sat there like a grey silk flower, wilting. Her head lifted, and Xanthe saw that her eyes were wet. She crumpled to her knees at her mother's feet, reaching out to grasp her gloved hands. 'Where is he? Is he all right?'

'Dr Miller is with him. He had – an attack. His heart. He hasn't been himself. Not for weeks. Longer. I knew it, I could see it, but he blamed it on his leg. He even got out that awful old stick!' She let out a watery laugh. 'I should have known it was more than that. I should have *made* him see the doctor, but he . . . he seemed so . . . *tired*. I didn't want to upset him.'

'I upset him,' Xanthe said bleakly. 'It's my fault, Mother, not yours. I quarrelled with him—'

'Bad things happen.'

The gravelly pronouncement made both of them start. Jonathan had followed Xanthe upstairs. He loomed in the doorway, his back as straight as a ramrod in defiance of his usual indolent slouch. 'Bad things happen. That's what he always says. You can't blame anyone.'

It had the sound of a phrase often repeated, yet there was no effect of comfort; his voice was toneless, and his face was still blank. Xanthe met her mother's gaze, and saw her own discomfort echoed there for a brief instant before it was hidden.

'Thank you, dear,' Caroline said, just as warmly as if he had wrapped her in his arms and assured her that everything would be all right.

The adjoining bedroom door clicked. Xanthe and her mother stood quickly as Dr Miller came in, greyer and more wrinkled than she remembered him. He'd always seemed effortlessly calm to her, when she was a child; now his eyes glanced over each of them restlessly.

'His Lordship is resting comfortably for the moment.'

Xanthe felt more than heard the exhalation of relief that had her mother sagging a little, leaning into Xanthe's side. She took Lady Kearsley's arm, clasped her hand in hers again. The doctor's attitude warned her that there was more, and worse, to come.

'Then he's all right? He'll be all right,' Caroline said, tremulous.

'For now,' the doctor repeated. 'The attack has passed. I've administered some medication – here is the prescription – and I would recommend that he have his valet sleeping in here at night from now on, in case he should need help. It's vital that he be kept quiet. No activity, no excitement, no stress. He should stay in bed if he can be made to. He will need tests, but they're beyond the scope of the cottage hospital. I'll refer him to a good man in Harley Street, a specialist.'

'A specialist? In heart conditions?' Xanthe asked. 'Is he likely to have more attacks like this?'

His gaze skittered away from hers. 'It's possible. I don't

want to alarm you. He must have the tests and receive further treatment as soon as he's well enough to travel.'

He took his leave with the usual blather of pleasantries. Xanthe was the one who remembered to thank him, who walked him down and handed him over to Bowdler. When she returned, her mother was crying in earnest. Xanthe couldn't even muster any shock over the inelegant sniffing and the way that Caroline's nose had reddened. She had no shock left. She made meaningless soothing noises and rubbed at her mother's arm, because that was what you were supposed to do. Jonathan was muttering again.

'Bad things happen. Bad things happen.'

In the back of Xanthe's mind, like a trail of ragged smoke, the dying vapour of something already burnt and lost: *I can't. I can't go. I can't leave now* ...

Sixteen

Jude, present day

I walk away from the art stall a little dazed. I don't realise I've taken a wrong turn somewhere until I reach the edge of the square and find myself in front of a sort of miniature stately home. It's not much bigger than a pair of semi-detached houses, but it has ornate white pillars and triangular arches and a golden clock above the front door. I'm definitely in the wrong place.

I sigh, put my bags down and rub my aching arms, bracing myself for going all the way back round to try to find Ben and Meg's stall. But, before I can pick my stuff up, there's a familiar voice calling my name.

'Jude! I thought that was you! Have you come to get a library card?'

It's Belle, from the bakery. She's leaning out of the bottom half of one of the mini stately home's windows.

Wrongfooted, I blink at her for a minute. 'Ah. No? I got a bit lost heading to – is this a library?'

'The central library. I volunteer here a couple of days a week.

Do you want to pop in and look around? You can leave your bags at the desk with me. Give your arms a rest.'

On the one hand, I would like to give my arms a rest. And I love libraries. On the other . . .

'Do you promise not to try to tell my fortune again?' If she's going to be offended by that, I'll be better off not trapping myself in there with her anyway.

She considers for a moment, then nods, unfazed. 'Deal.'

Inside, the place is just like any other public library, filled with ranks of utilitarian metal shelves and plastic-coated books. But the ceiling soars away into a white vaulted arch with elaborate plaster coving and gold leaf, and the walls are covered in gleaming dark wood panels. Tall windows flood the whole space with light.

'Wow.'

'I know, we were so fortunate to be able to save this place,' Belle says. She's perched on the edge of the reception desk, swinging her legs like a little girl. 'The council tried to sell it off. I think someone wanted to make it into a pub. Who needs more pubs?'

I put my bags down, and then she shoos me away. 'Go on and explore. I'll get your registration forms ready and fire up the card printing machine.'

It is always handy to have a library card.

At the last second, I snatch the A5 sketchpad and graphite pencil tin I've just bought and tuck them under my arm.

The place has a good few browsers for the middle of a weekday, but there's so much space and it's all so open that we just give each other friendly nods and mostly move easily around each other. There is one young man sitting on the floor against one of the Art History shelves, where I'm foraging for Rossetti. He doesn't move when I approach, face buried in a massive volume of, I see over his shoulder, glorious golden reproductions of Klimt. His legs are sprawled across the aisle and I can't get past. I wait for a moment for him to notice me, then clear my throat.

His head shoots up. I'm taken aback by how good-looking he is. Stupidly handsome, really. Like an actor. Dark hair and brows, full lips, all the cheekbones, a square, slightly stubbled jawline. He's even got a cleft chin. I feel a little twist of interest – but it turns to a chill of alarm almost instantly; he looks angry at being disturbed. Really angry.

He's wearing a cream cable-knit jumper, and he's on the floor with his head at the height of my waist, looking at art. He shouldn't be all that threatening. But the intensity in his dark, dark gaze nearly makes me back up a step. In fact, I'm about to turn round and leave when, without saying anything, he folds his legs out of my way and goes back to his Klimt. I skitter past, exiting the aisle without looking at the books. I have no idea what this guy's problem is, but I can search for pre-Raphaelite stuff another time.

I decide to avoid any further trouble and set myself up at one of the free desks, propping my phone on some books. I bring up a photo of the ruins of Kearsley Castle. It was taken in the room that I decided to call the orangery, looking straight out past the tumbled walls, through the drooping boughs of the beautiful, twisted old oak. The sea is a thin line in the distance, and there are fronds of wild grass spotted with flowers in the foreground.

Trying not to think too much – trying not to let it mean too much – I crack open the pencil tin and the sketchpad.

The first page is a wash-out. My fingers almost seem to have forgotten how to hold a pencil. My mark-making is too tight and everything looks cramped on the page, perspective subtly off. With a huff of frustration, I flick the page over.

I look at the image on the screen again, more deeply this time. I zoom in and out, squint a little. How did it feel to be there? What does it make me feel to look at it now? What do I want to make other people feel, looking at my impression of it?

It's been so long since I did this. Find a way in, Jude. Let your eye lead you.

The tree. The beautiful, weird shape of it, sweeping down, leaves dark against the sky, intersecting with the horizon line. The curved shadows falling over the trunk, and the texture of the trunk.

It's right this time; I can feel it sing. I quickly start to fall into that deep focus state, quietly humming the strange little tune that's been stuck in my head for days, turning the page this way and that to get at different angles, switching between pencils without overthinking it. I'm hardly even checking the reference picture any more, working from memory, from instinct. The sunlight from the tall windows is baking my back and hair, and I think one of them must be open – a soft breeze keeps bringing me the scent of the sea, and of roses.

I've completely lost track of time, fooling with the detail of one of the flowers – the way you do when you know that you're finished, really, but you're having fun and you don't want to let go yet – when Belle appears at my elbow. I smile up at her in greeting.

She's not looking at me. She's looking at the drawing, arrested. Pleased but self-conscious, I start to close the sketchbook.

'You've really captured her beautifully,' Belle says.

Does she mean the ruins? I turn the notebook straight again, and look at the sketch as a whole, trying to see what Belle's seeing.

I suck in my breath. Then hold it, staring in disbelief.

There's someone in my drawing.

She's standing in the dappled shadows of the twisted oak, one hand resting on the trunk as if she'd been looking out at the sea – but her head is turned, staring back over her shoulder at the viewer. The way I've shaded her hair and her body, and caught her pale, heart-shaped face, glowing in a splatter of light while the rest of her blends into the dramatic area of darkness beneath the leaves, makes her look otherworldly. Like a spirit emerging from the shadows of the ruin. Or disappearing into them.

It's Xanthe. The girl from my dreams.

Sometimes you draw things you didn't originally mean to. Sometimes art shows you things about yourself, or the world, that you didn't expect to see.

But this. It's as if my dream summoned herself into being on the paper.

Belle reclaims my attention by putting her warm hand briefly on my chilled one. 'Come with me.'

At the back of the library there are glass-fronted cabinets, filled with various bits and pieces. Local sporting trophies and pictures of a succession of mayors shaking hands with different people. A few pamphlets on local history. I don't spare any of it more than a glance; my attention is on the large, gilt-framed painting hanging in an alcove in the panelling.

It's an oil, in the style of a later Singer Sargent piece, although I doubt it can be. It's a little too soft-focus, a little too flattering. A real Singer Sargent wouldn't be hanging here in a small-town library, either. It's good work, though. Expressive.

A family portrait. The light falls starkly on the family, originating on the left, so that the right side is slightly deeper and darker in tone. There's an attempt at informality, naturalistic positioning. A thin, greying man sits on the curving wooden arm of a chaise longue, the tip of his polished shoe keeping him balanced. One hand rests proprietorially on the shoulder of a younger, pretty woman with dark hair, wearing a lacy dress. Both of them are smiling, and something about the angle of their heads, the pose, suggests that smile is aimed at the young man standing behind the sofa, close enough to the older man that their shoulders almost press together. The young man is slender, with an aquiline face and golden hair carefully smoothed back. His expression is enigmatic. You might even call it a smirk.

Perched on the other end of the chaise longue, on the right, like small pale bird about to flit away, is a girl. Younger than the one in my drawing. Her heart-shaped face is still a little rounded and her pose and the length of her limbs give her a gawky look. Her mouth looks pursed, as if she's about to speak. The artist has captured a brilliance in the large, lidded eyes, although I can't tell their shade. They're light – blue or green, maybe. She's the only one looking directly out of the painting at the viewer.

She seems out of place. Separated from the main family

group by more than the few inches between her knee and the other woman's skirts.

The plaque beneath the painting says: *The seventh Earl of Kearsley and family. Donated to the library in 1919.*

There are no names listed, but that doesn't matter. I already know who they are.

Seventeen

So – what? I'm being haunted?

I don't buy that.

If there was such a thing as a ghost, if there was any way for someone to come back – Ma would be here with me. I know that. If she could have offered me comfort when I was so afraid, when I needed her so much, she would never have left me alone.

No. I don't believe in ghosts. If she can't haunt me, then I don't believe that these people, these strangers, in this place that I barely even know, would be able to.

And maybe part of that certainty is that Xanthe, in my dreams, doesn't feel . . . ghostly. She doesn't feel dead. It's not like watching some sad spirit's faded old home movies play out in my head. It feels like something happening right now, vibrant and changing and unpredictable. Not set in stone. Not *finished*. It's not over for her. It's not her past. For Xanthe, it's the present, just as much as this moment is for me, right now.

My head is spinning as Belle – who hasn't said another word about my drawing, or the painting itself, or any of it – quickly guides me through my application form for a library membership, then hands over my brand-spanking-new card. But, just as I'm about to head out of the door, she passes me one of those local history pamphlets from the cabinet.

'Might be useful.' She hesitates, then adds, 'She looks so alone in the portrait, doesn't she? That girl. Like she needed a friend.'

I was in the library longer than I realised. Outside, the market day crowds have nearly disappeared, making the square seem suddenly bigger. Most of the stallholders are packing up.

Before I can wade into the maze of vendors, I see a movement in my peripheral vision; I startle. Someone has walked up behind me. It's that same man, the angry man, from the library. He's standing way too close for comfort. This time I give in to the urge to back away, putting space between us. My gaze darts towards the nearest stall, to the library entrance, uneasily wondering if I could catch someone's attention if I needed to.

But he's holding out . . . a sketchbook? It's my sketchbook, the one I was just using in the library. It must have fallen out of the top of my jute bag – there's a scuff on the leather.

'Oh! Thank you, I can't believe I didn't realise . . .' Flustered, I put down the shopping and try to take the book from him. Only he doesn't release it. My gaze flies up to his face, questioning. 'Er. Thanks?'

The dark stare gets more intense. Goosepimples tingle on my skin; why is he *looking* at me like that? Like he knows me? I want to let go of the sketchbook, walk away, but I can't – it's got the picture of Xanthe in it. My brows come together, and finally I say loudly: 'Will you give me my sketchbook, please?'

He opens his mouth. Shakes his head. Then he does let

go – jerks his hand away so suddenly that I almost drop the book – and stalks off.

What on earth?

I stare after him for a long moment, unnerved, before blowing out a breath and shrugging the strange encounter off. I tuck the sketchbook carefully back into my bag, determined not to lose it again.

By the time I've lugged my stuff all the way to the other end of the square, I'm not feeling too hopeful that Nick will still be around. I'd actually be grateful to have some time alone to try to work out if I'm finally losing my tenuous grip on sanity, but my arms aren't going to stand up to trudging several miles back to the cottage with these bags. I've just about decided that I'll try to grab a local to ask about taxis (and I will not feel guilty – it's not a waste of money) when I arrive back at the Kurtzman stall and find that they're all there, Meg and Ben and Nick, although they're in the middle of packing their stock away.

'Hi, Jude!' Meg says cheerfully, and Nick – who has his back to me – drops a box on his foot. While he's quietly swearing, Meg goes on:

'We thought you must have gone home when we didn't see you again. I don't suppose you'd like to buy any of this? Half off, since we didn't manage to shift it during the day.'

'Really? Yes, please!' I say, whipping out my purse. Nick still seems to be . . . sort of intentionally busy, maybe avoiding my eyes a bit. I remind myself that I don't have any right to be disappointed, and quietly ask if Meg has the number for a local taxi service.

'Taxis?' she says doubtfully, handing me back my debit card. 'I think I might have a flyer for one somewhere.'

'You don't need a taxi, love.' Now it's my turn to jump. Liz Fairley has crept up behind me. She pats my arm. 'Didn't Nick offer to drive you back? He was a bit worried about you earlier, in fact – went looking for you, just in case you'd got lost. Didn't you, Nick?'

Nick's shoulders, which have been creeping up around his ears, sag. He's a bit flushed in the face as he turns to look at us, but obviously determined to style it out. 'I did, yes. I thought you must have gone home.'

'I went to the library. Belle was there; we got chatting.' Somehow seeing his embarrassment over this gentle, motherly teasing is making me much more at ease. 'You do realise I come from London? I mean, it's a *little bit* bigger than Winterthorne, so if I didn't get lost there—'

'All right,' he says, suddenly grinning. 'All right, I get it. I'm glad you made it back in the end.'

A man appears from inside the stall and puts his arm round Liz's shoulder, giving her a squeeze. 'That's all the honey packed up, with room to spare. Hello! Is this Anne's little niece, then?'

He's tall, even for this family, with an unruly head of salt-and-pepper hair and an iron-grey beard.

'That's me,' I say, unable to resent being called 'little' by a man who must be six foot five. 'Are you Nick's . . .'

Liz flinches. At the same time, Meg flicks a look at Nick, her face suddenly anxious. My brain, working unusually fast, reminds me that I've never heard either Liz or Nick mention his father.

'I'm Nick's uncle, Alan,' he says quickly as I hesitate. 'How are you doing up at Anne's place? Not too lonely after London?'

Meg and Liz visibly relax. There's some sort of family hurt there. Something that won't stand prodding. I feel compelled to smooth over any awkwardness. 'I'm doing really well, thanks. I love the cottage. I like the quiet. And everyone's been . . . wonderful.'

'Oh, that reminds me,' Liz chimes in. 'You'll come to Sunday lunch this week, won't you? Welcome you to town properly, and you can meet my younger daughter. She's coming down with her family.'

'She does a cracking roast, does Mum,' Meg says with a decided nod. She goes back to stacking boxes. 'We can handle this, Nick. You get Jude on home. Her arms must be nearly falling out carrying all that around.'

☽◯☾

'Sorry for that weirdness, back there,' Nick says abruptly, as we bounce over a rut in the road. His eyes are fixed on the green corridor of the road ahead, shadowy in the dusk.

'Weirdness?' I say warily, looking down at the bag of art supplies in my lap.

'With my family. They thought you were going to assume Alan was my dad. People often – well – anyway – sorry. They were afraid I'd get upset, that's all.' His hands tighten round the wheel. 'My father died. When I was twelve.'

The starkness of it pulls at me. I know that ragged, patched-up feeling that makes his voice go rough. The struggle of trying to find words for a loss that can't be expressed in words, needing to tell people just enough to warn them off from the wound without exposing the raw, vulnerable edges of it.

There's nothing to say about a wound like that except: 'I'm really sorry that your dad died, Nick.'

He takes his eyes off the road long enough for a quick look. Surprise, then understanding. 'That's right. You lost your father, didn't you?'

'No,' I say wryly. 'I never had him. Never even met him. It's my mother I lost.' I snort out a little laugh through my nose. 'I don't really like calling it that, though. As if, you know, I just misplaced her somewhere. Forgot her on the train. I didn't lose her. She was taken from me.'

He nods slowly, as if I've said something profound. Maybe I have. 'Yeah. Yeah.' He clears his throat. 'I'm sorry too.'

Neither of us says anything else. It's enough.

There's a . . . moment, when the truck's parked on the verge and Nick's hopped out to help me with my bags. We're both still in the intimacy of the quiet in the truck, of that understanding. Our faces are close as I heft one lot of shopping up and he's leaning across to open the gate for me with his free hand and I can smell the clean smell of his skin – and when my eyes meet his, just for a breath, I think that he's thinking about kissing me. But he doesn't. We both sway back, then he steps away, tells me that he'll see me on Sunday. I go into the house as the engine starts up again, wondering: did I imagine it? Would I have kissed him back? I can't decide how I feel about it.

I like Nick a lot, already. I like his family. But I barely know them. I only just got here.

I'm unloading all my purchases onto the kitchen table when my phone wakes up. The capricious wifi has awarded me a signal, although I don't know how long it'll last. I have an email from Mr Swan telling me that he's sending some paperwork and I should call him if I have any questions. And another text from Penny, who has been in surprisingly regular contact since I left London.

She's sent me a picture, and it takes me a moment to work out that it's the second bedroom in the flat, the bedroom I was supposed to have. The piles of boxes and junk have gone, the walls have been stripped and painted and she's squeezed a little daybed into it.

> All done, at last! So if you ever need a place to crash when you're back in London or whatever, you know where we are ;p

I bet anything Duncan doesn't know about that offer. Surprised and touched, I text back quickly.

> Looks great! Congratulations on finishing. I might be staying here for a while, though. Maybe you'll have to come and visit me instead.

I didn't mean to say that. It's not like Penny'd take me up on it, though; Duncan would rather die than come here, and I'd kick him off the front doorstep if he did. This is my house, and I decide who gets to come in.

Exhaustion swamps me as I put the phone down. It's not even that late, but I feel like I've had the longest, strangest day. I can barely make sense of everything that's happened. I stuff the perishables in the fridge, and then give up on plans to cook, and eat focaccia with cheese, heritage tomatoes and ham. It is, once again, unbelievably good. Maybe there's something magic in the soil around here. Also: tea. Glorious, strong tea. I've never drunk so much tea in my life.

Sitting at the table with my second mug, I clear a space to open up my sketchpad again, and examine the drawing. It seems alien to me already. I can't make sense of the way I've constructed the figure, the way she swims up out of the dark. It couldn't have come from my fingers. But somehow it did. My fingers. My dreams.

She's looking right out at the viewer, just as she did in the portrait at the library. But unlike the lost, lonely look the painter gave her in his work, in my sketch her gaze is direct and meaningful. She's looking at *me*, the same way she did in that dream, on the top of the cliff, in the maze. In that... memory?

See, that doesn't make sense. If I'm reliving Xanthe's memories of the 1920s – setting aside the insanity of that, for the moment – then how could Xanthe have reacted to my presence? The past is done, and nothing I do, or dream, in the now should be able to affect it. But she saw me. I know she did. One minute I was just observing everything, invisible, and in the next she knew I was there. Like a light suddenly turning on. Like the poem Ma wrote down for my father all those years ago. *I have been here before, but when or how I cannot tell... But just when at that swallow's soar, your neck turn'd so, some veil did fall... I knew it all of yore.*

Sudden light. Shining through the past so that it casts shadows onto the present. Onto the surface of my mind. But the light is shining through me as well. I'm casting shadows onto her. Onto the past.

That's it. I feel it instinctively. I'm *not* being haunted. I'm being... connected.

'Why?' I whisper into my mug. 'Why me?'

The Moonlit Maze

As if in response, there's a rattle at the letterbox. I nearly send my tea flying. That's the problem with quiet, I admit to myself. In London, I wouldn't even have heard the sound, let alone had a heart attack over it. Leaning back, I squint down the straight corridor to see if a leaflet or something has been pushed into the brass mail cage. Can't see anything. I heave myself up, switch the light on and, no, nothing. I didn't hear an engine passing, either, although maybe I wouldn't have noticed. Frowning, I unlock the door and open it a sliver, peering out.

There's something on the doorstep.

After a cautious look around, I open the door properly and pick it up, bringing the mystery item into the light.

It's a jar of creamy, pale honey, exactly like the ones on the Kurtzman stall today. But if they'd wanted me to have some they could have handed it over before Nick and I left. And I doubt any of the family would have walked all this way to put honey on my doorstep without coming in for a cup of tea, at least. This jar doesn't have the cheerful bright red tin lid or the label with the stylised bee logo on it, either.

It could be from anyone.

I carry it into the kitchen and put it on the counter, then think again and hide it in a cupboard. Flowers are one thing. Anonymous edible stuff is another. It's not coming anywhere near my toast, or my stomach. You'd think whoever put it there would at least have left a note.

I pull out my phone and, since I still have reception, quickly google *language of flowers forget me nots*.

Oh, it's sweet. They're a symbol of love and respect, fidelity and devotion, just like their name suggests. I scroll down a bit, smiling – until I read the final paragraph.

Zoë Marriott

From the late Victorian period onwards these pretty blue flowers – also known as Scorpion Grass – often came to be laid as an offering on graves, representing a promise of remembrance to one who had passed on. As a result, they are now sometimes considered unlucky, having a double meaning: devotion and death.

Eighteen

Xanthe, spring 1924

The windows of the breakfast room were opaque, gold-tinged white. The hedges and rose gardens had been reduced to ghostly dark voids in the mist beneath an eye-smarting band of brightness where the sun steamed in the clouds. Xanthe and her mother sat silently on opposite sides of the table. Between them, another void: Lord Kearsley's empty seat at the head of the breakfast table.

Having at last been declared strong enough by Dr Miller to travel, he had been packed off the day before, with his valet, to London and the Harley Street specialist. Both Xanthe and her mother had begged to be allowed to accompany him. But in vain.

'I have no need for a nursemaid,' he had snapped with an irritability that bordered on viciousness. 'I am not an invalid, thank you!'

Xanthe turned over her scrambled eggs, wincing at the faint scrape of the tines on the plate. Her mother was shredding a piece of toast into successively tinier pieces. Xanthe almost wished for the distraction of Jonathan's taunting presence.

No, she took that back; actually, his absence was the only thing that made staying here bearable. Her 'fiancé' had disappeared from the castle the morning after Lord Kearsley's heart attack without, as far as Xanthe knew, even bothering to say goodbye. Damn him. If nothing else, her father would have been far more likely to agree to allow Jonathan to travel down to London with him.

She sipped at her tea. It was blessedly hot, and extra strong this morning. Cook must have taken pity and tipped in an extra spoonful of leaves.

Like the Sword of Damocles, Jonathan's name had hung above every interaction between Xanthe and her parents for the past week. Nothing had been resolved or even alluded to. She had wanted, so badly, to talk to Papa, to make peace. But common sense had sewn her lips shut. He was ill, and vulnerable, and therefore at his most pig-headed and infuriating. The angry, pig-headed part of her own personality was likely to make an appearance too, the moment that they disagreed. And how could they not, when what he wanted was impossible?

So she was trapped here in the place she loved best in the whole world, longing with every fibre of her body to go.

She took a mouthful of the scrambled eggs, grimaced and swirled them into a new circle with her fork. She couldn't back down. Not again. It was doing precisely that, and hoping they would relent, that had got her into this ridiculous mess in the first place. If she had only had the sense, the gumption to stand up for herself when she was sixteen.

But then what? No one in this house ever took 'no' for an answer, at least not from her, and she'd had even fewer resources to draw on five years ago than she did now.

Xanthe crossed one ankle over the other to stop her foot jigging. At the other side of the table, her mother had gone through most of the toast rack without eating more than two bites.

Outside, the mist was beginning to sizzle away under the sun's seething light. Local wisdom had it that an early sea fret on a sunny day meant a scorcher by lunchtime, and good fishing. They called it an echo tide, the fishermen. When Xanthe had asked about the name as a little girl, her governess had told her that men who went out on their boats before the mist had fully cleared would hear voices echoing in the tide, echoing everywhere the sea fret touched: those who had been lost at sea in centuries past crying out for their loved ones, for aid that any living person was years too late to offer . . .

Good grief, she was getting positively morbid, sitting here.

'I fancy a walk,' Xanthe announced. 'I think I'll go down to the town.'

Lady Kearsley reached for the bell. 'I'll have Higgins draw the car around.'

She sighed. 'No. Thank you. I'd rather go on foot.'

'Oh, darling, all that way, in the fog? Surely—'

'I know the way, Mother! Anyway, I'm used to long walks. I walk in Paris all day sometimes.'

Her mother's neck stiffened, like a doe scenting danger. 'Not by yourself, surely? Does Josephine enjoy long walks? What does her mother have to say about it?'

Xanthe hesitated minutely. She could have smiled and said something light, and Lady Kearsley might have cooperated and let it pass. But Caroline might just as easily decide to dig, and

Xanthe – always terrible at lying – would immediately appear childish for attempting to hide the truth.

Xanthe met her mother's gaze evenly. 'No, she doesn't. She doesn't usually come with me, and nor does anyone else. I walk alone, and have been perfectly safe doing so, because I am a grown woman, and able to look after myself.'

'Look after yourself? Wandering the streets of a foreign city at all hours!' She did seem genuinely shocked. Xanthe judged that was more about her admission of a breach in etiquette than by the actual substance of it.

'Young ladies spill out of nightclubs at all hours in London these days, you know. And, as far as I'm aware, no one was murdered in broad daylight at a cafe, boutique or gallery in Paris while I was there.'

Caroline opened her mouth and Xanthe felt a surge of such mixed irritation and weariness that without thinking she copied one of her father's gestures and lifted her hand, palm flat: *stop*. To her surprise, Caroline actually heeded it. Xanthe hastily put down her napkin and got to her feet.

'I am going for a walk. I doubt that I'll be mauled by lions on my way; if I am, you can comfort yourself by saying "I told you so". Have a good morning, Mother.' She paused. 'I'll make sure that I'm back before Papa rings this afternoon.'

The promise only deepened the worried crimp between her mother's eyebrows, as if she'd rather Xanthe didn't speak to her father at all. Xanthe felt her expression tightening in response, and quickly left the room.

She ran back up the stairs, feeling a ridiculous sense of relief at the prospect of even a small window of freedom. Her day dress wasn't suitable for tramping about the country, but she knew that her old clothes were still in the back of the closet, including her brogues, well-worn and soft as butter.

As she made to push open her door, it jerked away under her hand and one of the housemaids backed out, carrying a bundle of bedsheets. 'Oh! I'm sorry, miss – milady – I've just finished—'

Xanthe recognised the pretty face and wide eyes as belonging to the clumsy girl Ellen. 'Not at all, I know this is an awkward time of day for me to be getting changed.'

The bright, cheerful face peering above the heap of linens bore scant resemblance to the bruised and harrowed little creature that Xanthe recalled, even as the girl's smile slowly began to fade away under the continued scrutiny.

Ellen wasn't Suzette. Xanthe exhaled, letting go of the urge to intervene, to prod, to actually *do something* this time, and redeem herself in the process. It was too late for that and, anyway, this girl clearly didn't need her help.

Stooping, Xanthe retrieved a spilled pillowcase from the floor, and returned it to the pile in Ellen's arms. 'There you go. Run along now.'

The maid bobbed an unsteady curtsy and turned away too quickly to observe Xanthe's faint wince. 'Run along now,' she repeated to herself in disgust as she walked into her room. Good Lord, she must already have stayed here too long if Mama's voice was coming out of her mouth.

She changed into her walking clothes hastily, stuffing on the shabby felt hat that always made her mother scrunch up in disapproval, and the oldest, softest cardigan that still fitted. She pushed her arms into an ancient shooting jacket of her father's, rescued from the rag heap years ago because one of the inner pockets was large enough to hold a notebook, and after turning back the sleeves a few times, and tucking her journal and a pencil inside, felt fully comfortable for the first time since arriving home.

Xanthe exited the house via the French doors in the library, all the better to avoid her mother's censorious gaze. Just as she had expected, the fog was beginning to disperse already, but Xanthe knew the way so well that it hardly mattered; she could have reached Winterthorne safely even if someone blindfolded her. Slipping between the closely planted poplar trees, her feet found the well-worn path through the woods almost as if magnetised.

As a child, she had named the verdant tunnel of trees a fairy glade, imagining faces among the gnarled trunks and tumbled granite stones, friendly faces with lichen for eyebrows and moss for beards. The low, insistent coo of wood pigeons and the narrow bars of sunlight that pierced the thinning mists encouraged the stiffness of her shoulders and the tightness in her chest to melt away, leaving her suddenly aware of the strung-wire tension that had been vibrating through her body for days. In a week or so she might even see the bluebells come out, and wouldn't that be blissful?

She let out a long sigh.

There was someone ahead of her on the path. A young woman, rather shorter than herself, with curling, dark hair that drifted behind her in the same faint breeze that moved the mists. Answering a proprietary impulse – after all, ramblers and walkers were rare in these parts, and the woods were on Kearsley land – she called out: 'Hello!'

The woman didn't respond. She was moving swiftly,

soundlessly, flitting through the dappled sunlight and shadows like a wild creature. Xanthe kept losing sight of her, and realised with some surprise that despite her fast walk on the familiar path she was falling behind.

Perhaps the girl knew she was trespassing and was afraid of getting in trouble. Xanthe called out again. 'Hello! Are you lost? It's all right!'

Now a fair way ahead and downhill, the girl paused. She wasn't on the track any more, but under the trees, standing amongst the mossy grass and the forget-me-nots. A shaft of sunlight broke through the shifting mantle of an oak tree, and for the first time, just for an eyeblink, Xanthe could see her clearly.

She frowned at the queer clothes, the lack of both hat and rucksack. That hair, though ... surely ... a memory of the awful night of the 'engagement' party sprang to life, and she realised that this must be the same person who had been watching her from the maze. The woman who had run away in the moonlight. Who on earth was she?

Even as the question entered her mind, the girl turned. Xanthe glimpsed a pronounced widow's peak, heavy, dark brows, a retroussé nose and a pair of slanting, wide-set eyes. Just for a moment, as she looked, there was a noise like rain pattering on leaves, and she smelled the scent of petrichor. The girl lifted her hand, opened her mouth as if to call back—

Then the light shifted. The girl faded into the shadows again.

'Wait!'

It was no good. In the few seconds it took her to reach the oak tree, the girl had vanished so thoroughly that Xanthe couldn't even perceive a bobbing branch or snapping twig that would have given away the direction of her escape.

Nineteen

Xanthe stood beneath the oak, shielding her eyes from the light as she turned in a slow circle, wondering if the mysterious girl would come back, if she would catch sight of her somewhere among the trees. There was nothing, nothing but the dry whispering of leaves meeting and parting in the wind. Even the birds were silent. She was alone. A shiver contracted her spine.

After a moment, she shook herself, pulled her hat down more firmly and went on. A magpie cackled overhead, and a moment later a blackbird answered, and Xanthe felt the strange rainy-day chill fade from her skin.

Following the path downhill, she passed the red door of Mr Marten's little cottage, tucked away behind the hedgerows. No one would be there at this time of day. Mr Marten rose and got to work before six most mornings, Sally would be at her solicitor's office by now, and Tom? Well, he was miles away. Xanthe had never been allowed inside anyway. Mr Marten hadn't thought it fitting. She had always imagined it looked a happy house, even after Tom and Sally's mother died. A safe place, a little sanctuary in the trees.

Twenty minutes of brisk downhill walking brought her out of the hedgerows and into the bright glare of sunshine reflecting from the sea and the windows of the houses below. The water was a deep, cold blue today, the waves sharp-edged, and, sure enough, now that the fret had lifted, the curve of the bay was nearly denuded of boats. The road swept away to the left here, but Xanthe carried on, choosing the narrow zigzagging set of steps that ran steeply through the centre of the town. It was said that no one could ever count the number of stairs, that trying would drive a man mad, because the monks who had been displaced from the monastery on the hill by Xanthe's ancestors had cursed the steps. If so, the curse had long run out, for Xanthe had counted them many times going both up and down. There were one hundred and twelve. This knowledge didn't make the descent any easier on the legs, though. Especially on the parts of the stair where all the steps suddenly became random heights, or were worn in peculiar patterns.

The townsfolk, most of whom Xanthe knew by sight if not by name, were long up and about by this hour. She passed women of all ages out with their shopping baskets, beating their carpets and scrubbing their doorsteps, older gentlemen in shirt-sleeves tending their gardens, and the occasional person enjoying a morning stroll, as she was. She caught a few sidelong glances and suppressed smiles directed at her, most likely because of her choice of attire, but other than a few polite calls of 'Morning' and tipped hats that required nothing more from her than a quick nod and smile in return, she was left in peace.

In the town square, Xanthe surveyed the local shops, none

of which had changed in living memory. As a child, she would have run straight into Thurlestone's Sweet Shop and blued her pocket money on all the boiled sweets she could carry. The idea still held some charm, but after ignoring most of her breakfast Xanthe's eyes alighted with favour on Smethett & Sons, the bakery, instead.

Moments later, she was in possession of a pork pie wrapped in greaseproof paper and a bag of gingerbread. Mrs Smethett had even sold her a bottle of her homemade lemonade straight from the pantry. With the tangy sea wind tugging at her coat and hat and the shrill, almost human-sounding conversations of the gulls ringing out above, she made her way down to the sea wall that stretched out on one side of the bay.

She reached up and cautiously placed her food and the glass bottle on the wall's capstone, which was level with her shoulders. Then she planted her toe in the deep crevice between two huge, rounded stones of the sea wall and, with a groan of effort, heaved herself up to sit on top.

'Victory is mine!' She waved a fist in triumph, then looked around quickly to make sure she was unobserved.

The granite top of the wall was broad enough that as a girl she had been able to lie down flat on her back without rolling off it, and despite the chill of the stone and the sea wind that was already chafing at her face, it remained one of her favourite places to sit and think. Pulling her skirt down firmly to preserve her modesty and protect her stockings from the rough stone, Xanthe leaned forward to check the level of the water lapping at the piled-up boulders below, then spread the baker's bags out on her lap and took a bite of the pie.

She had missed this so much. No matter where else she went – no matter how exciting or beautiful – it simply wasn't the same. Not without the sea, her sea.

Paris wasn't really the way she'd imagined before living there. For one thing, Josephine hadn't warned her of the stink that wafted from the sewers by the Seine in the summer. For another, despite her hopes that a European city so dedicated to art, beauty and pleasure must be fundamentally different from England, Xanthe had still ... struggled.

People everywhere wore masks. They wore them as naturally as their own skin, it seemed to Xanthe: masks woven of stories, and intentions, ideas they had of themselves, that they wanted the world to identify with them. Even when the stories were obvious lies and the masks were a thin and unconvincing tissue paper, everyone was expected to act as if they were real. As if they were all that was real. Xanthe had a miserable time at boarding school before she was finally able to make herself accept that no one else was longing to have their true self excavated and understood, that poking at or pointing out the gaps or inadequacies in other people's stories about themselves won you only enemies. She had begun to wonder if, for most people, there was no true self at all. No original, genuine self. Just different masks, one succeeding the other. Masks all the way down.

A gull swooped low over Xanthe. Where one came, soon there would be a flock, harrying her for crumbs. She let out a high-pitched shriek that she had perfected years before, and the bird swerved in mid-air to avoid her, swiftly winging back out to sea. Xanthe smiled, knowing that the wind would have swept the sound away with the bird. No one would stare, no one would ask themselves: *Did you hear that awful noise? What is the matter with that girl? It's not normal!*

That was the trick she had eventually learned. In order to survive, she had to stop trying to discover other people's true selves, and instead disguise her own. She observed the way others presented themselves, the tricks of speech and behaviour that were accepted as normal and natural. Then she would adopt them, put on her own mask – though for her perhaps it was more of a shield – and suddenly people ... liked her. They made space for her. Or, rather, for her disguise.

Xanthe chomped on a bit of gingerbread, letting the crumbs fall. After a week at the castle, being observed minutely at every meal by everyone from her mother to the footman, it was a luxury to be untidy, to chew with her mouth open. The sea didn't care. Thank heavens for the sea. She wasn't sure, really, if she could ever be happy anywhere without the sea.

But she had tried.

Xanthe had become adept, while in Paris, at maintaining a mask that had just enough of herself in it, of her own natural thoughts and reactions, for her to feel she was being truthful, yet not enough that she was reduced to that miserable ball of self-conscious self-loathing that had been her constant state as a child and young girl. She no longer had to be consciously monitoring every conversation for that disbelieving quirk of the eyebrow, the mocking laugh or look of annoyance that signalled she had made a mistake.

She met people's eyes for just long enough, and not too long. Instinctively, she monitored the ticking seconds whenever she talked about a topic for which she felt enthusiasm, and cut herself off before others would become uncomfortable. If a sensation – say, a wrinkle in her stocking, or a label in her dress, or one of her hair pins – was driving her mad, she ducked into the bathroom and fixed it quietly, and if she couldn't she didn't dissolve into tears like the 'watering pot' that she had been as a child.

She was, as she had told her mother, a grown-up woman who was able to take care of herself.

But it was tiring. So very tiring.

There were times, even when she was with people she liked, people she thought of as sympathetic and like-minded – other writers, or artists or musicians, the Bohemian crowd that gathered in Felicie's drawing room, and at Les Deux Magots, and around the bookshops and excitingly seedy art galleries and theatres of Montmartre – that she began to feel less like a person sheltering behind a mask and more like a prisoner. A tiny, soft, vulnerable little thing that had been driven down deep into the darkness, left trembling with exhaustion and fear, peering out at the world through two small eye slits. And all that was left on the outside, all that spoke and laughed and moved, was that hollow mask, the relentless projection of normality.

This was why it was so hard to win fights with her parents. Because she was all too aware of the underlying strangeness in herself, this difference, while her parents . . . well, their masks were so close to their true selves that they were entirely unaware of the gaps between projection and reality.

The Moonlit Maze

All her life, Xanthe's father had told her, whenever she was fearful or upset: 'You must simply get back on the horse, my dear. It's no good fussing about things. Back in the saddle. It's the only way to get on in life.'

It wasn't until after her mother had raked her over the coals for giving him the cane, acknowledging the faint infirmity of his limp which everyone could see, that Xanthe realised: her father didn't follow his own advice. They didn't have riding horses on the Kearsley estate. She'd only learned to be an – indifferent – horsewoman at boarding school.

He lied. He didn't think of it that way, of course, because he was lying to himself every bit as hard as he lied to Xanthe.

Xanthe didn't seem to have the ability to lie to herself like that. It was a fatal weakness. How could that vulnerable little core of her, the fragile part that hid itself away, know what was best in the face of her family's complete certainty that they were always right?

But if she didn't listen to her real self, if she ignored it, starved it, abandoned it alone in the dark ... she feared one day it would be gone. All that would be left was the hollow mask made up of traits that other people wanted to see, and nothing of the true Xanthe at all.

And that was why she could not, could never, marry Jonathan.

Absorbed in her own thoughts, Xanthe didn't notice the invasion until it was upon her. A sound like a thunderclap startled her so badly that she almost threw the remains of her pork pie into the sea. Then a large, pale muzzle appeared in her lap, the shiny black nose making enormous whiffling sounds. The creature's dense coat was white, brindled with blueish grey, and it looked like nothing so much as a medium-sized wolf. The politely pleading expression in the blue eyes and the offer of a huge, sandy paw was all dog, though.

Xanthe's parents didn't approve of animals in the house; her mother was positively nervous around large dogs. But there were always plenty of pets and working dogs at Winterthorne, and Xanthe was used to them. Mr Marten had had a gorgeous collie, when she was growing up, whom Xanthe had especially adored.

'Are you expecting to wheedle my pork pie out of me?' she asked the giant dog now, laughing. She accepted a touch from the paw politely, then wiped the sand off on her coat front. 'You horrible beast! Who do you belong to? What's your name? Fang? Bonecrusher?'

She offered her hand again, this time to sniff. The dog made an eager dart towards it, then cast her a look of intense misery when it realised she offered only friendship, not pie. She scratched cautiously behind one of the huge ears – the coat was both soft and stiff, like bear fur – and then a shout made Xanthe start again.

'Don't feed her! For God's sake, Rowan, you've no manners! Hey – hello! Don't feed her, I said!'

She knew that voice.

With a rising sense of inevitability, she swivelled – holding the dog off with one hand – and stared down at Tom Marten as he appeared on the walkway below.

Oh. He hasn't changed at all.

Ludicrous. Of course he had. He wasn't a lanky freckled boy any more, with unruly hair that always looked like it wanted cutting, even after his father had hacked it short with the kitchen shears. He'd lost all the last of his skinniness, and the roundness of his face. He was nearly as tall as his father, broad across the shoulders, neatly dressed in a grey suit, and his hair was almost – almost – completely tamed.

But she felt exactly the same about him. The swell of instinctive affection and liking, the urge to pull him up beside her and offer him the bag of gingerbread, babble out all her worries and woes and do her best to tease his out of him in return. And what was strange, but not strange at all, was that he was staring up at her, his eyes filled with surprise and happiness – and she knew that he felt it too. It was as if no time had passed at all.

'The sixth of May,' she said softly. Sally's birthday. She had even noted it when she'd got up that morning. 'Did you get in last night?'

'Just now,' he answered easily. 'I came by car. Brought her a cake down from Harlow's tearoom. The one with—'

'The pink icing. I remember.' It had always been his sister's favourite.

The dog, perhaps annoyed at being forgotten, let out a deafening bark. It pushed its nose down insistently at the remains of Xanthe's pork pie. Xanthe elbowed it away, but it was too late. The moment was broken. Tom's gaze flicked from her to the dog, and she saw him recollect how long it had been, and that they weren't children any more. Maybe even that last silly almost-quarrel when she had been home from school at sixteen. The fact that he'd just shouted at her in public, and his dog had assaulted her.

His cheeks went ruddy and his eyes seemed suddenly wiped

clean of expression, like the shutters snapping closed in a shop window.

Xanthe wished she knew the right words to open the way back into that enchanted moment of easy recognition. Instead, the awkwardness attacked her too. She felt herself shrinking away, curling her legs up more tightly, pulling her shoulders back, suddenly aware of the shabby old clothes and tangled hair she was sporting. What a fright! Tom looked so grown up and respectable. He even had a decent hat in one hand. It made her feel a child. What must he think of her?

This was it, she realised. That familiar, bittersweet scene where the childhood companions met again as adults and went from friends, no matter how long separated, to strangers. It was natural and fitting. She was supposed to accept it.

She wouldn't. She refused to let it happen. Xanthe swallowed back the expected pleasantries, the polite disentangling words, the ones that would free them both from this self-conscious, interminable moment. She didn't care if she – if they both – had to cringe for the next half hour. She wouldn't let go.

Turning her attention back, deliberately, to the dog, Xanthe asked, 'So this monster is yours? What did you say his name was?'

Tom cleared his throat. 'Milady . . .'

Xanthe kept her flinch hidden, ignored the waiting silence that followed. He wanted to be released. Well, she wouldn't release him. She kept on scratching the base of the dog's left ear, watching its eyes narrow in pleasure.

'Her,' Tom muttered.

'I'm sorry, what was that?'

The Moonlit Maze

'Her!' he repeated, louder. 'She's a girl. Rowan, I call her.'

'Better than Lucky, or Patches – but I thought from the look of her she'd be a White Fang.'

'I found her under a rowan tree.'

Xanthe abandoned her pretence of nonchalance and turned her head to stare down at Tom. 'Found her? Was she abandoned?'

'Near as I could tell. She was filthy, probably only a couple of months old, nothing but skin and bones. Someone had dumped her in the woods near the cottage, we think. Either that or she ran off from somewhere. There was still a rope tied round her neck.'

'Oh, the poor girl!' Xanthe gave in to the desire that had been kindling all this time and pressed her face to the dog's large, fluffy cheek. 'Are you sure she can't have some of the meat, Tom? It's just pork. I'm sure it won't upset her stomach.'

'You don't know her,' he said, stubborn. 'She'll eat her own body weight and keep begging. If I'd known what it would cost to feed her, maybe I'd have left her under the tree.'

'Tom!'

'Fine, all right. A small piece, mind. Small, I said – for the love of God, woman!'

'I can't help it, it's not my fault if your dog's a savage,' Xanthe said unconvincingly, muffling her laughter. 'At least I managed to stop her eating the paper.'

'The paper's the least of my worries. If she brings that back up on the drive home, I'll know just who to blame,' he said, exasperated, shaking his head, his hat still dangling from one hand, the other shielding his eyes from the sun.

She smiled, engulfed in gladness. 'You can send me the bill if you like.'

He sighed, then, in a quick movement, clamped the hat down on his head. It didn't suit him. 'Xan, I can't stand about like this all morning. Come down off there, will you? Let's at least walk a bit, like normal people.'

At the word 'walk', the dog let out a yip of excitement and abandoned Xanthe immediately, descending the sea wall in an effortless rush.

Xanthe, just barely, held herself back from a similar response. 'Are you keen on being normal all of a sudden, Tom?'

He squinted at her, then grinned, the dimples she remembered so well carving long, deep lines in his cheeks. 'No more than I ever was. But I'm getting a crick in my neck.'

'Then I agree. Here, catch.' She shoved the empty pork pie paper into her pocket, and tossed the bag of gingerbread down to him, then managed a clumsy one-handed descent, while clutching the lemonade bottle. Her skirt rode up dangerously high and she looked around anxiously as she landed.

'No one saw,' Tom told her, his gaze fixed studiously on the brown paper bag in his hand. Rowan danced happily around both their legs. 'I was keeping watch for you. Here, is this from Smethett's?'

'Go on, help yourself,' she said airily. 'Where are we walking? No, no, never mind that – what I really want to know is what you've been writing lately!'

'Since you've been nice enough to give me biscuits, I'll tell you ...' he said, turning towards the slope down to the little beach. Fishing out a piece of slightly crushed gingerbread, he lifted it high to avoid Rowan's quick leap, and trained smiling-serious eyes on Xanthe's face. 'If you'll tell me what you're working on, first.'

Twenty

Jude, present day

Somewhere in the stillness of the dawn-grey woods beyond my window, a cry rings out.

It's a thin, pleading sound. Like a tiny, helpless creature, cold and afraid. Like a baby. The noise pierces straight through to some previously unknown back-brain instinct. I'm up out of the bed and dragging on yesterday's leggings and sweatshirt, shoving my feet into my trainers, before I've even realised I'm moving.

I skid down the stairs without bothering to turn on any lights, setting picture frames swaying as I pass. The sound comes again as I reach the back door, desperate, and I feel desperate myself, desperate to find it and help whatever it is.

'It's OK, it's OK, just wait, I'm coming . . .'

I fumble with the keys, shoving the door open just as the tiny voice fades into a weak whimper, and then dies away.

Standing on the back doorstep, I hold my breath, listening *hard*, listening with tensed back, with hands and teeth clenched. The trees are quiet, barely whispering among themselves. A couple of birds twitter. Nothing else moves.

'No. Come on, where are you?'

I go down to the bottom of the garden and listen there. Then back through the house and out to the front where the road passes by. The crying doesn't come again. For a few moments, I consider putting my coat on and going out looking, afraid that the silence means whatever it is may have used up all its strength, and is dying. But the cold air – and a faint vestige of common sense – gets to me, and I admit to myself that not only do I have less than no chance of 'tracking' something through the trees, but that, for all I know, the sounds come from something that doesn't even need help. What if it's just a fox in heat? Or a rabbit that was being killed by a fox? What am I going to do about it?

Neither common sense nor the cold can erase the weird sense that I've failed, somehow. That I was too late. Upset, and feeling stupid and annoyed with myself for being upset, I eventually trudge back indoors and put the kettle on.

But I keep listening. I can't help it.

☽◯☾

By the time the sun's up I've selected (and inexpertly ironed) my chosen outfit for Sunday lunch with the Fairley's, done my hair, tidied the house and am staring down the barrel of four empty hours before Nick is supposed to call to pick me up. I have just about managed to stop trembling with readiness to fly out of the house if the crying starts again. Mainly because in the increased noise of daytime I doubt I'll hear it. But I can't quite shrug off the restlessness.

Eventually, I force myself to stop wandering about the

house like a lost soul, and sit sensibly on the sofa in the front parlour with my third cup of tea. I've fetched my sketchpad and a pen, put on my glasses and picked up the pamphlet on local history that Belle gave me at the library. It's still mostly unread. I've started it two or three times, but I just can't get beyond the first few pages; it has a kind of smarmy, smug tone that makes me instinctively reluctant to believe anything its author says.

'Mrs Radley J. Pikestaff,' I mutter. There isn't a picture or author biography, but I've got a vivid image of what she's like. Though the pamphlet's dated 1967. She might be bossing everyone around and making passive-aggressive comments about people's tarts having soggy bottoms in the great W.I. in the sky by now.

Mrs Radley J. Pikestaff starts on local history at the time of the Norman conquest ' . . . when a tiny settlement was recorded in Domesday Book under the name Wynterspyrne, the Old English "p" being – as scholars of history will of course know! – the equivalent to our modern "th" sound. Wynterspyrne resided then in the hundred of Kaersley and was populated by 3.7 households. The village and surrounding land were the property of Norman noble William de Wynter, forefather of the earls of Kearsley.'

Xanthe's family really was around a long time. Before the fire.

I check my phone for bars, sigh when I see there are none. No Google for me. Back to the pamphlet.

Next there's a bit on some Cistercian monks who set up a monastery on the hill in the thirteenth century and 'were remarkable in their own time for their high standards of piousness'. Which

I thought was supposed to be the literal job description for monks? I mean, what would be the point, otherwise? Anyway, apparently they produced a saint 'who one day, while walking the maze in prayer, was blessed with an ecstatic vision that warned him of a coming disaster from the sea.'

Walking the maze in prayer. The phrase gives me a little thrill of interest. Not Xanthe's maze – the maze where I stood and watched her in my dream – that would have to have come much later, but ... maybe there's always been a maze of some kind there? A chalk maze, maybe? I've read about them, and I know they used to cut them into the turf. I can imagine it perfectly, a white knot of curves, stark against the mossy grass, with the sea crashing below, gulls screaming and wheeling above ...

The saint's warnings persuaded the local fishermen and their families to abandon their houses and take shelter in the monastery – just before a massive chunk of the cliff fell into the ocean, causing a tidal wave that swept the town away. Well. One point for being super pious, I suppose.

I'm guessing that nothing much interesting can have happened after that for a while, because Pikestaff skips straight to Henry VIII getting his knickers in a twist about his divorce. 'In 1538 the king entrusted Hugh de Winter with the dissolution of the monastery at Winterthorne and confiscation of the holy relics and treasures there – which at this date were believed to be of considerable financial worth – and with the disbandment of the monks and the Abbot, Roland Ippesley. The inmates of the monastery, however, were not compliant with the king's orders. Hugh de Winter's swift and efficient actions in harrowing the monks from the community and suppressing the local populace won him favour with the king.'

Wow, Pikestaff. Did you just describe a civilian massacre as 'efficient'?

The abbot was unsurprisingly a bit cross with de Winter. He took a break from piousness – and, presumably, running – and cast a curse on the steps that the monks had cut into the cliffside to make it easier to get up and down between the monastery and the village. The curse was supposed to make it impossible to count the steps without going mad. Unfortunately for the abbot, this didn't stop Henry VIII making Hugh de Winter a lord and granting him the right to build his 'country seat' on the site of the abbot's former home.

I skim through the next parts covering Lord John Winter (the family having dropped the 'de' by then) and his decision to back the wrong side in the English Civil War, through the Restoration of Charles II, which leads to Lord John's grant of the title of the Earl of Kearsley as a reward for his loyalty. According to Mrs Pikestaff, the Earls of Kearsley continued on in pretty blissful peace from that point until the Great War when basically every male under the age of forty carked it over in France. Except – and there I sit up straight, putting my tea mug down with a thud – for the oldest nephew of the family, the heir. Jonathan Alfred Fanshaw Winter. 'A decorated war hero, Jonathan Winter –' I turn the page with trembly fingers, *knowing* what I'm going to read next – 'became engaged to his cousin, the daughter of the Earl of Kearsley, Lady Xanthe Winter, sometime in the spring or summer of 1924.'

I can't believe my luck. There's a picture of them. Not a

painting this time. A blurry, brownish sepia photograph of the family. They're all dressed up to the nines, Xanthe and her mother Caroline in glittering evening gowns and white gloves, Caroline with a plume of pale feathers in her hair. The earl's face is downturned, hard to make out. He looks shrivelled, shrunken almost, leaning heavily on a cane. Both his hands are closed over the top of it and the picture quality isn't great, but I'd bet anything it had a silver hawk's head with garnet eyes. And there's Jonathan. God, he was a handsome bugger – even in the softened smudgy photo I can see it in a way I just can't in Xanthe's memories. He makes her too unhappy. I think the artist of the portrait in the library must have felt the need to tone him down a bit for believability's sake; either that or he, like me, had an instinctive dislike of that ever-present smirk.

Jonathan's not smirking here, though. I might be imagining it, but I feel as if he's clenching his jaw. The eyes are dark, intense. Could be a trick of the photo, or it could be that he really was furious. Because his fiancée didn't want to marry him?

I study his face, and Xanthe's. This picture is different from the portrait in more ways than one. Caroline stands close to Xanthe, one hand clasped over her daughter's elbow, as if trying to keep her close. But Xanthe doesn't look lost or sad. She's smiling. Just a faint quirk of her lips, but it says everything. Her posture, the tilt of her head.

Belle said she thought the girl in the painting looked like she needed a friend. The girl in this picture looks like she found one.

Photograph taken July 1924, at the Kearsley Castle Summer Ball, reads the caption.

The Moonlit Maze

And then, underneath, more treasure. Pikestaff says it was at the ball that the fire happened. Aha! So this picture might have been taken right beforehand.

'It is now believed that the fire may have been caused by outdated gaslighting in one of the castle's public rooms, which had been awaiting repair. No evidence was found of foul play, although at the time many wild rumours swirled, with some attendees of the ball claiming they had heard gunshots prior to the fire's discovery. These stories may have been prompted by famed beauty Lady Xanthe's reputation as a Bright Young Thing with many suitors in addition to her fiancé. She had spent several years living unsupervised in France, and was known to overindulge in champagne, and flirt.'

My jaw aches from clenching my teeth. Screw you, Pikestaff. Screw you. You didn't know her. You have no idea. Maybe this was what Nick was talking about, these rumours? But I can't imagine Tom, the Tom that Xanthe knew, ever hurting anyone. Maybe he did love her, that I can believe, but – to set fire to her home? No.

I really want to try Google again, but Ma always said that repeating the same action over and over while expecting a different result is a sign of madness and, frankly, at this point, I don't need any further threats to my sanity. I flip the page and read on until—

I actually throw the little booklet away from me. A useless gesture. It just hits the arm at the other end of the sofa and lands on the cushion. I can't unread what I read. I can't unknow it.

'While most of Lord Kearsley's family and his guests at the ball escaped the blaze unscathed, two servants and a local man – Thomas Marten, son of Lord Kearsley's gardener – were believed to have been killed when the roof caved in. But the greatest loss of all was that of Lady Xanthe herself, at the age of twenty-one.'

They were killed in the fire that destroyed the castle. They both died there, in that place, in the ruins I've been roaming through, taking pictures of and sketching. It's their tomb.

Xanthe was only the same age as I am now.

I put my face in my hands. My breathing is wet and ragged. *Not a ghost*, that was what I'd told myself. *I don't believe in ghosts*. Too vivid and real to me in my mind, so *alive*. But of course I was dreaming about the past, about history. I must have known that in some part of me. I just . . . I hadn't confronted it yet. I hadn't imagined that the people I was seeing would only have . . . what, weeks? Months, at most, left to live.

'Oh, this is shit,' I mumble, sniffing hard. '*Shit*.'

It's ridiculous to be upset about it. I know that. Just like I knew it was stupid to contemplate running out into the woods to investigate those sounds earlier. But it doesn't stop me feeling this. That's what feelings are like, aren't they? Inconvenient. When they're real, anyway.

I look vengefully at the pamphlet, wishing I knew how to start a fire in the big fireplace so I could chuck it in there. Bloody Pikestaff.

Oh God. Still over three hours until Sunday lunch with the Fairleys. I can't stay stuck in the house until then. I'll drive myself up the wall, across the ceiling and out of a window. I have to move. But the thought of rambling up to the ruins

The Moonlit Maze

with my phone camera and sketchbook makes me feel sick. It's different, now that I know.

All right. The town, then. I've not even been to the seaside yet. I'll go to the sea.

Twenty-One

The clouds are a high, brittle white, blanketing the sky. There's little wind this morning, and it's unpleasantly muggy – I regret putting on my coat within a few minutes of setting out. It's the first day since I arrived that the weather hasn't been bright and sunny, but in a way I'm glad, despite the stickiness gathering at my lower back and the backs of my knees. Or maybe even because of it. The unpleasantness suits my mood.

I've got my sketchbook and pencils in a tote bag slung over my arm, but it's mainly for form's sake. I don't want to draw anything: I want to tear something apart. My body feels as if it's vibrating, as if my innards have been invaded by wasps. I want to cry, but, more than that, I want to kick.

This isn't a good mood for turning up to Sunday lunch, is it? I wonder if I ought to text Liz that I'm off colour and can't make it. Without that to look forward to, though, I don't know what I'll do with myself for the rest of the day. I have to try to get it together. Somehow.

This is something I was always going to have to come to terms with. Come on, Jude. Xanthe is in the past. One hundred years in the past. It's all already happened. That doesn't mean it's not important, that it's not extraordinary that you've seen these things – that you've experienced this connection. But why? That's the question. What does it mean?

Why is this happening to me?

For that matter, what exactly *is* happening to me?

The vibrating anger and upset are draining away, but what's left is a strange sensation, one I can't really put a label on. The grass rustles thinly underfoot and insects buzz and zip in the hedgerows. The trees shift and dip gently overhead, moving in a faint air current that doesn't reach me. I feel disconnected from all of it.

I worried about getting lost amid all these narrow winding roads and hedgerows again, like I did when I first came. That's why I haven't been as quick to go and visit the town on my own, see the beach and the ocean, as I could have been. But in this strange mood, where perhaps I wouldn't care even if I did lose my way, it's easy to find it. Obvious which turns to take, which bend is a cul-de-sac and which will open out to the road into town.

There's a different route I could have tried, of course. Xanthe's route. The one that leads down from the cliff, those steep, curving steps. I wonder if I really could find them, walk where she walked again, if I could connect to her in her time that way. If I could make her hear me. If . . . if I could warn her.

She reacted to me, before. She saw me. Maybe it's possible. Does time work like that? Thinking about it makes my head feel echoey and hollow.

The town seems quiet, almost deserted. Sunday morning in the country. A dog-walker nods and smiles at me without recognition, tugging his little schnauzer away briskly. A couple of cars whizz past as I walk along the high street, absently cataloguing the differences between Xanthe's Winterthorne and mine. The pavements are different, the roads wider. The sweet shop is an Oxfam now. Smethett's is . . . Belle Croute. Huh. I waver, feeling a sudden need to seek Belle out again – 'psychic' Belle with her makes-sense-if-you-look-sideways statements and watchful eyes – but then I notice the closed sign in the bakery window. Beyond, I can finally see the water.

That strange sensation of being . . . not outside myself, but not fully present, washes over me again, stronger than ever, dreamy and sort of sickening at once. It's the same way I felt the first time I explored the castle ruins when I knew, just knew, that the room with the oak tree had been the orangery. Maybe it's because I'm already feeling a little out of it, or because Xanthe was looking at this same sea in my dreams last night and, unlike almost everything else my eyes rest on, it *is* the same, the same endlessly shifting thing, unchanged by time.

The clouds melt away. I can feel the warmth of Xanthe's sunlight touching my cheeks and hair. Cobbles, the shape of them beneath my boots . . . my shoes, the leather soft and worn, laces gently tapping. I'm moving without even thinking, my feet stepping where she stepped, as if my soles were magnetised to her path.

The quiet morning gets louder. Seagulls shriek and the wind roars, there's stinging salt in the air, and the sweetness of flowers, roses. My fingers are cold round the neck of the lemonade bottle, and the paper bags rustle in my other hand. I'll climb the old sea wall, like I used to as a girl . . .

'Watch out!'

The shout jolts through me like a punch. The day goes grey and dim. I stagger and my hands close on empty air. The sea lashes at the rocks below.

I'm at the very edge of the harbour wall, the toes of my boots poking out into the empty air. One step from going over.

A scream burns my throat. My centre of gravity is too far forward. I can feel what's going to happen, but I can't stop it. I can't stop myself. My arms wheel desperately at the air as I tip forward above the rocks, over the lashing tide. I'm going to fall – I'm going to fall – I'm *falling*—

A hand clamps down on my wrist. The world spins and I do fall, but backwards, away from the water, away from the rocks onto – onto a person who lets out a winded 'Ooof!' as we both go down.

'Holy shit.' A deepish voice, hoarse and accented. 'Are you OK? What were you trying to – holy *shit*! You nearly went over!'

'I'm all right. I'm perfectly fine, thank you,' I garble out, but the words are wrong, the voice is wrong. That's Xanthe speaking. Speaking out of my mouth.

'It's OK. We're going to get you help – nope, nope, I'm not letting go of you, that is not a thing that's happening right now,' the man says as I reflexively try to free myself from his grip, and I realise that he thinks I've just tried to kill myself, that he probably thinks I'll try again if he releases my wrist.

What just happened? I don't understand.

The harbour wall. It's not the same. It's – it's been reconstructed some time in the past hundred years. The shape is different, straight instead of curving. It's at least two metres shorter than it was in the twenties, missing the extra barrier on the top where Xanthe used to sit.

The Moonlit Maze

I tried to walk on a structure that doesn't exist any more.

There's cold sweat on my face. My eyes are blurry and my heart feels as if it's leapt out of place and is taking vital space that my lungs need. I can't get a full breath in. But I have to say something. I can't even bring myself to look at this person, but I have to *say something*.

With a massive effort, I tear my gaze away from the end of the harbour wall and turn towards him, keeping my eyes down.

'I'm all right.' The words feel the wrong shape in my mouth, but it's my voice this time, mine. Whatever – whatever was going on – it's over now. I'm back in my own head. 'I. Stupid. I got too close and . . . Vertigo. Really. I'm all right.'

'Oh yeah? Because this is the second time in like a week you nearly died, lady, so somehow I'm not buying it.'

I blink. Frown. Scrub at my eyes with my free arm and finally manage to force myself to look at the man crouched tensely on the concrete next to me, the man who's currently clutching my wrist with both hands in an effort to stop me escaping.

I know him. I know the accented voice, and the dark eyes. Know that stubbled jawline and cleft chin. It's the angry man from the library. He's the motorbike wanker. The motorbike wanker just saved my life.

Part Three

Twenty-Two

Xanthe, summer 1924

'What do you think? My editor says I don't have enough.'

The yearning cry of a kittiwake nearly drowned out the middle of Tom's sentence. Xanthe squinted up against the sun to see the bird dipping low above them, moving into the shadow of the cliff where they sat, perhaps curious about the visitors to the rarely used little spit of beach. Technically, the cove was private Kearsley Castle property, but none of her family had ever cared for it – the rough scramble down the rockface through brambles and nettles, with the path crumbling away alarmingly underfoot, the tendency for the sea to deposit massive lumps of stinking rack against the rocks and the late low tide and early high tide times had usually deterred even Xanthe's adventurous cousins from bothering much. Like the maze, it had always been a special place for Tom and Xanthe. Oh, and Sally, of course. Well. Mostly Tom and Xanthe.

'You don't have enough,' she said, still watching the bird.

Rowan, who was rollocking up and down on the edge of the tide, let out a sonorous woof, as if in agreement.

Tom finished taking off his socks and shoes, and wriggled his toes luxuriantly in the still-damp dun coolness of the sand. Xanthe didn't dare join him. If she got her feet wet and sandy, she'd never be able to make herself put her stockings and shoes back on again. And then, almost certainly, Finch or Bowdler would catch her sneaking back into the castle in a scandalous state, and report to her mother. There would be more thin-lipped scoldings and thrumming silences.

Xanthe knew that she was the only person upon whom her mother could vent her anxiety. Her father had now been in London for nearly a month, yet during his daily telephone calls he was apparently determined to offer up nothing more informative than pleasantries about old acquaintances and the weather. Even Caroline got short shrift if she tried to ask about how the tests were progressing, or what the doctors had said. Jonathan was still notable only by his absence. The atmosphere in the house was thick enough to slice up and butter for afternoon tea.

Shaking off the dark thoughts, she returned her attention to the crumpled typed pages spread across her lap. 'That's why you've got all this filler in the middle here, sources-hint-she-suggested stuff, isn't it? It's all guesswork. You need to talk to the mother – that's the only way – if you're not going to repeat the factory owners' line, like everyone else.'

'She won't speak to any journalists,' Tom argued, resting one elbow on his knee and then leaning his head wearily into his palm. His fingers, long and callused, with large knobby knuckles, covered almost the whole of his face – one eye peered out at her between them, and his voice emerged as a mumble. 'You think I've not tried? Blank refusal. You can't get at her.

She doesn't leave the house. Doesn't even answer the door. I managed to catch her sister-in-law in the street once – the woman threw a packet of herring at my head.'

The kittiwake cried once more, dipped its inky wings, and went soaring away over the cliff. Xanthe sat up properly. 'Serves you right! Don't knock on their door! For heaven's sake, how would you like it, if your family had gone through something like that, and the people responsible were telling lies about your dead son, and you knew all the neighbours were watching through their curtains? Write her a letter.'

'I'm not trying to invite her to a tea party . . .'

Xanthe waved the pages in his face until he took them back. 'Write her a *polite*, business-like letter. Introduce yourself and say that you're on her and her son's side and you want to get the truth out, not this farrago of nonsense that's all over the papers. Tell her you want to help.'

'I'm not an agony aunt. I just want the story,' he said, folding the article up and stuffing it back into the battered leather satchel beside him. He withdrew a bottle of ginger ale, and offered it to Xanthe, who wrenched the top off and let the fizz out.

'Bilge! You want to help her, that's why you're still trying to get your editor to publish this when half of it is conjecture. Write her a letter telling her the truth. She'll speak to you.'

'How do you know?'

She leaned her shoulder against his and pushed him steadily sideways until he had to slap a hand down into the sand to keep his balance. He shoved her away, letting out a deep, rumbling laugh. Rowan, attracted to the noise, executed a perfect figure-of-eight turn and arrived on top of them in a tail-wagging cloud of sand and salt spray.

'Because I know you,' Xanthe answered belatedly, after she and Tom had both fended Rowan off and dusted themselves down. 'And I know how convincing you can be. Now, do you want the tongue sandwich or the corned beef? I've got a couple of tomatoes too.'

'A proper lunch?' Tom tugged the greaseproof-wrapped tongue sandwich out of her hand, pushing aside the large nose of the dog with absent-minded ease. 'How did you get hold of this?'

'Oh, I've got a friend in the kitchens now. Ellen. She'll smuggle me out something good if I ask her specially.'

'Ellen?'

'Technically, she's a housemaid, but apparently Cook's training her up a bit. She's sweet.'

Tom snorted, one brow quirking. 'Your parents never quite managed to beat the taste for unsuitable company out of you, did they?'

'Unsuitable? I grew up with Jonathan – anyone's a step up from him.'

Immediately, she wished she hadn't spoken. Xanthe stared at the sea, biting her lip, feeling self-consciousness prickle like the nettle stings that had got her shins through her stockings. The water was churning up the beach towards them in frothy ripples, and a couple of oystercatchers were hopping around, harassing the tightly curled-up shape of a small brown crab. Xanthe hoped it was already dead. Rowan stared at the birds with interest, but the lure of tongue sandwich was apparently too strong.

'I – we heard about the engagement party, when you arrived,' Tom said eventually. His voice was crushingly neutral, and

Xanthe fought the urge to hunch up in defence, like the crab. 'Since it's been officially announced now, is the wedding—'

'No!' She took a furious bite of her sandwich, and fought not to choke on it. 'There was no engagement, and there won't be a wedding, either.'

'That's not what the rumours say. They say it was quite the occasion, all the local nobs in attendance—'

She didn't dare look at him in case she saw something in his face. Something she couldn't unsee. Something that might change things. 'It wasn't a party – it was a press-ganging. It doesn't matter what anyone else says, the whole idea's absurd. Jonathan and I can't stand each other! The only reason he's going along with it is because my parents have got it into his head that . . . I don't know, that it's fitting or something. You'd think they'd want something better than my flighty and disappointing self for their golden boy.' She tasted the vitriol in her own words and bit her lip again, feeling disloyal. More quietly, she added, 'I've told them. They just won't hear me.'

Rowan, with the ready sympathy of animals, thrust herself between the two humans and plopped her head down on Xanthe's knee. Despite the long streak of slobber the dog had deposited on her skirt, Xanthe scratched the large triangular shape of her ear gratefully.

'You might want to ask yourself why that is,' Tom said, and now she did turn to look at him. He was frowning, not in anger or irritation but in fierce concentration. His eyes, that striking warm hazel, were fixed on her with uncomfortable keenness.

'How do you mean?'

'It's not like he needs you for the title, and the property's all tied up in him too. So what's the real reason they keep pushing you together?'

'I don't know,' she said slowly. 'I . . . I mean, they've never . . .' *listened to me. Cared what I wanted. Taken no for an answer.* 'I don't know. Look, it doesn't matter. It's not going to come to anything.'

'Just think about it,' he said. The piercing look eased suddenly into a smile. 'And if you truly aren't interested in him? The next time they invite you to a party, run away.'

'I only wish. The next big party is the Summer Ball. If I try to escape from that, they'll disown me.'

He tilted his head. She ignored the unspoken question – *would that really be so terrible?* – and took another bite of corned beef.

☽○☾

The water was lapping at their heels by the time they abandoned the beach for the rocky path back up the cliff. Tom had Xanthe's scribbled suggestions for his letter to the mother of the boy who had died in the factory fire in his satchel, and Xanthe had Tom's suggested revisions to her uncomfortably autobiographical short story about a young woman getting lost in the streets of Paris stuffed into the inside pocket of her battered old waxed jacket. As they had done when they were children, they clambered up over the edge of the cliff path almost on all fours – the dog enthusiastically leading the way, her tail whacking grass seeds and dust and bits of grit into their faces – then skittered quickly into the leafy cover of the maze to avoid being spotted, passing an almost empty packet of Garibaldi biscuits back and forth between them as they crunched over the gravel between the plush green hedges.

'I'm surprised your editor doesn't mind you haring off back home on a Friday all the time,' Xanthe said, licking crumbs off her thumb as Rowan danced hopefully around her legs. 'I mean, I've never been allowed to have a job or anything, but that's the sort of bunking off that'd have earned us a couple of good whacks on the knuckles with a ruler at school.'

'Shockingly, having a job is nothing like being at school,' Tom said dryly. 'As long as my assigned work is done by the deadline, he's happy for me to hare off after stories. Welcome to the exotic real world, milady.'

She frowned at him in mock confusion. 'But you weren't after a story. You just came to sit on the beach and eat sandwiches with me.'

Tom tripped on the gravel, caught himself on the hedge that formed the entrance to the maze, then cleared his throat.

Xanthe felt a near painful, tingling warmth suffuse her body, a kind of internal quake of longing. She wanted – oh, how she wanted! – to reach out and touch the naked back of Tom's neck, flushed and vulnerable seeming, where his hair was shaved short above the rumpled collar of his shirt. Instead, she beckoned to Rowan and buried her hands in the dog's thick neck ruff.

'Well. I wanted your opinion, didn't I?' Tom said quickly. 'And very useful it was too. I'll make sure to credit you when I win my next award.'

'I'll hold you to— oh.' She ducked hastily away from the moon gate, pulling the dog with her, and waved Tom back as well. 'Oh damn. No – don't –'

Tom frowned at her, brushing the early buds of wisteria aside to see what had taken her by surprise. He stiffened. There on the driveway were two cars. One was the Morris, surrounded by the footmen and O'Connell, Lord Kearsley's valet, busily unpacking various cases and trunks. The other was blood-red, low-slung and expensive-looking.

'Your father's back,' Tom said tonelessly.

'And Jonathan.' She felt on the verge of tears, as if something she hadn't even known was precious to her had been snatched away, without any warning. This little spit of time, unwanted and unused by anyone else, when she had felt . . . free.

But Xanthe hadn't managed to cry in years. Her eyes were only aching from the sun and the salt air, and just as the little spit of beach didn't really belong to her and Tom – but to her father, to the estate – she hadn't truly been free, either. What a foolish thought. Jonathan was always going to come back.

And as for her father . . . Of course she was delighted he was home and well. He must be better. Surely they wouldn't have *let* him come back, away from the hospitals and the specialists, if he were truly ill?

'I have to head in,' she said, forcing herself to straighten up and stop clinging to Rowan. 'Mother will want me and – I don't want them wondering where I've been all this time. The last thing we need just now is more arguments.'

Tom gave her another long, keen look. 'Yes, I see that. I hope he'll be all right, Xan. Your father. I really do. You can always – I mean, if you want to talk to me about it. Or anything. Just pass on word with my dad, or – or ring Sally.'

He was doing it again: trying to give her a way out. Trying to slip off into her past, the fading shadow of an old childhood friend and nothing more. She sighed, attempting to banish the uncomfortable fluster the sight of the cars had caused, and take control of herself once more.

'There's no reason I should stop seeing my friends just because Papa and my cousin are here. I'll meet you next Friday. So long as you're able to get away, I mean.'

The dimple in his left cheek flashed briefly, though his lips were pressed too firmly together to call the expression a smile. 'All right. I'll head home, then. Sally's having her young man and his parents over to dinner at Dad's tonight and she'll want to fuss at me a bit about it. It calms her down. See you next week.'

'See you.'

He summoned Rowan to him with a snap of his fingers – the dog gave Xanthe a wet farewell lick on her leg – and loped off down the wall towards his father's greenhouses, where no one would question his presence. Xanthe drew in and released another slow breath, then slipped under the wisteria and ran across the lower lawn, heading for the French doors of the library. If she could get in, get herself up the back stairs, and quickly run a brush through her hair – maybe even change into a somewhat less rustic skirt and jumper – then the chances of a harmonious reunion with her family were vastly increased.

But, although Xanthe's entrance to the castle went unnoticed, her progress up the servants' staircase was arrested by the sight of a slight familiar form, crumpled at the bottom of the steps.

'Ellen?' She went down on one knee on the blistered lino, hands hovering cautiously over the other girl's shuddering back. 'What's the matter? Did you fall? Are you hurt?'

The girl let out a soft, hitched breath. She began to uncurl a little, and Xanthe saw that she was huddled over her left wrist. A wrist encircled by vivid red marks, already purpling at the edges. Finger marks.

Ellen met her gaze. Her lip was trembling, and tears stood out on the lower lids of her eyes, but although she was breathing hard she wasn't crying, or not any more. Her expression was one of resigned shame rather than distress or outrage. Xanthe felt the numbness of shock catch fire, roar up into an almost uncontrollable blaze of anger, her hands spreading out wide over her knees in an effort to avoid knotting them up into fists.

Someone was hurting Ellen.

Just as someone had hurt Suzette.

Twenty-Three

She didn't want to think about Suzette. Not now. But she couldn't help it, even though Suzette had been nothing like Ellen at all: not fair and small and gentle-seeming, but dark-haired and dark-eyed, with a flashing grin of slightly crooked teeth and a loud, honking laugh. Charming in a fervid kind of way. Most likely a few years older than Xanthe, though Xanthe had always been bad at judging people's ages.

Suzette had been one of a revolving group of pretty girls who hung around in cafes and galleries, at the fringes of the bohemian Paris parties and salons that Xanthe attended at the house of Felicie and her friends. They flirted and danced and hung on the men, young or old, cadging drinks and cigarettes. But Suzette usually came with one particular man – Laurence.

He was an elder of the set, in his late forties. Handsome and fit, faintly leonine, he was a poet and memoirist, and had been a British correspondent for various London newspapers in the war. Felicie and many of the other artists and poets on the scene, even those who were closer to his age, revered him.

Laurence would read people's work, if they dared approach

him, and give them thoughtful comments on how to rethink or improve it, phrasing his words so that even his harshest judgements fell on the listener like an honour. He would tell stories about the war, sometimes, sad and terrible stories that lingered on in Xanthe's mind for weeks. And often, while he did these things, he would pull Suzette down onto his lap and give her his cigarette to smoke. He would murmur things into her dark hair that made her laugh her appalling laugh. He would have her sit at his feet and rest his large fingers, with deliberate and conscious gentleness, around her slender sun-flushed neck. And the other women – the poets and painters and singers, even those who had their own men at the parties – would watch and bridle, or avert their eyes.

The one time that Xanthe had ever tried to talk to Suzette, out of that painstaking, polite impulse that sometimes forces women to attempt to be friendly to other women who make them uncomfortable, Suzette had looked utterly shocked. As if no one – save Laurence, presumably – had ever bothered to say a word to her at one of those gatherings before. And then the surprise was gone, transformed into a sneer, and she had blown a cloud of smoke straight into Xanthe's face.

'Never mind this little cat,' Laurence had laughed, only faintly apologetic, putting his arm round Suzette and drawing her away. 'She's not here for the conversation.'

Later, Felicie told Xanthe what she had been too naïve to work out herself: that Suzette was a prostitute, or the nearest thing to it. 'Oh yes, you are not the only one of us dying to give the slut a slap, I promise you – but what can you do? Poor Laurence seems to have conceived an unlikely passion for her. Ignore her! It won't last.'

Felicie was right, but not in any way that Xanthe had expected.

One evening, Laurence invited everyone round to his apartment. It was a vast, crumbling place – the top floor of what had once been a grand townhouse – where damp had caused the gilded paper to bubble up and peel off the walls, the parquet floors were marked with deep scratches and gouges that tempted the turning of an unwary ankle, and cobwebs hovered in the corners of the high, corniced ceilings like dusty, listless ghosts. The decayed grandeur of the setting suited him. He was in high spirits all night, even trying once to pull Xanthe onto his knee into Suzette's usual place. Xanthe – more surprised than offended – had let out a loud yelp and whacked him on the wrist hard enough to make him let go. He had let out a shout of his own, shocked, knocking his glass of whisky off the arm of his chair to shatter on the ruined parquet. Seeing that Xanthe was shaken, Felicie and a couple of others had intervened, laughing and downplaying what had happened: 'She is not your type! Leave the poor girl alone – you'll scare her to death!'

In the humid thunderstorm closeness of that early summer day, Xanthe had already been suffering with a headache. She'd only allowed herself to be coaxed out because Laurence was supposed to be reading that night, and his poetry was brilliant, beautiful and musical and often a bit shocking. Now it was clear that Laurence was too drunk to recite his own address, let alone any of his writing, and she just wanted to go home – at least, back to the quiet refuge of her attic room. But she knew if she told Felicie she was going there would be protests.

Xanthe tried to tell herself she wasn't bored of them, these people, her friends. Bored of the parties and this life already. She wasn't homesick. This *was* her home now. She had a headache, that was all.

Resisting the urge to apologise, to help clean up the smashed glass, she ducked out of the smoke-and-alcohol-fugged main room into a dark, quiet space. It was a bedroom; she could just make out a rumpled bed, clothes tossed on the floor. She didn't turn on the light. The darkness of early evening was a balm to her throbbing eyes. Across the way, there were glass doors leading to a balcony. She headed for them with relief, and lifted the little hook on the inside that bolted them closed to let in a gust of cool air.

Suzette was out there on the balcony, slouched on a little wrought-iron stool shoved into the corner of the small space, against the railings. She was wrapped in an oversized, threadbare man's dressing gown. Her feet were bare. Xanthe could tell at once she had been out there for some time. There was a cracked flowerpot, overflowing with cigarette butts marked with the rusty red imprint of her lipstick. Xanthe had noticed that Suzette wasn't in the apartment that night. Noticed and been glad.

The door had been bolted on the inside. On the inside.

Xanthe swallowed hard. 'You're not dressed, Suzette. Why don't you come in and warm up a bit?'

The other girl darted Xanthe an unreadable sidelong look, and stayed on the stool. Her arms were wrapped round her body. Xanthe could feel gooseflesh prickling on her own bare arms. 'He says I'm not allowed.'

'He?' An instant after the word came out, she wanted to bite her tongue.

Suzette let out a contemptuous snort through her nostrils and finally slithered round to face Xanthe. She lifted one hand to gesture at herself, but Xanthe didn't need the direction, she had already seen that Suzette's lip was badly cut, enough that it had swollen up, distorting one side of her mouth. It had bled everywhere; a gory mess of dried blood was flaking off down the side of her chin and neck. Suzette's hand was bloody too, the knuckles grazed, the wrist marked with distinctive bruises. Finger bruises.

'Who do you think, imbecile? Who do you think?'

The balcony doors had been bolted on the inside.

Xanthe nodded. Then without another word, without even another thought, she turned and left the balcony.

It took her longer than she had expected to locate her beaded evening bag, which was hidden beneath piles of carelessly dropped jackets and stoles on the rickety chaise longue in the hallway of the apartment. People kept trying to talk to her, pull her away. She barely heard them, or acknowledged them, and one by one they drifted off. Laurence himself came once, sheepish and charming. She thought perhaps he was trying to apologise for his earlier behaviour, but his words made no sense to her; it was all just a low, droning sound, like bees, like wasps. She shied away from him, unable to stand the thought that his reaching hand might make contact with her skin. She forced herself to meet his eyes, just for a moment. Then he left her alone.

It had all taken too long. When Xanthe returned to the balcony – ten, maybe fifteen minutes later – clutching the contents of her purse, most of her month's allowance from her parents – it had started to rain. The growl of thunder was in the air. The stool in the corner was empty. Of Suzette there was no sign except the pile of cigarette butts slowly wilting in the wet.

Too long. Too slow. Too late.

Slowly, numbly, she went back into the party. She looked – she knew it was useless, but she had to look – and of course Suzette wasn't there. She wasn't anywhere in the apartment. Eventually, Xanthe gave up, collected her things and walked home alone through the rain to her little room in Felicie's house.

The next morning, she told Felicie that she was never going to Laurence's place again, or attending any gatherings arranged by him. Felicie, convinced that Xanthe was overreacting to Laurence's drunken playfulness, tried to convince her otherwise. They had a disagreement, nearly an argument, over it, and Felicie was huffy with Xanthe for days. Xanthe didn't care.

Inevitably, though, Laurence did still turn up at many of the parties and gatherings Xanthe attended. He gave her a wide berth, and Xanthe did the same. But he had new girls on his arm now. Xanthe never saw Suzette again. As far as she could tell, no one ever even asked where the girl had gone.

Every time after that, when the papers contained some small, sad little reference to an unknown young woman floating up out of the depths of the Seine, Xanthe wondered. What if she had found her bag faster that night? What if she had been able to make herself accept Laurence's apology, to soothe him by pretending all was well? What if, what if, what if?

The summer passed, and the winter. In the spring, her mother's letter had come, asking her to return to Winterthorne. Now here she was in this cramped little vestibule with Ellen, staring at her bruises. And, this time, Xanthe would not be too slow.

'Will you tell me his name?'

The smaller girl shook her head frantically, tears spinning free of her eyes with the force of her movement.

Xanthe gnawed on her lip with frustration. She told herself it didn't really matter who it was. As the most junior housemaid in the place, it would be easy for anyone to take advantage of Ellen, even one of the boot boys. And there had been such a great turnover of staff since the war, since she'd left for Switzerland.

'But he is in this house?' That was all she truly had to know.

Ellen's breath caught, and after a moment she nodded.

'Do you want to leave here? To get away from him?'

Her face crumpled. 'But I can't, milady. My mam – I told my mam, I begged her – she told me to just be nicer and – and maybe I'd get a present ... She won't let me go home, she won't, miss, she won't. She doesn't want me – she'll kill me herself if I do—'

'It's all right. Hush now.' Xanthe clasped the other girl's thin upper arms as carefully as she could, rubbing them up and down, up and down. The coarse material of the uniform pricked against her palms. 'I understand. I won't make you go home. Listen, do you have anyone else who might help you? A friend or some other family?'

Xanthe's mind was already racing ahead, trying to construct some other solution, but Ellen breathed in, out, closing her eyes as she pulled herself back together. Then the tiniest light began to dawn in the hopelessness of her face, and she sat up straighter. 'My auntie. My aunt Heather. Da's sister. She was always good to me, really good. But after Da died, she and Mam rowed and she went away. To Durham. She wrote me a few times from there, but Mam took the letters off me before I could get the address straight. It was – it was Talburt or Turbot Street. I think. She'd help if she knew. Only I don't have the address straight and Mam takes all my wages and I don't know how—'

She was falling apart again, overwhelmed. Quickly, Xanthe said, 'Ellen, look at me. You're going to give me your aunt's full name and as much information about her as you know, and I'm going to find her.'

'Find her? Oh! Oh, do you mean it, miss? She's the only person who ever stood up to my mam. She wasn't afraid of her or anyone, and even my da was afraid of Mam. Do you really think you can work out her address?'

'I'm sure I can, Ellen.' Or, at least, she knew someone who could. 'In the meantime, any time you think this man is going to come near you, you drop what you're doing and you run away and hide in my room. Turn the key on the inside if you want.'

'But – Mrs Finch'll be so cross—'

'Tell them I gave you a job to do, make up whatever you like. They're not likely to tax me with it, are they? And if they do I'll back you up.'

The girl put her face in her hands. She looked as if her bones were dissolving from sheer relief. 'Oh. You can't know – Th-thank you.'

'You don't have to thank me. And don't you think it's about time, just when you and I are alone, for you to call me Xanthe?'

Ellen sniffed, rubbed her face, her brow crinkling. Then she looked Xanthe in the eye with a sudden glint of humour that took Xanthe by surprise. 'No, thank you, milady, I'd rather not, if it's all the same to you. I can never say any of those foreign sort of names right.'

Twenty-Four

Jude, present day

I don't want to be here. I don't want this to have happened to me. I don't want to explain myself to this person, of all people. It's too much. I need to get away. There's a moment when I'm ready to explode. Scream, hit him if I have to, hit him and make him *let go*. The violence of the impulse frightens me, and that – that shock of feeling – is what brings me back to myself, just enough to really look at him.

He's falling apart.

The voice, the grip on my wrist, they all indicated anger to me, like before. But he's not angry. His eyes are sunken, his face is wet and his breath is rattling in his chest, panicked. He's staring at my wrist, where he's holding on to me, as if he doesn't dare take his gaze off it for one second. Or as if he's seeing something – someone – else.

I'm the one who almost fell. But he's more scared and distraught right now than I am.

It comes back to me in a whisper of memory, Ma's voice. What she always said. People aren't what you can see on the surface. Every one of us is a whole universe, galaxies and worlds and colliding stars hidden under the skin. You don't have to understand what someone else is going through to have compassion. Stand up for yourself, yes, one hundred per cent, but be kind too. Give people the benefit of the doubt if you can. One day you might need it too.

'It's ... it's Aidan, isn't it? Listen. I wasn't trying to hurt myself.'

I make my voice as gentle as possible. It's not easy; he's hurting my wrist – actually, he probably did that dragging me back from the edge, but the death grip now isn't helping – and there's no hope of getting him to let go until I convince him I won't immediately leap up and try to jump.

He's shaking his head sharply. I keep trying anyway. 'It was a stupid accident. Thank you. I'd have gone right over if it wasn't for you. But I didn't mean to do it. I'm OK.' His grip's starting to relax, just a little. 'You can let go of me now.'

His fingers clench tight again. I let out a hiss as the forming bruises throb. Horror lashes across his face as he realises what he's done. He rushes into speech: 'I can't just let go. I can't let you go. I get it, but – we'll go to the hospital or something – OK? You've got to—' His breath catches. *'You've got to let me help you.'*

There's an ache in my chest. He's a mess, as big a mess as I ever was, this guy. What's happened to him to make him like this? I scoot a tiny bit closer to him on the – ouch, really cold and uncomfortable – concrete of the harbour wall. I put my free hand over his on my wrist.

'Look at me. Aidan. I need you to look at me. Come on. Please.'

He flinches. Then his gaze flicks up and to my surprise I see that his eyes, the eyes I thought were so dark, are actually blue. The most vivid, midsummer sky blue. Stunning, and totally out of place in his pale face, beneath those black, angry brows. Only . . . they're not really angry, are they? They're just worried. For me. Involuntarily, I smile at him, and he blinks at me, shellshocked.

'You already helped me. You did it – I'm safe. I'm OK.'

'You're OK? You're . . . you're OK.' His expression crumples as his fingers loosen, but I don't jerk away, I let him let me go. He scrubs at his face with both his hands, makes a noise that might be a sort of strangled laugh, shading into a groan. 'Is your *arm* OK? I didn't mean to hurt—'

'It's fine.' Much better now someone isn't squeezing the life out of it. 'It'd have been a lot worse if I'd walked over the edge of the wall like a numpty. I landed on you. Did I do any damage? No? Look, there's a bench over there – let's go sit.'

He seems to suddenly remember where we are and gets to his feet in a rush, leaning down to help me scramble to my feet too. I feel bruised and wobbly. My tote bag and the art supplies are, miraculously, still on my arm, caught round my elbow by the bunched fabric of my coat. I shove the bag up to my shoulder, talking all the time as if I'm trying to soothe a spooked animal. I almost don't recognise myself. This patient, kind version of me who's coaxing him to sit next to me on the metal bench. It's a Jude I haven't been for a while. Not Jude at all, really, the practical, tough Jude who always looks out for number one. More like that other girl, Juliet, that I used to be. The me that Ma knew.

'Here.' Once we're both settled on the salt-pitted metal seat of the bench, I shove the contents of a packet of tissues from my pocket at him. He huffs a bit and buries his face in them, his large, fine-boned hands scrubbing at his wet cheeks roughly. He's actually shaking with reaction. I get the feeling that he might also be blushing if he weren't so pasty with shock. I gave him a hell of a scare. He's not much older than me. Kitted out in dark leathers with a vintage Van Morrison T-shirt underneath, big manly combat boots, a big manly watch on one wrist. He's a Tough Guy, or at least that's the part he's dressing for. Roaring around on his big bike, annoying and scaring everyone in town. Including me. He wasn't looking for sympathy. He was looking for a fight.

I wonder what trouble he got into that he's ended up here.

I've gone silent and, despite the noises of the tide and the wind, it's starting to feel uncomfortable. What would Ma say in this situation? What would – what would Liz do?

'I'm Juliet,' I say, stilted. 'From London. Bit accident prone, as you've noticed. Staying here to sort out some family stuff. What about you?'

'You know who I am,' he says, voice gravelly, from behind the tissues. 'Don't pretend you don't.'

'I know you're Aidan something and that your motorbike is considered a local terror. That's it. Why don't you fill me in on some more details? Last name. Where you're from. Why you're here?'

The broad shoulders under the black jacket jerk a bit and I hastily back away from this touchy territory. 'Or you can just sit – it's fine.'

More silence.

'You know what, I came out to do some sketching so, since I'm not dead – thanks again – I'm just going to do that.'

I rummage in my tote for my sketchpad and pencil tin and then I have a sudden spark of inspiration. A memory of Ma pressing paper and pencils on me when I had cried myself into a state after a nightmare and couldn't even speak. I rip out a page and offer it and the pencil tin to him. 'You want to give it a go?'

He doesn't react. I nudge at his arm with the tin. Slowly, he lowers the tissues and stares at me, those blue eyes delivering the kind of glare that convinced me he was homicidal – when was it, only a day ago? It's not quite as effective now, but I have to admit it still makes the small hairs on the back of my neck want to lift.

'It'll help,' I tell him. 'Just draw something. Doesn't matter what. If you're going to sit there, you might as well sit there and draw.'

He keeps staring. He's tensed up. Abruptly, he stuffs the tissues into his jacket pocket and leans forward with an aggressive movement as if he's about to – I don't know – tell me to stuff it, get up, stalk away. But then he hesitates and a puzzled look comes into his eyes. He snorts.

'You serious? Is this a rom-com?'

'A – a what?'

'Like a rom-com! What are you, some kind of manic pixie dream girl?'

'I have no idea what you're talking about. I'm just trying to help.'

He waves his hands around. 'With – what – spontaneous fucking art therapy?'

'I'm not your therapist,' I snap, out of patience. 'In fact, I happen to have had a pretty horrible day myself, so you can either take the fucking paper and draw something, or I'll give up and go home and you can stay here and be miserable by yourself.'

He's leaned back again, his eyebrows going up, the sudden aggression replaced with surprise. 'All right, all right, I'll draw. Wow.'

I shove the paper and tin at him and turn determinedly away, focusing on the view of the foaming tide, the headland, the clouds and the birds circling above. Since I've given Aidan (if Aidan is indeed his real name) my pencils, I grab a black fine-liner out of my tote and start in on those jagged spires of rock that stick out of the ocean by the cliffs. The Thorns, that's what Xanthe calls them.

Against all odds, within a few minutes I'm starting to relax, a hum – that strange song that's been stuck in my head – rising in my throat. Xanthe would like this, I find myself thinking as I experiment with cross-hatching to try to catch the effect of shadows on the moving water. She loves the sea.

Wait. Should I be thinking that? Should I be letting her into my head again – after what just happened?

No. No thinking. Just drawing. Take your own advice, Jude.

'It's Aidan Antonenko.'

I try to control my startle. 'Nice to meet you. Like I said, I'm Jude.'

There's a pause. 'I thought it was Juliet?'

I clear my throat. Why did I introduce myself that way? It was weird to hear him say the name, weird to hear anyone use it but Ma. But . . . it doesn't hurt, exactly. Or not as much as I expected it to. 'Yeah. Most people call me Jude, though.'

Another few minutes of quiet. A seagull wings overhead, crying mournfully. I hold up the sketchpad and squint at it a bit, trying to figure out the perspective.

'You're not from round here, you said?'

I keep my eyes on the sketch. Apparently, art therapy does work. 'Nope. Londoner, born and bred. I only arrived a week ago. I'm staying at my aunt's house. What about you?'

'Been here a few months. Nearly six now. My folks are back home, I mean, back in New York.'

I snort, then hastily explain: 'Talk about culture shock.'

'You could say that. I guess you're used to it, right, since your aunt lives here?'

I look up from the page to see him folding his piece of paper into a neat square. He's used it. There are marks, impressions, showing through. But I can't see what he drew.

'Not really. This is my first time in Winterthorne. My aunt – my great-aunt – is dead. I'm here cleaning out her house and . . . stuff.' If you could count starting on one room and then giving up immediately as *cleaning out*. He's looking stricken again.

'Oh. Oh man, I'm sorry.'

'I didn't know her. It was complicated.'

He gives me a half-smile that conveys sympathy, wry understanding, a tinge of apology. It's a nice smile, the first one I've seen from him, and it transforms his face: I'm caught off guard, just like before, by how attractive he is. It makes me shy away, shifting uncomfortably on the bench. I can't trust that kind of handsome.

'Complications. Yeah, I get that.' He sounds worn out. The smile fades, takes that flash of dangerous attraction with it. I go back to my sketch.

'Hey, listen,' he says a minute later. 'Maybe it sounds – weird – but is there – I mean, is there any chance we've met before?'

I look back up at him, surprised. 'Have you ever been to London?'

'Ah, a few times, when I was a kid, yeah. My mom's actually a Brit.'

'Then I suppose it's possible. I don't remember it, though, sorry. Do you—'

'Yeah, no. No, it's stupid. You just seem sort of familiar.'

'Well, you did nearly run me over. Maybe that made an impression.'

'Right. That's what it is.' He slumps back next to me on the bench, holding on to the pencil tin, balancing one booted ankle up on the opposite knee. 'Finish your drawing. It's good.'

I squint up at the clouds – they're gathering over the sea, making some dark, dramatic shapes that bode ill for the weather later on – and add a few marks to the page. Then I date it on the bottom right and scrawl my initials. 'I'm finished. Thanks.'

'Ah. OK. Well, I guess – can I give you a ride home? I mean, I already know where you live. Oh, shit – that sounded creepy.'

I quietly put my art supplies away, taking my pencil tin from his unresisting fingers as he writhes in silent, badly concealed mortification. I should absolutely turn him down and walk back – I know that. But. *But*. I've got an instinct that if I do, that'll be it. He'll take it as a judgement, a rejection. And after what Nick told me about the local gossip and what Aidan's said himself, I think I could be the only person he knows here.

'All right. But I've never been on a motorbike before. I don't know what to do.'

'I'll go real slow. It's easy,' he assures me, relieved. 'You can just hang on to me – or on to the back of the seat – whatever you're comfortable with. I've got a spare helmet.'

Which is how I arrive back at the cottage ten minutes later, a little bit breathless and windswept, but in one piece. I clumsily climb off the bike as Aidan puts the kickstand down, and then fumble with my helmet. He keeps his on. I get a feeling that being able to hide his face is probably a relief. But since he's pushed his visor up I can see him roll his eyes as he helps me untangle the fastener under my chin.

'I've not worn one of these before and I can't see what I'm doing. If I hear one word about pixie dream girls . . .' I warn, gulping in the cool air with relief once the heavy plastic is off my head.

'Nope, no ma'am,' he says. 'Not one word.'

'Well, thanks. For the lift and for rescuing me,' I say. Then I hesitate. 'And, listen, since we're both visitors, we can keep in touch if you want? I mean, don't come zipping down past my house at six thousand miles an hour again with no warning, please—'

'Six thousand miles an hour,' he repeats, mocking, muffled by the helmet. 'It's literally the public highway—'

'Shush.' I offer the sketch that I did, on which I'd quickly jotted my number when he wasn't looking. 'You can ring if you want a chat. Or just drop by. To talk. Whatever.'

He looks down at the piece of paper for a minute, making no

move to take it. Embarrassed, I'm about to turn away when his gloved fingers suddenly close round mine. The gauntlets make his hands seem so huge that they totally engulf my smaller one, and the leather creaks, cool against my skin. I let out a tense breath, but relax as I realise that he's barely touching me, hasn't even crumpled the sketch. He's being careful of the bruises forming on my wrist. Just . . . holding on to me.

'Hey. Thanks.' He sounds almost choked. 'Sorry.'

Before I can work out what's happening under the visor, he's taken the sketch and handed me something in return. Then he's swinging back onto the bike, revving it up, roaring away in a cloud of acrid smoke.

I cough, and through watering eyes stare down at the thing in my hand. It's the neatly folded piece of paper that I gave him to draw on. When I unfold it, I don't know whether to laugh or run after him, waving my fist.

It's a little caricature of me, with an oversized head and hands and feet. The face is quite cleverly done – annoyingly so – with heavy brows drawn down in an exaggerated scowl and a hint of fangs around the mouth, as if the sketched version might be about to bite. There are pencils clutched in each hand, but the caricature is holding them more like knives. Above my head there's a curved banner, an untidy scrawl naming me 'Manic Pixie Danger Artist' and a speech bubble originating from my mouth proclaims: 'Fear my pencils! Fear my wrath!'

Underneath all this is a phone number, and a slashing signature, of which the only decipherable letter is a large capital 'A'.

Then I notice the drawing's extravagent nest of curling hair, sticking out in all directions. A tentative poke at my own

The Moonlit Maze

head confirms my suspicions: my careful plait is completely destroyed. It's a knotted, frizzy nightmare.

I shove the sketch into my jeans pocket and head back inside the house at a run. Sunday lunch is still on and I need to try to look like a normal person, even if I don't feel like one, by the time Nick arrives to pick me up in – oh God – half an hour.

Twenty-Five

Sunday lunch at the Fairley house doesn't start promisingly, if I'm honest. I'm already primed to be jumpy and distracted after the truly weird day I've had so far. When Nick knocks on my door, there's something different about him. It takes me a minute to get it: not only has he made an attempt to comb his hair, but he's wearing a collared shirt under a smart suede jacket, and clean trousers, rather than the worn jeans and T-shirts I've come to associate with him. He looks good.

'Er. Do your family dress up for Sunday dinner?' I ask warily, plucking at the knee of my jeans as I get into the truck.

'What?' He stares at me uncomprehendingly from behind the wheel, then laughs. 'No, you're fine.'

When we arrive at Liz's house – which is much larger and much grander than expected, a rambling redbrick farmhouse all the way over on the other side of Winterthorne, surrounded by fields and woods on the approach, and with a sea view behind – everyone spills out to greet us. I note with dismay that both Nick's oldest sister, Meg, and the new-to-me middle sister, Jess, are wearing dresses, nothing too fancy, but with tights and nice shoes. Liz is dressed in a silk shirt and a circle skirt with sandals. Even the two little kids who are chasing around everyone's legs are in nicer clothes than me, in my Mary-Jane Doc Martens (literally the most expensive item in my whole wardrobe, bought second-hand off eBay), blue jeans, sloppily ironed shirt and hand-me-down jumper. The third child – Jess's baby, who passes between at least three people's arms in the time it takes me to be introduced to everyone – is wearing a onesie, which, since he's under a year old: fair enough.

They look as if they're about to head out to a party. Or, worse, to church.

'You are a lying liar who lies,' I mutter to Nick. He gives me another confused look.

How? How are men so infuriatingly clueless?

Everyone's perfectly nice. Nick's uncle Alan, his beard more neatly trimmed than the last time I saw him, asks me how I enjoyed the Kurtzman farm produce, and Meg's husband, Ben, beams when I say it was amazing. Jess even compliments my Docs. Then, as we trek back indoors to the light-filled, open-plan living room, Alan hands the baby to me as if it's the most natural thing in the world.

Luckily, I quite like babies, just as long as they aren't shrieking their heads off. This one is a good one – smiley and goggle-eyed, with a little tuft of soft, dark hair. I try not to squeeze his reassuring baby-scented weight too hard, and in return, as I hitch him up a bit higher, he slaps me gently in the face. And then someone takes him away again, leaving my arms empty. At which point I realise that I ought to have brought something. Flowers, or a cake or – wine?

Dressed like a hobo and no gift. I walked in the door two minutes ago and I've already messed up *twice*.

The Moonlit Maze

I realise, somewhere dimly under all this surface-level panic, that the real issue is that I've imagined the family wrong. I thought, what with Nick's rusty old truck and Liz's working as a cleaning lady, that they were like me. Hard workers, yes, but also hard up. That was why it had been so easy to let them befriend me.

The house alone makes it clear how wrong I was. For the first time since I arrived in Winterthorne, I feel out of place, and because I wasn't prepared I know that it's showing, which makes it even worse.

Liz gathers me into one of those ridiculous hugs, murmuring, 'They're a bit much, aren't they?' as she whisks me away, warding off her family with a shooing motion: 'You lot all stay out here, you're neither use nor ornament and you know it.'

Nick follows us anyway, his face settling into a stubborn expression. They exchange a long look, and she sighs. 'Oh, all right. Not that you'll do anything but get under my feet.'

Her meaning is revealed when I see that she's bringing us into the kitchen. It's a long, low room, the walls and ceiling criss-crossed with honey-coloured beams, a dining table positioned in front of modern folding doors. Beyond, there's the sea, and clouds swelling into deep slate-grey banks. A storm is coming.

Before I know it, I've got a mug of tea – the Fairley family medicine – in one hand and a fistful of cutlery in the other and I'm helping Nick lay the table while Liz busily stirs flour into her gravy over at the hob. I can hear that the chaos continues in the living room, but the kitchen is much quieter, filled with cosy sounds of bubbling pots and Liz's whisk, and with the scent of roasting lamb, and garlic and rosemary. There are already two bunches of flowers in there – tulips and daffs – both in proper vases without an old pickle jar in sight.

'Ah!' Liz swears under her breath. 'Look at this, all down the front of my top. Too late for an apron now. And the damn gravy's all lumpy again, and still not thickening! Why does this always happen?'

Nick smiles slyly at me over the table, whispering: 'Every Sunday. Like clockwork. Next panic will be the roast potatoes, just wait.'

'Have you tried a cornflour slurry, Liz?' I ask, then bite my lip. Ma never much appreciated my backseat cooking when things were going wrong.

Liz, on the other hand, appears delighted. 'Can you cook? You can, can't you? No one else except Alan can boil an egg – this is a miracle!'

'I can boil an egg,' Nick protests.

'Oh yes? And when was the last time you bothered to?' Liz retorts. Nick opens his mouth, then wisely shuts it again. 'Exactly. Jude, you come here and have a go at this, and I'm going to check the roast potatoes.'

In minutes, I'm wielding a carving knife, draining vegetables and setting serving plates on the table. As the rest of the family drift in, drawn by the intensifying smells, Liz squeezes my arm. 'This is the least stressed out I've been on a Sunday in years. You can come back any time, love.'

Nick pulls out a seat for me at the table and waits for me to sit. As he pushes the chair in, his hands come to rest on my shoulders. I pulled my jumper off in the kitchen's heat, and opened a couple of shirt buttons – his warm, slightly rough fingertips press lightly against my collarbone, and his little finger brushes the bare skin at the base of my neck. A bright shivery feeling sweeps through my body. Behind me, I hear him draw in a deep breath. Then he takes his hands away and sits down on my left. He's a bit flushed.

'Oh. There's no lumps in this!' Alan says in wonder, pouring some gravy out onto his plate, where he's already helped himself to roast potatoes.

'That's because Jude sieved it. Let me sit down before you start, you heathens – who raised you?'

'No one to blame but yourself, Mum,' says Meg cheerfully, before shooting a worried look at Nick. He doesn't seem to notice.

Alan tells me, 'You can come back again any time.'

'I've already said that!' Liz sits down next to me at the head of the table. As if that's the signal, everyone digs in. Since I'm the one who carved that roast, I'm not shy about making sure I get a decent-sized portion.

Conversation shifts around me in waves. On my left, Nick is quiet, but that's all right – Liz makes me laugh with an account of an argument between two elderly ladies at the charity shop where she volunteers, then draws me out, asking me what I've been up to. I tell her about starting to tidy up the house, how it was harder than I was expecting, that I found some things related to my mother.

'Well, you've got plenty of time, haven't you?' she says. 'Sometimes it's all right to let the hard things go for a bit and just do what you can for now.'

I've been trying not to think about today, the most unsettling and inexplicable day, but somehow out of nowhere I hear myself asking, 'Do you ever think that . . . I don't know, maybe time . . . doesn't only move in one direction? I mean, maybe it doesn't even move at all? Maybe it stands still and we're the ones moving about, making waves in it. Maybe we could even move backwards, somehow.'

Liz leans her elbow on the table and her hand on her chin. Her face is thoughtful, as if this is totally normal Sunday-lunch conversation. 'What an interesting way of putting it. I suppose you'd need a philosopher to answer that, really, but it's a nice thought in some ways, that everything that ever happened and everyone we've ever known is still there. But I don't think we can go back, no. I know – well, I know I've tried hard enough, worrying about things I wish I'd done better.'

'It's actually simpler than that,' Alan says from the other end of the table. His deep, slow voice falls into the conversation like a heavy stone that brings ripples of silence with it, as everyone pauses what they were saying to listen. 'Time is an aspect of space, as far as we can tell. It's real, and it's all around us all at once, so yes, in a way, you're right that everyone who's ever been and everything that ever happened is out there. Nothing's ever lost in that sense. Our experience of time passing is just . . . a sort of local effect, a peculiarity of our perception. But that doesn't mean time stands still, precisely. We're not insects trapped in amber. Everything is always *happening* all at once. You see, lass? The present isn't any different from the past or the future – that's just the way we see it. The past is not behind us. It's here, with us. That's why wormholes and time travel, theoretically, are possible.'

And then, having said his piece, he puts a roast potato in his mouth.

The Moonlit Maze

Nick's frowning, staring blindly out at the sea. 'So does that mean—'

'No, don't set him off again!' Jess laughs. 'Come on, why don't you tell me about how things are going on your course?'

Everyone slides gently back to their previous chatter. Liz reaches over and tips the last couple of the roast potatoes onto my plate. 'Our Alan's a physics teacher, in case you hadn't guessed. That was probably more than you were really wanting to hear, though.'

'No. It's interesting,' I say, perhaps a bit too fervently. Because . . . if I'm interpreting what Alan said right, then it's not only the future that can change. It's not only the past influencing the present; what we do and say and think in this moment could actually carry *in both directions*. And that would explain . . . well, not everything, but it would make the tiniest bit of sense of what I've been going through, how it could be possible for me to connect to Xanthe, and her to me.

It would mean I was right. What I felt. She's not a ghost. She's really still out there. Separated from me by time, like people can be separated by physical distance, but as alive and real as she ever was. Just as capable of changing the future. Her future.

So maybe. If I could just get her to hear me in my dreams, the way I can hear her. Maybe.

I could save her.

☽◯☾

Later, after we've eaten slabs of a massive homemade Victoria sponge – supplied, I'm told, by Alan – and I've spent a little bit of time sitting cross-legged with Nick on the floor next to the coffee table, helping Liz's grandchildren to construct a terrifyingly complex 3-D puzzle, I end up back in the kitchen with Liz.

'You can never go back to guest status now, I'm afraid,' she tells me cheerfully as I hand her the rinsed pots to stack in her dishwasher. 'Only family helps with the dishes.'

I try to return some light answer. It won't come. I clear my throat, turn my face away, but she's seen. She makes a little clucking noise of concern, rubs my arm with one damp hand, but doesn't say anything, for which I cannot even express how grateful I am. After a couple of minutes – punctuated by shouts from the living room that are probably to do with some variety of sport – I manage to get myself together.

'I – I actually wanted to ask you some things. About . . . I mean, about family.'

It's been bothering me, what Nick told me about Tom Marten. About the local rumours, the gossip, that Tom started the fire. Pikestaff's pamphlet didn't mention that and I just can't believe it's true. But before I can work out how to ease into the topic, Liz completely derails me by saying: 'About your dad? I thought you might.'

I gape at her, and then my brain kicks into gear, my jaw unhinges and the question jumps out. 'Did you know him?'

'Only a little bit, I'm afraid. I would have been about twenty-two – yes, because I was expecting Jess – when Anne brought him home. He was maybe ten then, I think. Oh, I'm getting ahead of myself. You know that Anne was his aunt? Have you wondered about why she raised him?'

'Yes, I have. Ma said he was orphaned. What happened to all the rest of his – to all the rest of our family?'

'The extended family? I don't know. I do know that Anne and her sister – that was Meredith, your grandmother – were very close at one point. And then, this won't be nice to hear, but she got into a relationship with a man who was . . . well, reading between the lines of what Anne told me, he was controlling. Even violent. Anne tried to get Meredith to leave, and I think she did a few times, but she always went back to him, your grandfather.'

'That's horrible.'

'Yes, and then it got worse, because she got pregnant and he insisted that they get married and that Meredith cut Anne off. Which she did, for years and years. Then . . . Anne told me that Meredith died of an infection. Something that ought to have been easily treated. And her husband just picked up and left. Left Stephen behind there in the rented house, all alone. Thank God the neighbours got worried and called the police.

'The poor little boy ended up in care, lost, for over a year before they tracked Anne down. Can you imagine? Not even knowing what his home life was like before, but then to have his mum die and his father abandon him. When he came here, he was like a small ghost. He didn't speak for weeks.' She looks up from popping in a dishwasher tablet and her face changes. 'Oh, Jude! Quick, sit down, here.'

Lightheaded, I wobble my way to the dining chair Liz pulls out and sit down with a thump. 'I'm OK. I'm OK. I'm not going to faint or anything.'

'You're shaking. I'm so sorry, love, I didn't think. You've never heard any of this before. I shouldn't have just dumped everything on you. Do you want a—'

I burst into jagged laughter, hiding my face in my hands,

hiding the tears that squeeze out against my will. 'I can't drink any more tea.'

'Are you all right?'

Foster care. Left behind like luggage by his own dad. A dad who had hurt his mother and isolated her and maybe even stopped her getting medical treatment that she needed, causing her death. Maybe he had hurt Stephen too. Maybe that was what Stephen and my mother had in common, the thing that drew them together at college, even if he didn't tell Ma everything – that they had both been abandoned. Maybe that was why . . . what had Mr Swan said? 'Stephen was adamant that you and your mother would be better off without him.'

Oh, Dad. Oh, Dad, you *idiot*. We weren't better off without you. Not ever.

'I'm all right. Or I think I will be,' I say after a moment, trying to discreetly wipe my face. Of all the days to put on mascara. Liz silently passes me a bit of kitchen roll, and I take it gratefully. 'Thanks for telling me. I'm glad I asked. I think I understand him a bit better now.'

The hairline cracks inside me, the ones that I was too stubborn to ever admit to, the ones that have always been lurking there ready to shatter, even since before Ma died, feel as if they're beginning to heal a little. The carefully saved photo album started the process. This might be enough to finish it. I needed to know. I had to know, even though it's awful. But it aches.

I sniffle, then on impulse I look up at Liz and ask her something else that's been bothering me. 'Liz, I'm not offended or anything – and no offence to you, either – but that first day when you were showing me the house and Nick came in . . .

what was going on there? I felt like there was a weird vibe, almost as though . . . you didn't want Nick making friends with me? But you've been so good to me. I can't work it out.'

She looks surprised, then resigned. 'I hoped you hadn't noticed that.'

With a sigh, she pulls out a chair at the table next to me, easing herself into it wearily. I know she's a decade older than my own parents would be, but this is the first time she's seemed older. Tired.

'It wasn't anything to do with you, darling – don't think that. It's just that Nick is one of life's fixers. Do you know what I'm talking about? Ever since he was a kid, he would come running to me with unfledged birds that had fallen out of nests or hedgehogs that had got run over, asking me to help him nurse them back to health. If there was another child at school who was being left out, Nick would go and make friends with them, even if they picked their nose or peed their pants.'

I let out a little snort of laughter, and after a second Liz joins me, guiltily. She turns her gaze to the glass doors, where the iron-grey sea is thrashing under the clouds.

'He takes responsibility. He can't help it – it's just how he's always been, and it's not necessarily a bad thing. But after his father died . . . well, things were rough for a while, and he struggled. He couldn't fix it. Couldn't make us . . . whole. Since then, he's sometimes had a problem giving people space. If it had been up to him, he'd have camped out at your house to make sure you didn't have nightmares.' She huffs at my expression. 'Well, exactly. And, honestly, I didn't want him to scare you off. I didn't think you needed him swooping in. That's all it was, love.'

I nod, then – feeling brave – I put my hand over one of hers and close my fingers round it. 'Thank you.' *Thank you for everything.*

She smiles, then leans in. 'I know you said no more tea, but there's a couple of slices of that cake left in the tin. What do you say?'

I push my chair back. 'I'll put the kettle on.'

☽◯☾

'I didn't grow up there, you know,' Nick says, out of the blue.

'Hmmm?' I blink myself out of a half-doze and look at him enquiringly.

We're nearly home – nearly at Anne's house, I mean – and the ride's taken place mostly in restful quiet, since both of us are full of good food and tired out from playing with the kids. The rain hasn't come on yet, but it must soon. It's not even six, and the evening's as black as night.

'We lived in a terrace on Cornick Street. Dad was a bricklayer and Mum had her little cleaning business. It was only after Dad died ... He had a heart attack. He was clearing out the gutters, and he fell. He might have survived the attack, but he didn't survive landing on the paving slabs.'

'Nick. I'm so sorry.'

He shakes his head, shrugs it away. 'He had insurance, right? Not a huge policy, but just what they could afford, just in case. The insurance company tried to get out of it. They said that he killed himself. Mum had to take them to court. She had to sell the house to do it. We ended up living in Alan's place up in Durham for a bit. We didn't have anywhere else to go, but it was only a two-bed flat and he and his boyfriend broke up over it. So he was heartbroken. We were grieving. It was the shittiest time. Anyway, in the end Mum won, and they were ordered to pay compensation. It was enough to pay for the new house, and get Meg and Ben started with their farm. Now Mum runs the cleaning business almost like a charity, jobs for people who are struggling, because we struggled, and we know what it feels like.'

He pulls up outside the cottage and we sit in silence for a minute, both of us looking at the headlights shining on the trees and hedgerows. Nick's face is almost invisible in the gloom, only a thin line of gold limning his profile, but I don't need to see it to imagine how he's feeling; I feel a little bit sick myself at the idea of relating all my history, laying my most painful and tragic wounds out to anyone like that.

But he did it. Like Liz said, he's a fixer. He realised I was uncomfortable there, at the Fairley house, and he realised why. So he's trying to fix it.

'Thanks for telling me.' It's not enough, just words. I snap off my seat belt and lean over the gearstick. I want to – I don't know – touch him, show him what it means that he shared that – rub his arm, the way his mum did mine—

I don't, though. Because Nick's hand is reaching for mine through the shadows, at the exact same moment. Warm, callused fingers close round my wrist just a little too tightly – he doesn't know about my bruises – drawing me closer. The rustling of his jacket reaches my ears and then his shoulder is there and it feels so natural for me to lean on it. His face is next to mine. His hair brushing my forehead. Breath warm on my cheek. Our lips meet.

Twenty-Six

Xanthe, summer 1924

Xanthe peeled off her sandy, doggy clothes, brushed her hair – removing a spray of sticky burrs that had somehow ended up embedded behind her left ear – washed her face and hands and pulled on a respectable dress. She arrived at the bottom of the grand staircase ten minutes after leaving Ellen, only slightly red-faced and out of breath. In one hand, she was clutching a book that she had picked at random from her bedside table, in order to have an excuse for being late. She quickly checked the title: *The Mysterious Affair at Styles*.

When she walked into the Pink Saloon her excuses died on her tongue unspoken; it was clear they hadn't missed her. Jonathan was keeping Lord and Lady Kearsley so well entertained that none of them even looked up when she pushed open the door. She ignored the familiar pang, and drew on her brightest smile.

'Hello! How long have you been home? How are you?'

Her father, correct as always, pushed himself to his feet. Jonathan followed behind a moment later. Xanthe resisted the urge to try to wave her father back down. To her eye, he looked no better than he had when he'd left, still grey and hollow in the cheeks, with that new hunch in his shoulders. She'd never thought she would learn to hate the sight of her gift, the cane, so much.

Despite her worries, Lord Kearsley's eyes were twinkling with good humour and when she instinctively reached out towards him, he caught and pressed her hand, unusually demonstrative. 'Don't worry, I've only just been washed ashore. And I've brought you a surprise, look!'

He indicated Jonathan, who stepped in to kiss her on the cheek. He managed to brush the corner of her mouth with his. She jerked away, disguising the movement with an inelegant bump down onto the edge of the chesterfield sofa. Jonathan raised an eyebrow, then sprawled out gracefully beside her, nudging her ankle with his toe. She forced herself not to react, instead fixing her gaze on her father as he eased himself back down beside her mother.

'I notice you didn't answer my other question, Papa. What did the doctors in London say?'

Lord Kearsley sighed, but Caroline beamed. 'All tests were negative. A touch of angina and a touch of overexertion. They've given him orders to rest. That's all.'

'That's all?' Xanthe couldn't quite keep the doubt from her voice, and from the corner of her eye she saw her father's expression darken.

'They've given me some more blasted pills and threatened me with house calls if I don't take them,' he interrupted testily. 'I am not an invalid. I'll thank you not to talk over my head!'

'Unless the doctors shrank you, I think the ladies would

have to grow quite a few inches before they were capable of that,' Jonathan said, swinging his foot lazily.

Lord Kearsley shook his head, then gave a wry chuckle. 'Oh, very well, then. Stop bristling at me, Xanthe, and I shall do the same.'

'I wasn't aware that I was,' Xanthe said quietly. 'I was just worried about you. We all were.'

'Speak for yourself, cuz. I knew he was fit as a fiddle. Dr Miller is a fussy old woman.' There was a viciousness to the last sentence that made Xanthe and Caroline both look at him uneasily. Xanthe remembered the mention in one of her mother's letters that Miller had tried to treat Jonathan when he first came back from the front, and Jonathan had threatened to bash in his teeth, or some other ridiculous threat. She also remembered the grave worry on the doctor's face after her father's attack. Xanthe didn't think he was the overly fussy type.

'There's really no need to pester your father any further,' Caroline said quickly. 'He's had the all-clear and now we can focus on other things, like the Summer Ball. I'm so looking forward to it this year, aren't you? Alfred, do you think we should make the effort to invite the Bradshaws again?'

Xanthe's hands, clasped neatly on her lap, tightened slowly into a knot. There was a sustained note of tension vibrating through her; she didn't know what it was, but something wasn't right. She looked longingly at the French doors as Caroline and Alfred and occasionally Jonathan picked over the details of the Summer Ball. Jonathan nudged at her ankle again, a look of mocking enjoyment on his face. She kept her expression immobile and didn't let herself edge away from him.

'Do you think you brought anything suitable home from Paris, Xanthe?' Caroline asked.

Xanthe swiftly ran the conversation back in her mind and realised Caroline was talking about clothes.

'Nothing floor length, but if you're inviting anyone under the age of forty I imagine I won't be the only one daring to flash her ankles,' she said, trying to sound mildly interested instead of desperate to avoid being dragged away from Winterthorne to London for dress fittings. 'That green dress with the beading you liked so much, perhaps. I'll need to get some shoes dyed to match.'

'Daring. The next thing you know she'll be refusing to wear plumes in her hair . . .' Jonathan said, examining his nails.

She allowed herself a glare. 'It's a party, not my presentation to the queen!'

'We shall have to see what Pinchbeck says about that.' Caroline sounded amused.

'I rather think I am *de trop* for the remainder of this conversation,' said Lord Kearsley, heaving himself to his feet. He seemed to waver for a moment, and Xanthe saw the effort it took her mother to keep her smile in place.

'Are you going up to rest before dinner, dear?'

'No, I am not,' he said forcefully. 'I have called Mr Ogilvy to deal with all the estate affairs that have been piling up while I wasted my time in London! The mere thought of the mess he'll have made of things in my absence is enough to cause nightmares.'

There was a faint wheeze in his voice by the time he finished. Caroline's smile was ghastly. Beside Xanthe, Jonathan's gaze had taken on an eerie, faraway blankness.

'We'll see you at dinner then, Papa,' Xanthe said, perhaps not brightly enough, but it was the best she could do. 'Don't work poor Ogilvy too hard.'

He gave a faint, perfunctory chuckle, and went from the room. Outside somewhere a blackbird trilled, the note rising and falling in a piercing, liquid refrain. It went on and on, and then abruptly petered out, leaving silence.

Caroline cleared her throat, smoothed her dress down over the bony shapes of her knees then stood. 'Well. Your father may be indefatigable, but I should have a little lie-down, I think. Do keep chatting, won't you, darlings? It's so nice to see you getting on so well.'

She drifted off, patting Jonathan gently on the cheek as she passed.

Xanthe wished the blackbird would start up again. She reached for her book, but found that Jonathan's hand was resting firmly on top of it as he leaned towards her. He gave her an amused look, eyebrow raised.

'Not running away so soon, my dearest? It's been an age since we spent any time alone.'

He would like nothing more than some kind of childish tug of war, she was sure. She consigned the book to the past and sat back, crossing her arms. 'Must you always communicate at the level of a twelve-year-old, Jonathan?'

'A gentleman must attempt to please his company,' he said, still smiling.

'You're insinuating that the women you've been trying to marry for the past five years is a child. I don't think that's quite the slight to me you intended.'

A faint spark of temper lit his eyes. 'Not all women can

hope to match Aunt Caroline's maturity and graciousness, regardless of age.'

'And now you're implying that you'd rather marry my mother than me.' She raised her hands and clapped three times, the sound echoing around the room. 'Well done. So witty.'

For an instant, she thought that he was going to fly into one of his tempers, storm from the room, as he had so often when he was 'courting' her. Then he lifted his hand from the top of the book and resumed his previous sprawl across the sofa. 'Put your claws away, sweetheart. If you wanted your filthy potboiler back that badly, all you had to do was ask.'

Xanthe was suddenly so tired of him – of both of them, of this snide dance of veiled meanness – that she could have burst into tears. She nearly gave in to the urge to pick up the novel and fling it into his face. Instead, she shook her head, looking away to the garden again.

'What do you actually expect to gain from going along with this farce? How do you imagine this will end? If Father got his way and I agreed to marry you, the result would be misery for both of us.'

Jonathan's low chuckle was unnervingly like her father's. 'Do *you* actually imagine that happiness is the point of marriage, for people like us? Or are you so naïve as to think that if you can see me off you'll be free to gallop into the sunset with your dirt-stained gardener's boy?'

Slowly, so slowly she felt each individual muscle of her neck crack and strain, she turned her head to stare at him. 'I beg your pardon?'

He blinked at her contentedly, like a cat. 'I'm afraid you haven't been quite as discreet as you believed. These things come with experience, but a word to the wise: a hotel in Bournemouth is the usual trysting place, not the family estate. You might also consider the consequences to the livelihood of your little friend's family, should word get out. They all work for us, directly or indirectly, you know. And Uncle Alfred's temper is so uncertain these days.'

Xanthe couldn't supress her disgust this time. She met Jonathan's gaze and held it. 'I often wondered who it was, all those years ago, who slunk around spying on us, then went running to my parents with stories about my spending time with Tom and Sally, and convinced my father to send me off to that second-rate boarding school. I thought it must have been some sad busybody with a dirty, nasty little mind. And, apparently, it was. Just when I thought I couldn't despise you more.'

She had never dared speak to him so plainly before. A snarl pulled at the corner of his lip before he forced it back into a smirk. 'We've already established that you have low tastes.'

Xanthe remembered the drunken flailings, the fights, the local scandals he had caused, and let out a scornful laugh as she rose to her feet. 'I think we both know I'm not the one with low tastes, Jonathan.'

Before she could move, he was on his feet. Hands clamped painfully around her upper arms, and alcohol-scented breath gusted hot over her face. She barely had the chance to make out the look of savagery twisting his mouth, the dilated pupils that turned his eyes black before he shook her viciously. 'What do you mean by that? Who's been tattling to you? Who?'

He shook her again, harder. And then, as if he couldn't help himself, he did it again. He didn't ask any more questions; there was no way she could have answered. Her feet scrambled at the floor, trying to regain balance. Her fingers clawed involuntarily at his sleeves. She couldn't even get the air to cry out as her head snapped back and forth. The world dissolved into silver mist before her eyes.

Xanthe had disliked Jonathan and the future he represented. She had never truly been afraid of him until now. As she felt the blood vessels breaking in her arms where he crushed the skin, felt her neck and skull grind and crack, she knew she had been a fool.

Her mother had warned her.

Years ago, in her letters, and again when Xanthe came home. They couldn't keep housemaids at Kearsley Castle. The girls kept leaving. Even when threatened with no references. Even when, like Ellen, their own parents abandoned them.

The. Maids. Just. Wouldn't. Stay. Since. The. War.

Her heel dug into the carpet. For a second, she had leverage. In a fever-hot burst of desperation Xanthe flung herself forward, hurling her full weight at Jonathan. She was only a little shorter than him; he stumbled, caught off-guard. The moment his hands loosened on her arms she clawed at him, feeling the searing in her fingertips as the cloth of his collar tore under her hands. She slapped, kicked, heard the harsh huff of his breath as at least one of her blows handed somewhere.

And then – at last, at last – she was able to suck in her breath. It burned all the way down into the bottom of her lungs, and then out into the air, a scream in a voice that didn't even sound like her own. 'Get your *hands off me*!'

He did.

'Steady – steady on now.' He lifted his hands, palms open, shocked out of his violence. Sweat glistened on his upper lip.

A trio of long, raw marks from her nails slashed down the side of his neck. His shirt was torn.

Xanthe backed away, wary. She wanted to go for the door, but didn't dare turn her back on him. She would never trust she was safe – not with him still in the room – ever again. She saw him realise that, and then realise how much he had given away. The danger he was in now. Would any of the servants, perhaps even her mother, come running to investigate her scream? Would anyone see what he'd done?

As Xanthe, lightheaded, staggered and caught hold of the arm of the sofa, Jonathan strode to the French doors, flung them open hard enough to crack one of the panes, and disappeared into the garden. She stayed upright, clinging to the leather of the sofa with her fingers curled into talons, until she heard an engine start, the wheels roaring away down the drive. Only then did she let herself fall onto the seat.

'Milady?' Bowdler asked from the doorway.

She wondered, had the butler waited, outside? For how long? Had he rehearsed in his mind what he would say? How to hit the perfect tone of unconcerned servility, as if he had heard nothing, guessed nothing – felt nothing?

'Milady, did you call?'

She didn't look up. After a few moments, the door clicked gently shut behind him.

Twenty-Seven

Jude, present day

It's nice. Kissing Nick. It's comfortable, and I feel . . .

He makes a little noise, a sort of purring rumble in his throat, the same noise he made when he took a bite of the Victoria sponge. A laugh bubbles inside me, and I feel his lips curve up too, against mine. It's nice. I feel—

We're both leaning slightly awkwardly over the gearstick. Nick shifts sideways, trying to get closer. My eyes open and I see that the windows are steaming up, which makes me realise how hot it's getting in here, how loud our breathing is in the enclosed cab of the truck. Then Nick's hand shifts, spreading across my back, and suddenly, vividly, I remember, exactly as if the memory was my own: Tom's hands on Xanthe's back when she was sixteen, that embrace she never wanted to end, the shimmering heat, the smell of roses and the sea . . .

A fierce, liquid pull goes through the centre of my body. I gasp, shudder. My left hand lands on Nick's thigh – I feel the warm, heavy muscle jump under my palm – and he kisses me harder, his tongue touching mine. But I'm not kissing him any more. I'm not me at all. I'm Xanthe, and those are Tom's hands on me, Tom's lips on mine, and in that instant, before I realise what's happening, I feel like fire.

My back collides with the window behind me as I jerk away from Nick, desperate to put space between his face and mine. I bring my hand up, then slap it down, clamping my hands together. I wanted to scrub at my mouth, erase the kiss from my lips.

'Jude?'

'Sorry. Sorry. I can't—'

'Are you OK?'

His voice is even, concerned. I can't see his face well, but I know that gentle look he'll be aiming at me. He's not even annoyed. I can't stand it.

'I'm not ready for this,' I blurt out. It's probably true, but it's also the only excuse I can think of that won't make me sound delusional. 'I – I like you – but I just got here – I don't—'

'Hey, hey! It's all right, I wasn't trying to—'

'No, I know, you're really nice, it's not you—'

'You don't have to make excuses—'

We talk over each other in a confused babble until we both just – stop. Then there's silence in the steamy dark of the truck, awkwardness crystallising between us. If I stay too long, it will freeze me in place.

'I had a nice time. I've got to go.'

I lunge at the door, forget how high the drop is from the truck to the ground, and nearly fall out onto the grass outside the cottage. I can hear Nick moving hurriedly behind me and there's some mad part of me that thinks if I can get myself through the gate of the cottage before he can get out of the truck I'll be – safe.

'Jude. You dropped this!'

My hand's on the gate. I turn back to see him standing a cautious distance away, his own hand extended. I can see better out here, see the worry he's trying to hide. A bit of paper dangles from his fingers. As I watch, he tilts his head in that curious little movement, and frowns down at it.

'Is this you? Did you draw this? It's . . . Oh.'

It's Aidan's drawing. It must have fallen out of my jeans pocket, where I forgot that I stuffed it earlier. And he's just seen the phone number scrawled at the bottom.

I don't owe him an explanation. Besides, Nick loathes Aidan, and, actually, if Aidan's been anywhere near as rude to the locals as he was to me when he nearly ran me over, then he probably deserves it, so talking about him is hardly going to improve the situation.

'I made a new friend. Down in the town,' I say casually. I reach for the bit of paper, still hanging on to the cottage gate with my other hand. Nick gives it up without a fight.

'So I guess you don't need me any more, then,' he jokes feebly. Hurt. I did that.

What am I doing right now?

I shove the paper back into my pocket without a glance, let go of the gate – fingers tingling from how tight my grip was – and grab his hand before it can fall.

'Nick. You're the first friend I made here, and . . . I'll never forget how good you've been to me. You're my favourite. OK? And even if we kissed – and then I got panicked and awkward about it – that will never not be true. Look, you know what I mean, right?'

There's a pause that goes on just long enough to make my

teeth ache. Then Nick lets out a snort of laughter, and his face, his whole frame, suddenly seems to relax. 'Yeah, I think so?' He gives my hand a friendly little shake. Then he says, 'Favourite except for my mum, obviously.'

'Obviously.'

He laughs again. 'OK, that's fair. See you later, then, Jude.'

☽○☾

It pierces through the silence, a knife in the shadows: the cry. That pleading, desperate cry, ringing out in the darkened woods. I cling to my pillows, burrow down under the duvet, try not to listen. I can't do this again. It's the middle of the night. It's just an animal, clearly, some animal that – that happens to make a sound that – that sounds like it's in pain. Like it's alone, and terrified, and needs help—

I stumble out of bed again, hurriedly dress in yesterday's clothes. Run down the stairs. And again, by the time I get to the door, the sound has died away, leaving me lost and filled with a sense of awful emptiness.

But this time I find something waiting for me on the doorstep. It's another flower, I realise, squinting blearily. A rose, the pink petals of the heavy bloom just beginning to unfurl. It reminds me of the one Jonathan gave Xanthe when she was sixteen, the one her mother pressed between the pages of a book. La Reine Victoria.

The third gift in a week, just laid there across the stone step. Maybe this is a collective 'Welcome to Winterthorne' effort from the whole town, like the big box of baked goods from Belle? But I don't really believe that. Exhausted, I decide to accept the offering and take it into the kitchen with me, where I plop it into the empty green glass jar, add a splash of water and put it on the windowsill. I had to throw the forget-me-nots away yesterday; they'd withered.

There's no point going back to bed. I put the kettle on, surrendering to the cliché, though it's a large mug of instant coffee I make this time, not tea. I defiantly add two spoonfuls of sugar and eat the remaining cookies from the farmer's market while slumping wearily over the table.

It's time to have a long, hard think about what's been going on since I arrived here in Winterthorne. What I've seen and felt. What it means. And what I'm supposed to do about it. I'm going to rationally examine this whole experience and make some sense of everything, because if I don't and weird, extraordinary things keep happening to me like this, I'm going to lose my grip. I can feel it starting to happen now, exacerbated by lack of sleep: the sliding sensation of unreality. Dreams that might be real. Visions when I'm awake. Screaming in the night. Flowers at my door . . .

I wake up four hours later with a crick in my neck and a numb backside. The kitchen fills with the sounds of my groaning as I *crack-crunch-crack* my way upright, off the table and out of the seat, and then attempt to stretch the aches away. Even though I seem to have completely zonked out, I don't feel the slightest bit rested. The day outside is ominously dark and gloomy, the heavy, swollen clouds tinting the light a strange yellowish shade. It's muggy, and everything feels faintly damp even though the rain hasn't come yet. I'm tempted to go straight back to bed.

As I slope wearily over to the counter to wash my mug,

and then the eight teaspoons that appear to have bred in the bottom of the sink, my eyes absent-mindedly latch on to the rose, drooping over the edge of the green jar. In the warmth of the house the flower has begun to open, flattening out into a deep cup shape. There's ... wait a moment. What is that? A glint of something bright in the centre, almost concealed by the frills of the petals.

Gently, with two fingers, I part the velvety swirl of purple-pink. Driven deep into the golden centre of the rose is a jagged shard of glass. I swallow hard.

Without looking away from the rose, I reach up to open the overhead cupboard where the mugs live. It's where I hid the pot of honey that I was too suspicious to eat, but not quite suspicious enough to throw away unopened. I grope around until I find it, then wrench the lid off and shove the jar into the sink, turning on the hot water. The honey is the pale, set kind. The stream of water pouring into the jar takes a moment to begin to eat away at it. But, as it does, something dark is revealed, hidden at the centre.

It's bees. Dead bees. Dozens of fragile little corpses spilling up out of the pot like a dark tide, flooding the sink. Death everywhere. I slam the tap off with one hand and back away, breathing through my mouth; the sweet stink of the melting honey is sickening.

That posy of forget-me-nots. Innocent-looking little flowers with an ambiguous meaning: devotion and death.

They were never gifts. Right from the start. They were threats.

Jude. Don't be afraid. That's what Belle said. What was she warning me about?

The Moonlit Maze

I look around at the kitchen. It's unfamiliar, filled with shadows that are too deep, too secretive. I don't know the nooks and crannies, what might be hiding in the backs of the darkest cupboards. I don't know who else might have a spare key to the door. I don't know this place at all. This house, this town. These people. I've let myself be fooled. I let myself think it was safe. But it isn't. I'm not.

It all hits me at once. What I've refused to admit to myself: how dangerous it is, what's been happening to me, these dreams and memories and visions. Why did I let myself get sucked into them in the first place? Caring about Xanthe, empathising with her? Even if any of it is real, if she is, I don't know her. She's nothing to do with me. I nearly died letting her into my head. Nearly threw myself right off the edge of the sea wall because I was *hallucinating* – and I was still trying to think of ways to help her. And help Aidan, even more of a stranger. Help anyone but myself. Why? What's the matter with me? When did I turn off my common sense?

When did I decide to try to be Juliet again?

There's a reason I started going by the name Jude. Juliet was my mother's little girl. Juliet thought she was tough, but that was a laugh; she'd never been alone for a day in her life. She was idealistic, soft. Gullible and stupid. Romantic, exactly like the name sounds. Jude was hard, and cynical, and angry, and maybe that's not what Ma would have wanted for me. But Jude is the one who survived.

It's time for Jude to be in charge again.

I made the decision to come here, to see the place, to find out about my family if I could. Well, all right. I've done it, haven't I? I've found out more than I knew there was to know, maybe even more than I wanted to. There's nothing else here for me. So why am I still hanging about, being polite to people's relatives, trying not to hurt anyone's feelings? Why am I putting myself through any of this?

It's time to stop dancing around in forests and pottering in this cottage like some deranged cartoon princess, and go home. Back to London, where I've never experienced a single delusion, and no one is stalking me.

Back to reality.

Twenty-Eight

Xanthe, summer 1924

They weren't going to believe her. She knew without considering it for more than a second. Or at least, if she showed them her arms – already throbbing – and told them Jonathan had been responsible, they might believe that. But her parents would never believe that he had hurt her on purpose, that he was ... what he was. They would make excuses. Make up stories, just as they had been doing ever since he came back from the front. That he loved her and he was only human, that she had provoked him, that he had got carried away. It wasn't his fault. He didn't mean to. It didn't count.

No one blamed Xanthe, of course, but really, after treating him so cavalierly, what had she expected ...

Just be nicer to him, and maybe he'll give you a present.

Mother must suspect, Xanthe thought. She *must*. Caroline wasn't stupid; she ran this place, she knew what happened within its walls, and Finch knew, of course – all the servants knew, and knew to turn their eyes away and keep their mouths shut. But Caroline would die before she admitted it to herself, wouldn't she? Her father had already accepted that the drunkenness and fights were inevitable, the price to pay for having Jonathan alive and here instead of interred in the family mausoleum with all the other Winter boys.

They would cover his debts and cover up his scandals, arrange flowers and plan balls and complain about how difficult it was to keep the staff these days and lie to themselves and everyone else, and they would pin a white veil in place over Xanthe's bruises with their own hands and deliver her to Jonathan with a smile, if that was what it took to keep the lie alive.

The only way her parents would ever accept her, love her, was if she joined in. If she lied for Jonathan too. That was the price she had to pay.

'No,' Xanthe whispered, lifting her head to look out at the long, green sweep of the lawn, at the sun glinting on the white ripples of the sea beyond. 'No more.'

☽○☾

It took a while for her legs to stop wobbling and her hands to still. For her chest to loosen enough so that she could breathe full breaths again. When she was sure that she was steady on her feet, she went into the hallway, where the brass and Bakelite telephone gleamed on its stand. She picked up the handset, tested the signal, and heard the operator's voice crackle to life.

A discreet shuffling noise behind her. 'Can I help, milady?'

'You can give me some privacy, Bowdler. Thank you.'

She waited for him to leave, then lifted the telephone up close to her mouth so she could speak quietly. 'Hello. I need to be connected to Braithewaite and Carlisle's in Winterthorne, please.'

It only took a few moments for her to get through to the solicitor's down in the village, and be passed on to the head typist there. A few moments more to say what she needed to say.

'That's fine, milady. I'll be sure to pass on the message,' Sally said, brisk and correct – people would be listening, of course – but with an audible smile. Tom must have told her that he and Xanthe had been . . . talking again.

'I won't have caused any problems by ringing you at work?' Xanthe asked.

'No, not at all. Thank you for letting me know. Goodbye.'

Xanthe hung on the line just long enough to hear the faint echo of Sally's unconcerned voice saying, 'Just some business for the estate . . .'

She took a deep breath as she replaced the phone and hung up the handset. Footsteps rang sharply on the tiles behind her – she jerked round in sudden alarm, but it was only Ogilvy, his document case under his arm, with one of the footmen. He looked worn out and faintly shamed, as always after a meeting with her father. Xanthe empathised.

'How nice to see you, Mr Ogilvy. Is my father still in his office? Good.'

She dodged the usual pleasantries with a smile, slipped past them and made her way to her father's study, where she pushed open the door without knocking.

'Did you forget something— Oh, Xanthe.'

Her father returned his attention to his papers, his pen moving in elegant loops. 'Has your mother sent you to chivvy me into resting?'

'No. I need to talk to you.' She took the seat opposite him, crossed her legs and waited for the silence to prickle. It took several moments. She counted the throbbing of her bruises, rubbing absently at her sore neck. Finally, the movement of his pen began to slow. He sighed.

'I am rather busy, my dear.'

'This shouldn't take long.'

His eyes – the same shade as Xanthe's – narrowed. He capped his pen, folded his arms across the piled papers, and inclined his head, taking on the familiar mantle of distant paternal patience. She'd always thought it was rather like having to deal with Moses.

'I would like an explanation. Why are you attempting to force me to marry my cousin?'

The faintest flicker of unease crossed his face before annoyance and exasperation slotted into their places. 'Are we really going to rehash this tantrum again?'

'I'm afraid so – and you won't stop me talking by accusing me of hysterics this time.' She ignored the restive movements, the eyes rolling up to the heavens, simply raised her voice over his attempted interruption and rolled on. 'However, what's really important is this: I will not marry Jonathan. I never wanted to marry him, and even he admits that we would not be happy together. Now, as you've assured me that there's nothing medieval about this arrangement, that should be the end of it.'

'Should it, indeed?' He sighed again, weariness personified. 'And what, may I ask, do you intend to do with yourself after you have broken your engagement and publicly humiliated your cousin? Run off to Prague or Russia or perhaps the

Antipodes this time? I meant what I said, Xanthe. If you do this you will have no allowance from me.'

She drew in and then exhaled a long sigh through her nostrils. 'Well, that will make things harder. But I'm sure I'll make do somehow – everyone else who lives out there in the big wide world manages it. You can tell all your friends that your daughter is a shopgirl. Won't that be fun.'

His mouth worked, patience beginning to evaporate. 'Don't be ridiculous. You're acting like a spoiled child.'

'And you're acting like a tyrant. You can't actually think that Jonathan's breaking his heart over me—'

'You stupid girl! It has nothing to do with Jonathan!'

Xanthe stared at her father. He stared back, frozen, mouth still half open as he absorbed his own admission.

'Papa, until you give me an explanation, one I can actually believe, I will not be getting out of this chair. And, please, no more lectures on honour, responsibility, duty. I have no intention of being preached at by someone who has been *lying straight to my face.*'

The last words came out with a whiplash of rage, with that strange flat intonation that she didn't recognise as her own voice. She watched him flinch, then flush, the pallor of his face taking on an almost purple blotchiness across the cheeks. To her eyes now, the battle between his outrage at her rudeness, and the realisation that she wasn't going to budge, that she wouldn't be belittled or dismissed this time, was visible.

'I am not used to being spoken to like this.'

She settled back, folded her hands. Met his eyes. 'Tell me the truth.'

He raised one hand to his mouth, the fingers clenched.

Behind it, he swallowed – she heard the dry click. The line of his shoulders didn't slump. There was no other visible sign of distress.

At last, he spoke. 'The estate is badly off.'

It had not been what she was expecting to hear. 'How badly off?'

A tiny, bitter chuckle, reminding her painfully of Jonathan. 'Very. You accuse me of lying to you? Well, my dear, I'm afraid it's got to be a habit of mine over the last decade. I'm forced to lie to the bank, to our creditors. To our friends. The estate is bleeding money. This house is bleeding money. The roofs are on the verge of collapse, the kitchens are damp, the foundations on the north side are unsafe, I've had to have the orangery closed off because the gas pipes are probably leaking – and I can't afford repairs because none of the local tradesmen will give us credit any more. We are, to put it bluntly, on the verge of bankruptcy.'

Xanthe swallowed down the questions that wanted to bubble out of her: how, why, what? They would have to be asked, but at this moment they were only distractions, and he probably hoped that they would divert her. It wouldn't work. She would not be diverted.

'And in what way is this . . . this disaster related to your –' *obsession* – 'determination that Jonathan and I should marry?'

He reshuffled papers, rearranged the pen and inkwell. Xanthe felt her brows crimping as a suspicion twinged at the back of her mind. 'Is there some way that . . . ? Is there some financial advantage—'

'You are a wealthy young woman.'

He made it sound as if it were obvious, some fact she had stupidly forgotten. She had not forgotten anything.

'Am I? And this is the first I've heard of it because . . . ?'
'The money is in trust.'
'What trust? From whom? Why don't I know about it?'
'There was no need for you to know. Your maternal grandmother left her fortune, everything that remained after your mother's dowry payment, to Caroline's children. If boys, the money would be paid when they had their twenty-first birthday. If girls, they would receive it at the age of thirty-five, or—' He took a breath as if to say more, then pressed his lips closed.

'At the age of thirty-five – or when they married,' she finished for him.

Xanthe's head rocked back and she stared up at the ceiling. Wanting to imagine that he wasn't there just for a moment. Needing to feel that she was alone as every sharp, jagged little piece of the puzzle of her life fell into place.

'*Of course.* And when I do marry, my money will become legally my husband's. So once the estate got into trouble you needed me married off as quickly as possible. But only to someone who would take my inheritance from me, and spend it the way you told him to.'

'Kearsley is our home, Xanthe. Our family's estate, our legacy. It's everything we have, and all we have.'

She came out of the seat in a rush, noting her father startle. 'Kearsley is Jonathan's! Not a single stick or stone of this place can ever be mine – that's what the entail says. And that's why you lied to me, isn't it? Why you and Mother never said a single word to me about Grandmother's money. Because you wanted that to be Jonathan's too, and I might have felt that I had a right to it. Were you ever even going to tell me, or would you have just had me sign some mysterious papers and then—'

'For God's sake, it's not a matter of *stealing* anything from you! I am trying – Jonathan and I were trying – to preserve our home, our name! It's my duty, your duty, every member of our family's duty to protect the Kearsley holdings and pass them on to the next generation.'

'How noble!' she jeered. 'Let me ask you this: in your quest to preserve our family's legacy, did you consider ... cutting down on parties? On staff? Selling Jonathan's car or the townhouse in London?'

The blotchy flush rose to his cheeks again. 'We auctioned some of the land.'

'I'll bet. The worst bits. Very, very quietly.'

'If we start retrenching, selling our assets, the bank – our creditors – they'll realise how badly off we are and come demanding immediate payment.'

'How terrible – people would talk. Much simpler and less unpleasant to take your daughter to the church, and then the cleaners.'

'No!' He hit his hand on the desk – a flat, unimpressive thud that barely made the inkwell tremble, but it was enough to interrupt the flow of her fury, and he leapt into the opening, voice softening. 'Xanthe, this is your home. It doesn't belong to you in law; there's nothing I can do about that. But it still belongs to you, as one of the family, by right. It *is* yours. When you were a girl, you would go out walking for hours, through the woods and the fields and by the sea. You would come home with stories from every corner of the estate, everything you had seen and everyone you had met. There wasn't a corner of this house you didn't explore. Would you really want to see it all gone? The farmers thrown off the land that their people have worked for generations, the fields turned into cheap little housing estates, this place bulldozed or made into a ... a hotel?'

'No,' she admitted softly. 'No, of course not – it would break my heart.'

'Then surely you can—'

'But not as much as being married to Jonathan would.'

'I – Perhaps ... it needn't – there might be some talk, but if you truly don't want to marry Jonathan, maybe we could find someone else – if they would agree, beforehand, to sign the trust over ...'

She stared at him, and after a moment the torrent of words dried up and a look of defeat came over his face. He nodded, his head sagging down wearily. 'I see. Yes, that is the problem, the place where we differ. If our ancestors had not been willing to fight and struggle and sacrifice for this place all the way back to William the Conqueror, none of it would be here. We wouldn't be here. I've always felt we owe it to them, and to the generations that come after, to do what needs to be done. Whatever needs to be done. I wish, how I wish you understood that.'

She did understand. That was what made it so awful. He was weary and pale, the flush long faded from his face. Sympathy and misgivings wanted to rise up – could she really see Kearsley Castle and the estate brought to ruin? – but she couldn't let them take hold. This was a mess not of her making. And she was so tired of being made to feel shamed and guilty over things that weren't her fault.

Resolution settled within her.

'I will not be your sacrifice. Or Jonathan's, either. You'll have to find another way.'

There was silence between them for long moments. Lord Kearsley's gaze rose and examined Xanthe. She stood still under his scrutiny, refusing to fidget or flinch. He would see that she meant it.

Eventually he spoke again. His voice was low, and each word seemed painful to him. 'It was a mistake to send you away, to boarding school. I realise that now. And to ... to try to ... manage you. Without telling you the truth.'

This was the closest thing to an apology she had ever had from him. She sat down on the edge of the seat again.

'Your mother and I have made many mistakes. We weren't prepared for you. We had stopped hoping, you see. By the time you arrived. Even when your mother was expecting you – we thought it would be like all the other times. After you were born, when you lived, it didn't seem real to us. I suppose we were so used to loss that we simply never stopped expecting it to come. I never quite let you in. In here.' He gestured at his chest. 'That was wrong of us. Of me. But to lose everything, everything I've spent my life trying to protect, that would be a harsh punishment indeed.'

Back to that.

She repeated: 'You'll have to find another way.'

'I don't have time.' He smiled, a crooked, thin expression. 'I lied to your mother and Jonathan too. I'm dying. My heart is shot; I won't make it past the end of the year, the doctors say. And when I'm gone the truth about our financial affairs will all come out. No help for it. Everything will be gone for good.'

The Moonlit Maze

At nine o'clock that night, after enduring the most painfully uncomfortable dinner – one where Jonathan's absence and Lord Kearsley's sagging face and her mother's helpless, pleading confusion made Xanthe want to pull her own hair out strand by strand, just to have something else to focus on – she threw her tweed travelling coat on over her evening dress and left the house.

The clear, bright day had led to a chilly night. She hugged the coat around herself, palms cupped gingerly over the bruises. The welts, mottled red, purple and near black against the white, untanned skin of her upper arms, had shocked her when she was dressing for dinner. She had had to put on her longest evening gloves to try to hide them; some still peeked over the top. But she needn't have worried. Her father, absorbed in his own tragedy, didn't notice. Her mother might have done, for all Xanthe knew, but, of course, she wouldn't, couldn't ask.

Xanthe trod cautiously over the lawn, walking on the balls of her feet in her heels, making for the entrance to the maze and the topiary owl. She had to hope that her cryptic message had made it to Tom, without being subject to Chinese whispers. She had to see him. He was the only one who could help.

The moon wasn't yet up; the sea was an opaque line on the horizon, seemingly unmoving in the dark, though she could hear its surging against the cliffs below. She could tell from the sound that it must be nearly high tide. It was a sound so familiar that it counted as a kind of silence to her ears. Everything else was quiet in the mothy, windless night.

Until it wasn't.

Xanthe heard the noise as rising wind at first. But the rose bushes, the hedges and wisteria, didn't stir. No breeze brushed at her face or tugged her hair, even as the sound grew louder. Louder. Drowning out the sea.

Rain. It was the sound of a downpour. But the sky was cloudless; she could see the stars. Bewildered, she held her hands out before her. Nothing.

'*Xanthe*.'

Her name rippled up, indistinct and echoing, as if through water. There was a shadow there, blocking Xanthe's path into the maze – a shadow, and then more than a shadow. A girl. The same girl Xanthe had glimpsed before, twice before now.

Her form seemed to shift, to distort and bend, there one moment, gone the next. The only part of the girl Xanthe could be sure of was her face, that intent, serious face. Dark hair drifted around it in a non-existent gale. Her eyes were fixed on Xanthe, and they were the colour of moonlight.

'What are you?' Xanthe breathed, the sounds of the rain almost drowning the thinness of her voice. 'Are you – are you a ghost?'

The figure didn't answer, but she lifted her hands, echoing Xanthe's own pose. Beckoning her closer.

Xanthe realised with astonishment that she wasn't afraid. She ought to be gibbering, she ought to have run away already. But there was no sense of menace, no threat. Xanthe's heels sank down into the grass as she stepped closer. 'What is it that you want?'

'*Fire*.' The word seemed to come with enormous effort. '*Warn. Time.*'

'What fire? I don't understand. What are you trying to tell me?'

The Moonlit Maze

The figure rippled again and the hands made an urgent, grasping gesture. Those pale eyes seemed to brighten, like the moon breaking through clouds. Rain blossomed in the shadow of the girl, shaking the hedge, pattering in the grass at Xanthe's feet. Xanthe felt the cool spray across her own face and hands and heard, somewhere impossibly distant and close at once, a deep rumble of thunder. As if the girl had brought a storm with her from . . . wherever she was.

'*Xanthe – listen!*'

Xanthe started. All at once she recognised that voice. She had heard it coming from her own lips as she screamed at Jonathan, shouted at her father. Impossible. 'Who – who are you?'

'*Don't be afraid—*'

Without thinking, Xanthe reached out. Her warm fingers brushed against human skin, chilled and damp, but real.

'Xan?'

There was a low, threatening rumble of thunder, a flare like lightning, bright enough to make her wince. Her eyelids snapped shut. Xanthe's fingers closed on nothing. When she opened her eyes again, the girl was gone. The shadow was gone. There was nothing there.

But her hands and face were wet.

'What's happened?' Tom stepped out from under the wisteria, face creased with concern. 'Are you all right? Sally said— Have you been crying?'

'No,' she whispered, touching her cheeks. 'No. You know I never cry.'

'Then how did your face get all wet?'

She drew in a deep breath, feeling it tremble in her lungs. 'I don't . . .' *I don't know*. No, she couldn't say that. He would ask more questions. *Fire. Warn. Time.* 'It doesn't matter. I . . . I need your help, Tom.'

'Of course, if I can. Come here. Good grief, you're freezing.' His fingers cupped her elbows, the heat of them burning through the wool of her coat. He drew her close, into the shelter of his body, and she realised she was shivering as his arms closed around her. 'Xan, just tell me.'

She swallowed hard, tried to pull herself together, remember why she had come out here in the first place. What she needed to do.

'I have to find someone, Tom. For my friend, Ellen. I need to find a woman called Heather Shackleford.'

Twenty-Nine

Jude, present day

I'm lucky: there's a signal on my phone. I email Mr Swan in London to let him know that I'd like to discuss putting the house on the market, and ask him to get back to me. I hesitate for a second, then send a quick text to Penny to see if her offer of a spare room is still open. No big deal if not, but I'd only need to stay for a few days, and it would speed things up. Plus, I find I'd quite like to see her. Just to see how things are going for her.

I start to pack. My clothes and toiletries don't take long to roll up into my case. I didn't bring very much. It's a bit of a squeeze to fit in the new art supplies. I find the leather sketchbook that Ma gave me all those years ago, and hold the cover up to my face; it hasn't offered the faintest trace of her perfume in years, but I love the smell of the leather anyway. I tuck it back tenderly in among my stuff. I don't know if I'll ever be able to open it, or use it, even now. But I'll never leave it behind.

Once my cases are stuffed full, I go into Stephen's room.

My dad's room. Even the blandest of his possessions mean something to me now. I gather up the precious photo album, his books, a couple of little bits and pieces, and lay them out on his bed. It's more than I ever had before.

Then I fetch my new hardback sketchpad, open it to a fresh page and start to make a list of the things in the house I want to take with me. All Anne's art, obviously, and the Japanese woodblock prints from the bedroom, the lovely big print of Rossetti's *The Beloved*, probably the Rackham illustrations . . . A practical little voice tells me that I ought to take the pictures down now and make a neat stack of them in my father's room too, where they won't be in the way. I can't quite get myself to do it, and I don't really want to examine why. The thought of the blank spaces on the walls just makes me cringe.

Anyway, first I'll have to go down into Winterthorne and buy some sturdy boxes and packing materials. Then, when Mr Swan gets back to me, I'll see if he can arrange a moving service, so I can take some of the furniture. I'll have to rent storage space until I find a permanent place, but I love Anne's bed, and the chair in the living room is really comfy too.

The little voice reminds me that the Fairleys would probably be happy to help me. Only I don't even want to think about how that conversation will go, telling Liz that I'm dismantling Anne's home, selling up and running for the hills. Or how Nick'll take it.

They'd be kind about it. They've always been kind.

I just can't face them. Not yet. Not now.

I pace around uneasily, forcing myself to mentally separate out and remove the contents of my house – Anne's house – and slot them into a new home, a new place, miles away from here. The problem is that *this* feels like home. It's only been a week, but I don't want to imagine being somewhere else any more.

Tough, says the little voice. Jude's hard, ruthless voice. You can't stay. Someone is stalking you here. You are losing your grip on reality here. This place is clearly no good for you, and the fact that you're getting all wobbly-lipped about it is an obvious clue that it's messed with your head too much already. You need to get out while the going's good.

I can't even argue with myself. It's true.

After I've dealt with my list for the kitchen and finished counting through pots and pans, I decide it's time to tackle the artist's studio, Anne's little cabin hidden in the back garden. I never did get around to exploring it. I told myself I had time. Well, time's run out now and, anyway, I've been drawing again lately, so there's nothing stopping me. I take the keys from the hook by the back door and go out.

It's only midday but the garden's hushed, dim as twilight, the air dense with a fuggy forest smell – rotting leaves, dampness, mushrooms. The silence of the trees seems pointed. Unfriendly. Even the birds are quiet, and I thought they never shut up around here.

The atmosphere almost sends me straight back indoors. I shake my head at myself. Marching determinedly down the paving-stone path, I don't hesitate when I get to the door, unlocking it with a brisk jingle of keys and pushing straight inside.

A gentle sigh of air greets me, scented with the same dry rose-petal scent that was in the bedroom when I first arrived. I haven't noticed it there for a while. I hit the light switch and then let out a sigh of my own. Maybe only another artist would get it, but this . . . this is a kind of heaven. I can physically feel the humming tension slip out of my bones, leaving me suddenly peaceful and relaxed.

The small space doesn't have too much in it. The peaked, white-painted ceiling makes it feel light and airy, and a small skylight floods everything with good, even light despite the gloomy day. A long, pale pine worktable, pushed under one window, is streaked and scarred with drips of ink, paint stains. Old jam jars and cracked mugs hold paintbrushes and pencils. A tilted draftsman's desk sits in the corner. Sketches and studies in all different mediums – pencil, pastels, watercolours – are pinned to the walls. At the back of the space, next to a sink, is a business-like metal shelving unit filled with boxes of different paper, charcoals and pens and paints, and a few well-used books on art history and technique. I can see the Post-Its and markers fanned through the pages. A tiny filing cabinet is topped with the bent furry finger of some kind of cactus, its blue-and-white pot the twin of the one that holds the African violet in the hallway of the cottage.

I move to the draftsman's table and sit down, running a reverent finger over the rough edge of the heavy watercolour paper pinned there. She was working on a prep sketch, a view I recognise: the curved line of the ancient steps winding down through the centre of Winterthorne with a few quick lines suggesting houses of different shapes and sizes on either side, and then, taking up the top half of the sketch, the bay, the new modern sea wall, and beyond that the jagged spires of rock, the Thorns, extending out from the headland. It's a fantastic sketch, conveying so much with just the careless flicks of Anne's pencil. The unfinished quality, the abundance of negative space, give it a dynamism, a sense of movement.

I wish I'd known her when she was alive, instead of just through these fragments she left me. I wish that I could stay and learn as much from the fragments as possible, instead of running away. I wish—

Outside in the preternatural quiet of the still day, the cry rings out.

The chair topples over as I leap to my feet. I don't waste time picking it up. I only stop to grab the bunch of keys; the big brass one is for the gate in the garden wall, Liz told me that, and also that the garden backs onto the woods. The sound is coming from the trees, I know it, and this time I'm going to find the source.

The gate – blistered green wood set in a pinkish brick wall – opens with a low, juddering creak that doesn't drown out the eerie cry when it shreds through the air again. The sense of urgency, of desperation, makes me fumble as I try to close it behind me. It won't shut – there's something caught under it, leaves or blown dirt. I leave it, like the chair. The scream drags me out.

I've never gone through the gate before. There's no path here. Underfoot, the ground is rutted and rough, and my boots don't have much grip on the damp leaf mould. I nearly stumble down a little dip, catching myself on a thick, spiralling tree branch that's low enough to sit on. The trees are strange shapes, bent and twisted, their roots sticking up out of the mossy ground in tentacle loops, just waiting to catch my feet as I pass. Xanthe would know what kinds of trees they are; I have no idea. I'm too busy forcing my way through as quickly as I can, running whenever there's a couple of clear steps, feeling twigs and whippy stems catch at my hair and clothes as I go. The cry comes again, urgent, irresistible, tugging at something down deep in my chest.

Then, through the thump of blood in my ears and the sounds of my wheezing breath, I hear something else. A deep, rushing roar. Like a – a wave, a tidal wave, coming closer and closer. Thunder rocks the air and ahead of me the trees are bowing down as a wall of glassy silver sweeps over them.

I only have time for a single look back – and I only realise how far I've come away from safety when I can't see anything, not the cottage or the garden wall, no trace of home – before the rain drowns me.

I'm soaked through instantly, and shivering. Clinging to a tree trunk, I listen without much hope; I can't make out anything above the sounds of the rain battering down, the low creaking of the trees. The cry was ahead of me. I know it was. This might be my last chance to find it, whatever it is. To help.

It might also be a really good chance to wander around for hours, catch pneumonia and die. I don't even have my phone. I'm out here without a coat on.

Frustrated beyond belief – with myself, with this bizarre place and the weirdness it keeps throwing at me, with the stupid rain – I swipe roughly at the water running down my face. Then slowly, wearily, I turn back the way I came.

Two steps later, the ground suddenly disappears.

A scream tears out of me as my feet skid uncontrollably on a near vertical slope. I lose my balance, go face-first into the mud and roll down, down, down, slipping and slithering over tree roots and wet moss. The world dissolves into a terrifying blur. I've come loose from gravity. I'll never stop.

Then I do, and the thud knocks a hard grunt from my lungs. I'm a huddled ball, gasping for air, unable even to move at first as the rain puddles in my hair and the small of my back. I'm waiting for the pain to kick in, to realise that I've broken or torn something. It doesn't come, though. I think I'm OK. The main throb of hurt is coming from my knee, that same unlucky knee that I bruised nearly getting run over by Aidan, and then again yesterday when he dragged me away from the sea.

It takes me a good few minutes to get my breath back. Then I heave myself stiffly to my feet, my socks squelching in my boots, and stare around me. 'Where the hell . . . ?'

It's a hollow. Trees bend overhead, their canopies shadowy and cloudlike. Curling roots, thicker than my wrists and green-gold with crusts of lichen, stand out of steep mossy slopes on either side of me. Fine ribbons of rain patter down between the dense branches, swaying gently as the trees shift in the wind. Embedded randomly up and down the slopes – like a handful of gravel tossed by a giant – there are rocks, massive rocks, probably taller than me once, but tumbled down now in beds of ferns and wildflowers. I'm lucky I didn't roll into one as I fell. I'd have broken my ribs, or my skull.

I can still hear the wind, and the rain. The storm is roaring up there above the trees. But there's a kind of quiet here, a different quiet to the ominous one before the storm hit. It's . . . a waiting quiet. Like the quiet in the ruins of Kearsley. As if the trees are listening.

There's a swift, darting movement to my left.

I jump, jerk around. For an instant, I see a tall girl with

slender white limbs, wearing a green dress. And then . . . she's gone. The blur of green and white in my vision resolves into a slim tree with a pale, papery trunk, vivid green leaves and masses of tiny, starry white blooms. It looks incongruous, out of place at the bottom of the hollow, young and tender, sprouting among the roots of the giant dark behemoths.

I hear a thin, whimpering cry and see movement down by the base of the tree. I crouch – wincing as my knee crunches in protest – and there's a puppy, a shivering little ball of thick grey and white fur. Huge, pointed ears far too big for its skull. And blue eyes.

'*I found her under a rowan tree . . .*' Tom had said.

'Rowan,' I whisper, looking at the strange tree spearing up towards the light.

Impossible. Anyway, there's no rope round her neck, not like Tom said. But she looks so similar . . . A descendant? It's the only explanation I can imagine.

The puppy cries again. Its tiny voice is hardly loud enough to hear even in the stillness of this place. There's no way, no way that I could have heard it back in the cottage, in my bedroom, in the middle of the night.

And yet.

'It's OK, baby. Come here, come here,' I murmur, and the little pup snuffles tentatively towards me and lets me gather it up, bony and icy-cold under the wet fur. Tiny sharp claws scrabble unhappily at my chest and arms, then relax as I get a good grip. It – she – is shivering. I'm shivering too. 'I've got you, baby. We need to get somewhere dry and warm.'

It is not easy to climb the slippery, mossy side of a deep hollow, in the rain, with a wonky knee and a puppy's weight taking up both of my hands. It's nearly impossible, in fact. But I don't dare fall again, not with Rowan in my arms. I'd crush her. I dig the toes of my boots into the ground, breath sawing in my throat, and push, and push, bent double, and finally, we're up. Out in the full force of the storm again.

The puppy – might as well call her Rowan for now – shudders against my chest, and I sense rather than hear her little whine of protest. I can't even wrap her in my sweatshirt; it's too wet. I have to get us home, and fast. I take two steps forward before it occurs to me to look back.

There's nothing there. No strange hollow in the ground, no mass of dark clustered tree giants, no fallen stones. No slim rowan covered in starry white flowers. Nothing.

The wind howls around us, tossing a gush of rain directly into my face. Rowan squirms and whimpers. I take the hint and get going again.

Movement helps, generating a tiny bit of warmth, but my toes and fingers are completely numb, and my face aches with chill. Visibility is basically down to what I can see under my feet and maybe a foot ahead now. But this isn't the middle of nowhere – there are houses peppered all over the place. Surely, I'll eventually find one, or get to the sea, or maybe stumble over the path to the castle. Then I can work out which way home is.

At least the trees are thinning out. They're less twisted too, taller, their branches overhead instead of reaching out to bar my way as I walk. There's shrubs, undergrowth, grass and weedy bits instead of just thick moss. It's brighter ahead. Three, four more steps and I break out onto a road. A real road, tarmacked, wide enough for a couple of cars to pass each other. There's even a white line down the middle. I could almost cry at the evidence that civilisation still exists, even though the shaggy hedgerow stretches out in front of me on the other side of the road, barring any kind of view. I get a flashback to dragging my case down the road in search of Winterthorne – was it only a week ago? It feels like eternity. The road has to go somewhere. A bus shelter, a house, a hamlet. Anything. I'd take anything at this point.

'You're OK, Rowan. We're going to be OK,' I say, shifting her increasingly uncomfortable weight in my arms. She burrows further into my chest, and I allow myself to stroke her ridiculous ears gently. She likes it. Even as the rain continues to batter us both she pops her little head up and licks me, tongue a shock of heat against the chilled skin of my chin. 'Oh, you're a good girl. Yes, yes, you are. Good—'

There's a familiar engine noise – the mosquito drone of a motorbike. I hustle back off the tarmac onto the mud under the trees just in the nick of time as a black motorcycle screams round the corner and then screeches to a halt a few metres past us.

It's Aidan.

He rips his helmet off and twists to stare at me in disbelief, rain flattening his dark hair to his head, seal-like, as he watches me trot – well, squelch – towards him. 'What in the hell? What have you done now? You look like you've been in an earthquake! What is with you? Can't you be trusted on your own for one damn day?'

It's a shame my arms are full, otherwise I could scrape a handful of mud off myself and chuck it right in his judgemental face. 'Does it really matter? Can you just give us a lift home out of this rain?'

The Moonlit Maze

'No way am I letting you get on my bike in that state! You must have at least three inches of dirt everywhere. Not to mention animals can't ride!'

I cannot believe it. 'Fine! At least point us in the right direction, then, since you know where I live.'

He scrubs his face with one hand, a rough downward swipe. 'For God's sake, I didn't mean – my house is literally right here!' He waves at a gravel driveway leading off the road. I hadn't even seen it. 'I've got dry towels and a shower! I'm not a monster: you've literally got a puppy. Did you just get it?'

'It's a very long story,' I tell him grimly. 'Lead me to the towels first, and then I'll tell you whatever you want to know.'

Thirty

Xanthe, summer 1924

Xanthe was already awake and dressed when the tentative knock came at her door. She rushed to unlock and open it, praying that the gentle sound hadn't disturbed anyone. Jonathan, who had arrived late last night – ready for the Summer Ball this evening – was only at the other end of the corridor.

'Quick, come in. Do you have everything?'

Ellen slipped through, raising a bulging carpetbag in answer. Xanthe was glad to see that she was wearing a beret and a coat over her dress. The sea fret was thick and it would be chilly until the sun scorched the mist away, especially under cover of the trees.

'You're sure? Because I don't think they'll return anything you leave behind.' She remembered, all too well, Caroline's petty refusal to give the maids who left a reference.

'I'm sure, milady. After I came here, Mam sold most of what I'd left at home, so I don't really have enough to forget.'

Xanthe resisted making a sharp comment about Ellen's mother – Ellen didn't need to hear it – and quickly shrugged her father's old waxed jacket on over her own jumper. 'Then we should go before the whole house is up.'

'Annie will be in the kitchen a bit longer with Cook. They've got to get the bread started for the finger sandwiches for tonight. And Bertie's always running late. He won't see us if we go out the front,' Ellen murmured, hugging her bag against her chest.

'Ellen.' Xanthe stopped the other girl with a touch to her narrow shoulder. 'You don't need to worry. We're only sneaking out this way because we didn't want a fuss. You've every right to go, and if anyone does try to stop us then they'll have to deal with me.'

Ellen swallowed, then nodded. 'Yes, milady. And – Auntie Heather's really here?'

'She's really here,' Xanthe said. 'Sally got a message to me last night after the train arrived. She let Mrs Shackleford have her bed. Your aunt's looking forward to seeing you.'

The furtive tip-toed journey down the grand staircase, through the empty hall and then the furious sprint across the gardens was accomplished in silence. The girls kept a tight hold on each other's hands the whole time. Despite her reassuring words, Xanthe had her own private fears about being forced into a confrontation with any one of her family over what she was doing. She knew it was the right thing. She wouldn't let them stop her. Yet this summer the household seemed to tremble on the edge of some unimaginable cataclysm, and the faintest breath of conflict could be enough to send them all over.

But there was no sudden hue and cry. No one saw them, or tried to stop them. When they reached the cover of the woods, they stopped to catch their breath, Xanthe leaning on a tree as Ellen braced her hands on her knees. Ellen let out a weak little giggle and Xanthe joined her. The mist and the leaves muffled the noise. After a minute, they clasped hands again and went on, Ellen following Xanthe almost blindly down the steep, winding track through the trees.

'You're a local girl, aren't you?' Xanthe asked, seeing Ellen's nervous glances at the dark, twisted shapes the trees made looming out of the sea fret.

'Mam never let me play out here. She said the woods were full of vermin and muck.'

From a fishing family, maybe. 'I expect you'll be a lot happier living in Durham.'

Ellen nodded, shying from the rustle of a shrub that had overgrown the track. Xanthe found her eyes searching the wood keenly too. Some part of her expected, as she always expected now, to see a shadow of a girl, fleet and silent, slipping through the mist ahead, a shadow with dark drifting hair, carrying the smell of rain and the sound of thunder with her . . .

She didn't see anything. There was no one in the wood but them.

Ellen hung back as they approached the little gardener's cottage tucked into the trees – where Tom's car was parked on the grass verge – clasping her possessions to her chest again, like a shield. With a feeling of strangeness, of unreality, that almost exceeded her relief, Xanthe gently nudged the other girl through the gate, down the path that crossed the neat front yard to the red-painted front door. It was the first time Xanthe had ever opened that gate, or knocked on the door. She had imagined it so many times when she was little. And now—

The door rattled, then opened. A tall, slim woman stood

there, her greying blonde hair neatly pinned up under a rather square hat. Her expression was stern, bordering on pugnacious. Then she caught sight of Ellen as Xanthe hastily stepped back, and her dark blue eyes went wide.

'Ellie?'

'Auntie Heather!' Ellen dropped her bag and launched herself across the doorstep.

The stern expression melted into one of sudden, fierce joy, like sunlight illuminating a saint's face in a church window. The woman enfolded the smaller girl in her arms. 'Oh, haven't you grown up! My girl! Look at you, look at you.'

'I'm sorry I never wrote back,' Ellen said. 'Mam wouldn't let me.'

'Never you mind that now, Ellie. We won't lose track of each other again.'

Xanthe's eyes prickled, and for a moment she almost thought that she might cry. But her lashes stayed dry, as always. She smiled instead.

After a few moments, Tom's head appeared in the doorway, looking pleased but a tiny bit ill at ease with the emotional reunion taking place on his threshold. Then he spotted Xanthe and grinned.

'Mission accomplished, Captain?'

She felt her smile widen and gave him a crisp nod. 'Mission accomplished.'

At the sound of Xanthe's voice, the dog Rowan pushed her way past the legs filling the front step and galloped out into the front garden, jumping and dancing and thwacking everyone with her heavy tail as Xanthe tried in vain to get her to stand still long enough to give her ears a scratch.

'Oh, goodness me, my manners!' Ellen's aunt seemed to remember herself and broke away from Ellen, wiping self-consciously at her face with a lace-edged handkerchief. 'I'm that sorry! I forgot you were there! Only it's been years and I was afraid I'd never see my girl again—'

'Don't worry, Auntie, Lady Xanthe doesn't mind,' Ellen said, giving Xanthe a beaming look. 'Do you?'

'Not in the slightest!' Xanthe said, straightening up. Rowan sat heavily on her foot, grinning a wide grin as her tail swept back and forth over the grass. 'I think you're entitled after such a long time apart.'

'Sorry to be a wet blanket,' Tom said, apologetic, as he edged past them and came to stand next to Xanthe on the path. As soon as he was near, and without having been aware of her hand reaching for his, Xanthe found that their fingers had entwined. She knew she ought to let go. She didn't. 'Only if you two want to catch the seven o'clock train then we need to get going soon. I'll run you down in the car if you don't mind squeezing in a bit?'

'Well, and we shall, but first I'll say my piece,' said Ellen's aunt, her jaw firming up again. 'Which is this: I did wrong by letting my sister-in-law drive me away after my brother died, and not taking Ellie with me. And you've gone out of your way to set that right and help my girl, and there's not many of your kind of folks who would, if you'll pardon me, my lady.'

Xanthe shifted uncomfortably, eyes darting away from the older woman's face. Tom's grip tightened on her fingers, a gentle squeeze-squeeze, and quite involuntarily she felt herself relax.

'So, though it might sound unlikely, if either of you are ever wanting help – if you're ever in a fix or you need something – you make sure as you come to me. You know where I live. You'll always be welcome.'

'Thank you,' Tom said after a moment, seeing that Xanthe was speechless. 'And we'll stay in touch anyway, won't we?'

'Yes,' Xanthe managed to put in. 'I want to know how you get on, Ellen. Don't be a stranger.'

And that was that. Only an hour or so after Xanthe and Ellen had fled from Kearsley Castle, Ellen and her aunt were returned to Winterthorne station, loaded onto the right train for home and waving goodbye from the window with teary smiles. After the train had departed in a cloud of steam with what seemed to Xanthe to be a triumphant toot of the whistle, she and Tom walked back to his car in silence. They didn't talk as he drove her up the bumpy rutted road, or as he pulled the car to a stop outside his family's cottage.

'Phew,' she said finally, into the quiet.

'I almost can't believe it went off so well. I expected something dramatic to happen. I'm not exactly sure what,' he admitted.

'Me too. I think we've both read too many novels.'

'Maybe. But . . . now you've got to go back there, and pretend to tolerate that cousin of yours at your parents' ball. He's going to notice eventually that Ellen isn't around any more. Do me a favour, would you? Take Rowan with you. She'll look after you.'

'But what am I supposed to do with her?' Xanthe asked. 'I can't let her wander around the castle, my father would—' The words caught in her throat. *Have a heart attack.*

'Please. Just until things have settled. I'll worry about you all the time, otherwise. She's all right on her own for a few hours with a bowl of water and a blanket to lie on, or you can let her roam in the gardens. She does that all the time anyway with my father.'

'All right,' Xanthe agreed reluctantly, her heart squeezing at the thought of shutting the sweet-natured, boisterous dog into her bedroom and leaving her alone. 'But you don't have to worry about me, you know. I won't inflict an invitation to the ball on you—' He let out a scornful 'Ha!' at the idea and she hurried on. 'But why don't we meet up at the maze, at say . . . ten o'clock, like we did before? You'll be able to see I'm all right, and I can tell you if Jonathan's given me any trouble.'

'More clandestine meetings after dark,' Tom said. There was a note in his voice that jarred. 'People will start calling us Romeo and Juliet.'

They were both staring determinedly out of the windshield at the hedgerows, rather than look at each other. Xanthe felt like a fly trapped in amber. She didn't dare move. Or say anything else. Or even breathe. What was he thinking? Why did this moment, just a little fragment of time like any other, feel like this – like the most important moment there had ever been, or would ever be?

Tom's hand found hers where it rested on her knee, and closed around it.

'I don't suppose . . . you'd like to come in for a bit. Have a cup of tea?'

She breathed out, freed. 'Yes. Yes, please.'

Xanthe walked through the red door like someone in a dream, turning in circles as she took in the little front hall with its whitewashed walls, the terracotta tiles underfoot. Rowan greeted her as she peeked into the front parlour, and Xanthe sighed at the sight of the comfortable chairs drawn up before the fire, the hooked rug, the upright piano and the pile of old tartan blankets that served as a dog bed.

'It's just an ordinary house, Xan,' Tom said, half bemused, half grinning, as he watched her skip into the kitchen and examine the dresser, the table, the battered old range. 'Not a fairytale palace.'

'It might as well be, to me.' She leaned over the sink to stare out of the window, down the garden, at what she assumed was Mr Marten's potting shed. She even opened the door at the end and looked into the tiny lavatory. 'Forbidden territory. Your father didn't want me to get into trouble.'

'He didn't want us in trouble, either,' Tom admitted, rubbing the back of his neck. 'I remember him fuming after Bowdler tried to have a word with him, once. We should remember your station and not take advantage of your friendliness just because . . .'

'Just because I was too strange to know better.' Xanthe blew an extravagant raspberry. 'That's for Bowdler. For all of them. Not one's worthy to clean your father's boots.'

'He'd not like to hear you talking that way,' Tom said, but he was really grinning now.

Xanthe smiled back. 'I know he must already be at the greenhouses, cutting flowers for the ball, but where's Sally? Still asleep? Did she have to share your room last night?'

'Ah. No.' He rocked back on his heels, eyes drifting away from hers to stare at some fixed point on the ceiling. 'She – er – she stayed with her fiancé's family. Down in the village. They have a spare room. She'll be spending the weekend there.'

Xanthe stared at Tom's exposed throat as he avoided her gaze. Alone here together. He hadn't told her that when he'd invited her in.

Tom seemed to brace himself, his shoulders heaving with a long, slow breath as he finally looked at her. In the shadowy kitchen, where the morning light hadn't yet reached, his eyes seemed endlessly deep. 'You did mean it, didn't you? What you said before, at the cove. You wouldn't marry Jonathan. Especially not now, after learning about Ellen.'

'Of course I meant it. I don't say things I don't mean. Not any more. And not to you.'

'Promise me?'

She hesitated, caught by the look in his face, a look that seemed to be asking some other, some greater question. 'Promise you what?'

He took another deep breath. 'That if you marry anyone, it'll be me.'

She gasped, fear and disbelief warring. Then she threw her hands up. 'What kind of a – sideways, half-hearted proposal—'

'Xanthe.' He caught her flying hands, and drew one up to lie against his chest, holding it there, pressed flat, as he brought the other to his face. In the quiet, he pressed his lips tenderly to her palm. Her heartbeat hammered through her entire body, shuddering in the tips of her fingers, in her throat, every vein.

'You can't mean it,' she whispered. 'They . . . they're horrible. They'll fire your father, wreck Sally's job too if they can. They'd ruin your life—'

'My father's been getting job offers from other toffs for years. He owns this place too. He's not going to end up destitute. Sally's getting married in six months, and moving away. My newspaper would laugh in your father's face; they're Marxists. They can't get at us, Xan.'

'I'll be rich,' she blurted. 'When I get married. I'm not sure how rich, but – it's a lot of money, apparently. My father wants it for the estate.'

'So? He can have it. We don't need his money. We don't need anything from them.'

Was it true?

Could it be true?

'When?'

His fingers ghosted softly up along the side of her neck, his thumb touching the lobe of her ear, toying with the pearl stud there. His feet were nudging either side of hers, the battered brown leather of her brogues scraping the polished black of his. Their knees touched. They had drawn so close together, somehow, so close, without either of them ever even seeming to move.

'Not today. Not next week. Just . . . when you want to. Whenever you do. Promise it's me.'

The words breathed out of her. 'I promise.'

☽○☾

Tom's bedroom was tiny. The window was tiny too, but it faced east, flooding the small space with sunlight and warmth in the early morning.

Tom's hands were fumbling, trembling. Xanthe realised hers were too, that she was shaking all over like a racehorse that didn't know if it wanted to bolt out of the gate or back to the quiet darkness of the stable. Tom saw her staring and ducked his head, a shy, jerky movement. She kept looking, struck by the freckles across the tanned bridge of his nose and the bump, that dear, familiar little bump from where he had broken it once. She tried to lean in to kiss it, and Tom reared back, taken by surprise – exactly like a horse himself – and Xanthe couldn't help it, she let out a kind of trill of nervous laughter, high-pitched and silly, almost a titter. Tom blinked at her. Then let out a harsh bray of his own, snorting through his nose.

Time had stopped, gone still. They were touching each other, standing in each other's space, but unmoving. The sun had turned the dust they'd disturbed into slow-turning spirals of gold, turned Tom's eyelashes and the ends of his hair a kind of tawny.

His freckles really were almost orange.

A hard cramp of laughter folded Xanthe over where she stood. She nearly headbutted him. But – miraculous! – he was laughing too, hands steady now as he held her. It was all right. It was all right, laughing like this. It made everything better, like champagne bubbles trailing under her skin wherever he touched, bursting, bright, in a rush that made all the tiny hairs on her body bristle up. She could touch him back now. Fingers slipping the buttons of his shirt open. Feeling the little patch of coarse hair in the centre of his chest crinkle under her fingertips. Feeling the smoothness of his skin, and the way he flinched, just a little, as she brushed his nipple. The trail of gooseflesh that sprang up under her hands.

'Am I giving you the shivers?' she gloated into his neck.

He laughed, soft and low this time, rumbling against her. 'Too right you are. Give me a chance, will you? I'm only a mortal man.'

'You're not "only" anything,' she whispered, her throat suddenly tight. She pushed her forehead hard against his collarbone, squeezing her eyes shut against the ache, the burning under the lids that she thought she would never feel again. She had cried so many tears of confusion and sadness and loneliness, before they all dried up. But there were tears left in her still, it seemed. For joy. For him.

'Only a mortal man,' he repeated. His hand was under her jumper now, lifting it up, and she had to pull back to raise her arms. His face changed as he registered the tears. Tenderness moved across his expression, making his lips hard and his eyes gentle.

'And you're a mortal woman.' He threw her jumper away and drew her against his bare chest. 'And that's enough. Enough to build a life with, Xan.'

Yes, she thought as they laid down together on the narrow bed in the golden light. As she moved against him. As he kissed her. Yes. It was enough. More than enough. Everything.

Thirty-One

Jude, present day

By unspoken agreement, Aidan and I both shut up as I follow him onto the gravel driveway. I'm shocked, a little, when I see the place, round the bend of the drive: it's basically the twin of my cottage – Anne's – but extended to one side, and with a kind of hideous glass and steel box bolted on. There's a cutesy sign on an American-style mailbox calling it 'Keeper's Cottage'.

'Old gamekeeper's place,' he grunts. Aidan wheels his bike under the overhang on a carport off to the side of the house, then unbolts the front door and ushers us in.

The quiet is so sudden, I almost feel I've gone deaf. It's such a relief not to feel the rain battering down on me, and it's warm in the hallway – a bigger, brighter version of Anne's, with a lot less art on the walls. But I'm still wet, and Rowan's dripping mud everywhere, whimpering and struggling, and I don't really know what to do with myself.

'Here, hand that over,' Aidan says.

I clutch the puppy to me; she yips in protest. 'She. She's called Rowan.'

'Relax, I respect her personhood,' he says, rolling his eyes, but smiling too. 'I've had dogs all my life. There's a bathroom down there, at the end of the kitchen. There are towels out, and spares under the sink. I can leave you some clean stuff to put on.'

'Your stuff?'

My face must be a picture. He sighs, reaches over and firmly removes the sopping burden of Rowan from my arms. Despite his complaints about how dirty we were, he doesn't seem to notice the smeary muddy footprints Rowan leaves all over his leathers. 'My mom's stuff. This is my folk's house – my mom grew up here. I promise I'm not gonna skin and eat your puppy, OK? Will you just go? You are going to wreck the floors.'

I look down. The floors are hardwood, and probably expensive.

'Fine. I mean, thanks.' As I walk through the kitchen, I glance back and see Aidan lifting Rowan into the butler's sink, murmuring quietly to her. He does look like he knows what he's doing.

I officially let it go. The whole experience of running into the wood, finding Rowan, the storm ... it's starting to feel like a dream, like so many of the other things that have happened to me here. It's also starting to feel like if I don't warm up soon I'm going to lose the ability to stand up or even talk. Everything hurts. Being cold for this long *hurts*.

The bathroom is a wet room, tiled in beige marble with twin sinks, backlit vanity units, and a heated towel rail larger than the bed I slept in as a child. There are several showerheads. Refusing to be intimidated, I hit buttons and turn dials randomly until the waterfall head bursts into life, then fling my wet, mud-caked clothes into the corner, and dive under the water.

☽○☾

Dry, and dressed in the clothes I found waiting for me outside the wet-room door – a T-shirt, an oversized women's flannel shirt, jogging bottoms and thick cotton socks – and with my loose hair drying in long twisting curls around my shoulders, I emerge into the kitchen again. Both boy and dog are absent, but I can hear movement from down the corridor.

They're in a large, airy room next to the kitchen – inside the glass and steel box. There are sofas and chairs scattered around, all a bit mid-century modern and uncomfortable-looking. In one corner is a complex Scandinavian-style wood burner. Aidan's sitting on a rug in front of it, leaning back against one of the sofas, with Rowan. She's clean and dry and looks like nothing so much as a greyish-white dust bunny, all fluff and ears. The remains of some chicken sit on a saucer nearby. She's draped across Aidan's legs, nearly comatose under his stroking hands. When she catches sight of me, she lets out a tiny, joyous bark and scrambles clumsily off him. He lets out a grunt as she tramples his lap, but doesn't complain. She skids across the wooden floors to greet me, jumping and dancing around my feet. She's such a sweet little girl. The memory of her lost and alone in the woods makes me flinch. I crouch down to make a fuss of her wriggling little body, then pick her up again to hold her against my chest.

There's a strong smell of breakfast about, although it has to be mid-afternoon by now. My stomach reacts predictably with a massive, audible gurgle. Aidan squints at me, then points wordlessly at the low coffee table next to the rug, where there's a cafetière, a pile of toast, pastries, a couple of jars of preserves and butter in an actual butter dish. There are even napkins. I sort of want to look around and see if there's a butler hiding out somewhere.

But I'm only human, and those are *pains au chocolat*.

Aidan adds to the evidence of having a hidden civilised streak by distracting Rowan so I can demolish a full plateful of food, and finish a mug of coffee, before he starts interrogating me.

'Time's up. Come on, what was it this time? You were chasing butterflies through the meadow with your puppy and you just didn't notice the rain coming on?'

I swallow some toast. Clear my throat. 'I wasn't chasing butterflies. I heard crying coming from the woods near my garden – I've been hearing it on and off for a few days. I went to look and found the puppy abandoned out there, but when the storm broke I couldn't find my way back.'

'Don't you have GPS on your phone?'

'Er . . .'

He squints at me, then points an accusatory finger. 'You didn't take your phone, did you?'

'I was in a hurry! I can hardly ever get reception around here anyway.'

He's not listening. 'Let me just make sure I've got this straight. You ran out into this weather, without even a freaking coat on, no phone, no idea where you were going, because you heard noises in the woods? You could have died! Jesus Christ, tell me you're a spoiled princess without telling me you're a spoiled princess.'

The Moonlit Maze

Very gently, I put down my coffee cup and piece of toast and sit back from the coffee table. I'm tired. Too much has happened lately and none of it makes sense. The weariness, the throbbing pain in my knee – the ever-present ache of my decision to leave this place that was just beginning to feel like home – only adds to the slow-burning fury that I can feel flushing my face. I have tried to be the better person, the person Ma would have wanted me to be. But it seems like, once again, Juliet is just here to get slapped down. So now it's Jude's turn to deal with this guy.

'Do you actually think that you know the first thing about me, Aidan Antonenko?'

He rolls his eyes. Again. 'Clearly I know at least a couple of things.'

'Let me ask you something, then: do you know how many family members or loved ones I have left on the face of this planet?'

He opens his mouth, then pauses, exasperation suddenly tinged with uneasiness. 'What kind of a question—'

'Go on. Guess.'

'I don't know, OK?'

'Weak, but fine, I'll help you. The answer is zero. None. My mother is dead. My father is dead. My grandparents and my foster grandparents are dead. My aunt too. There's literally no one who cares if I'm alive.' He sucks in a breath as if to respond. '*Shut up,* I'm speaking now. After my ma died I ended up in foster care. Do you have any idea what that's like? I've spent the last four years working dead-end jobs to afford a place on a sofa in a mouldy flat, always knowing that I was literally a single emergency or illness away from being on the street. *One good thing* happened to me, one good thing – my dad's aunt left me her cottage in her will. But I don't even get to stay because . . . because weird things like this keep happening to me, and it's dangerous, and, yes, sometimes I hear screaming in the woods. I have to go back to London, where there's nothing and no one waiting for me and try to start again *all over again*. So don't you tell me I'm spoiled, you little shit. You think you're tough? With your luxury holiday cottage and your folks back home and your shiny motorbike, running around ruining everyone's day because you can't deal with feelings? You'd last five minutes where I come from. Grow the fuck up.'

I'm speaking in a sustained, vicious hiss by the time I'm finished. He's leaning back away from me. The dog lets out a little whine and I realise she's trembling. Fantastic. I'm out. I start trying to coax her back to me so we can leave.

'Wait. Wait!' Aidan has a stricken sad-boy face again, like a kid who pulled a butterfly's wings off to see how it worked and only just realised that it can't fly now. He reaches across the table to try to grab my arm, then stops and holds his hands up. 'I'm sorry, I'm – I'm really sorry. You're right. Don't go back out there – it's still pouring. Please don't leave.'

There's so much temptation to turn on him properly, really rip him up. I could do it. It's too easy to go for another person's weak spots, find the places where they're bruised already and hurt them more, if you're hurting yourself. If you don't care. I take a deep breath. Then another.

'I will stay,' I say deliberately, 'if you tell me what your deal is. Why are you *here* instead of at home in New York?'

His gaze flickers away and he shifts in place, only stilling when the puppy, released from my hands, crawls her way onto his lap again. 'It's – Look, I don't . . . You win, all right? Your – your tragic backstory is better, I concede—'

'Aidan.'

He snorts a breath out through his nose, scrubs his hands roughly over his face, his long, pianist's fingers digging in cruelly at his temples. 'Why do you care? It's not fucking interesting.'

'People's tragic backstories are never that interesting. That doesn't mean they're not important.'

'Jesus. OK. Fine.' He pours himself the dregs of the coffee, and drinks them straight down like a shot. Then he coughs and thumps his own chest. And then, finally, he starts to talk. 'I – I had two friends growing up. From elementary school. They used to call us the Three Musketeers, the Three Amigos. Me, Amy and Arthur. Arthur came out – we were there for him. Me and Amy got together – Arthur was there for us. We were really close. We all got into the same college upstate, like . . . like some wholesome movie.'

He stops, and I can hear the breath tremble in his chest, on the verge of a sob.

And I'm sorry. Suddenly, completely. I want to interrupt. Tell him it's OK. But clearly, clearly – it's not OK. I want, in an uncomfortable, squirmy way, to let him, let us both, off the hook and say that he doesn't need to talk about this. But again, very clearly – he does.

So I do what I suppose I always wished someone would do for me, after Ma died. I just . . . sit there. And when he darts a look at me, I make sure that my expression's calm, not too eagerly interested. That I just look like I . . . care, I suppose. Because, for some reason, I do.

'At college. That was when things started going wrong. We drifted apart. Maybe – I don't know, maybe it was natural. Except we didn't want to let each other go. We kept clinging to each other even when we weren't making each other happy any more. Arthur even came on to me, one time when Amy and me were "off". We both knew we weren't into each other like that, and it was just so awkward and wrong. Then, like an idiot, I told Amy and she couldn't let it go. She was always needling at both of us about it until one of us blew up.' He shook his head.

'I was so sick of them both by the time we were ready to graduate. I could see this future where we all just split up and maybe saw each other once a year at Christmas and it hurt, but it was a relief too, you know? Maybe they could see it happening as well. Amy convinced me we should give it another try as a couple, and then Arthur persuaded us both to come to this party. One last fling, right? He even volunteered to be the designated driver, which was usually me, because I was the one with a car. Anyway, we argued. We always argued. I can't even remember what it was about, but Amy demanded to go back to the apartment, and she and I had both had too much to drink and Arthur had the keys and . . .' He runs out of steam. Whispers, 'I didn't know.'

I wait for a minute, then two. The rain drums gently against the windows of the steel box and, lying across Aidan's knee, the sleeping puppy whimpers and kicks a foot. Aidan lays a hand on the back of her small head, and she quiets.

When it's clear he's run out of steam, I prompt him. 'What didn't you know?'

'I didn't know Arthur had a problem. Later on, it came out

The Moonlit Maze

he'd been struggling for . . . a long time. He was high that night. He was probably high most of the time, but I didn't even notice. He was good at hiding it.' He strokes Rowan once, a slow, smooth stroke down to the base of her tail, and then looks at me. His eyes are wet. 'Amy got in the front with him because she didn't want to be next to me in the back. I didn't bother to argue with her about putting her seat belt on like I always did, because I was drunk and angry. And Art crashed into the side of a truck.'

I hesitate, then shuffle sideways a little to where I can lean against the sofa next to him. I put my hand down on the puppy's back. When he doesn't move, I shift my hand sideways until it covers his.

He takes in an uneven breath, scrubs at his eyes with his other forearm. He doesn't take his hand away. 'Arthur had a serious head injury, broke his collarbone, messed up his hand. When they found the drugs in his system, the school expelled him. Two months from graduation. He stayed out of prison, but only barely. His parents put him in a rehab programme. They put him in about three, I think. He comes out and goes back in.'

I don't want to ask. I don't want to know the answer. 'What about Amy?'

He makes a jerky motion with his head. 'She went through the windshield. Never woke up.'

'I'm sorry. And you? Were you hurt?'

He lets out a wet laugh. 'I walked away. Literally walked. Everyone felt so sorry for me. My best friend killed my girl-friend – poor kid, what a good kid. I didn't even get lectured for drinking. The university gave me a pass on finals. I graduated with honours. My two best friends, my best friends . . . She's in the ground and he might as well be, and I just walked away.'

'Did you?'

'What?' He frowns at me, angry and embarrassed, his eyes red-rimmed, just like when we were on the sea wall.

'Did you walk away? I think you're still there, Aidan. In your head. I don't think you ever left them behind.'

'I didn't even need stitches! How is that fair?'

'Is this why you're here? Because you think you deserve to be exiled or something, punished for what happened?'

His eyes won't meet mine any more. 'I couldn't be there any more. Not – not at home, not in the city. Everywhere I went, it was like . . .'

'They were there. But they weren't there.'

He nods jerkily.

I stare blankly at my socked feet for a minute. Am I really going to share this? Am I really going to tell him this secret, something I've only barely admitted to myself?

Yes. He needs to hear it. I have to.

'Listen. After my ma died . . . I had a choice. I was on track to get good A levels, get into a great university. Everything was horrible, but I knew I could pull it together – people were sympathetic, people were ready to help me. I could still have the future that she and I planned. But . . . I didn't do that. I dropped out of college. I let it all go. I stopped talking to my friends, I didn't fight the debt collectors when they took all our stuff. It wasn't until later on that I realised what I'd done. There was some mad little part of me, so deep down that I didn't even recognise it back then, that thought if I just fucked my life up badly enough, she would have to come back, right?

She would have to come back to yell at me and help me fix it. And by the time my brain straightened out enough to realise she was gone, really gone for good . . . it was too late.'

'That's messed up,' he says, low and serious.

'Yeah. It was. Aidan, by the time you end up coming off that bike and break your neck going into a ditch somewhere, it will be too late for you. Your friends aren't coming back. Your old life isn't coming back. You have to make a new one.'

He stares at me, frozen. Then he takes a breath, makes a kind of coughing noise, like I've punched him in the gut. Like, after all our ranting and posturing, something in there, something I said, actually got through to him. I wonder if he's going to break down, or if it's going to be too much and in two seconds Rowan and I will be out on our ears, rain or no rain.

But eventually he sighs, sort of slumps back, as if he's too tired to sit up straight any more.

'OK. I mean . . . thanks. Hey – you know what?' He lets out a kind of teary chuckle, and his hand squeezes mine. 'Next time, I think I'll take the art-therapy option. It was gentler.'

Thirty-Two

Xanthe, 19 July 1924

Xanthe steps through the moon gate.

Overhead, stars drift among wisps of summer cloud like handfuls of lustrous pearls tossed carelessly on a midnight cloth. A warm wind moves through the leaves, sending the pale green silk of her evening dress fluttering around her calves. She brushes back a few strands of hair that have escaped the beaded scarf wrapping her head.

'Tom?'

No reply. No movement at the entrance to the maze.

She glances back through the curve of the moon gate at the castle. Light streams from the tall windows, painting gold squares on the lawn. The only place on the whole building that's dark is the carefully roped-off space of the orangery. She can hear the faint trilling of the string quartet in the ballroom. The party's in full swing. Even if anyone notices that she's gone, no one will be venturing out here to look for her. She can't stay away too long, though; she doesn't want to have to endure another scene.

But she won't go back without seeing him, either.

She moves away from the lower lawn, towards the topiary maze. Gravel crunches faintly underfoot, treacherous and shifting. Her new heels, specially dyed the perfect shade of *eau de nil* to match her dress, were not designed for midnight strolls. Beyond the maze, the sea is booming as the tide comes in on the cliffs below. Salt makes the air tangy.

'Tom?' A little bit louder now. She knows he must be there. He's always there – always waiting for her. He especially wouldn't be late tonight, after what they promised each other. After . . .

A memory. Skin sun-flushed and sticky, glazed with light. Tom's nose trailing down the tendon on the side of her neck, ticklish, his breath warm, voice ragged as he recites to her, '. . . *you have been mine before – how long ago I may not know: but just when at that swallow's soar your neck turn'd so, some veil did fall – I knew it all of yore* . . .'

A tiny smile creases her lips. This, this happiness, is what she was searching for without knowing it, for so long – a search that sent her all the way to Rome and Paris, and brought her back again. A kind of freedom that she's never experienced before. It no longer matters what her mother and father say. They can have the money in the trust – they can do whatever they want with it. And in return she and Tom will have each other.

She knows the life she wants. She knows the person she chooses to be.

There'll be no more arguments, no more shame, guilt, shouting or pleading. Tomorrow she'll explain everything to them, and Tom will be by her side when she does.

Well, if he'll have the good grace to show his face now.

One hand trailing over the carefully trimmed curve of the yew hedge, she follows the path deeper into the maze. Overhead the familiar shapes of the cockerel, the peacock, the owl, the swan, the albatross – Mr Marten's life's work – loom against the starlit sky. She blows them a kiss.

The gravel sounds ahead of her. A shadow moves out of the dead-end hidden in the hedge ahead. She laughs as she rushes towards him, stretching out her hands.

'Playing hide and seek? You should know that I'll always find you.'

'Oh really?' says a deep, masculine voice. 'Now that you mention it, I didn't know that.'

Xanthe stumbles to a halt, heart knocking hard against her ribs. She takes a hasty step back, her heel turns under her – wretched shoes! – and before she can turn to run a large, long-fingered hand closes on her wrist.

How did he find out I'd be meeting Tom here? Did he tell my parents? Stupid, I should have brought Rowan with me instead of turning her loose!

And then, piercing through everything else: *Where is Tom?*

'What are you doing lurking out here?' The words emerge crisply, not giving away her fear. 'I thought you were welded to the wall. Or did the footmen stop bringing you drinks?'

'I came looking for you, my dearest, darling fiancée.' His voice is low, deliberately menacing. 'And now that I've found you . . .'

'What, Jonathan? What exactly are you—' She gasps as he wrenches her arm up, dragging her close enough to smell the whisky on him. Hear his fast, excited breathing.

His grip tightens on her wrist, slowly, calculatedly, until her bones protest with hot, elastic twinges of pain. He could break her hand like this. He wants to. His gaze is on her face – the moonlight is so bright – and she knows the sight of her pain there would excite him. Fear will arouse him even more. She tries, desperately, to hide it all, keep her expression blank.

'I haven't decided yet,' he whispers. 'But whatever it is, whatever it is . . . Oh, Xanthe, I promise you will not enjoy it.'

A shudder of disgust moves through her, cold sweat springing up all over her body. She yanks at her arm, ignoring the pain. 'I did you the favour of not showing my parents the bruises last time – but I'm not going to protect you any more, Jonathan. You are pathetic. Give up!'

'Protect me?' He sounds genuinely surprised. Then a laugh tears out of him. '*Protect* me? You spoiled, vapid little bitch – I waded through mud and shit and blood to protect this place – to protect this country and this family – and now everything's going, everything I fought and killed for – it's all going to ruin *because of you*! Because you'd prefer to fuck a grubby gutter-snipe in a hedge than marry someone of your own class—'

Xanthe's free hand flies up before she's even realised she's moving. It's no ladylike slap – her fist crunches into the side of Jonathan's face with every bit of force she has, and he lets out an exclamation of shock and pain, reeling sideways.

The painful grip on her arm loosens, just for an instant. She whirls and runs, the gravel scattering under her feet, blood hammering in her ears. She has to reach the house – she has to find out where Tom is—

Jonathan catches her in five steps. Pinions her arms to her sides, lifting her to her tiptoes, almost off her feet. 'You shouldn't have done that,' he breathes hotly in her ear. 'Now my blood's up. You're for it.'

His hands are on her. She feels the beaded lace at her shoulder tear. She screams. It's hopeless and she knows it: no one can possibly hear her. No one except him, and he'll like it. But she can't help herself. She can't hold it in. Her long, wordless shriek of fury and terror echoes tinnily through the empty gardens.

Hard fingers clamp down over her face, over her nose and mouth, cutting off her air. Silvery ripples slide across her vision. She fights. She fights until everything goes dark.

Thirty-Three

Jude, present day

I gasped awake on Aidan's sofa, shaking all over. Xanthe's scream echoed in my mind. He was going to – it was the night of the ball, the night of the fire – Tom was missing – and Jonathan was going to—

I rolled over onto my stomach, hiding my face in both hands. There was nothing I could do. I had tried to reach her, to warn her. It hadn't worked. I hadn't even known to warn her about *this*. She was there, and I was here and it was too late and there was *nothing I could do*.

The trembling gradually eased off, replaced by a deep sense of weariness, hopeless resignation. This was what you got for caring, allowing your emotions to get all tangled up with other people. You couldn't save anyone; most of us couldn't figure out how to save ourselves. I knew that, but I'd let myself get involved anyway, and now here I was, wounded inside by the fate of a girl I had never even met, a girl who had died a hundred years ago. It was all so pointless.

I ought to have packed up my stuff and left the cottage, left

Winterthorne, first thing this morning, after I saw that rose on my doorstep. Or maybe I should never have come here at all. Maybe I should have just stayed in London where I was safe, and alone.

I dried my face on the sleeve of the borrowed shirt and sat up. Neither Aidan nor the puppy were in the room. There were no voices, and no movement in the house. All I could hear was the deep drumming of the rain on the glass walls. Where were they? Why had he let me fall asleep?

'Aidan?' Nothing. 'Rowan? Aidan!'

In the quiet left behind by my shout, something sparked in the back of my brain. An instinct that made me want to hunker down small, to stay still and quiet. My skin tingled with rising awareness of danger.

Where had he gone? Where had he taken the dog? Why, why, why had I run out of my house without my bloody phone?

I spotted a cordless housephone sitting in its cradle near the wood burner and snatched it up, wracking my memory for the number that I had seen pinned on the fridge every day for a week in Liz's neat, round handwriting.

The call connected. The phone rang. Once, twice.

'Hello?'

Not Liz: Nick. He sounded breathless, a bit harried, but his voice filled me with relief.

'Nick, it's Jude—'

'God, Jude – are you all right? I went to your house to check on you – the door was unlocked, the garden gate was standing open and I found your phone—'

'I'm OK. I'm fine. But I . . . went out in a bit of a hurry and

I got turned around in the storm. I've . . .' I stopped, trying to figure out how to phrase it. 'I've ended up at Aidan's house.'

'Aidan?' Blank, like he has no idea who I'm talking about. Then: 'The arsehole?'

'Yeah, him. He let me dry off and – he's actually been OK – but now I seem to be alone here and I'm getting a . . . a weird vibe. I'm just not sure I can find my way home from here by myself. And he's taken my puppy.' That last bit slips out plaintively.

'Puppy? Look, just – stay where you are. I'll be there in about ten minutes. We'll sort it out.'

'OK. Thank you.'

He hung up. Keeping a firm grip on the phone, I moved cautiously – not quite tiptoeing, but slipping across the floor as quietly as I could in my too-big, borrowed socks – out of the glass extension into the hallway. The kitchen was empty too, and the room on the other side of the stairs, some kind of study or snug. I forced myself to shout again, up the stairs. The sound echoed back at me without a response, not even the sound of little puppy nails scrabbling.

I didn't know what I was afraid of. Not Aidan, specifically; I'd actually have been really glad if he turned up right now and told me I was being a weirdo. Maybe it was a reaction to what I saw happening to Xanthe, but . . . I couldn't explain it, this suffocating, awful conviction that something bad was coming for me. Getting closer and closer by the second.

I just wanted to get my puppy and go home. No, not home. Back to Anne's house. Oh, whatever.

The wait seemed a lot longer than ten minutes in the stillness of the strange house, with only the battering rain and my deepening paranoia for company. By the time I heard the sound of an engine outside, I was so wound up that I nearly flew into the hallway and flung the door open. Nick jumped a bit, his hand still raised to knock, then – probably because of my expression – reached out to grab my shoulders.

'He didn't do anything to you?'

'No, I—'

From behind me there was a crash – running footsteps – and suddenly Aidan was crowding up behind me in the doorway, his hand making a fist in the back of the baggy shirt he'd lent me as if he wanted to drag me away from Nick.

'What the fuck is *he* doing here?'

'Where were you all this time?' I started to ask, looking back over my shoulder, incredulous. There was still no sign of Rowan, but Aidan had a coat on, splattered with rain. Had he been just – *outside* or something?

My voice was drowned out by Nick's, so harsh it was almost unrecognisable. 'Get your hand off her.'

I jerked back round to stare at him. He was glaring over my head at Aidan, face twisted up in an expression that seemed completely foreign. Murderous. 'Nick, it's OK.'

Aidan's hand tugged at my shirt. 'Who'd you think you are, Fairley? This is my house—'

Nick's grip tightened on my shoulders, pulling me forward, off balance. I had to catch hold of the door to steady myself. A swoop of apprehension – *something bad, something bad* – made my stomach turn over and when I spoke the words came out less forceful than I intended. 'Both of you stop it. What's the matter with you?'

'This bastard nearly killed me with his truck the first time he saw me.' Aidan tugged at me again, more insistently this time. 'Jude, I am serious. He's a psycho!'

'That isn't true, Aidan.' I tried to swallow down my rising fear. *Something bad.* I thought seeing Nick would make me feel safe, but sweat was standing out on my lip and forehead and my gut was churning. *Something bad!* I couldn't understand what was wrong with me. 'Nick, can you please—'

Without any warning, Nick released me – and lunged at Aidan. Taken off guard, Aidan yanked on the back of my shirt again at the same time that Nick barged roughly past me. Dizzy and off-balance, my fingers slipped off the wet door handle as my socked feet slid on the hardwood floor. I crashed backwards.

Nick and Aidan's startled faces blurred in my vision, black holes for eyes, gaping voids for mouths.

Something glanced off the side of my face, an impact that set my skull on fire. The last thing I heard was the sound of a dog's frenzied barking.

Thirty-Four

Xanthe, 19 July 1924

The first thing I see when I open my eyes is Tom.

He's lying sprawled half on his side, his back to me, maybe six feet away. There's a terrible spreading wetness across the tiles beneath him, viscous and dark – the orangery tiles, I realise distantly – and he's not moving. I can see that soft, vulnerable skin above the collar of his shirt, I can see one of his familiar callused hands lying palm up like an empty shell on the beach. But I can't see his face. I can't see him breathing.

I scream again, scream like I never stopped. Nothing comes out but a muffled moan – foul cloth is stuffed in my mouth, tied cruelly tight round my head. My arms are fastened behind me somehow, my legs hobbled. I'm six feet away and I can't get to him. I can't help him. *Tom.* Tom. Wake up. *Wake up!*

'I don't think he can hear you just now,' Jonathan says unsteadily, and the dim shape of him bends over me. His hair flops over his forehead as he prods at my cheek with something sharp, cold. 'Joining me at last? I thought I might have squeezed a bit too hard on your lovely neck. What a shame. You'd have missed all this excitement.'

The space is cavernous, shadowy, filled with Mother's distorted, twisting trees. He's only turned a few of the gas lamps up – not enough to attract undue attention. The ball is going on right there, just on the other side of the orangery's curtained doors.

I scream again, in rage and sorrow. My head throbs with it, my hands – crabbed and numb where he's tied them – ache as they twist and scrabble. I kick and struggle, but I can't move anywhere. No one can hear. No one's going to find us here. No one will help us. Not until it's too late. We should have run. We should have gone when Ellen did.

I was stupid. So stupid.

'I expect you think I've gone mad,' Jonathan says conversationally, turning in a smart little circle, stumbling, and then catching himself on one of the windows nearby. It's the first time I realise he has a gun. He's pressing the ugly black shape of it up against the glass as carelessly as if it were a handkerchief. In the other hand, there's a half-full bottle of spirits. He takes a long pull. 'I'm just sick of all of it. Sick of you, dearest cousin. You never ought to have been born. I should have been their son. What are you? Nothing but a mistake!'

He swings round, quick as a snake, and aims a kick at my stomach. I crunch up with a guttural grunt of pain as his polished shoe connects with my body. My knee takes half the impact, but he gets the bottom of my ribs. I feel a sickening *twang* as something gives way inside me. Nausea surges up and I desperately try to force it down. If I'm sick behind the gag, I'll choke.

'When I came back from France, I could barely walk. Barely breathe. All they could talk about was you. Oh, poor Xanthe, does she like her boarding school? She's such a sensitive soul! Such a funny, sweet little thing!'

He staggers away, laughing bitterly. Breathing through the agony, I uncurl, shuffling painfully to try to keep him in sight.

'I did everything I was supposed to do, and I suffered for it. I watched them all die. Do you know the sound someone's skull makes when it gets smashed open? How it feels, how it smells, when someone's guts come out in your hands? You can't wash it away. Some things. Shit and mud and blood. Shit and blood and mud. I can still smell it, every day. It soaks into your skin; it stays. And there were you, all clean and neat in your sweet little frock, expecting everyone to pander to you. You never did anything you were supposed to. You were never what you were supposed to be. They all died, all of them, and you're here. It's not fair.'

He collapses down into one of the wicker chairs. The gun dangles from his fingers, hanging loosely over the edge. For a few moments all I can hear – above the faraway sound of music, of people making merry beyond the curtained glass – is my own dry, gasping breaths and his, fast and shallow. He's almost wheezing. Almost . . .

Crying. 'I didn't even mean to shoot him,' he says quietly now, raggedly. He lifts the arm with the gun and swipes his inner elbow over his face. 'I never wanted to use this. Never again. I brought it back with me, from the war. Uncle Alfred took it away. He was afraid of what I might do with it. But he forgot about it, and it was mine, so I took it back. I only brought it along to give your little boyfriend a bit of a shock.

Make him see sense. I would have paid him off. That's the expected thing. All he had to do was . . . what he was supposed to do. Show respect. Show that he understood what was at stake. Why couldn't he understand? He laughed at me. He laughed at me like you always did. The fucking gardener's boy, laughing in my face.'

He takes another swig of the liquor, sets it down and, quite deliberately, his hand steady, takes aim at me. I look into the dark void of the gun and wait for him to pull the trigger. Wonder if he'll miss. If I even want him to.

Tom. Tom. *Wake up*. Please, Tom, wake up.

'Bad things happen. That's what Uncle Alfred always says. Bad things happen. No one's to blame. They'd forgive me for this – I'm sure they would. If I could save this place.' Jonathan's muttering. 'Uncle Alfred. Said he'd rather see it all fall into the sea than watch some disgusting millionaire buy it. He said that. But I can't save it without you. And you won't do what you're supposed to do. You won't do it. What am I supposed to do with you, then? You might as well die if you're no use.'

But the gun barrel is wavering. Slowly, he lowers it. 'I never liked guns.' He swipes at his face again, frowning, his head rolling back. 'Damn stuffy in here. Stinks. Hot as hell. Hot as blazes, sorry, Aunt Caroline!' He lets out a hiccupping laugh, sagging in place.

Stinks.

The gas. The gas pipes. Father had said it was dangerous in here, and Jonathan's turned up the lamps.

I'm on the floor. Gas is heavier than air; I ought to be affected. Maybe I am, but I'm already hurt – I can't tell how much of my aching head is what Jonathan's done to me, and what might be something else. I think I can smell it now, smell that eggy, sulphurous hint of coal gas. But there are cracks in the glass down here, close to the floor. A cool breeze is flowing in from the sea. I can feel it blowing in my face, disturbing my hair. It's what woke me up. It's driving the gas upward, inward. Towards Jonathan, in his corner, in his low chair.

'Hot as blazes ...' he mutters. Will he sit there until he suffocates? I'll suffocate too, eventually. I can't even warn him.

I close my eyes, my dry, unweeping eyes and laugh into the gag stuffed into my mouth, a harsh, croaking noise barely escaping the cloth. My hurt ribs throb, my head throbs. My heart, my heart ... my heart is gone. It's lying bleeding on the tiles where I can't reach it. I can't stop laughing. This is what they mean by 'hysterical'. He's going to kill us both and it won't even be on purpose.

Jonathan doesn't notice. He nods to himself suddenly. 'Air.'

It takes him a couple of attempts to stagger to his feet. His weaving about knocks over his bottle of whisky, slopping it everywhere, and disturbs an empty bottle that rolls across the floor towards me. Muttering and swaying, he reaches for one of the orangery's outside doors, the doors to the garden. The gun's still clutched in his other hand.

The door creaks open. Cool air blasts my face, and I gasp in as much of it as I can around my gag.

Then there's a low, tearing growl. I recognise it instantly. *Rowan.*

The huge grey-and-white dog streaks through the open door like lightning and strikes Jonathan square in the chest. He goes down under her, screaming – a high, unholy wail of pain. She's snarling, savaging him, tearing at him as he falls. His hand opens and – the gun – the gun sails across the room – I watch it – watch it arc towards the ground in strange stutters and blinks – knowing, knowing what will happen—

Wake up. Tom. *Wake up!*

Jonathan's gun hits the tiles. There's a flash. A surprisingly dull pop. Then a noise so vast that it unfolds into echoing, endless silence. The orangery explodes.

Thirty-Five

Jude, present day

Wake up.

Wake up!

Xanthe's voice in my ear, echoing strangely like sounds heard at the bottom of a swimming pool. My head was throbbing, a slow, vast throb like a heartbeat. I couldn't get my eyes to open properly.

Wake up!

Sleep paralysis. Like before. I could feel my body, feel my arms and legs, feel that I was lying down on a rough, uneven surface. I couldn't move. But I could see, through barely cracked eyelids. And I saw that the world was on fire.

The castle loomed above me, quiet and still, shadowy shapes of twisted metal in the sinister dusky light. The leaves of the bent oak rippled gently overhead. The orangery. Somehow, I was in the ruin of the old orangery again.

But there was fire. Fire glowing through all of it, the way a guttering candle would glow through opaque glass. The familiar jagged shapes of the broken towers were lit by lashing flickers of spreading flame, the flame that had already destroyed them. My ears were filled with a faraway roaring sound. The sea coming in on the cliffs below, or the sound of fire devouring the castle? Or both. As if I was in two places at once.

In two times at once.

Caught between them.

Jonathan. He killed Tom, he was going to shoot Xanthe – oh God – the castle is burning down. It's happening here. It's happening now.

Painful tingling, like the world's worst case of pins and needles, swept over my skin. The heat of the blaze faded in, out, in again. And there was something pressed against my side. Someone. Xanthe. I could feel her, I could *feel* her breath, her torso heaving as she fought for air. With an effort that made cold sweat spring out all over me, I lifted my hand. It was clumsy. Too heavy. My fingers passed through the place where she had been. But I could feel her. She *was* there. She was still here.

Everything is always happening all at once. That was what Alan had said. *They're all still out there.*

It was true. It had always been true. I had seen it. I had felt it.

I closed my eyes. Reached, reached, seeing in my mind a clear, pale light – a sudden light – opening up a pinhole, a gap, a space between, a space through. *It's all happening at once. It's happening now. Now.*

'Xanthe,' I whispered. 'You're not alone this time. I'm coming to save you. Don't be afraid.'

I began to cough. Heat singed my throat, my nostrils. I could taste smoke and blood. The fire roared, clawing at my ears. The heat was indescribable, suffocating, billowing around me as if I had been shoved headfirst into an oven. My hair crackled.

Forcing my eyes open, I saw the trees, the tiny oaks, burning in great tall cones like flaming torches. The walls of the orangery had been blown out by the explosion, but, above, the glass dome of the roof was black with roiling smoke, spiralling orange sparks and cinders. And not far away, sprawled across the floor, there was a still, dark shape, lying in a pool of blood.

Tom.

There was nothing I could do for him.

Squeezing my eyes shut, I turned back, lifted my hand again, and – she was there, next to me. My hand closed on her elbow, bony and awkward. She was real.

I dragged her face to my shoulder, put my arms round her, just for a second. Her hair was wiry against my cheek, and beneath the overpowering stink of smoke there was the faintest smell, the sweet, dry smell of sea salt, of roses.

She was limp. Unconscious. There wasn't any chance I could lift or drag her without help – she was taller than I was. I had to get her free, then wake her up.

Already gasping for breath as the smoke clogged my throat, I laid her back down, turned her onto her front, scrabbling at the ropes that held her wrists behind her back. It was no good. The ropes were wrapped and knotted. They had never been intended to be undone. The bottle, I had seen the bottle – there! I caught the neck, smashed it against the tiles with a sob of desperation, smashed it again until it broke, used the broken end to saw at the knots. I was cutting her, I could see blood seeping across her skin, but there was no time – no time – no time – too much time between us like a surging ocean that would swallow us, drag us apart if I stopped fighting its current. The moment her hands were free I moved on to the bindings round her ankles. As the leg ropes began to fall away, I felt her back heave with a deeper breath, and suddenly she was helping me, squirming and struggling against the bindings, pulling them away with her bleeding hands.

'It's you – you're real – who are you?'

I wheezed out, 'I'm Juliet.'

She ripped her foot free. One ankle was still tangled in the rope, but she was able to bring her legs up, push herself upright. She dragged me up with her, swaying. We leaned on each other for balance. Her hair was tangled and matted, and a starburst of blood stained her headscarf near her forehead, drying in a tarry black trickle down the side of her face.

'Tom? Where's – Tom!'

She lurched towards him. I wrapped my arms round her again, struggling to hold her back.

'You can't! He's gone!' I was dizzy, my lungs on fire. But the orangery's glass walls were open, the way out was right there. I couldn't see any sign of Jonathan. He must have fled. She could get out. She could live. Tears were pouring down my face as I begged her. 'Xanthe, don't die here! You have to go, go now! Please!'

'Juliet . . .' She stopped fighting me. Her eyes met mine.

They were grey. Silver grey with dark rings round the pale iris. They were *my* eyes. How could I never have noticed before? As I stared, she caught hold of my face in both hands. Her lips were dry as they pressed against mine. 'Thank you.'

There was a feeling like vertigo. She was right in front of me, but I was falling away, going numb and heavy again. Darkness spiralled in my vision like ripples spreading in a pool, sucking away the light. The sound of the fire faded out of my ears, the heat dying in a damp chill. The noises of the sea rushed in.

I couldn't feel her fingers on my face any more.

The last I saw of her were those eyes. Her pale lips tugging faintly up at the corners. She let go of me, and ran back across the burning room towards Tom's body.

'No!' But it was too late. It had always been too late. Time was still moving and we were slipping past each other, tiny fishes caught in different currents, carried away in opposite directions. In the final instant, I watched it happen. The great gout of fire overhead. The groan of buckling steel. Then the impact, like an earthquake, shaking the foundations of the cliff itself, as the orangery roof crashed down.

☽◯☾

I'm on the ground again. It's dark. Tall grasses are whispering around me, and the sea is booming below. The wreckage of the orangery is above. Stars are glittering then dying into darkness amid the streaming clouds. They blur before my eyes. *Xanthe.* Tears run down the sides of my face, pool in my ears, hot and sticky. I try to blink them away, but they keep coming.

In the midst of my grief there's a faint stirring of alarm.

What's happened to me? Who brought me here? Why *here*?

My limbs feel so heavy I can barely move them, and my head is fuzzy and dull. I'm not restrained in any way, not tied up like Xanthe was. I don't need to be. I'm so weak, so dizzy I'm struggling to even see straight, let alone move. I bite my lip to hold in a groan, my right temple throbbing as I slowly roll my head sideways, squinting against the shadows. I don't dare call out.

There's someone lying near me. They're huddled, still. Tom? No – Nick.

He can't be dead. History can't repeat itself like that, it can't. It can't.

His hand's lying palm up on the grass. It's the only part of him close enough for me to really make out. It looks very pale. I stare at it for long moments, stubbornly blinking away the tears that keep welling up, and welling up. Slowly, too slowly, I realise that the hand is wrong. The palm is soft, not striped with rough brown calluses like Nick's hand. The fingers are long and thin. Not blunt and square. That's not Nick's hand. It's not him lying there. There's the glint of a chunky metal wristband; Aidan has a watch like that. Aidan? Where's—

There's a crunch amid the rubble and the grasses nearby. Footsteps. I roll myself onto my front, get my knees under me, weave forward again as dizziness surges, catching myself on both hands in the rocky dirt. I'm not going to be able to get to my feet. This is as much as I can do.

I look up. I look up into Nick's face. Into the barrel of a shotgun.

The gun's broken over his arm. He's holding it pointing down. But he's holding it.

Maybe it's from the farm. Maybe he has a good reason to have it. But not now. Not here.

'You're alive,' he says. His voice is flat, toneless, nothing like the Nick I know. 'I thought he'd killed you. I'd killed you.'

'I'm alive,' I say slowly. 'Why are we here, Nick? What happened?'

'I thought we'd killed you.' He swallows – I can see the movement in his neck. 'Like before.'

Light flickers behind him. Out over the sea, there's a low, echoing rumble of thunder.

I have to force the words out. I'm quaking, actually quaking in place, my body wracked by long, convulsive shudders. 'What . . . what do you mean . . . before?'

'Back then. Back when this place was still standing. Don't you remember us? I was sure you did. You called me by his name.'

'I don't . . . I don't know . . .'

My voice is wavering, but his is firm with certainty. 'You do. It's why you love it so much here. Like she did. He loved it too. He . . . I didn't mean to destroy it. It was like once I'd started hurting people, out there, once he'd been made to do it, I couldn't stop. Something broke in him and he couldn't stop himself any more. I couldn't stop myself.'

He's talking about Jonathan. Jonathan Winter.

I started to get these dreams, these visions, as soon as I came here. As if something in this place, in Winterthorne, awoke a part of me that was the same as some part of Xanthe, and that connection just arced between us, unstoppable. But I was so, so caught up in myself and what I was going through that I never even asked myself, not once, if I was the only one. If anyone else was experiencing the same thing as me.

'Nick.' I can't believe I'm saying these words. 'You're not him.'

'I'm all of him that's left.'

'You'd never hurt anyone, not like he did.' My eyes flick to Aidan, unmoving among the tall grasses. I take a breath, keep talking. 'Your mum told me about you. How you've always tried to help everyone, the little birds and animals you brought to her as a kid—'

'You don't get it. I was trying to prove I was different. Trying to make up for it.' He lets out a wet, shuddering sigh, sits down on one of the blocks of fallen stone. The gun rests over his knee. 'My first memory, the first thing I remember from being a little boy ... it's not trying to walk, or playing with my sisters on the beach, or – or anything from my own life. The first thing I remember from being a kid, is remembering what *he'd* done. I don't even know how young I was. I just knew my fingers, round her neck. Your neck.'

'Jesus Christ ...' I whisper.

Nick was *born here*. Grew up in Winterthorne with these shadows of time, the traces of what came before, trauma and terror and violence. Long before I ever arrived, this story was playing out, connecting Nick to the past. I'm a part of it too, but it was never all about me. It wasn't even about Xanthe, not really. Not completely.

It was always about all of us.

'I'm so sorry.' I'm sagging in place, more tears pouring down my face. Will I ever run out, like Xanthe did? My head hurts so much. I've only been here for a week. Nick's had to live with it since he was a child. He's never known a day of peace. 'I'm so sorry, Nick.'

'As I got older, it got better. The ... the memories seemed to fade. I tried to be – good. But then. My dad. I found him, on the paving slabs. His head was all broken open. And it all came back. The war. Mud and shit and blood. Mum sent me to therapy, but I couldn't tell anyone the truth, what I'd seen, what I'd done. Mum selling the house helped, being away in Durham helped. By the time we came back, I had a handle on it.'

No wonder his family tiptoed around him, gave him wary looks, shied away from mentioning his father. But even Liz never had any real idea why he was struggling back then, or what he's been going through now. He hid it all, because how could she ever understand? How could she help him? 'God, Nick, I can't even imagine—'

'But you can.' His gaze swings back to me. Lightning flashes overhead, silver-white veins through the purplish clouds. Thunder follows. The storm is coming back, getting closer. 'You can imagine. You, and him.' He points the gun barrel to Aidan's silent form.

'Aidan? How? He's nothing to do with – any of this.'

'He's the other one. The other one I killed.'

My head jerks to stare at the hunched stillness of Aidan's body. He couldn't be. He was nothing like Tom, nothing at all.

Maybe it sounds crazy . . . Is there any chance we've met before? You just seem sort of familiar . . .

'As soon as he came here, I recognised him. That's why he came. Why he hates me so much. Why he tried to be friends with you, when he's not had a good word for anyone else here since he arrived. He couldn't help himself, either. None of us could. The three of us . . . We were always trapped. We can't get out.'

Is it true? The despair, the sheer misery in Nick's voice, makes doubt sweep over me like frost.

No. No, I refuse to believe that. I refuse to believe that we don't have a choice. But maybe . . . this *is* why I was drawn here . . . why I was shown everything that happened to Xanthe: so I *could* understand. So I could save Aidan from Nick this time, but, even more than that, *save Nick* from this trap in time that was never his fault. From the echoes of the terrible things Jonathan did. Save all of us from having to go through this again, and again.

I have a chance this time. A chance that Xanthe never got. I can set things right.

'That is not true,' I tell him fiercely, willing him to listen. Slowly, swallowing down the swoop of nausea, the thudding in my skull the movement brings, I wobble to my feet. 'You are not trapped. You have a choice. You haven't hurt me. I just fell, like an idiot. You are not Jonathan Winter. You're Nick Fairley, and you're a good person.'

'Maybe I was,' he says. He stands up too, and I can't help it – I flinch back from the gun, from his weary, miserable face. 'Before he came. Before you did. But it's too late now. I hit him. After you fell. I hit him, and he's not moving, and I brought you both here because I can't stand it any more. I can't stand it. I need it to be over. There's only one way out. For all of us.'

'You don't mean that,' I say steadily. 'This isn't you, Nick. Let me check on Aidan. Let me see if he's all right. Then we can decide what to do.'

'It's too late.' He's not listening to me. Lightning and thunder come again, shaking the ruins as one, almost drowning out his desperate, rambling voice. 'It was always me. I'm the one who left you grave gifts at your door – didn't you work that out? I was trying to frighten you away, because I was too much of a coward to warn you to your face. Because I liked you too much and I didn't want to see you stop smiling at me. I didn't want to hurt you. But I have. I can never make up for what he did.'

'You're not responsible for what Jonathan did. You haven't done anything you can't take back,' I cried over the thunder. 'Let me check on Aidan—'

'No!' He snaps the gun into one piece suddenly, the metallic click echoing as the thunder dies away, and steps forward so that he's standing under the twisted oak. Almost on top of Aidan. 'He's trying to take you away from me! You were mine, I knew you first, you were always meant to belong to me! Why couldn't you choose me this time instead of him? Why couldn't you do what you were supposed to do?'

I reach my hand out towards him, pray that he will hear me. 'I told you before. You're the first person I met here, and you will always be my favourite, Nick Fairley. Always.'

He stares at me, grip on the gun seeming to loosen. 'Except. Except for my mum, right?'

'Obviously, yeah,' I say with a watery smile. Please, please. Come back, Nick. Come back . . .

And then Aidan groans, shifts in the grass. 'Shit, my head. What the hell?'

Nick's eyes grow cold so fast. It's like watching his soul die out of him, like watching the person I know die right in front of me. For the first time I see Jonathan in his face, and I am truly, truly afraid of him. 'Don't – Nick, *don't*—'

Aidan groans again, oblivious. Nick lifts the stock of the gun to his shoulder.

It's happening again. Still happening. The same tragedy, echoing on and on. Xanthe couldn't stop it then, and I can't stop it now.

Please. Please. Help me save them. If I could see across time, touch Xanthe across time, there must be a way. There must be, or what was the point of any of this? Out in the streaming wind, in the clouds, among the darkness and the sea and the hidden stars that Xanthe loved, there must be a chance. *Someone. Please. Help.*

Behind Nick, beneath the twisted oak – the place where I drew Xanthe staring out at the sea – there's a shift in the darkness. I see something come alight. A tall, slender shape, shining with a strange internal glow. As the glow touches the ruins, for a breath, I see . . . the past. I see this place as it once was, one last time. The orangery as Xanthe knew it before everything went wrong, full of light and warmth, music and laughter. There's a tinny echo of melody, that song I haven't been able to get out of my mind. I smell sunlight on the sea, and roses.

Nick's eyes are huge. He's frozen. He sees it too.

This is the only chance I'm going to get. I lunge for the gun.

Nick staggers back. Shocked, he raises the barrel above his head like a kid playing keep away – then, with a snarl, he snaps it down to point at me. At my chest.

Behind me, Aidan lets out a hoarse yell. The world spins as he grabs me at the waist and pulls me down. And in that instant, as he puts himself between me and Nick's gun, the pale sudden light – the light of the past – streams away, upwards. Up to the dark, flickering clouds.

Then it comes back. As lightning. The night explodes. Thunder comes again, claws apart the shadows. Everything is black and burning white, a photo negative of time standing still. I clamp my eyes shut, flat on the ground, my hands curled over my head, feeling Aidan's arms tighten round me as the noise goes on, and on, and on.

When it finally dies away, when I can finally lift my head, the oak tree is burning, and Nick is lying beneath it. The gun is gone, lost somewhere amid the grasses.

'Are you hurt? Juliet, look at me, are you hurt?' Aidan's hands are pawing at me.

'I'm OK, I'm OK – what are you doing?'

He's not listening. He's frantically patting at my body, searching for injuries, as if he can't believe I'm in one piece. The light from the tree is barely enough to see him by, it's so dark. There's no blood on him, not even any bruises that I can make out.

'I'm OK!' I say again, struggling away from him, ignoring his protests, to crawl over to Nick. I put a trembling hand on his neck.

He looks as if he's just asleep. Like Aidan, there's not a mark on him. I can't see any burns. Did the lightning hit him or just stun him? There's a pulse. He's breathing. I think . . . I think he's all right.

As abruptly as if someone had turned a bucket over, it starts to rain. The thunder rumbles again, growing distant already. The fire among the oak leaves goes out with a low, hissing sizzle.

There's nothing here now but Nick, and Aidan, and me.

And they're alive. They're both alive.

I flop down with my head on Nick's chest, unable to hold myself up any more, and let out a single, hard sob of relief. The raindrops patter on my face like tears, but for the first time since I woke up here in the ruins there are no tears in my eyes. There's nothing to cry about any more. After a moment, I manage to get my voice to work again.

'Aidan. Please, please tell me you have your phone? Can you call an ambulance?'

He crawls up next to us, fumbling in his jeans pocket with a shaky hand. 'Yeah. Yeah, I – listen, what the – What's going on? How did we even get here? I don't remember—'

'It's all right. I promise it's all right.' I smile as I realise it's true. 'It's finished now. We're all going to be OK.'

Thirty-Six

I'm stuck in the hospital for three days.

It's mainly because of the concussion from my fall. The doctors think there might be a chance of a skull fracture, and they need to wait until the swelling goes down so that they can be sure the scans will show it up. I don't think they'd have kept me in just for the bruised ribs or sprained knee.

But for those three nights, for the first time since I arrived in Winterthorne, I don't dream. Not once.

It really is over.

I ought to be glad. I mean I am, really. I am. To be safe. I just miss her too. And I grieve for her. Aidan was saved from Nick's gun – and Nick from using it – but I failed Xanthe. I failed her, and she was taken from me.

When I wake up that first morning on the busy ward with a splitting headache, the sun streaming through the vertical blinds, and a taste like charcoal in my mouth, I find Liz sitting at my bedside. I nearly dive off the other side of the bed and try to crawl away: how can I possibly look at her? How can I meet her eyes?

'I'm so sorry,' I start to say, covering my face even though it makes the huge, swollen bruise distorting most of the right side of my face throb like fire.

A firm grip on my hands pulls them away and down. Liz's green eyes are looking at me, steady as always, unsmiling and serious. She's been crying.

'Don't. Don't you ever apologise for someone else having hurt you, Jude. No matter who they are. You trusted us, and we—' Her voice breaks. 'We let you down. I'm the one that's sorry.'

'It wasn't your fault. Nick didn't know what he was doing. He didn't want to hurt me. He just needed help.' Probably only half of this is comprehensible to her. My throat is so swollen up from all the tears, from the cold and rain last night. From the smoke.

She sighs wearily, still holding my hands. 'Well. I think you're right there. I've spoken to him – yes, don't worry, he wasn't hurt. Physically, at least. But he's not even really sure what happened, only that he ... started to think he was someone else. Like when he was little. Like when his father died. I ought to have noticed he wasn't well. We all should have.'

I can see there are a million words she's not saying. She looks so small, and hurt. I turn my hands round to hold hers. 'If you need anything—'

She lets out a watery chuckle. 'The police told me that you're not intending to press charges. That's more than I could have hoped, love. Don't worry about me. I'll get through it.'

Liz has been down to my house – Anne's house – collected the keys I left stuck in the garden gate like a total numpty, and locked the place up for me. While she was there, she also

The Moonlit Maze

found my packed suitcase, and brought it to the hospital. She leaves it by my bed – without any comment on why I was so conveniently prepared – which means I have clean pyjamas and my own bodywash, toothbrush and shampoo, the things anyone would give their kidney for when they're stuck in the hospital.

'They let that boy Aidan out last night,' she tells me before she leaves.

I actually already know this. Aidan came by to see me before he went home. He made it through the whole ordeal with a bit of bruising, and his usual performance of surliness was not up to concealing his worry, or his relief.

'Did you see it?' he whispered abruptly, after pushing a packet of Jaffa cakes, a crossword book and a magazine – all from the 24/7 hospital giftshop – at me.

'See what?' I murmured back. The woman in the bed next to me let out a rattling snore.

'The light. Back there in the ruins. That *light*. It made everything look . . . I felt as if I saw things I'd dreamed about. Like a memory. I knew it.'

I knew it all of yore. The fine hairs lifted up on my arms. I hesitated, then said: 'Yes. I saw it.'

'What was it?'

I closed my eyes. It didn't help my headache much – even the backs of my eyelids ached. 'I don't know. Something like . . . a gap, between times. Or maybe the imprint left by one. Or maybe you're right. It was just a memory.'

'Uh. You – uh – you know that makes no sense, right?'

'Well, I might have a fractured skull, so . . .'

I started laughing first. We both giggled manically for nearly ten minutes, until the nurse came to throw him out. He promised me that he would look after Rowan for me until I was released, then left me with a gentle squeeze-squeeze to my hand that somehow made every tense muscle in my body relax all at once. I stared at my hand for a long time after he left, the words of the poem – Ma's poem, Xanthe and Tom's poem – circling round and round in my head.

Now, Liz goes on: 'He's not pressing charges, either, the police said. They said you talked him out of it.'

I start to brush it off, but she gives me a look and I shut up.

'The point is that Nick's got a hard road ahead of him now. He's going to need treatment, and it might be a long time before he can come home. Before he's the person we knew again. But you made it a bit – no, a lot, easier on him. So just remember what I said before: you're not going back to being a guest. Or a stranger. You're family. Just like Anne was.'

The whole Fairley clan visits me at some point over the next three days. It's . . . difficult. Definitely awkward. But since Ma died I've been a person who didn't have other people. Not anyone who really cared. No one who would visit me in the hospital. I'm grateful that's changed.

☽○☾

The morning that I get the all-clear to go home, Liz insists on driving me back to the cottage. She updates me on Nick, who's just settled in at a private psychiatric facility. He's still shellshocked by what he did, but beginning to be willing to talk. I ask her to tell him that I'm fine, and thinking about him. Other than that, we're mostly silent on the drive, and

The Moonlit Maze

Liz seems comfortable with it, tapping her fingers absently on the steering wheel of Nick's truck. I'm thinking hard, barely seeing the sunlit countryside as it passes us by. After charging up my long-abandoned phone, I had a call from a concerned Mr Swan on my last night in the hospital, wondering where I was and why he hadn't been able to reach me.

'I assume,' he said gravely, after I'd offered him the barest outline of what happened, 'that you will want to go ahead with the sale of the property as quickly as possible? I could arrange temporary accommodation in London for you, if you'd like, to speed up your departure?'

'No,' I found myself saying. 'No, I think . . . I think I want to stay.'

'For how long?'

I hadn't known how to answer. I don't know what I want now. Eventually, I just told him that I would wait to make any decisions until I was fully recovered. Could I really stay in Winterthorne after all this? But after all this, could I honestly bring myself to go?

The cottage is quiet after Liz leaves. That restful, unquiet-quiet I noticed when I first arrived, all the sounds of birds and trees and wind blending into a kind of peace I don't think I ever knew in London. I've got a large box of bacon, eggs and butter, courtesy of Ben and Meg, and Aidan texted me he would bring Rowan home this evening, so I'm free to make myself a messy omelette for lunch – glorious after hospital food – and eat it at the kitchen table while finally reading the rest of Pikestaff's pamphlet.

There's no mention in it that Tom Marten was ever implicated in the fire, despite what Nick told me. I learn that after the destruction of the castle Jonathan was hailed as a hero; he claimed his injuries, the injuries Rowan inflicted, were the result of having tried to save people from the disaster. As usual, everyone seems to have swallowed his lies whole. But just one year later – after moving to the South of France with a heartbroken Lord and Lady Kearsley – he drowned. It was ruled an accident.

Lord Kearsley died later that same year. He lasted longer than the doctors ever thought he would. Long enough to see everything he had dreaded and feared come to pass, almost entirely through his own actions. The money from Xanthe's trust could have saved his home, if he had been willing to let her live her own life. If he had been willing to see Jonathan for what he was, and hold him responsible for the wrongs he did.

Lady Kearsley lived to nearly ninety. She never returned to England.

There's nothing in the pamphlet about what happened to Tom's father, Mr Marten. Or his sister, Sally. I do at least know she must have had children eventually, because otherwise the Fairleys wouldn't exist, but whether her fiancé stuck around after the fire . . . who knows? There's no mention of the first dog named Rowan, either. I wonder if I could find out. Then I think it might be best not to know.

Unpacking my case in the bedroom, I come across the sketchpad Ma gave me again. I find myself opening it at last, flicking through it, running my thumb down the edges. The paper is the best kind, textured, with uneven deckle edges. All at once it seems so obvious to me that I should use it. Leaving it untouched in the bottom of my case isn't any way to honour

Ma. I fetch some pastels from Anne's art studio, a box she had barely touched, and settle down in the living room.

It's a couple of hours before I stop to stretch, clean my hands, examine what I've done.

I've rarely ever experimented with portraiture, which is part of why Xanthe's unintended appearance in my sketch of Kearsley Castle shook me so much. This – this was a deliberate choice, though. A soft-focus head-and-shoulders, full of colour, heavily influenced by the style of Rossetti, but with my own modern twist. I've caught her in a half-smile, the face in quarter profile, light glinting from the vivid red curls of her windblown hair. Her eyes, those moonlight eyes that look so much like mine, are filled with mischief. This is how she looked on the beach, teasing and talking with Tom and Rowan. This is how she looked when she was happy.

It's probably the best piece of art I've ever made in my life.

As I look at it, I know I want to do this for a living, like Anne did. I want to go to university – not just because that's what Ma planned for me, but because it's what I choose for myself. Maybe I'll need to go back and redo my A levels, and, one way or the other, it'll be a lot of work, but I'm ready. Ready to start again. With the time and space that Anne gave me, that my father indirectly paved the way for, and the ambition and love of art that my mother taught me, I can do it. That's the life I want to build. I can build it here.

It's then, as I smile down at Xanthe's smile, that my fingertips feel the dents inside the back cover of the sketchbook. I turn the pages over and stare. It's Ma's handwriting. She inscribed the sketchbook for me. I never knew.

Time may sweep away much that you have loved – but if

you wait long enough, time will return that love to you, even if in a different form.

It sucks all the breath out of my lungs. She meant *me*. With everything I've learned since I came to Winterthorne, I understand exactly what she was trying to say. My father may have left her, but love returned anyway, because she had me.

Beneath the quotation is neatly noted: *Zan Thomas:* The Lights Around the Shore.

Zan Thomas. *The Lights Around the Shore*. I'm sure I've seen that somewhere before.

My eyes stray to the window seat where the book Anne must have been reading when she died has lain untouched since she left the cottage. I first noticed it there as Liz showed me around the house. The bookmark is still poking out. As I approach and pick it up, I see that the bookmark is an old train ticket, which is exactly what I always do with train tickets; that makes me smile again. The book's a much-thumbed old paperback, the pages starting to yellow and curl back at the corners. The cover art is a black-and-white photograph of the Valley of the Kings, with a small group of people – Indiana Jones types in jodhpurs and knee boots with big moustaches and big grins – clustered in front of the Great Pyramid of Giza. At the centre of the group is a person on a camel, and it takes me a moment to see that it's a woman, kitted out the same as the men except for the massive hat that shadows her face. One hand is lifted in a wave, or a salute.

The Lights Around the Shore: The Memoir of Zan Thomas, by Zan Thomas, ed. E. Erskine and Dr J. B. Thomas.

Erskine? It's not all that common a name. I wonder if they were a relation of Anne's – of mine – and that's why she had this book. That would be really interesting to look into, see if I can find out more. I flip it over to read the back copy.

'An account of the convention-defying life of war correspondent, civil-rights campaigner and novelist Zan Thomas, in her own words.

'In 1925, a fiery, ambitious young journalist called Zan Thomas submitted a story about corruption and corporate manslaughter to the *Durham Herald*, and was taken on by the newspaper as a freelance writer. It wasn't until two years later that the owners of the paper discovered Zan Thomas was a woman. By then, she was, as she herself stated "too indispensable to fire".

'So began the astonishing career of the only female journalist to report from the European frontlines during the Second World War, a ground-breaking novelist whose works have sold over 100,000 copies. In *The Lights Around the Shore*, Zan Thomas talks with scintillating and sometimes painful honesty about her journey to make a life on her own terms, offering insight into her time spent in Africa, India and Tibet, her controversial decision never to marry and her late-in-life adoption of two orphaned children. Although her early life remains shrouded in mystery, Zan Thomas serves as an inspiration for both women and men in the twentieth century.'

At the bottom, in smaller print:

'Zan Thomas died in 1993, surrounded by family and the friends she had made over a lifetime. This memoir, on which she worked until the last days of her life, was published after her death with the permission and assistance of her daughters, Eleanor Erskine and Dr Juliet Thomas.'

It takes a moment for everything to come together in my

mind. I nearly drop the book. Fumble to catch it, and end up with it pressed against my chest, where my heart is pounding.

Zan. Xan. That was the name Tom called Xanthe. Zan, short for Xanthe – and Tom, short for Thomas. Zan Thomas.

Everyone thought she'd died there. That the fire took her. But no one ever said they found her body, did they? It could be. Maybe she did escape and make a new life. A long, extraordinary life. I want to believe it. I want to believe that so much. That she adopted two daughters, and one was named Juliet, and the other was an Erskine, part of my family. That Xanthe was part of my family. Surely it can't be coincidence?

No. None of this was coincidence.

Book still held against my heart, I rush to grab my phone, hoping for a signal. There is one, but before I can jump on Wikipedia I see a string of texts from Penny. I ignored the alerts earlier, too busy working on the portrait.

Jude, are u around?
Jude?
I had a fight with Duncan. Things are bad.
He won't leave the flat. I can't get him to leave
I can't stay here. I don't think it's safe.
I'm really sorry but did u mean it when u said I cld come stay w/u?

I stare at the phone. Then, slowly and reverently, I place Zan Thomas's book down on the sofa, just for now, so I can quickly text back. Because . . . I know now what I want to do with my life. But, more than that, I know the kind of person I choose to be.

The Moonlit Maze

Of course I meant it. Just ring me whenever you can. It's going to be OK, Penny.

'... *if you wait long enough, time will return that love to you ...*'

It's so exactly right that Ma wanted me to read that. It's so exactly right that I've found it now, now that I'm here, after everything that's happened. Ma always liked to say that you have a chance, here on this earth, to make a life that is about love. Not some grand, romantic love, but the kind of love that encompasses everything, that makes a person joyful, and generous, and brave. She said everything we do affects everything around us. Everyone around us. Like infinitesimal grains of sand tumbling a great rough boulder to smoothness, each of us changes the world by being here. By who we choose to be here. And that change changes everything, in time.

There's so much unhappiness and pain in life, and I don't know why it has to be that way. But unhappiness and pain don't last for ever. They can't. They don't create anything. They can't endure.

Love is what creates, what allows us to make every human thing that makes up a life – art, and homes, and friends and, eventually, families. Lives may end in time, but love doesn't. We are love. And love remains.

I know who I choose to be.

I'm Juliet. My mother's daughter.

Author's Note

Dear Reader,

The book you've just read took over a decade to write.

The central idea for *The Moonlit Maze* – that of two brave young women, reaching for each other through time – appeared almost fully formed in my mind during one of the darkest periods of my life.

My father had just died. I was his carer during his last, terrible illness. For a long time, the doctors would not admit that his diagnosis was terminal, and so I hoped that by following all the medical advice, looking after him with all my love, I could save him. Hold him in this life with my own two hands. When the end came, I was not ready to let go. In the midst of that bleak, dripping-grey autumn, the sun never seemed to shine, and all hope was gone. I did not write a word for many, many months.

Then one day, out of nowhere, a vibrant, evocative scene unfolded in my mind.

A warm midsummer night. A hedge maze on top of a cliff, the sea booming below and the stars bright above. And a beautiful girl, her heart full of love and hope. I couldn't resist the call of this quirky seaside setting, called Winterthorne – an imagined landscape made vivid with memories of childhood holidays in York and Whitby – or the unforgettable character of Xanthe. I sat down and, in one go, wrote the prologue that greets you when you turn the first page of this manuscript.

When I realised the kind of story I had begun, I was flabbergasted. This complex, bittersweet, dual-timeline narrative of enduring love and historical trauma was, very clearly, not a Young Adult novel like those I'd written before. I was already badly behind deadline on a book for children I was contracted to write, and the bills were mounting up. Grateful for the spark of creative joy and hope it had given me, I nevertheless put the project in a drawer.

But I couldn't let go. Every now and again I'd return to the hastily scribbled notes, add a new idea or image, and feel the story's life still stubbornly beating behind the words like a tiny fragile heart.

Years passed, and in 2019 I finally found the courage to take a break from my career as a writer for children. To take a leap of hope, and go back into education. A working-class Northerner, I'd left college at the age of seventeen without completing my A levels. To my astonishment, I graduated with Distinction in my Master's degree, and that motivated me to pursue a PhD, one that would blend Creative Writing, Art History and modern theories about the workings of time. When I received the life-changing news that I had won my PhD place, I knew there was only one story to which I wanted to dedicate the three years of doctoral study. It was *The Moonlit Maze*, the book in front of you now.

I'll tell you a secret: when I wrote the final lines of *The Moonlit Maze* I cried as if my heart was breaking. Not with sadness. With love. Love for this story, for my brave, hurting characters – and for every imagined reader out there in the real world, whom I hoped would find this book and perhaps be comforted. Because I have comfort to give now. I have found hope again.

I couldn't have written this book ten years ago. Back then I hadn't begun to confront my own undiagnosed autism – a condition that informs the character Xanthe, a fiery, talented young woman of the 1920s, raised in immense privilege but stifled by the rigid expectations of her family. I hadn't admitted to myself how the uncertainty and financial precarity of my working-class upbringing had marked my life – which was vital to the development of the character of Jude, a down-on-her-luck Londoner who has lost the last of her family, and her connection to her art, but who is brave enough to seek a new life when the chance presents itself.

Most of all, to write *The Moonlit Maze* I needed to learn the persistence of love. Love in all its forms. Not only romantic, but familial, and platonic, and perhaps most important of all the all-encompassing love for the world that takes the form of hope. It was hope that allowed me to recover from the loss of my father, and understand that the love he had gifted me would always remain. Hope that allowed me to pursue my PhD, and my autism diagnosis. To write this deeply personal book, and work to get it into your hands.

Reader, I don't know you. I don't know your heart, your struggles or your grief. But in sending *The Moonlit Maze* out into the world, I want more than anything to pass on this message:

Hold on to love and hope. Hold them in both hands. Feel that tiny, fragile heartbeat. Don't be afraid, and don't let go of them ... until it's time to let them fly free.

Sincerely,

Zoë x

Acknowledgements

Writing acknowledgements is both a gratifying and tricky business at the best of times. But when a book takes over a decade to see the light of day, the writer must face the sad fact that they cannot possibly fit all of the people who have contributed in one way or another to the process into the small space allowed for such thanks (in many cases because ten years is a long time and said author's memory just isn't what it used to be). And so the first thing I need to do is sincerely thank each and every person who helped me along the way ... but whose name isn't on this page. I'm truly grateful.

Huge thanks to Kate Shaw, my phenomenal agent, who has gently guided me into the turbulent waters of grown-up publishing, and continues to keep me afloat. I am so lucky to have you.

Equally huge thanks to Sherise Hobbs, a publishing legend, for falling in love with Jude and Xanthe's story and championing them so passionately. I can still hardly believe it. And to the rest of the brilliant team at Headline, including but not limited to Imogen Taylor, Isabel Martin, Kashmini Shah and

Samantha Stewart, who have made the process of getting this book ready for release into the wild a genuine pleasure.

Thank you to my PhD Supervisors at the Open University, Dr Ed Hogan and Dr Joanne Reardon, for challenging me to make both versions of this book the best they could be, and everyone at the Open-Oxford-Cambridge Doctoral Training Partnership, without whose support the book would not exist. And to all my fellow doctoral candidates in the department of English & Creative Writing, for so many inspiring discussions both in real life and online: you are wonderful.

Thank you to my writing group, the funniest, cleverest and most talented group of damned scribbling women anyone could ever be lucky enough to stumble across in the publishing wilderness. Special thanks to Emma Pass and Sheena Wilkinson who read and offered much needed feedback on the first draft of this book. Please forgive me for any historical inaccuracies I may have perpetrated, Sheena. Mea culpa.

Lastly, I need to thank my mother, Elaine Marriott, for gifting me with a lifelong love of reading – her decision to offer my eleven-year-old self a copy of Barbara Erskine's timeslip epic *Lady of Hay* changed my life – and my late father David Marriott, for passing on his storytelling gene. Whether I say it or not, everything I have ever written has always been for you.

RAISING READERS
Books Build Bright Futures

Dear Reader,

We'd love your attention for one more page to tell you about the crisis in children's reading, and what we can all do.

Studies have shown that reading for fun is the **single biggest predictor of a child's future life chances** – more than family circumstance, parents' educational background or income. It improves academic results, mental health, wealth, communication skills, ambition and happiness.[1]

The number of children reading for fun is in rapid decline. Young people have a lot of competition for their time. In 2024, 1 in 10 children and young people in the UK aged 5 to 18 did not own a single book at home.[2]

Hachette works extensively with schools, libraries and literacy charities, but here are some ways we can all raise more readers:

- Reading to children for just 10 minutes a day makes a difference
- Don't give up if children aren't regular readers – there will be books for them!
- Visit bookshops and libraries to get recommendations
- Encourage them to listen to audiobooks
- Support school libraries
- Give books as gifts

There's a lot more information about how to encourage children to read on our website: **www.RaisingReaders.co.uk**

Thank you for reading.

---

[1] OECD, '21st-Century Readers: Developing Literacy Skills in a Digital World', 2021, https://www.oecd.org/en/publications/21st-century-readers_a83d84cb-en.html

[2] National Literacy Trust, 'Book Ownership in 2024', November 2024, https://literacytrust.org.uk/research-services/research-reports/book-ownership-in-2024